PRAISE FOR ESTRANGED

"In *Estranged*, history comes alive. Charles Lamar Phillips' voice is immediate and urgent. This novel will suck you in and you'll want to spend as much time as possible with the complicated and interesting world he's built."

—Andrew Gifford, founder and director of the Santa Fe Writers Project

"In sentences that capture the sensory specifics of late-1940s America, from 'rotten fruit and stale shoe polish' smell of printers' ink to the greased hair and cheap suit of its hack politician villain, Charles Lamar Phillips's novel re-creates a low and dishonest moment in our past that uncomfortably resembles the depths to which we have since fallen. In "Red" Randall Harker and his fall, persecuted by a puffed-up anti-Communist midwestern Senator, Phillips gives us the view from inside a witch-hunt's target, the lived experience of the political scapegoat. If we're lucky, Phillips's powerful rendering is as close as most of us will get to such experience. With this hard-boiled and compelling portrait, that's close enough for me."

—Michael Thurston, former fiction editor of *Massachusetts Review,* author of *Houses from Another Street*, and Provost and Dean of Faculty, Smith College

"From the first page of *Estranged*, Charles Lamar Phillips taps into the very best of the noir genre. And then he cranks it up to eleven. This is the story of Randall Harker, an ex-Communist, city editor at a Midwestern newspaper, who finds himself in the crosshairs of a shady senator during the Red Scare in the 1950s. Point-blank, it's obvious that Harker's career, marriage and reputation are toast. But readers will keep turning the pages to find out if he can survive a ruthless smear campal, intact.

In a novel eerily reminiscent tmare, Phillips's snappy prose weaves a sticky k-full of gangsters, grifters and heroes with l of newspaper ink, Scotch and fear oozes ter to the last. Estranged is a heckuva good book for anyone who loves quality fiction. And Phillips is an author with talent."

— Adam Kovac, author of *The Surge*

"In *Estranged*, Charles Lamar Phillips anchors the reader in the Midwest of 1950, a time when politicians made deals in smoke-filled rooms, hard-drinking journalists sparred with them, and reputations could be ruined by extramarital dalliances, one's sexual orientation, or a youthful affiliation with the Communist Party. The crackling plot, full of spot-on period details and dialogue, propelled me forward, but the sentences were so well crafted, I slowed down to savor them. This is one of those novels that perfectly recreates another place and time while also under-scoring universal truths."

— Jan English Leary author of *Thicker Than Blood* and *Skating on the Vertical*

"Charlie Phillips is a smart, funny, open-eyed writer who salts his pages with discarded illusions. Tough and good: we could use more writers like him."

— James Whorton, Jr., author of *Angela Sloan, Frankland*, and *Approximately Heaven*

"There should be more novels about that scary time and place for any-one with a questioning mind—McCarthyst USA. *Estranged* sprints along, drags you convincingly into the times, injects the ice of dread into your veins. These were the times when leveling an accusation of 'Communist!' could save any public figure from allegations of corruption. Lord, how familiar this feels! A great yarn, and how very appropriate for our own times it is."

— JL Crozier, author of *What Empty Things Are These*

ESTRANGED

Charles Lamar Phillips

Regal House Publishing

Published by
Regal House Publishing, LLC
Raleigh, NC 27612
All rights reserved

ISBN -13 (paperback): 9781646030552
ISBN -13 (epub): 9781646030569
Library of Congress Control Number: 2020930422

Interior and cover design by Lafayette & Greene
lafayetteandgreene.com
Cover images © by C.B. Royal

Regal House Publishing, LLC
https://regalhousepublishing.com

Printed in the United States of America

For Patricia Hogan

Part 1: THE WORKING DAY

Men make their own history, but they do not make it just as they please ... .

—Karl Marx, *18th Brumaire of Louis Bonaparte*

1.

Kid Guthrie—I'm sorry, *Andrew* Guthrie—my pint-sized young protégé at the paper and I went to the memorial auditorium for Larry McKnight's speech in November. It had been a little less than a week since the senator flooded the state with his press release about the *Capital News* and the Communist on its staff. Though he named no names, he meant me of course, Randall Harker, Dell for short, the city editor who happened to be writing a series on the sorry-ass job McKnight was doing in Washington.

I was mostly just chronicling his career—his disinclination to show up on the Senate floor even during important votes, his constant campaign-financing irregularities, the bribes he all but bragged he took from special interests. That and his character—his two volatile marriages and quickie divorces, his immense fondness for distilled spirits. The senator struck back just as the Chinese invasion of Korea claimed the lead in the *News*, so forgive me if we took too little space to defend ourselves in print. But our publisher John Tuckerman—a thin, stooped, aging gentleman socialist (he preferred the word Progressive) who wore English tweeds under a swirling mane of white hair—flatly denied McKnight's vague allegations in a rare appearance on the editorial page. Nice of him, since it was his idea to attack McKnight in the first place.

Old Man Tuckerman, I have to hand it to him, warned me off the memorial auditorium. He said he didn't like it, my going was a kind of provocation, it might be dangerous. (He didn't mean it was dangerous for me, naturally, he meant it was dangerous for him and the paper.) He said the last thing we needed was for trouble to start with me there. When I told him it was my story and I was going regardless, he said if I went, he'd bust me off city desk. When I ignored him, he said to take that kid with the chin whiskers—and a fast car.

"If anybody," he said, "and I mean anybody points a finger at you, or even looks at you too long, you hop in that car and—better yet, leave the kid outside at the wheel with the engine running." As he

3

talked, he took out some matches and stoked his pipe. "We can still pull this thing off, Dell," he said between smacks on the stem, "if you don't do anything stupid. The attorney general's investigating the senator's campaign finances, and the Republican leadership wants to bounce him in '52. The whole point is: Get McKnight. For Pete's sake don't play to his hand."

I shrugged and left for the meeting, the kid in tow.

The memorial auditorium sat on the edge of downtown, at the mouth of the North Side. From there out, till you reached farm country, the neighborhoods grew swankier and swankier, the houses bigger and bigger, the country clubs more exclusive and grandiose. The worst of the Republican big money and the best of the Progressive old money lay there. Out there, they all drank cocktails together, played tennis together, golfed together, planned for the education of their children, and seduced each other's wives. The few friends my father once had in Capital City lived out there now, too, but I never saw them.

And neither did McKnight. Oh, there may have been a couple of lawyers from the North Side there that evening who also happened to sit on the state Republican central committee. But most of the crowd came from the western suburbs and the South Side—the Knights of Columbus, and the Shriners, and the small businessmen, a few chamber-of-commerce types, a real estate agent or two. And lots of women, lots of married women, who joined the PTA and played bridge and canasta and had their hair done just for the occasion. Tonight, they brought the children.

The rest of the press was already there, and some of the boys got uneasy when the kid and I showed up. The memorial auditorium was a modern affair with a sweeping domed ceiling, concrete walls, and a blond-wood plank stage. Behind the podium, in cheap tile and pale washed-out red, white, and blue, was a mosaic of the American flag. The place was filled, the atmosphere relaxed, like a high school talent show. I heard a steady buzz of neighborly conversation, the occasional squeals of tykes trying too hard to have fun, and rare barks of discipline. The lights were up, and people looked around in the glare to see who they knew.

I knew McKnight mostly from photographs—the picked-over glamour shots of newspaper copy—but I had seldom seen him in the flesh. I got that mild twinge I always get when I come across the abstract people I write about in all their corporeal splendor. Real bodies can sit, for example, on a metal folding chair in a row of folding chairs behind a podium, and twitch, and shift position, and lean over trying to make strained conversation with persons left and right. McKnight wore a dark, conservatively cut, not especially expensive suit, a white shirt, and a blue club tie. He sat with his legs crossed, one hand always resting on his top knee as he flopped legs back and forth between the older, graying man—the geezer no doubt condemned to introduce him—and a younger, severely handsome, swarthy guy I took to be his aide, Daniel "Slick" Freeman.

McKnight was shorter than I had imagined, around five foot nine. He had black well-oiled hair, parted low on one side, the other combed straight back across the top over a bald spot. A string seemed permanently to dangle down on his forehead, dangerously close to the right eye, and he constantly pushed it back with his hand. He had a cowlick grease failed to conquer. If I had ever been tempted to buy a used car, McKnight would have been the man I expected to find standing across the hood from me.

He saw us come in while he was talking to the older man, but he did not let on. When he finished what he had to say, we were already seated, and he turned to Freeman to point us out, but before he did, he took one long, hard look at me. His face was sardonic, and his eyes—if I had been close enough to see his eyes—would hold the look of the huckster who has just spotted a newlywed walk onto the lot with his wife. His tongue flicked out across his lower lip, wetting it some more, as he smiled and spoke to the aide. Freeman's eyes, dark and luxurious even at this distance, shot up immediately, involuntarily, at us.

The introductions consisted of mindless patriotism and half-baked eulogy. Some of us pledged allegiance to the pale-tile flag, and the gray-haired geezer, president of the city's chamber of commerce, told a lot of silly jousting jokes playing with McKnight's name. Finally, having spent what little dignity he possessed, the local joker

5

gave, broadcast-commercial style, a brief pitch for free enterprise and the American way. The lights, which had remained up during the introduction, went down when McKnight rose to speak. Under the concentrated illumination of the stage, I noticed for the first time McKnight's eyebrows. As he sat and talked casually to Freeman on the platform they were unremarkable enough, but when he spoke to the crowd they both arched dramatically, adding to the weasel-like sharpness at the center of his bloated face and to the satanic grin he deemed appropriate for his stance as a political crusader.

Later, of course, his voice and manner of speaking would become famous. All good Americans would recognize the fast, blurred, almost monotonous tone and the long, rambling, illogical style that occasionally built to a kind of ersatz intensity before he made some wild, sensational charge. The national press would claim average folks found him exciting. But that night he was still a local phenomenon, a fast-talking, small-town businessman who had somehow been elected to public office. And the audience was bored. They were bored as he repeated the charges he had made in his week-old news release. They were bored during his dissertation on the evils of International Communism. They were bored as he outlined the plot hatched by Stalin and those Soviet stooges, the Red Chinese, to conquer the world starting with Korea.

Then he stopped his slurred monologue and carefully poured himself a glass of water.

"I have here," he said, "I have here in my hand a photostatic copy of an editorial written by Mr. John Tuckerman, owner of the *Capital News*. The editorial is dated March 14, 1941."

He pulled the paper down and held it out in front of his face, as if he were straining to read it. "And in this editorial, Mr. Tuckerman says, and I want to quote this to you. He says: 'Now let's get down to cases. Mr. Harker—' and by that he means Red Randall Harker, the same Red Randall Harker who now works for Mr. Tuckerman as his city editor—he says, 'Mr. Harker is a Communist, and I defy him to publicly deny that statement.'"

It was the same kind of crap he'd been tossing around for ten minutes already. And I doubted very seriously that he held in his hand anything but another page of the speech the polished young Freeman had written for him, or even that five people in our crowd knew what photostatic meant. But the difference was this: he had supplied a name and now he had his audience. A breeze of hushes silenced the restless noise of the children.

"And let's get down to cases. Before I came here tonight—early this morning, in fact—I sent Mr. Tuckerman a wire. And in that wire, I told him, I said, 'Mr. Tuckerman, I have a question to ask you. WERE YOU LYING—'" The shout made most of us jump, and almost immediately one or two of the children started to cry. McKnight went on: "Were you lying, I asked, when you said Harker was Capital City's leading Communist? If so, I said, tell us, *please* tell us WHEN HE CHANGED. And I did even more than that. *I* got down to cases. I went even further than he did in his editorial. I did not merely challenge him to publicly deny that he made that statement. No, I URGED him that if a single word of what I say is not the truth, I URGED him to sue me for libel, and I will gladly pay the damages."

Yep, he's got us now, I thought. Right in the wallet. I had been with Tuckerman all day, and no such wire had come for him. Still, McKnight had those of us in the audience now, in the moment, regardless of what I could disprove tomorrow.

"Let me quote something else to you," he said, frenetically searching through his notes. Since I was positive that whatever he was looking for did not exist, the search must have been an act. But it was convincing. Why would a man act out incompetence, why would he openly reveal how unprepared he was?

"Let me quote you something else. Only this time let me quote you something from a great American—J. Edgar Hoover, the head of the FBI. I know Mr. Hoover personally, and he is extremely concerned about this case. Extremely concerned about what is happening in communities like this all over this great country. Here it is, here it is." Again, he held a sheet of his speech out as if he were reading it. "Mr. Hoover says, 'The primary aim of the Communist Party at the present moment in the United States is to plant party members in important newspapers and radio stations, especially in college towns.' Now think about that—did you know that in addition to the *Capital News,* Mr.

John Tuckerman owns controlling interest in your city's major radio station, KNET?"

I finished his thought for him: And the renowned and progressive University of Wapsipinicon was just down the street. Every person there could finish that thought for him, now, or tonight at home, or tomorrow on the way to work. Yes, he had brought his bottled fear home for us. Now, he went in for the kill. "Now I don't want to frighten anyone here tonight," he said. "And when I tell you what I must tell you, now, I want you all to remain seated. And I want you all to remain calm. But you read the papers, and you know what's been happening with the labor unions in this state and around the country, the strikes, the violence, the threats. So, I have to tell you this TO PROTECT MYSELF. Let me say now that when the time comes that I quit exposing things because I might bleed a little in return, I promise you here tonight, I will resign from the United States Senate. There is someone here tonight, right here in this audience, who would do me great harm if he thought he could get away with it. Yes, out there among you, in the dark, maybe sitting right next to you, is a Communist—"

The whispering and the sporadic whimpering, and the hushings, created a kind of tremor through the audience.

"You better go start the car," I whispered to Guthrie. "Now."

"Right, Chief," he said.

"Yes, he is here tonight. Let's have the lights up! Turn them up so we can see him! Yes, Red Randall Harker! The very man we've been talking about!"

The lights came on. If folks did not know where to look to find me, the boys in the press made it clear enough. And as the eyes of the crowd began to search me out, a reporter no doubt on McKnight's payroll made it final by pointing and shouting, "There he is!" A couple of the women screamed out, the way they used to on dates at a double-feature horror show, and I remember worrying how I was dressed.

"I want that man searched!" McKnight shouted. "I want him searched!"

As the shock of light wore off and I could focus on the faces around me, I got a very, very unpleasant feeling in my gut. These people—these housewives and shopkeepers—seemed to suffer from paralysis, from the slowness of action you find in dreams. Or was it me, me who felt the leaden clamp of fear, the unreality of the moment? I should have known, I told myself. I should have figured that if McKnight was getting to me, his effect on those who knew nothing about the dark alleys of real politics would be that much worse.

I was surprised to find myself standing. I could not remember having stood. Then, I saw the men hanging around the back entrances moving down the aisle toward me. Oh, they would search me all right, and they would find on me, no doubt, one of the guns they now carried under their own coats.

I looked at McKnight and said as calmly as I could, "I am a U.S. citizen. Where is your badge?"

He smiled sarcastically. He said: "Oh, so you are a U.S. citizen? Okay, boys, you better forget it. Let Comrade—I mean Citizen Harker hide behind his legal rights. He would not dare to try anything against me here, now. But Citizen Harker, before you go…"

I had already started to move awkwardly down the row toward the aisle. The crowd was buzzing now, and people jerked their legs out of my path—but, at least, they were letting me pass. I stopped in the aisle and turned to face McKnight's ellipsis.

"Since your boss, Mr. Tuckerman, does not like to answer inquiries," McKnight said, "I'll ask you. I'll ask you to do the same thing he asked you to do back in 1941. Only, I'll ask you to answer the question in the proper way. To answer the question Congress will put to you if we are ever fortunate enough to get you out there in Washington, D.C., on the witness stand. The question all Communists refuse to answer. Are you now, or have you ever been, a member of the Communist Party?"

To this barrage, I responded: "I am not a member of the Communist Party."

"That's not the question!" he shouted as I walked out. "That's not the question! The question is, were you a—"

Outside, I took a long breath and thought about the crowd. They had sat there, frozen. By that clown. Guthrie pulled up, and I got in the car. Before he could ask what happened, I said, "Let's get out of here. Tuckerman's not going to like this."

9

❧

I was shook up, but it wasn't fear or dread I felt. I felt embarrassed. McKnight had thrown a spotlight on the foolish enthusiasms of my youth. He had not so much unmasked my nefarious past as exposed its juvenile naïveté. Again, I was reminded of a dream, of that odd mixture of excitement and shame you get when you look down to discover you are suddenly standing in front of a crowd of folks buck naked. In reality that night, I was much more concerned with my private life than McKnight's public one, more worried about my crumbling marriage than his political posturings. After the speech, for example, I didn't relish going home to Kathy, so the kid and I stopped for a quick drink or two at one of his hip but dimly lit dives. Once I was well lubricated, I had him drop me off at Sharon's.

She was a tall ice-cool blonde with pale Scandinavian skin and sky-blue eyes, when they were open. But she was asleep on the couch when I let myself in. She was wearing a dark green silk nightgown that perfectly matched the apartment. The place was a breath of the tropics. The furniture was all bright green foliage on a stark white background with white wicker chairs and tables and so many plants placed in corners, hanging from the ceiling, arranged on walls, that you had to check twice to make sure you did not hear the caws of toucans and the chatter of monkeys. The temperature must have been in the eighties. I was amazed she could sleep amid the hiss and clang of the steam radiators, painted a bright green. She heard me close the door behind me, and she moved off the couch toward me with a grace most women only dream of.

"You're wet," she said. "And late."

"Very late," I said. "I got caught in a storm with Guthrie. A kid from work." I stepped back, displaying with a movement of my arms my overcoat, soaking from the heavy snowfall outside.

"Always the patter," she smiled, and the smile stretched into a yawn. "Even at midnight."

"You're right," I said seriously. "Shouldn't have come. I know you have to work in the morning."

"My, my, aren't we considerate? You must be drunk. You do reek of

10

alcohol. And don't you dare apologize. I haven't seen you in almost a week, Dell. You are staying?"

"I'm staying," I said. "Couple hours?"

"Then let's get you out of those clothes." She snatched my hat. "And get you a bath. There's time for that. Let's put it this way, there better be time for that."

"Lady," I said, "I am at your command."

She floated toward the bedroom's bath to run the water. When she came back into the tropics, she smiled, turned sideways, hitched up her hip and revealed her shoulder, winking and motioning with her head behind her.

"I know what's wrong with this room," I said.

"There's nothing wrong with this room," she said.

"It's not really a room at all. It's a display. Like one of those things you do at work. Like it's in a glass case at the Emerson Museum. In the section marked American Decor. Entitled: Exotic Nights."

"Life," she laughed, disappearing again into the bedroom, "is an aesthetic phenomenon." This time she left the green nightgown behind with the wicker.

Sometime after that, much later, when Sharon was asleep again and I began to think again, I thought about long ago in Chicago where my wife and I first slept with each other, and I wished I understood how it was that you once loved somebody and then no longer loved them. Now I could not think why I had ever loved Kathy. Her father was a retired banker, and her mother an emeritus professor named Dr. Rose Spencer, who I'd had a schoolboy crush on back before the war when I attended her class on Shakespeare. Dr. Spencer had seemed the height of sophistication to a farm boy like me, so maybe it was inevitable that once I met her daughter I wound up marrying her. I certainly loved the memory of our first weekend in Chicago. Kathy had seemed to enjoy so spontaneously the big city nights and the rush of fear that accompanied our plunge into pleasure. We saw the Whitehead Band and whispered about the gangsters at the tables around us. One minute she wanted it all—the cars, the furs, the money—and the next she wanted to run home and set up a refuge for the two of us where I would struggle to write my fiction and she would finish her degree and work to support us till I got published and we would never see or need anyone else. As we steamed up the nights and slumbered away the days, I guess I mistook her lust to escape girlhood for passion and imagined I loved her.

These are certainly not thoughts to share with your good-looking mistress, so at Sharon's I drifted along, not thinking about tonight at the memorial auditorium or tomorrow at the office but about marriages—how all marriages depend on prevarication, and how, for me, marriage, like politics, had turned out not to be a base for building anything, much less a decent life. Eventually, I let myself out and caught a cab back to our apartment, regretting a little all the times I had been unfaithful to Kathy in the last fifteen years. She had stood by me, I told myself, she had accepted my notion of who I was. Now it seemed I didn't care if she believed in me or not. I only cared that Sharon would sit up nights in her tropical digs, waiting for me to come over late and take a bath. When Kathy asked me where I had been, I would lie to her about McKnight's attack, tell her how Guthrie and I went back to the *News* building, elaborate with a story about our getting caught in the snow on the way home. But would that have taken us all night?

This time Kathy was not up waiting for me. For a moment, I wondered if this was even our apartment. Shreds of white covered the living room floor and furniture. They ran willy-nilly down the hall and into my office. The floor in there, too, was sprinkled with the white sheets of paper. And the desk. And the typing table. Some of the sheets had been ripped into small pieces, some of them crumpled and tossed away, many of them whole sheets dropped here and there, others in careless bunches of irregular stacks as if they had been dumped in reams on the hardwood.

Clothes, too, had been tossed about the place, and some of them shredded. And broken glass dotted the floors. It looked as if we had been ransacked. I shouted out for Kathy, rushed from room to room searching for her. About the time I realized she was gone, I had calmed down enough to notice the ripped-up clothes were all mine. And to discover the bits of paper all had words written on them. Typewritten words. I began picking them up, and reading them, and reading them without understanding. Then a phrase became clear. Paragraphs suddenly familiar. All words I had once used. Words I had once written. Their disposition gave me the scene. Every page of the fiction I had long since abandoned for newspaper work, every typed and stored page was here. Then I knew: no burglar, but Kathy herself had done this. She had trashed our home with a passion I assumed completely vanished. I wondered if she had tried to read the fiction again as she paced about the apartment. How she had felt about the passages she shredded. If she felt differently about the pages she merely crumpled into balls. If she was oblivious to the sections she only tossed around, but left whole. And if she had read them all again, how long would that have taken. Would something like that take all night?

When I checked the bathroom her makeup and toothbrush were gone. And some of her clothes seemed to be missing from the closets. So, she had heard about Sharon. And McKnight had dug up more dirt on me than a checkered political past.

2.

To my surprise Tuckerman stood by me when the event at the memorial auditorium made the next morning's radio babble. Maybe he had no choice. After all, what McKnight said was true no matter how much we tried to gloss over it. I had indeed been a Communist for a couple of years in the 1930s before Stalin and Hitler got together and stabbed Poland in the back. And, yes, once the Old Man had called me a Red in print. I'd dropped out of school after my father killed himself, and I went to work for Tuckerman's paper. I joined the Newspaper Guild and came under the influence of a CIO organizer and party recruiter named Vladimir Padikoff ("Vlad Paddy" to the Irish jokers in the union). I helped organize the *News* for the Guild, and the Old Man almost never forgave me. But so what? When I was director of the local CIO's PAC, I had called *him* a cocktail socialist, a warmonger, and a Red-baiter. All that, of course, was before the war and before Tuckerman made me city editor. Now, I simply worked for the man. But it didn't matter to the bullyboys on the right, still searching for the specters of the Comintern, that these events belonged to another era and concerned mostly dead issues. Besides, I'd lost my faith not my pride. Just because I was no longer pals with the Bolsheviks didn't mean I suddenly believed Karl Marx an idiot nor all capitalists choirboys.

Trudging my way, hungover and spent, to work the next morning through the wake of the early winter storm that hit our burg last week like a slap in the face, the city room promised a refuge. But buying a pack of cigarettes in the lobby on the way upstairs, I noticed a disapproving frown from the cute girl at the cash register who once flirted so freely with me. Still, when I caught Tuckerman in his office, searching for something with which to stoke up his pipe, he just mumbled, "I warned you." I grimaced and shrugged, and he shook his head and asked me to close the door for a minute.

"We need something fresh for your next piece on McKnight,"

he said. "The man's obviously desperate. It's a fact the Republicans hate the idea of renominating him." Tuckerman knew the GOP top brass well, for he, too—like my father and every other inhabitant of Wapsipinicon old enough to vote and buy a drink—had once been a Republican back in the old "Prince" Albert Collette days when Progressivism was the breathtaking new political phenomenon. He'd switched parties sometime during the New Deal.

"I'll check with Guthrie and Hoops," I said. "Last night the kid tried to tell me something about the bogus tail gunner crap, but by that point I wasn't paying much attention."

"Just see what you can come up with," Tuckerman said. "Let's shut down the son of a bitch, rather than answer his charges." All this time, Tuckerman kept looking for a light. It was an odd habit—and irritating. His desk, his entire office, was as orderly and clean as his soul. Then he produced a match from God knows where, lit his calabash, and the face underneath his mane went blank. He impassively started to shift around the few odd trinkets on his desk. It was his way of letting me know that he was ending our little story conference. I stood for my exit.

"Right," he said on my way out. "Send Bill Dyers in, will ya?"

The newsroom's fluorescence wobbled at the edges of my eyeballs, and the routine clack and clang of its typewriters tested my temper. Looming wisps of tobacco smoke, like dirty angel hair, decorated the space, its desks paved with unruly stacks of loose-leaf drafts and the orphan scrolls of old proofs. The sweet smell of newsprint and printer's ink—some spot between rotten fruit and stale shoe polish—hung in the air, too, as staffers hustled about with evident purpose. But Bill Dyers, our managing editor, had simply disappeared into the morning din. I tagged a copy boy to deliver the Old Man's message to him. Hoops, our political reporter, was nowhere to be found either, so I left a note on his desk to let me know if he ever returned. Then a miracle occurred. I caught Guthrie on his way out.

"Man, you look awful," he said.

"C'mon, Guthrie, don't fuck with me. I'm in no mood. Tuckerman wants something new this minute on McKnight. What was all that nonsense last night about our pal Larry's war record?"

He screwed up his face. "You mean," he said, carefully, "the jazz with those bogus war hero clips about his famous mission behind enemy lines?"

I looked at him.

"Okay, okay, I'll run it past you again. Something's kinky with the narrative," he said. When Guthrie talked, he shifted his small frame from one leg to the other, and his shoulders moved as if keeping time to the beat of brushes on drums, a blues tattoo *chu-chu chu-chu-chu chu-chu-chu*. "Like I was trying to tell you, McKnight had this pal, worked for the *Stars & Stripes*, and he evidently talked him into writing up the story as a gas one night they're both high. But there was nothing to it, daddy-o. The mission, according to this buddy—Haugen, Jack Haugen—was nowheresville, a milk run; McKnight could not have been any safer if he'd never left base. Evidently, man, everybody but the brass was in on the act. I don't see the laughs, but then I wasn't there."

I looked at him.

"And," he said, "next thing you know, the cat's got the clipping published in his hometown newspaper. State Republican honchos, don't know shit from Shinola, are looking at him as a good candidate—war hero chucka-chucka-boom—to challenge Collette's son for the primary. Suddenly, the thing's no joke, and the pal wrote the article? Out of the Army, working on McKnight's campaign, running PR, hauling in the dough. Hoops has the dope on Haugen, who works for the *Wapsipinicon Times*. Got the story off him listening to bebop together one night, Haugen bragging how hip he is, how he *made* McKnight a big shot. But he won't confirm it sober, won't even answer our calls."

"I didn't hear this last night," I said, staying focused by will alone.

This time it was the kid who gave me a look. "You were real gone, man. Didn't want to talk about McKnight or the speech. Seemed to me you were looking to chill out, you dig? So I shut my trap. Then we got to talking about chicks, and, you know . . ." Now, he was the one who shrugged.

"Sorry," I said. "In any case, story seems pretty stale to me."

"Seemed that way to me too, dad. But talk to Hoops. He's got me hotfooting it all over, checking shit out about it."

"I will if he ever shows up for work," I said. "Meantime, haul your butt over to Republican headquarters, will you, and find somebody in the dump-McKnight camp who's hoarding an eight-by-ten glossy of the senator accepting a large stack of greenbacks from one of the manufacturing lobbyists."

When he somehow nodded sarcastically and took a pause, I snapped my fingers a few beats. "Go, man, go," I said. He went, and I was stuck with the din of work and a stack of unedited stories.

Last night's long stew settled into my bones like the flu, and I went about the business of putting out today's paper. To this morning's local headlines charging I had tried to disrupt McKnight's speech, we responded that I was there covering the story for the *News*, trying, we said, simply to do my job. We ignored the newspaper accounts claiming I had refused to answer a direct question as to whether I had "ever" been a member of the Communist Party. And, believe it or not, *Get McKnight* wasn't our only story. To my mind, it wasn't even our most important. There were the off-year elections, which Truman's critics had predicted would spell disaster for the Democrats but hadn't been all that bad. There was, too, the President's Russian-roulette foreign policy (dubbed "containment" by the administration), especially the so-called police action in Korea, and the impact it was having on political life in Capital City. Also we were in the middle of a big decertification and recognition battle between the Electrical, Radio, and Machine Workers of America—yet another powerful union the Congress of Industrial Organizations had recently drummed out of its ranks for being Communist infiltrated—and the United Electrical Workers, which the CIO honchos formed to replace the ERMWA.

The strike started at the General Electric plant on the East Side, but it spread until a group of contractors had to close down a job rewiring the city's municipal buildings, including city hall. And the mayor didn't like taking a dump in the dark.

Tommy Rojack, head of the new union, was a good friend from my days on the PAC, and Vlad Paddy, leader of the old one, was the man who, as I said, originally recruited me for the party and, even today, despite all that had come between us, remained one of my heroes. For a lot of people like me, including most of the workers involved in the strike, whatever their current loyalties, we weren't talking about abstract historical forces but about people, people we knew, people some of us had worked with, not mindless puppets with strings to the Kremlin, on the one hand, or naïve idealists on the other.

The ERMWA strike—that was a story I could get my teeth into instead of yet one more hatchet job for the Old Man on Larry McKnight. It was an important story, a vital story. But it was not the story our labor guy, Charles Wilson, wrote.

He had landed his job shortly before I made city editor, so I had inherited him, and I had been trying to get him to understand the rudiments of wage earning and class struggle ever since. By now I was convinced he never would, and I longed to fire his ass. But he was a Tuckerman hire, a favor for a family friend, or so I had heard, and I kept putting it off, telling myself that marginal, liberal dailies like the *News* have to do the best they can with what they've got. His copy today, as usual, was terrible, and after the morning's regular staff meeting, I told him to stay behind as the rest drifted away to their desks.

"Boss," Wilson said.

He was about five-seven or -eight, with limp dishwater hair, his face once mildly scarred by adolescent acne, which he half attempted to hide with a Vandyke, and he had a contemptuous air about him he took from reading white-shoe detective novels. He seemed...affected, a sissy. No surprise the boys down at union hall wanted nothing to do with him.

Lillian, my secretary, interrupted. "I've got Hoops on the line," she said.

"Take his number. No, just tell him to get his hiney in here."

Wilson was leaning casually on the corner of my desk.

"Wilson, this stuff is shit. But I don't suppose that surprises you."

"Boss?"

"Jesus Christ."

Where do you start with some people? They've been spoon fed on free enterprise and the American Dream, and they think they know what they want and can get it. They've no economics, no history, no politics, not even a retarded class consciousness, yet they think they know what they want and can get it. A whole generation of these jerks, a little older maybe (and a little manlier) than this one, had come back gung-ho from the war to a simplified world with a simple-minded notion of success. They read some Nietzsche before and some Niebuhr after, and they went back to school in political science or business management or, worse, journalism. They had the spurious snobbery of a Philo Vance and the celluloid polish of a David Niven. Arrogant, ambitious, and clueless, they worshipped raw power, enjoyed mindless consumption, and expressed a kind of pride in conforming. Just thinking about a slug like Wilson alive in my city was enough to start the blood thumping along my forehead again.

"All this here," I said without hope. "This crap about Reuther and Murray and the great purge of '47—"

"Background," he said. "I—"

"Yeah, well they got an anti-Communist platform written, and they held a few elections. But on the local level, they lost as many as they won."

Wilson put on his sneer. Easy enough to read his mind if you could get past the sour kisser and the silk shirt and the finely shaped hands: *Right, I hear you, Mr. Red Randall Harker.*

"You can wipe the smirk off your face," I said. "I burned my Party card a long time ago."

"That's not what they say down at union hall."

"Fuck off. How would you know? You've never been to union hall."

"Vlad Paddy, on the other hand, says you sold out to a job."

He ran his finger along my desk like some damn ingénue in a Howard Hawks movie. I realized he was baiting me, of course, and I tried to control my temper.

"We're not talking about me," I said. He was leaning back, stretching his insolence the length of his body. Outside, the snow swirled, and the routine buzz of the newsroom you come to register as quiet the way you register (but don't really hear) Canada geese flying south on a windy day seemed suddenly muffled, which is when I noticed the people nearest us had stopped typing. I knew I was speaking too loudly, but I couldn't stop myself. "We are talking about this piece of crap I'm holding in my hand some fool wants me to believe is a news story. Where do you get this shit, this international conspiracy, blind dictates of the party? Huh? Don't tell me. I know. You've been reading *Time* magazine on the Dies Committee. You even know what a Communist is?"

Wilson lowered his head as if he were embarrassed for me. He made motions with his hands to keep it down. Then he looked over at Lillian, smiled a tolerant little smile, and shifted his eyes from her to me instead of nodding his head.

"No, you wouldn't," I said. "He's the guy standing next to you on the job who was just a little ahead of you in high school and a little tougher than you on the picket line."

"You ought to know," he frumped.

"Do you even understand why the CIO wants to expel them? Sharp guys like Reuther and Murray noticed Harry Truman won the election, that's all. So they wrote an executive council order barring anyone advocating the overthrow—excuse me, the violent overthrow—of the United States government from holding office in CIO locals. And guess what? Suddenly nobody seems to be advocating the violent overthrow of the United States government any more, not out in the open anyway. That, Wilson, is basically what your purge amounts to—prudence."

"And I suppose you're going to tell me Vlad Paddy's not behind the trouble at G.E."

Instead of giving in to my urge to smack him, I said in as flat a voice as I could muster: "Mr. Padikoff is one of those who can't adapt to the new CIO. He won't take the pledge, period. That's it. Him and lots of others. They don't like Walter Reuther, they don't like Phil Murray—"

"How about you, Mr. Harker? Do they like you?"

He was smiling. I took a breath, ignored his sarcasm, turned back to the typescript, and said: "What are your sources for this article? I mean, where do you get this crap?"

We both looked at his copy as I speed mumbled through the lead paragraph.

> City officials have refused to recognize the Communist-led Electrical, Radio, and Machine Workers of America (traditionally

abbreviated ERMWA), the largest and most militant of the electrical industry unions involved in the current strike that has closed down much of the construction underway in the capital, including the rewiring of City Hall. Many claim that ERMWA does not have the interest of the rank-and-file at heart in the eight-week-old dispute involving hundreds of workers, General Electric, and the company's city plant. Instead, they say, the ERMWA's bosses are desperately clinging to their dwindling influence in the current atmosphere of almost universal distrust of the Communists and their champions in labor.

"What's wrong with that?" he demanded.

"It misses the point."

Even I was surprised by the passion in my voice. One of the staffers walked over, obviously intending to step between us if trouble started. I held my hand up to him, and he stopped. And waited.

"No," Wilson said, "the point is—"

"The *story*," I said, "is not the dwindling influence of the Commies—"

"The *point* is," he jumped in, "that you used to argue with Mr. Tuckerman about this same thing when you were a lowly labor reporter."

He was right, of course, just like McKnight. Once upon a time the Old Man and I had fought regularly about such coverage, and Wilson was simply following one of Tuckerman's typical diktats. I knew that. But I could read subtexts as well as the next guy, and the subtext here was Wilson's unspoken claim he didn't answer to me at all any more after last night but only to the man who hired him. It was a mistake not to have gotten rid of the asshole long before today.

"There's nothing lowly about it," I said more quietly. "I was never stupid enough to think that."

"Of course not."

By now the entire bullpen had come to a halt. Everyone was watching us, listening to us.

"That's the second time you have tried to imply something without actually saying it."

"Oh, I can say it, *sir*, if you want me to say it. There is nothing wrong with my copy. Nothing except that it does exactly what Mr.

Tuckerman wants. It documents the fact that you and your ilk are having your asses kicked out into the street where you belong."

"No," I said, over the throbbing. "You're wrong. It's your butt getting kicked into the street. Get out. Go back to your desk, put on your fucking Empire coat, and go peddle your journalism-school fantasies and your balanced periods somewhere else. You're fired."

For a moment, his smile vanished. Then it was back, brighter than ever in the dotted pattern of his face, and he walked away with three fingers of one delicate hand hung in a vest pocket, the other swinging freely at his side, as he nodded his head to—and smiled superciliously at—everyone he passed on his way out. They stared back at him without expression.

When he had gone, people got back to work, and I caught Bill Dyers's eye as he stood by the Old Man's door. He laughed, shook his head, and waved his hand loosely from the wrist. I couldn't tell if he was trying to say it had been a heated little scene or if he was making fun of Wilson's mincing exit.

Five minutes later Wilson stood in front of my desk again, encoated, behatted, and very indignant. He had some news to impart, at last. I hadn't seen him using any of the telephones on the city desk, so he must have called union hall from downstairs. Because he said: "The copy would never have gone in anyway."

His voice quivered a little, and I thought he was going to cry. Dreading it, I ignored him.

"I said—"

"I heard."

"Oh, screw you. They settled the strike an hour ago."

When he was gone again, I waved to Lillian and told her to try to reach Tommy Rojack—and if she couldn't, to leave a message for him to meet me at The Cove for lunch. I marked up what copy I had left on the desk, sent it down to composition, and—after Lillian reported she couldn't get through to Tommy—allowed the pounding in my head to drive me toward my hat and coat and the newsroom elevator.

"I'll call him from the Cove. If Hoops or Kid Guthrie check in, tell 'em to leave a message where I can get in touch with them." Lillian avoided my eyes. "And if Hoops doesn't show soon, tell Gene to start rounding up the copy for the afternoon deadline just in case I'm late getting back."

Her *yes, sir* was as cold as the weather outside.

Jesus, I thought. Jesus. Does she actually feel sorry for the idiot?

God, I needed a drink.

3.

The Cove kept my tab. I ordered a scotch and found a back booth to avoid the lunch crowd. A couple of clowns from the *Times*, playing darts, waved to me smugly on my way back. I knew one of them, an old coot named Jenkins, but the other was the reporter who had pointed me out to the crowd last night at the war memorial. When I felt myself again, I thought, maybe I'd ask the bozo a couple of pointed questions, but before I even took a sip of my drink, a wait-ress—let's call her Charlotte—came back and told me I was wanted on the horn.

The two *Times'* reporters stopped me on my way to the phone booths and Jenkins introduced me to his pal. Turns out his name was Jack Haugen, the name of the man Guthrie told me about this morning who had been in the army with McKnight and run publicity for his first senate campaign. After joking about the snow, Jenkins asked me as a sort of garbled challenge to help them think of more adjectives to describe the kind of day it was.

"Miserable?" I suggested.

"Yeah," Jenkins said. "Slate-gray, looming, miserable."

We all took a slug. One gulp finished my drink, and I shrugged, put it down among a crowd of cups and glasses and ashtrays on the red-checkered tablecloth covering their wretchedly wooden table, and turned toward the bank of phones. Slurring still and obviously want-ing to extend their Writers' Holiday, Jenkins said, "Hey, Harker, I was telling Haugen here about how you made city desk."

"That's nice, but I gotta get moving if I want to keep the job."

"So do we," Haugen said, pointedly, and the two stood up.

I mashed out my Camel and started again for the booths but stopped and tried to tug Haugen a little off to the side. He snatched his arm back. He was another of the Philo Vance–David Niven kids, only a little sharper and tougher than Wilson—and better looking. He had a square handsome face, blond hair made darker by the oil he

24

used to comb it back perfectly straight over his head, and he wore a new, expensively tailored suit in muted grays, a light gray shirt, and a charcoal tie. I just couldn't warm up to these guys, guys like Wilson and Haugen, a feeling clearly mutual.

"One of my reporters tells me you used to work for McKnight," I said.

"I work for the *Times* now," he said, glaring at Jenkins.

"I can see that," I said, looking at their debauched tabletop. "And working hard, too. How about last night? You slaving away like this for the *Times* then or just shilling for the senator?"

"Let's move," Haugen said, grabbing the old fart by his arm and jerking him along at a gait addled by the alcohol they had both consumed. On their way out, I caught Jenkins's *Yeah, an' he was plenty Red back then, too,* just before I closed the door of the telephone booth I used as my hideaway extension at The Cove.

The Old Man barked in my ear. "Harker, what the hell is going on? Dyers tells me a young man is running around downstairs, threatening to blow your brains out, that you've dashed off to cover the story he's supposed to be covering, and that the secretaries are signing a petition protesting the paper being directed from Moscow."

"Sour grapes. I fired him."

"Who?"

"Wilson."

"Who the hell is Wilson?"

Nice try, I thought. I knew misdirection when I encountered it. I figured he was calculating whether, under the circumstances, he should let me get away with booting the little creep.

"The jerk who's been covering labor for the last two years," I said.

"The pansy?"

The Old Man was a good dissembler, I'd give him that.

"You know who he is," I said. "You hired him."

He gave me one of his pipe-smacking pauses.

"Dyers says the women think you were unfair."

"The women don't have to edit his copy," I said.

"This Wilson kid seems disturbed. Seriously, I mean. Mentally.

Dyers said he had a gun." Again, I didn't respond, and, after another long pause, he said, "Well, you know what you're doing, I don't." I took it he was done musing. Charles Wilson indeed no longer worked for me, nor for Mr. Tuckerman's newspaper. "If you get shot," he added, "don't try to collect workman's comp from this outfit."

When I neither laughed nor replied, he said, "So, they settled the strike?"

"The company agreed to a contract. I'm having lunch with Tommy Rojack."

"You mean they settled with the UEW. Very good. Very good. Go ahead, run with this today, but don't let it interfere with the piece on McKnight, understand. Get Hoops to help on this thing, this strike piece, too. Try talking to that Bolshevik pal of yours, Vladimir Padikoff, find out what the Communists think about having the rug pulled out from under them. You know, the—"

"—dwindling influence of the Communists on the labor unions."

"That's right. And, Randall, seriously, watch out for this Wilson character. Dyers is no worrywart, and he seemed concerned."

Which meant the Old Man knew a thing or two about Wilson I didn't.

"You bet, Mom," I said, and hung up.

I got twenty nickels from the cashier and stuck one in a hole.

"United Electrical Workers."

"Hello. Let me speak to Tommy Rojack."

"May I ask who's—"

"Randall Harker."

"One moment, please."

I lit a fag and waited. Maybe I'd cheat the telephone company my next call. When I was a boy, we used to wet pennies and slip them down the nickel slot. Lately, I'd seen kids twist off the voice end of the receiver and short the circuit, or whatever you call it, against the metallic top of the coin box.

"Yeah."

"Hey, Honky. Harker. I hear you done some good today."

"Harker. Well, the mayor exercised some muscle, and GE certified us, then agreed to a contract. Bing, bing, bing."

"Congratulations. When did they settle?"

"Ten this morning. The snowstorm helped. But the contract's still got to go for a vote, and—"

"Bet they're breathing easier down at city hall."

"Tell the truth, Harker, we couldn't have done it without them. Vlad Paddy is pissed as hell. If he can keep defections down, he's staying out on strike. I don't know we got the votes. If we have to face them over a picket line, anything could happen."

"You've got the votes. You get my message about lunch?"

"Can't do it, Dell. Gotta man the phones. My people are calling anybody who ever walked in the door."

"That's all right. I'll catch you at the celebration. Where you throwing it?"

"If we throw it."

"Where are you throwing it?"

"Waldorf on the Wharf."

"Guess I'll see you tomorrow night, eh, comrade?"

I didn't cheat the phone company on my next call.

"Hello. Mayor's office."

"This is Randall Harker. Of the *Capital News*."

"Yes?"

"May I speak to Mr. Toland, please."

"One moment."

One moment was all I needed to see Hoops trundle through the door and stop to talk to a waitress, who pointed first to the telephone booth, then to the booth where I had been sitting before I beat my retreat into Ma Bell's womb. The brim of Hoops's fedora had been flattened back above his forehead by the wind outside, and now he moved his bulk over the shiny big black-and-white linoleum squares heading toward the rear.

"Well, well, well," Paul Toland said into my ear. "Red Randall Harker."

So, he had heard about last night and wanted me aware of it. Paul was the city manager. He had a PhD in civil engineering, political science, city planning, some damn thing, from the state university. I had known him since he was a graduate teaching assistant and I was an undergrad. He had been hired straight from school by the mayor, a Democrat, a few years after His Honor came into office during the first Roosevelt landslide in '32. That was the election that put Prince Albert's Progressive ailing coalition out of its misery after Collette had careened into the U.S. Senate. With Toland's technical and academic training and the mayor's political savvy, these two New Dealers were supposed to transform our town into a model of humane urban development and efficiency. They fucked it up, of course, but Paul hung on to his integrity despite his ambition.

He was young enough at forty still to go far. He developed the city manager's job from an appointed, mostly advisory position to a seat of real power, getting himself elected along the way first as Democratic Chairman for the city, then State Democratic Chairman. As a civil servant, a merit employee, he was technically supposed to keep his hands off politics, but it soon became clear he was the real brains behind city hall, and nobody paid much attention to his title. From the city manager's desk, he did what good he could for the place while biding his time for something better. Most of us generally assumed McKnight's senate seat was now that something better. Paul Toland seemed to me the one man in state politics, Democrat or Republican, truly capable of picking up the Prince's fallen Progressive mantle, which made him meanwhile an awfully good contact.

"Hey, Paulie. How's the oppressing business? I hear the lights are back on in the city johns."

"Not quite. You people still must decide who it is you want to bargain for you this week. Eight weeks you've been trying to make up your minds who should talk to me."

"Yeah, well, you can drop the *you*, friend."

"Oh, yes. That's correct. You quit the Party, you quit the PAC, and—what? You're calling to tell me Tuckerman fired you after last night and you want a job."

"No such luck. I need to talk to you, though."

I let him breathe for a few seconds.

"I want to pick your considerable brain about The McKnight."

He let me breathe for a few seconds.

"U. S. Senator McKnight?" I said. "He represents you in Washington these days?"

"Some folks think so. Not today, Dell. The new contract, as I'm sure you are aware, goes up for a vote today. I have to see His Honor in forty minutes, and I am supposed to tell him—reassure him—this thing has been settled. Whether, in fact, it has been settled or not, that is what I'm supposed to tell him. Look it, we'll speak tomorrow, after this thing is settled one way or the other."

It was bullshit. He was dodging me. I needed something for my piece on McKnight now, not sometime in the distant future like to-morrow. "How about this afternoon, after your little confab with His Honor?"

He exhaled, then said, "Two o'clock. Earliest I'll be free. Five minutes, ten at the most."

"Two then," I said.

&

That Hoops was a fat man—given his name—was either funny or cruel or sad, depending on my view of the world at the moment. Dressed in a wrinkled shirt with curled collars, a print tie halfway down his belly, and a brown sports jacket, he was sitting in my spot next to the heap of our overcoats, looking toward the door, smoking a Lucky Strike and drinking a Miller High Life on my tab when I finally burst the confines of the phone booth. At rest, he appeared on the verge of slumber, but when he inhaled tobacco fumes into his swelling mass, he seemed to suck light and oxygen from the room.

"You didn't make the staff meeting," I said. "Lillian told you to get your keister into work. Instead you show up here."

"M'larky," he responded, spewing smoke as if startled awake. "I spent my morning over at Democratic headquarters listening to all the buzz about the off-year election results, which is where I was when I called you the first time to let you know I'd be a little late coming in, and you kissed me off. Jesus, I should get a damn medal just for calling in. None of the telephones at Democratic headquarters work, and not just because of the snowstorm. I found a public phone, *again*, and called the city desk, *again*, only to discover you had destroyed the place and run off. So, I rushed on over to your infamous hideaway."

I looked around for Charlotte and gave her my own version of a nod. Then, I sipped my scotch as Hoops fell silent. At length, I said,

"Did the Democrats have anything new on McKnight?" Charlotte, looking sexy and standing by, had her pad out. "Want another?" I ordered two more when Hoops bobbed his head slightly to the second question.

"New? Nah. They got a sharp political staffer name of Hickenlooper, Hickeydooger, sumpin, shoveling mud into buckets for your boy Paul Toland, I guess, to sling next time around. He told me about those famous Republican campaign irregularities, dirty tricks and what not; how in '46 some of McKnight's boys, army buddies, rounded up a gang of farmers back in the hinterland where you still don't have to register to vote and carted them from poll to poll in army troop trucks. Hoositburger is outraged. Gosh darn."

"Ain't that something," I said. "I see he's been reading the *News*."

"I got that impression. I didn't want to bust his bubble, so I didn't say: 'Well, Happendrop, old buddy, yeah, you know Randall Harker wrote all about this last August in his column.' He's new to the job and don't know no better. You'd probably just give him the sack."

I sighed and worked on my drink. Hoops fell quiet again, one hand on his beer. "Boss," Hoops said, "what's up?"

"I need something, anything, for us to hit back with after last night. Tuckerman says, 'Attack, don't respond,' quote end quote."

Hoops laughed.

"Just review it for me, okay," I said.

He made another slight gesture I might interpret as a shrug. "All right. Where do you want me to start?" I looked at him. "Tell you what," he said "I'll start at the beginning." As Hoops talked, I found myself half listening, drifting off to the sound of clinking silverware, lunchtime chatter, and short-order shouts. Hoops talked about how McKnight started out on his father's chicken farm back in 1928, abandoned that when his old man died, and took up the sale of farm implements. When this new business went bust in 1930, somebody— Hoops thought it was the Farm Bureau or the milk lobby—cleared off McKnight's debt and backed him in a campaign for state treasurer later that year. The Republicans featured him as 100 percent American—small-business guy from the heartland, standing out by his plow in his business suit, honest as the day is long—versus those gangsters in our state who called themselves Democrats back in those days. But Albert Collette, the great Progressive leader of the state's Republican Party, did not care for McKnight. In fact, he thought McKnight had been crammed down his throat by the party's conservative wing. By the time McKnight first ran for office, Collette was in the U.S. Senate, and the New Dealers had won the Wapsipinicon statehouse. When they decided to go after Collette himself, the corrupt little asshole state treasurer named McKnight became Prince Albert's natural Republican fall guy.

"So, you get the income tax evasion charges in '32," Hoops was saying. "But somehow, McKnight comes up with the money and pays off the back taxes—and, tell the truth, avoiding them to begin with don't exactly make him anathema with a lot of Republicans. In any case, now he thinks he's untouchable. Divorces his plain old ugly farm wife of seven years in '35 and takes up with a number of Capital City floozies."

"One of whom was underage," I said.

"Right," said Hoops, a little uneasy with the topic for some reason, or so it seemed to me. "And when the Democrats slapped him with a morals charge, Prince Albert had had all he was going to take of this little walking disaster."

According to Wapsipinicon political lore, Collette made a backroom deal with the Democratic DA to drop the charges and forced McKnight to marry the girl, enlist in the army, and rush off to free Europe. I was pretty sure the Prince had counted on McKnight getting shot dead over there, which would save him, and the Wapsipinicon Republican Party, any more political worries from the twerp. Of course, Collette had no way of knowing that he would be the one who failed to last out the war.

"Jesus Christ," I said. "Now McKnight's a U.S. senator."

"Yep," Hoops said. "Because, in the end, Republican voters picked the asshole, despite all his baggage, to carry their grand old banner."

The food came piled high. The Cove had filled up with the lunch crowd, and I was anxious to be on my way. Instead, I watched Hoops eat and sipped my drink. "Most of my life," I said, "we've been electing idiots to office."

"What can I tell you, man was a war hero," Hoops laughed. Hoops grew more animated as he ate, eyes sparking, forking food down with one hand and slicing the air up and down and back and forth with the other as he talked. "Besides," he was saying, "Hoboken thinks we've done some real damage."

"Hoboken?"

"Hickenlooper, the Democratic flack."

"I think you've gone from Platt Deutsche to Dutch, mangling this guy's name. Damaged how?"

"Before the war, all the Republican special interests—State Manufacturers' Association, Farm Bureau—backed McKnight to the bitter end. So, inevitably, when McKnight returns from Europe, he announces he intends to fill Prince Albert's seat now his majesty was, how to put it, kaput. He wins the Republican primary just barely over Collette's kid. But come the general election, the party moneybags and the special interests are nowhere to be found. They had dropped him like a live grenade."

"Wait a minute," I said. "Guthrie said something this morning about the Republicans courting McKnight? They thought he looked good because of his war record?"

"That's what Guthrie gets for listening to anything a *Times* reporter tells him. Remember, this was 1946. Truman has just dumped the Big One, and a Collette has been in office somewhere in this state since before the damn First World War. Nobody knows what the hell is going on, least of all the fucking Republicans. Here comes McKnight waving his Purple Heart and his Distinguished Flying Cross, and he's had it with being a party hack, a fall guy. He thinks he can be his own man now. The interest groups have absolutely zero interest in the man, war hero or no, because he's known to be a walking textbook on corruption, and they don't want to give Albert Junior even more ammo against them. But McKnight refuses to call it quits. Folks tell me he talked to every single farmer in the whole north half of the goddamn state. Walked his ass off during the primary."

I remembered the campaign well. McKnight constantly in uniform, wearing an aviator's cap, a machine gun belt wrapped round his belly, touting the thirty-two missions he'd completed against Fortress

Germany and asking how his opponent, Albert Collette's son, had spent the war, despite the fact Albert Junior was far too old to enlist by the time the Japanese bombed Pearl Harbor. McKnight accused Collette the Younger of war profiteering, too, though the only investment the boy ever made was in trying to fill his father's shoes.

"Your point?" I asked, rubbing my forehead.

"My point is, old Tail-Gunner Larry did it without them, without help from the rich bigwigs and special-interest groups. Christ, the CIO unions—including your old pal Vlad Paddy's outfit—even backed the man during the primary, despite his pitiful chances, because Prince Albert's kid was such an adamant anti-Commie."

I recalled the primary election night, too, of course. How stunned we all were that McKnight actually won. Barely, by about five votes, but he won. Then, Albert Junior, knowing he was the better man and hurt deeply by the dishonest and truly nasty personal attack against him, his always overwrought dignity destroyed by the shocking and embarrassing defeat, retired shamefaced from politics. Before the year was out, the depressed and despairing fallen native son committed suicide, though not so straightforwardly as my father had, so there were still those who proclaimed the overdose of sedatives an accident rather than self-slaughter. But I remember thinking he probably hoped to join his father in paradise, where—as we know—all politics are progressive.

"So, McKnight wins the general," Hoops continued, "defeating some Democrat nobody these days cares about, who everybody back then thought would lose to Colette, Jr., anyway, instead of to this guy. And off The McKnight goes to Washington. By 1947, 1948, the SMA and the Farm Bureau are back in his camp making up for their mistake, pouring money into his coffers, buying his every vote."

When I made a face, Hoops cut to the chase. "Okay. Okay. So, here's *Hoboken*'s message—we've been ragging the guy for over a year, my news pieces, your columns, bringing up all these old beefs, and have you heard an objection out of the special interests? Not one peep. They are preternaturally quiet. See it? They never liked the man but they once upon a time held their noses and backed him *after* he won *because* he won. But not now. Now they're not backing him at all."

I got it. "They don't think he can win come '52."

Hoops dipped his head slightly, like the Buddha congratulating a slow-witted pupil.

I added, "That's what Tuckerman says, too."

"It's all of a piece." Hoops finished his meal with a swill of beer and a belch. "The rise and fall of a turd, right? If you let me tell my story, the way I want to tell my story—"

"They *want* him to lose reelection," I said. "They really, really don't like him very much; they figure they can't trust him. But he is, after all, the incumbent, and they are afraid they can't dump him."

Hoops smiled. "They are definitely afraid they can't dump him. How do you dump a sitting senator? If the Republicans can't figure a way, I think they plan to all but concede the election. Your boy Toland could be sitting pretty. He should beat McKnight easy, no sweat."

"So, they want us to do the dumping for them. That's why Tuckerman has been on my ass. His old Republican pals are feeding him the story. Why don't they give us something, then? It's not enough for the party to be off hiding in the bleachers every time we throw a bean ball at McKnight."

"Yeah," Hoops said. "But they are. Just in case. They learned their lesson last time around."

Hoops motioned to Charlotte as she passed by. He ordered apple pie for desert.

"And you better bring him another of those," he said. He met my stare. "So, I eat too much? You drink too much. What else is new?"

"It's my tab."

Ignoring me, he said, "But wait, there's more. According to Howdy-high, the man's getting new money from somewhere. Now, we know it's not the traditional Republican groups or special interests. Some, it turns out, maybe, from the Catholic groups."

"Catholics?"

"Yeah. Surprise. He's a closet Roman. Didn't hear much about that before on account of the small-business people and Prince Albert's crowd being such blue-nosed Protestant teetotalers and all, but the man *is* Irish. The Papists knew it all along, and that's why he sounds a little like Father Coughlin now and then. But, from what Howdy

Doody says, he's getting a lot more money than that. This is the point where Hobby Boots drops his voice to a whisper and rasps on about some big meeting the other night, some group of right-wing senators, including McKnight, and a priest or two. Oooh. Scary.

"Our junior senator," Hoops summarized, "is a man who's lost what little power base he had in the state, a man without an issue or an idea or a scruple of any kind, vulnerable on every front, owing nobody round here nothing, and getting money—lots of it—from somewhere. If we can trust what the Democrats say, McKnight's a desperate man, made more desperate by us dragging up his spotted past all the time. Folks round here think he's a sitting duck, a cooked goose. I don't know, Dell, he looks to me like a dangerous man. Look how he's gone after you."

I laughed. "I am not worried about little Adolf McKnight, okay?"

"Hey," he said, growing lethargic again. "I fought the Nazi madmen, same as the next guy. Except Albert Collette, Junior, of course—and you."

Fuck you, I thought. One of my brothers had died on Omaha beach, but a childhood bout of rheumatic fever had left me with a heart murmur and a military deferment. I suspected Hoops still resented my being promoted over him while he was off fighting for his country, but maybe I was just being touchy. I said, "I've got to run."

"So, run." He made no motion to move in response. As far as I could tell, he planned to hibernate in the booth for the winter, living off my tab. I downed the last of my scotch, took out my pad, and started making a list.

"Argh, matey, yer famous list. My advice, look into McKnight's army record. Something's up there."

"The kid said that, too, this morning."

"It's his rank. He was a captain in the Army Air Forces, according to his official bio. But he's trying to have it both ways. The tail-gunners on bomber crews were enlisted men. So how could he be both Captain McKnight and 'Tail-gunner Larry'? We can't get the armed services to respond to our kind queries. Maybe a well-known patriot like you can do better. On my way in, did I happen to hear you had been chatting up front with his old army pal, Jack Haugen?"

I nodded, made a face.

"Cooperative bastard, no?" Hoops laughed.

"See if you can't find something to back up Hickenlooper's gossip about McKnight's mysterious newfound friends and contributors," I said. "Talk again to this Schultz; tell him if the Republicans—no, if the SMA—wants us to get rid of McKnight for them, they better come up with something we can actually use. You're a reporter. Find out about that meeting in D.C."

"Aye, aye, cap'n. And where will I be finding yourself?"

"Leave whatever you find on my desk. I'm going to try to write the next installment of the *Rise and Fall of the Turd McKnight* tonight with what we've got." I told him he needed to work the labor beat, too, for a while. "I'll do something on the strike this afternoon, the contract tomorrow. After that, you pick it up. I'll get Wilson's notes to you, a list of my sources. Any questions, just ask."

"Sure thing, boss," Hoops said. I could discern no sharp edge, no resentment, in his voice, but then it came, and when it came—as always with Hoops—it was indirect, joking. "Oh." He snapped his fingers. "Just one thing. Does this mean you plan to fire me next week?"

"Give it a rest, Hoops," I said.

I took up my pad, headed for the door, stopped, went back to the telephones. Hoops had somehow managed to reach the cash register to get some cigarette change despite the lunch line, and he looked at me on my way back, tilting his head ever so slightly toward me, saying confidentially to the cashier, the delicious Tish, for me to hear, "Mild-mannered reporter for a great metropolitan newspaper."

Tish giggled. "Funny, he don't look faster than a speeding bullet."

4.

Outside, the punch of our cold weather returned like a bad memory, its chill almost unimaginable, even in Wapsipinicon. The light, as always in the Midwest, was weird—perfectly flat, level across the horizon, the kind of light you saw in Grant Wood paintings—and it fed the emptiness left by Kathy's absence, which grew in tandem with my drinking. I tried not to think about her, or about the marriage. Thinking about it changed nothing. Automobiles and buses and trucks had churned the salt-sullied snow into a gray, brackish slush that yearned to rise over my rubbers. Lights had been clicked on in the office buildings, though it was the middle of the afternoon.

I had the sense I was trapped in an eternal twilight. Beyond the horizon—marked by the ragged shape of my city's toy skyline—lay the edge of the world, I told myself, a drop so steep no one ever dreamed of trying to escape any more, even into the future, no matter how miserable the place became. Oceans, seashores, mountains seemed to me fanciful things, born of strange desires, and I ached for something more, something other than just my job—for delicate, private acts, to touch the nipple of Sharon's perfect breast, to follow with my hand the arc of the calf on her well-shaped leg. Such things—and time for them—defined freedom for me. At least that's what I thought then.

When I got back to the office, Bill Dyers filled me in on what had happened with Wilson. He said the boy seemed crazed, and Bill finally called the police to remove him, over the objections, he added, of the typists and the secretaries and the receptionist and even a few copy editors. They were angry with me. Thought I was unfair. That it was politics, not work. Dyers said he told them he had a job to do and couldn't accommodate nuts running around his newsroom.

When I laughed, he warned me to watch out. "Even a cream puff is dangerous heavily armed," he said, with comic sententiousness, as though nothing could be funnier than the image of Wilson toting a gun.

I polished off a piece about the strike coming to an end, and at two o'clock I went to see my old school chum, the city manager. Despite his feral bureaucratic caution, Paul Toland trusted me—we went back that far—and in an expansive mood he might tell me anything, especially about the candidate he expected to run against come 1952.

City hall expressed the scariest moment in the Gilded Age's neo-Gothic nightmare. Constructed of massive dark-red blocks of stone, a huge gold dome sitting atop its menacing façade, four turrets—each topped with its own smaller dome laced in gold—sweeping away from its stolid square center, all made the thing a fiendish ogre of a building. Seen through the scrim of falling snow, its ominous dry-blood walls and the smirking gleam of its top gave one chills. Poe on a good day would have felt malevolent forces at work. Little kids cried when teachers took them there on field trips. I liked the place.

Its insides defined extravagance—a matter of expansive, arched ceilings and fat veined-marble pillars; plush red carpets on polished marble floors; elaborately colored tile trim on dark-wood walls decorated by oversized historical paintings; curved wrought-iron staircases and heavy red drapes pulled away from stained-glass circular windows. You knew it had been built by men out of control and greedy, cold, and indomitable. It put you in mind of top hats, canes, and big aggressive bribes. Paul's office, because he actually did some work, was tucked neatly away in the extreme backside of the building downstairs behind the last round staircase, the only office in the place without an echo.

Paul's secretary, Janice—a simmering brunette with whom he had been sleeping for a while now and who hid her charms in severe business suits, a bun, a pair of dark-rimmed glasses, and an air of total efficiency—actually smiled at me.

"Hey, Jan, is Paul in?"

"Yes, Mr. Harker," she said, lowering her eyes, "he's expecting you." She always seemed embarrassed around me. When I once asked Paul about it, he said she thought I was the only one who suspected what went on between them. That got a laugh, but he let her keep believing it.

"I knew he would be. All right if I let myself in?"

"Sure," she said, automatically pushing the button on her intercom. "Mr. Harker is on his way in to see you."

"Hi, Paulie," I said, closing the door behind me as she finished her sentence.

Paul's office was higher than it was wide, parsimoniously, but tastefully, furnished with hand-me-down arts-and-craft desk and chairs. A row of small pictures—one of the mayor, one of FDR, and one of Harry Truman—lined one wall along with three framed degrees from the state university. On another wall sat a politely pastel map, very large, of a planned annexation north of the city. Glass-fronted bookcases and a small conference table took care of the rest. Paul's gang had followed Prince Albert's old handpicked reform government into city office in the landslide of a New Deal that replaced it, so they were still very careful about costs and very deliberate in disassociating themselves from the Democratic mob that had run the city amid a state full of GOP Stand Patters in the years between the Civil War and Collette's earlier ouster of the East Side gangsters in the late '10s and early '20s .

"The specter who haunts Capital City," Paul said, trying to be funny.

We shook hands, mine cold, his perfectly manicured. Paul always seemed neatly dressed, even coatless in his vest and rolled-up shirtsleeves. The gold chain and watch fob led to a nice expensive Swiss job given to him by Janice during a Christmas Eve office party. On one of the rare occasions I had seen him drunk, he told me she said she gave him the watch to make him appear distinguished. He had been in his mid-thirties, then, and looked like a boy. Now, with his handsome, square, fortyish face, he seemed distinguished. Once again, I managed to marvel at his being sucked in by Roosevelt. He would have made the perfect Collette civil servant—intelligent, coolly egalitarian, a little aloof.

You know, better than you and me.

"I understand Vlad Paddy is very angry."

"Distressed, I'd guess."

He smiled tolerantly at my deadpan response and said, "I understand he plans to keep the ERMWA off the job, despite the clear election and the fact we have settled with your people."

"There you go with that 'you' shit again. As if I'm going to benefit from this thing. You worry too much, anyway. Forget Vlad Paddy. Everybody else has. Give me something I can use about McKnight."

"Sounds to me as if you are trying to change the subject, Randall."

"Me? I'm just a newshound trying my damnedest to get a story. Give me something I can use about McKnight."

"My, my," he said, glancing at his Swiss ticker. "If I weren't a merit employee, I would be tempted to offer you a drink and advise you to slow down. But what I can offer you is approximately five minutes."

"McKnight," I said.

He waved me into a chair under the picture of Harry Truman. He played around with the junk on his cluttered desk, finding under a stack of invoices a clipboard he pretended to glance over. Like most bureaucrats he had the ability to make you feel that he was only half listening to you—that he had more important things on his mind—but he did it all somehow without being a jerk. The skill was a perfect defense against anyone seeking information, help, or the truth, and Paul used it automatically, with no malice toward me, ignoring if not forgetting I had known him when he still wore wool sweaters and chinos, when we were both too callow to understand that every choice you made cost you more than you thought.

"Who?" he said, finally.

"We went through this on the phone already. Luckless Larry McKnight. You read about him in the *News* now and again. He's the man whose job you want."

"The asshole," Paul said, dropping his clipboard.

"Now that's no language for a merit employee."

"Words for his ilk exist not in my vocabulary, Horatio. I despair to think of the kind of voter who could put such a *thing* in office."

I find it hard to believe Paul is actually older than I am. Most politicians are assholes, egotists like McKnight whose lust for power allows them to suffer the humiliation of running for office, which as a human endeavor is one of the better arguments I can think of against man's innate dignity. But then comes that rare politician who through some kind of stubborn grace actually believes in the electoral process and his mission to represent the interests of those who elect him. His aura of belief, like the softness at the center of the embittered and disillusioned Romantic, makes him worth knowing, and voting for, if only to protect him from ourselves. I wouldn't say I actually admired this quality in Paul, but I liked him for it. It made him seem perpetually young to me, despite his aging good looks, his Swiss watch, his political savvy, and his self-conscious—if academic—tough-mindedness.

"How the hell did he get to Washington?" I needled.

"There you have me. You'd have to seek out the ghost of Prince Albert for that answer. McKnight's a mystery to us vacillating mortals."

"Yeah, whatever. Tuckerman says to get him."

"John Tuckerman always did have his heart in the right place. I mean we need these gentlemen of the old school, correct?" There was a peculiar curl to Paul's lip. "*He* was a Collette man back when McKnight got his start. Ask him."

"So maybe Tuckerman feels guilty," I mused. "Maybe that's why he wants McKnight's balls so badly. Look, Paul, do I detect a reluctance on your part to reach back in that file of yours before you were city manager—or whatever your bogus title is now—and give me the crud you got on our boy Larry when you was just another little part-time New Dealer in the DA's office? I'd think you would be glad to give me mud to sling—"

"Times change."

He went through his act again. Looking at the clipboard. Checking his watch. Rustling paper. Glancing at his intercom. Any minute Janice's voice would announce an appointment waiting to see him. Paul should have been a happy man. He had everything he needed—a gorgeous girl; an office without echo; a good shot at a senate seat; a strike finally settled; and a friend at the *News* ready to blast his ailing opponent off the field. Information should have been flowing like hooch at an Irish wake. Instead, he had started to tell me something, stopped, and decided to keep it to himself. *Christ*, I thought, *he's rattled.*

"Whatever that means," I said.

"Look it, Randall…" He caught himself, paused, wasted some time thinking.

"Hoops," I said, "says a guy name of Hickenlooper told him the big state Republican money has dropped our man. They think he's irresponsible. Or unresponsive. Says McKnight's being greased, and greased well, by someone else, out of state maybe?"

The way Paul pulled his neatly clipped fingernails so smoothly back from the button let me know I had hit a nerve somewhere. I could almost see the veil dropping down across his face as his expression became fixed.

"I wouldn't know. I no longer follow partisan politics."

"Spare me," I said, but it was no use. Since last night, maybe, the times had changed indeed.

Very carefully now, Paul said, "And I don't know this Hickenlooper either."

"Jimmy Mortenson's flack. Mortenson thinks it will be himself, not you, running against McKnight next year."

"He's entitled to his opinion," Paul said, stiffly.

"Will it be him, Paul?"

"He's entitled to his opinion. Of course, I recognize Hickenlooper now. And I will say this, for the record if you want."

"At last."

"What our friend Jimmy Mortenson's interim subaltern says sounds logical enough. McKnight has followed the usual pattern. They arrive out there, contract Potomac fever, and you don't hear a peep from them for six years, until reelection time comes round."

"Then the peep's being paid for by these flashers they find hanging around Fourteenth Street?"

"I didn't say that."

"You haven't said anything," I pointed out, then went on speculating. "It'd be pretty bad in McKnight's case. He went out there owing nobody nothing. If you won't tell me more, at least tell me who's picking up his tab these days."

"I can't. Honestly, Dell, I'm not privy to that information. The Republicans don't keep me abreast of the sources of their financing. I'm just an academic *manqué*—" he smiled. At least he tried to. It was a pathetic thing to behold. "— one who went wrong and works for the city. Don't look at me like that. Did it ever occur to you that you might not be the best person in the world to give information to today? That somebody who might be running for office sometime could get into real trouble just talking to you right now?"

42

"It won't wash, Paul. If you won't tell me, tell me who would know who will tell me. We'll do it that way. I'll question him and use you as background, my unnamed second source high up in city government."

"Dell, I—"

"Know what I just noticed?" He wouldn't meet my eyes. "How nicely your hair is cut. And what a nice blue three-piece suit you have on. And your hands. Look at your hands. They've been manicured."

"Cut it out, Dell. Okay, okay. I know, I know. I owe you. You always remind me how much I owe you. Okay. There is this fellow. Employed by the National Democratic Party. Worked for Truman until recently. Now he's keeping tabs on what the political right is doing in the Midwest."

"You mean he's working for you."

"No, I didn't say that. There is the possibility that, sometime in the future, he might serve in some advisory capacity to whomever we nominate for the U.S. Senate, but—"

"He works for you," I said.

"Tell me where you want to meet him, and I'll give him a call. He'll know what's going on. If he wants to give it to you. *If*..."

I told Paul to have him meet me at the Cove. The city manager put one of his elegantly buffed fingernails into a Bell aperture. When the party at the other end answered, Paul used no names, no greeting at all. He said, "Remember the person I mentioned might wish to see you today? That person is in my office now and—"

"Paul says you're okay for a pinko."

Paul's friend was a tough guy, name of Bob Weaver. He had a blue jaw, short-cropped hair shot with gray, close-set eyes, no neck to speak of, and a nose that might have been broken half a dozen times a dozen years ago. He wore a cheap dark suit, a shirt made out of something other than natural fibers, and a very thin black tie. He looked like a lot of things. The one thing he did not look like was a political operator on a U.S. Senate campaign.

"But I don't like it," Bob Weaver said. "It ain't no good, this social revolution crap. Shit, you own a car, I mean, like the rest of us."

"No," I said. "I don't."

"Oh," he said suspiciously.

"Never learned to drive," I explained.

"Oh," he said, suspiciously.

It was a lie. As a kid, like every farm boy, I began to drive the instant I was old enough to climb behind the wheel of a truck. But the guy intimidated me, which made me want to mock him. Rough, straightforward, apparently not too bright, he wore that peculiarly American brand of moral rectitude more easily than the ill-fitting suit from Montgomery Ward.

We did not meet at the Cove, the only place I can always afford. Paul said Weaver insisted it be somewhere else, somewhere away from downtown and nowhere near the campus. I took a taxi to a dockside restaurant on the spit between Lake Sac and Lake Fox. With its intimate cocktail lounge done in rough wood and black leather, it was called back then the Lewis and Clark and decorated with faintly suggestive drawings of big-eyed Indian maidens in scanty buckskins. The place has since become one of those steak-and-brew chain joints.

"All a man really wants," Bob Weaver said, with the emphasis on man, "is a wife he can trust, a decent future for his kids, a couple of friends to shoot the shit with, and a few...um...luxuries, get me? Don't guess you own no house, neither?"

"Nope," I smiled. "My *wife* and I rent a flat." Thank God I'm married, I thought, but I felt uneasy using Kathy as collateral, given last night.

"Uh-huh," he said, knowingly. "No kids." He paused. "Hell, you drink?"

I smiled a wide smile. "Make mine scotch."

"Sal," he called. "Two J-and-Bs."

We did not talk much while we waited for the drinks, using the natural pause to size each other up. When he was finished—and he was quicker than I with his assessment—Weaver kept looking around the lounge, drumming his beefy fingers on the wooden tabletop. It was early afternoon, and a small crowd from the docks had begun to drift in. The Wharf Waldorf, where Tommy Rojack would be holding his celebration tomorrow night, was just down the street, and I looked around for familiar faces, but I didn't see any. Most of the men sitting nearby were not dressed in cheap suits like Weaver, but in work-ing-class flannel shirts and denim jeans. Still, they could have been his cousins. Home for him, here or in some other Midwestern city or second-tier port-of-call was dockside or the stockyards. That was the thing about the New Deal, I thought. Guys like Weaver and guys like Paul met each other and somehow got along. When the drinks arrived, Weaver saluted me and watched nonchalantly as I tipped the glass. He leaned back a little in his chair. It was safe. I drank, all right.

"Did Paul tell you what I—" I started to say.

"See, I got to know the score," he interrupted. "I mean I got a family and kids, like I said. And I don't wanna be no Commie dupe, get me? I mean all this labor trouble, it ain't right. A man should get what's coming to him, but the other guy has got to make a buck. All this shit about the ruling class and all that? Just a guy trying to make a buck. Long as he's honest, and you give the next man the same breaks, then this shit with the labor unions ain't right, get me? I mean, I got to know the score. I don't want nothing I say being printed in no pinko newspaper with my moniker attached to it, get me? Now Paul Toland, he says you are okay, and Paul Toland is a very great man. He's got brains, if you know what I mean. This city is a whole lot better since he's been planning it, you know. Not great, maybe, but a whole lot better. Yeah, he's got brains, but sometimes I wonder how much horse sense he's got. Take him being pals with you, for instance—"

"Want another drink?" I interrupted. He stopped short, stared at me with distrust, and grinned.

"Yeah," he said. "You figure to get me drunk. Maybe get me fucking loose tongued. Okay, mister. Yeah, I'll have me another drink, I sure will. How 'bout you?"

"Most definitely."

"Oh, most definitely," he mocked.

Before he could raise his hand, I called out, "Sal! Two more!"

It didn't fly. I had thought I might get a little camaraderie going in the lounge between me and Weaver and Sal the bartender: just two pleasant customers drinking the afternoon away, served by the friendly local toastmaster. But Sal, a miniature version of Weaver, was just as taciturn, just as suspicious. His cheap white shirt, tieless with the sleeves rolled, was shining in the afternoon slant of sunlight through the Venetian blinds, lakeside. He had more hair than Weaver, so I figured he was younger. When I called to him, he did not pretend he did not hear me. That would have been bad enough. Instead, he acknowledged he had heard me by putting down the glass he held in front of a regular at the bar and glaring at me. Then he glanced over at Weaver without changing his wooden expression, but the movement alone was enough to say what he meant: Who is this jerk? Then Weaver nodded and Sal shrugged his shoulders in response and made the two drinks.

"Whatever you say can be off the record," I said. I tried to sound professional and unembarrassed. "I won't print a word of it, unless I can find a corroborating source—someone else who'll back it up, or the general drift of it, anyway."

"Like Toland?"

"Like Paul."

"So, I tell you what Toland won't tell you so you can go back and get Toland to tell you what I tell you."

"That's about it," I smiled. That was not exactly it—I hoped to leave them both comfortable I was quoting the other—but close enough. Hey, it's the job I do.

"That's some business you're in, buster," Weaver said, shaking his head. The drinks arrived. I said nothing. "Yeah, well, Paul says you are okay. But it don't do him no good, being pals with you, you know what I mean? These days?"

"Times change?"

"Yeah," he snorted. "And let me tell you something else. It ain't because he's Catholic. I mean, the fucking Catholics care about the poor, just like everybody else. And the working man, too. Wasn't for us, Roosevelt would never of been elected, and we'd all be drinking milk, like that pansy-ass Albert Collette. That's what he drank, you know, *milk*. He's not even a good Catholic."

"Are you talking about Paul, McKnight, or Collette?"

"McKnight, pal. Who the hell do you think I'm talking about, the king of Siam? You didn't hear nothing about him being Catholic when he was getting them fucking divorces, did you? Did you? Okay. So, I don't want to hear nothing about it being because he's Catholic, get me? I mean he's listening to a couple of priests now, and they are fucking right wing as hell, but a couple of priests don't mean the whole damn shebang, and besides he's only listening for show, to get votes. Way Truman is, he'd probably get them anyway. Truman don't give a damn about the Catholic voters. He figures where the hell they gonna go."

"You know a lot about Truman?" I tried to make the question as casual as possible.

"You kidding me? I was with him, right from the start. You ever hear the name Pendergast?"

"I know the Pendergasts run, or maybe ran, Kansas City."

"I used to work for Tom Pendergast, till Truman came along. You read a lot about Tom being some kind of gangster nowadays, but he was just one of the old-style politicians, get me? He didn't wear no white gloves and drink milk, for chrissakes. He drank whiskey, used his knuckles, and protected his people. Gave Truman his start, for all the damn good it does him now."

"So you've been with Truman right along."

"Oh, I just sort of keep an eye out for him. I'm kind of a Midwest weather vane, get me?"

"What is 'it'?" I asked, casually.

"It?"

"You said *it* wasn't because McKnight was Catholic. What did you mean *it*?"

"Oh, Jesus Christ. I thought you was supposed to be some kind of ace reporter. It? *It* is what Larry McKnight is doing. *It* is McKnight's fucking game plan."

At last we were getting somewhere—maybe. I sipped my scotch, waiting for Weaver to go ahead and reveal McKnight's game plan to me. If he had been part of the Pendergast machine, he was probably every bit as tough as he looked, and since he was on Truman's bankroll, that must have meant he knew a hell of a lot about Democratic politics. Paul was running with a fast crowd these days, and no one cozied up to Truman's hometown thugs for their culture or their charm.

"Maybe you guys out here really are outta touch," Weaver said. "It sure as hell looks that way to me, though you could have kicked me in the butt if I would of admitted it a month ago. Maybe out here, you don't feel it the way we do in good old Washington, D.C. The cold, I mean, the real cold, as in Cold War. Truman don't own the town no more—J. Edgar Mr. Hoover owns it; House Un-American owns it. These days, Harry takes his little morning stroll and there ain't nobody out and about. They all hiding behind their damn front doors, waiting for the summons. These days Congressional hearings look just like Uncle Joe's old show trials. Hell, you know a man by the name of Lefty Mills?"

"Lefty Mills. He's local. Some petty mob guy, right?"

"Yeah. He sort of runs things out here for some goombahs in Chicago. Kind of a Upper Midwest branch manager."

"Italians. You mean the Syndicate, like bang-bang you're dead? Al Capone?"

"Jesus Christ," he said, making a sour face, a broken-nosed, ugly face, at the drink in his hand. "What do you think about this weather we've been having, Harker? Terrible, ain't it."

I was on the verge of disliking the man, wondering why Paul sent me to see some dumb-ass bigot. If he knew something, why not simply tell me? The tough-guy coyness, all the jawboning about the big time in D.C. and Harry Truman instead of the useful dirt about McKnight I had come for started to get on my nerves. And I was tired, too, of hearing how it wasn't good for me to be pals with Paul. After this, I swore, I wasn't going to be pals with Paul. Trouble was, some guys are cagey. One of my shortcomings as a reporter was my impatience. Weaver had the air of telling me something, however obliquely; and, at any rate, I was enjoying the booze and the time away from the bullpen, so I played along.

"You been back East too long," I said. "Getting soft. This is good Midwest weather here. I love it. Especially being away from the office all afternoon and boozing it up. Brother, you do not know the meaning of routine till you sit behind a city editor's desk sending all the hotshots out into beautiful weather like this, while you stay cooped up, gabbing about headlines and hot leads."

"Don't like that office work, eh?"

"Not at all. You sit there, listen to the office gossip, watch people get sore at each other for stupid crap like not dropping a couple of pennies in the coffee box—"

"There's these fucking families of goombahs in Chicago, Detroit, Toledo, you name it," he interrupted, evidently done with the chitchat. "They are into construction or they own restaurants. Linen supply shops. Trash-pickup companies. Shit like that. And maybe once they used to know somebody named Capone; maybe he used to answer the telephone when they called him; maybe when they lived somewhere like Buffalo, or New York, or Minneapolis. Now they run restaurants and such. In Chicago. Other places. They are just trying to make a buck, get me? And maybe it's a lot easier to make a buck if some U.S. Senate committee, looking for some kind of issue, don't get too goddamn curious about how they are making that buck, right?"

He was referring, I supposed, in his roundabout way, to the hearings Estes Kefauver had been holding since May, which looked as if they'd run forever and get nowhere. I suspected Weaver would know all about them—Kefauver had called the hearings after a Kansas City gambling kingpin got himself gunned down in April in the local Democratic clubhouse. Maybe that was why Weaver was here now, to keep him far away from the committee's klieg lights. Anyway, before Kefauver's hearings, few folks—especially in the Midwest—had any real idea of the extent of organized crime in America. But back to *my* problem.

"Making money," I mused. I seemed to get more out of Weaver by pretending I wasn't paying complete attention to him. "Now there's something I don't know a whole lot about. My father was a farmer, and during the Depression, things went bad—"

"Okay. Okay, with your father, for chrissakes, Harker. Try to keep up with what I'm fucking telling you. Maybe a way to keep these nosy-parker senators off your back while you're making these fast bucks is to get them looking at something else. Maybe if everybody, you, me, the voters, maybe if we was worried about other things, real worried, get me, then we wouldn't much care about a few goombahs who owned a few restaurants and some other businesses. And that's why it ain't good for Paul Toland to be seen with you, let alone being your pal. Or me neither."

"I hear you," I said. "Les' have 'nother drink. You like this place here? The way the old sunlight peeks in through those venetian blinds?"

"You're supposed to be the smart one. Hell, you can't even hold your goddamned likker. I'm going to break Toland's fucking neck. Sal, two more! Yeah, Harker, I like this place. I like the nekkid Indian twists some pansy painted on the walls. Though I'd like to know where you'd really find a gal looked like that..."

"I found one," I said, smiling idiotically, I hoped. "Only she doesn't have olive-dark skin and coal-black hair, and she never wears rawhide. She's blonde, and blue eyed, and as tall as you are, but a damn sight prettier. Yes sir, a damn sight prettier, and she works—"

"How does your wife feel about that, Harker?"

"I don't know," I laughed. "I never asked her."

"No good, Harker. No good. You should treat her—your wife— better than that. Might consider something like having kids. I mean, I don't know this girl, see, and she might be all you say she is, but you married the other one. Kids. Kids'd do you good. You may not believe this, Harker, but Mildred and I had some hard times, too, before we had kids—"

"No!" I said. "*You and Mildred?* I don't believe it."

Maybe I had pushed him too far. He suddenly fell silent, brooded a while over his drink.

"So, you're a Commie, right?" he finally said.

"Not right," I shrugged. "Not right at all. I—"

"Okay, Okay. But people think you're a Commie, right?"

"Some people, who have shit for—"

"Right," he said. "So, you don't own nothing, right?"

"Well, I wouldn't—"

"And I own a house in Kansas City and a car and maybe two cars and I've just bought me a television set, and my kids, my kids want to go to college, right?"

"Right you are!" I cried. "Let's have another drink! Celebrate your kids going to college!"

"Okay. Okay. Settle down." He was thinking to himself again, only a little less morosely. Trouble was, we had both been putting the drinks away. I was getting a good buzz, and I liked the pleasant way the dark wood tables had begun to take on soft, muted shadows, and how the other people in the bar seemed more and more lovely, even cuddly.

"So, you—" Weaver went on, "the Commie—want to take away my house, maybe, and one o' my cars, my nice fucking Nash, maybe, and the television, yeah, the goddamned television I worked my butt off to afford, and give it to some comrade or other, so we'll all have a little bit of the same thing, right?"

"Now you're talking!" I fantasized what I would do with all of Bob Weaver's worldly goods. I'd give his Nash to Kathy to use to commute back and forth to the university for the degree she always planned to go back for, the one she gave up to marry me. His television, well, that would have to go to Guthrie. Guthrie could use it. Keep him off the reefers and the bad, imageless poetry. Now, the house. That was a tough one. In Kansas City. Who the hell wants a house in Kansas City? Hoops. I'd give it to Hoops. Why, I didn't know. This redistribution of wealth was a lot of fun. Better yet, I'd give the house to Vlad Paddy. Give him some place to retire to and reread *Eighteenth Brumaire.*

"So there are these other guys," Weaver said, a little blearily. "In Chicago. And some other places. Maybe even right around here, trying to make a fucking buck. Like me and you—like me. Like me. Only they are trying a little too hard, and too fucking fast, so maybe they are what we would call crooked, but I can still understand it, right? Not *like* it, maybe, but understand the impulse, get me?"

"If you say so, Socrates," I grinned.

"What kind of a crack is that?" Bob Weaver demanded, slamming down his drink. His eyes were beginning to droop a little, and he had set his square jaw in granite. "Is that supposed to be some kinda crack?"

"No, no," I said smiling. "I just meant—" But looking at him, I couldn't finish. I was laughing too hard.

"I mean do you want me to talk to you or not? I mean, what is so goddamned funny about this, Harker? You should try to stay fucking sober, man. What kind of reporter are you, for chrissakes? I mean, *fuck it!*" He slammed the glass down again. "*This* ain't doing me no *fucking* good, man. Paul said you was okay…"

"Look," I said, trying to draw myself up. "I'm sorry. I apologize. I'll listen to what you have to say. Promise."

"Okay. Okay. Let's have another."

"Sal!" I shouted, laughing.

"Sal!" he growled, throwing one shoulder away from the other, as if he were shrugging off an attacker. "Okay, Mr. Ace Reporter. So there are these three kind of people." He held up one beefy hand and counted them off on his fingers with the other as he named them. "There's the Commies." Then he pointed at me. "You. There's the crooks." He stopped counting and gestured outward with his hands, as if to include the entire world, but for us. "And then, three, there's people like me." He gestured at himself with his thumb, not the third finger he had counted. "And there is a lot more people like me. People trying to make an honest dollar. We understand number two—the crooks—a lot better than we understand number one, the Commies. Because the number twos, they are like us, get me, in a way, only a little bent, so that it don't matter to them if the dollar they are trying to make is honest or not. But the number ones, the Commies, they don't want to make no dollar at all. I mean, fuck it, I don't understand you, mister. You don't own no fucking home; you ain't got no kids; you run around getting drunk and getting paid for it."

It was my turn to steam a bit under the collar, and I placed my glass down on the table extraordinarily carefully. Dignified, I thought, be very dignified. "Now, wait a fucking minute," I said. "If you think being some goddamned political flunky for Truman makes you—"

"Aw, c'mon," he laughed. "I was pulling your leg, Socrates."

He smiled, and I realized he had me. He, too, had played the game I was trying to play and played it well. The sun beamed into the bar, catching the crooked smile on his ugly mug. I liked him now. We were good buddies. A thug capable of irony is a rare phenomenon, and I began to think maybe Paul knew what he was doing.

"You're Socrates," I said, leaning over and punching him with my index finger. "I'm Glaucon." I hit my chest with my open palm. "And we are having a real philosophical dialogue here. Let's get two more, what d'ya say?"

"You jaw a lotta gibberish, know that, Clawgun, ole buddy? Okay, two more. Sal!" I talk gibberish, I thought. *I* talk gibberish? What was all this about Truman and Lefty Mills and all this dime-store ideology? What was that, if not gibberish?

He was going on: "So these crooks"—he held up two fingers—"these number twos, they know they shouldn't oughta be making money the way they are. Some people, like me, the number threes, they are going to get awfully fucking upset when they find out about it. And one way to find out about it is if the folks on Capitol Hill start investigating the number twos. But the number twos are always thinking"—putting two fingers to the side of his head. "Maybe the senators and congressmen might be persuaded to look into the number ones"—pointing a finger at me—"instead, then—" but I wasn't listening. I was drinking and thinking, I talk gibberish? *I* do?

"All right," I said, as soberly as I could. "All right, I get it. So the mob, through this local crook named Lefty Mills, is underwriting McKnight's '52 campaign, and McKnight in return is going to pick up on the current misunderstanding about communism and start a second red scare, like after World War I, and while the rest of America chases after Reds, the Mafia moves into more restaurants and other businesses and nobody is the wiser. That's about it, right, Socrates?"

"Not so neat maybe as that, Harker, but like the kids say, you are getting warmer."

"And to tell me this you had to go halfway round the world and talk about Truman and your Nash Rambler and your new television set?"

"Hey," Weaver said. "Hey. Wait a minute. Harker, you are sober. Sober as a judge." Weaver had slunk lower and lower onto the table as more and more of the drinks had come, getting himself into some kind of conspiratorial slump, a lump atop the dark wood, and now he tried to pull himself up. I smiled condescendingly.

"You been stringing me along, by God," he said. "All this time you been stringing me along."

"No," I said. "You've been stringing me along. I could have got this from Paul with a lot less grief. Is this why Paul wouldn't talk to me? Is this the big deal?" I moved my chair back a little from the table, out of range, halfway expecting Weaver to make a lunge at me. Instead, this time, he was the one who started laughing.

"You been stringing me along all along, and I thought you was just some scribbling fool pinko intellectual. By God. Paul said you was okay. I bet you don't even have no beautiful blonde babe."

"But I do," I said. "Which is beside the point. Why don't you cut the crap, Weaver, and just give me what you got straight out. We'd waste a lot less time that way."

"Hey," he said. "Hey, Harker. Calm down. Back off a little. I'll give it to you. But, look, man, you got to be back at that little desk of yours or something? I'm just beginning to fucking enjoy this, you know? How's about we make an afternoon of it, maybe a night? I got a few hours to kill, and you can tell me more about your hot blonde bombshell and your poor old daddy farmer."

He could barely keep himself from hugging me. I tried to calculate the advantage of sloshing away the afternoon with him, but I was already too fuzzy-headed to do the math. There was work waiting back at the office—the afternoon deadline, a slew of irresponsible subordinates loving every minute I was out. True, Tuckerman had told me get something new on McKnight, but he hadn't meant me to do it to the exclusion of my duties as city editor. But I wasn't thinking clearly enough, I reasoned, nor was I sober enough to spend the rest of the day cooped up in the office, coddling Tuckerman's team. *So.* So I said: "Okay. But let's get out of here. Go somewhere I can afford."

"Let's go to a couple places you can afford, Harker. Show me your town. Thaz what I'm here for. Yes, sir. Thaz what I'm here for. Weather Vane Weaver. Test the wind."

"As in three sheets to," I said, plopping my hat on the back of my head. We were standing, crawling into our overcoats. Weaver laughed and whacked me on the back with a blow hard enough to take the wind he was testing out of me.

"Yes, sir," he said. "Yes, sir. Paul said you was okay."

5.

We drank. We took a cab the three blocks to the Wharf Waldorf, and I introduced him to Jerry and the boys and told him about the celebration planned for tomorrow night and explained to him who Vlad Paddy was to me and how I understood the situation in the city between the AF of L and the CIO, and we swapped stories about working for the *News* and the Pendergasts and Truman and Tuckerman and we drank. We left the Wharf and headed for the Cove, and I showed him my famous method for catching cabs in the middle of winter, which was to take him by the arm and push him in front of an oncoming taxi, and he threatened to break my nose in as many places as his was broken, and we drank. He talked about Paul and the off-year elections and how Truman was running scared, and then we talked about the Communist Party before the war and why people like me joined, and what the United Front had meant to the New Deal during the war, and we drank. He asked me about Sharon and then about Kathy, and out of politeness I asked him about his wife and then his kids, and then we talked about our fathers, his who was still living and mine who was dead, and what we had done during the Depression and during the war, and a little about our careers, but we were both too touchy and too cautious to say very much, though we did mention how a job changes you without you knowing it, and then we went back to our wives, and how they changed, too, but you always knew it, and we drank. We caught an afternoon strip over on the East Side and ran into a couple of his old Democratic cronies from the Kansas City days who had moved north through the years doing, I took it, a few grifts, but still hanging around the shadowy edge of the party where a lot of petty crooks spent their lives, and we drank. Late in the afternoon he began to work the conversation back toward McKnight and Lefty Mills, and when I told him I had probably better get a move on because Tuckerman was going to have my ass as it was and besides the chairs and tables, the very glasses we were drinking out of, were beginning to take on a life of their own, and it was better for a man not to be at the mercy of his surroundings, he said:

"Seriously, Harker. Now, seriously, before you go. I told you I was fucking going to give it to you straight and, goddamn it, that is exactly what I'm going to fucking do now, get me?" He drew himself up again from the puddle of flesh he had made on the table and tried through bloodshot eyes to find sobriety somewhere in the room behind me. All he actually managed to do was to put an artificial rhythm to his speech, to talk more choppily in tiptoe sentences, as if he were trying to prove he could drive soberly by walking a straight line.

"You don't seem to be taking all this too seriously. So you'd better listen pretty damn close. And try not to tie it up neat like you did before. At—what the hell was the name of that fucking bar—the Lewis and Clark? The Injun joint. This ain't just some newspaper conspiracy, Harker. Goddamn it. It just don't work that way. Harry Truman, he's trapped in this Mexican standoff with the Russkies, and the Korean thing he started last summer has finally gotten outta hand. Meanwhile, the country's been moving right since the war, and guys like McKnight, dumb as they are, plan to cash in.

"McKnight—you listening, Harker? Forget the damn scotch for a minute—McKnight had himself a fucking high-level meeting about two, three weeks ago—to talk about policy—with a couple of real right-wing senators." I started to listen. This was the meeting Hoops, too, had mentioned. "A big-shot New York cardinal was there, and McKnight's new aide, slimy little fuck named Freeman. They discussed what issue was up for grabs that would get him re-elected come Fiddy-two. Hell, with the Russians testing the goddamned A-bomb they stole from us and this clown Nixon out in California, I guess the answer was pretty damn easy. Something else, too. McKnight and Hoover. J. Edgar—I mean, who, seriously, Harker, just about runs the goddamned show in D.C. Mr. Hoover and Senator McKnight eat lunch together in public now. Real pals. Like you and Toland."

"So," I laughed, getting to the point *for* him, "they decided to come after me. Why me?"

"You and your paper kept squaring off with them," he said.

I must have looked befuddled, because he got that finger-counting expression again and said, "Listen, what you got here, Harker, is your basic clean city. Oh, sure, you got a little vice, some high-stakes gambling and loan sharking, but it's all Methodist crime, get me? The biggest thing going is policy and that's run, as you no doubt know, by a goombah name of Calenti. Nephew of the old Moustache Pete Liquor Baron Giusseppi Calenti. Now these wops in Chicago, they are part of a big family of goombahs been moving into organized crime all over the country. I don't fucking follow it all—I guess Calenti, he's from the wrong part of Italy. But he's got the numbers and the vice sewed up, and these other goombahs, these Sicilians, they are looking for a lever. And this punk Lefty Mills looks like he's gonna be their lever. To get the job, Lefty has to bring something to the table, so he'll have to set up shop where there is slack in the system. See where I'm headed? Around here, the unions is that place. Because guys like you been wiping out all the old Commie kingpins like this Padikoff fella. And that leaves, good buddy, you and your glib pals running the CIO. They can't shoot you all, which is what they'd do in Chicago. Not right now, anyway, not around here, not with the heat from Kefauver and all that shit. But maybe they don't have to shoot you to shut you up."

"Just paint us Red, huh?"

"Yep, like he did to you big time last night. And when McKnight's got you off in Washington answering fucking questions about your old comrades, your old pal Vlad Paddy, the goombahs will buy Lefty Mills a new Cadillac and young Calenti a pair of concrete boots and nobody'll even notice. And Paul and your Mr. Tuckerman and the rest of the city hall New Dealers won't be able to do a goddamned thing about it even if somebody does notice, because the crap they sling at you is going to be splattering all over anybody who stands behind you."

"You're the one who got to Paul, right? You're the one who scared him. Told him he shouldn't be talking to me."

"You're damn right I am. You and McKnight. You are one and the same, Harker. You're both part of the same shit storm, and when the time comes I'm gonna dress our friend Paul Toland up in a white suit and I'm going to aim him at Lefty Mills and at the goddamned unions and he ain't never going to mention McKnight, who he's running against, or you, who used to be his buddy. But I can't do that, he can't wear the goddamned white suit, if you are standing next to him getting doo-doo all over it."

"Jesus," I said. "Let's have another drink."

We ordered, drank, and plopped down the empty glasses ritualistically.

"You know, Socrates," I said. "You're not as dumb as you act, are you?"

He smiled that great smile of his again, and then he did the oddest thing he had done all day—he crossed himself.

"No," he said. "You on the other hand are a lot dumber."

I hadn't gotten much I could legitimately use, despite all the time I'd put in, but some days a newshound's life was like that. Images, and not much information, were what were on offer today. Paul in a white suit. Me covered in filth. Truman, a bespectacled cold warrior in a bowtie standing on the edge of the Free World, hurling A-bombs like some low-rent god throwing thunderbolts. That's how Bob Weaver sold his saga, I realized, with cartoon sketches out of Herblock. But not me, boy, not me. I sought a more sophisticated tale—one that made sense, that adhered, that reflected life as I understood it. McKnight? Christ, he was a nightmare coming out of the fog along the Potomac that the Old Man wished me to blow out to sea. Even if I ignored Bill Weaver's fancies, I had to take Tuckerman's needs seriously because he paid me—a paltry sum, true, but mine own—*and* because that nightmare was mine own, now, too.

I looked for the taxi this time without Weaver's help, and I stood in the cold for a good five minutes trying to sober up before I hailed one. I took the cab back to the *News* building, a squat, dull Mussolini-like object, constructed as a three-story office building in the 1930s. By the time I got there, the streets were deserted except for a few late diners caught in a distant halo of neon and swirling snow as they passed a stumbling old wino. Some of the afternoon slush had frozen over, producing the squeak and crunch of people walking on hard snow, and light streamed from windows at two levels. Downstairs, just below ground, the glow from the typesetters' world of webs and hot lead fought its way up and out across the steps, the sidewalk, the street, all blurred together by the snow. Upstairs, from lights in the newsroom, a glare caught the buggy swirl of November flakes as I stood on the sidewalk and looked up. I sighed, walked up the steps, and tugged on the door to the lobby.

Behind me I heard up close now the screech and crackle of footsteps. When you have covered as many strikes as I have, you begin to think about it in a vague, abstract way. When it will come. How it will happen. Who it will be. I used to imagine bludgeons or knives, because the company goons carried the one and strikers the other. Since I had missed the war, true combat was a mystery to me, bombs and grenades and machine guns as unreal as my own childhood memories; rods, gats, pistols, six-shooters, I knew only from the movies. And you can think about it all you want; when it happens, you are not ready for it. Maybe Bob Weaver's paranoid talk had made me skittish. By the time I realized it was Wilson behind me, I knew he had his gun out and aimed at me. And by the time I knew that, I knew he would shoot me the first move I made, and that I would be killed. But by then, I was already turning, and it was too late to stop.

Drunk, I imagined the impact as Bob Weaver whacking me on the back again. And I heard the tinkle of breaking glass before I heard the roar of the shots. The last thing I remember thinking was, So, this is it. This is the thing that is to happen. And the last thing I remember hearing was a sound like the ocean hitting the shore, an ocean I knew I would never see.

Part 2: DEPRESSION

A sick toss'd vessel, dashing on each thing;
Nay, his own self:
My God, I mean myself.

—George Herbert, *Miserie*

6.

"George 'Lefty' Mills," Hoops said, "is one mean son of a bitch. He owns part of a construction company with his brother out in East End. He used to ride shotgun in the spotter for a bunch of rumrunners out of Canada. Provides muscle for the dockworker's union and the local Teamsters on a sort of pay-as-you-go basis. Good bit of the time, the pay is a position for one of his muscle. A shark, Harker, with a real appetite. Contributes regularly and heavily to members of both political parties. As a young man, he was expected to go far with the East Side mob Collette chased out of office. All this from our very own crime reporter, Gene Gibson."

"Who asked you?" I said.

"You did. Yesterday. I was explaining how all my illusions had crumbled when the bullet failed to bounce off, and you ignored me, as is your way, rolled over and groaned, and then said, with morphine-induced clarity: 'Find out all you can about a hood named Lefty Mills.'"

"I don't remember."

I remembered someone chanting over and over *Who is he? Who is he? Who is he?* And a voice, the sound of ice—of ice and something almost sexual—and numbness. *We'll have you fixed up here in no time. No time at all.* There seemed to have been a lot of noise in No Time at All—it sounded like the clack of tableware and the muted gab at a Thanksgiving dinner, but now I recognized it instead as the professional murmuring and mechanical clicking of an emergency room. And I was thinking *what fresh hell is this* because I remembered the burning, my skin crinkling in its blaze, a hot strand running across my chest, that had accompanied some earlier, different quiet babble, like the whispering of the damned all around me. The ambulance crew, maybe, or the crowd at the *News* who first found me lying on the ground? At some point, there had been the crackle somewhere of electrical short-circuiting and the smell of scorched ozone, along with that roar like the ocean still in my ears and suddenly a big, odd-shaped black spot rushing toward my face, followed by some kind of annoyance that turned out to be overwhelming pain… I remembered the pain in No Time. And the silence. And a light out in some hall beyond a door that blinked slowly, rhythmically … In No Time, too, I remembered voices like dreams saying impossible things: the copper, Mike Shaunessy—*Damn me, Harker. We have all the luck. Looks like you'll live. The bullet passed right through you as if you did not even exist in the first place, a fiction, a piece of thin typing paper. Whose bullet was it anyway?* And someone who sounded just like Bill Dyers—*You get hit by a cream puff or what? Tuckerman says no workman's comp for the ghostly and the damned, for the near-to-life and the wretched, for the once-were and the in-pain.* And maybe Shaunessy again—*They can't find him. He has vanished from the face of the earth and from time into time without end where ye shall seek in vain.* And Tuckerman, for sure—*Jack Haugen is having a field day with the story. It's not good, Dell. It's not good.* And I dreamed I saw Kid Guthrie in a ditch with his face gone. Beside his body lay a copy of the *News* declaring McKnight had won reelection by a landslide. But it wasn't me who saw it. It was Vlad Paddy… Waking meant being aware of pain, bare walls, a sterile white room, and pain. A crucifix hung just in sight. Catholics and corridors and tormenting pain.

Now Hoops, benign Buddha, sat there blocking my vision of the hospital room. The crash of ocean had subsided, and I could hear clearly and see whole, and I was experiencing something other than the burn of confusion, which still simmered, a dull ache in my left shoulder. Behind Hoops's mass, I made out Kid Guthrie's unshaven little face, all Celtic and pale. Alive, I had returned to the world of men. With an IV stuck in my arm.

"Hey, man. How do you feel?"

"I dreamed you got shot, too."

Hoops laughed. Kid Guthrie looked confused. Nothing had changed.

"That's like saying you dreamed he got laid."

"Shut up, Hoops," I said. "How long have I been here?"

"Couple of days. It's Friday."

"How did the union vote go?" I asked. "And what's happening with McKnight?"

"We've gone over this," Hoops said with some frustration.

"Pretend I don't remember," I said.

"You asked about the UEW vote, which passed as expected, and I told you all about Vladimir Padikoff's Waterloo down at union head-quarters."

"You covered the celebration?"

"Yes, boss." Hoops resorted to his standard sarcasm. "After I gave up doing your work for you trying to squeeze information on Turd McKnight out of constipated politicos—must a been after dark by then—I headed down to the riverfront for a nice, relaxing dinner of rotten carry-out with Tommy Rojack and the gang. Tony Martin, Bilinski, that bunch. Rojack was nervous as a cat counting the ballots. I think he thought he was actually going to lose to Vlad Paddy. Yep, nervous as a cat. A big cat. A big blond hunky cat. How can he be so big but look so innocent, like he never had his cherry popped?"

"Just tell your story, Hoops," I said.

"They finished counting the ballots about ten o'clock. Enough of 'em, anyway, to know they had won. Then they started whooping it up, slapping me and Rojack on the back, Bilinski smashing his fist into the wall, stuff like that. You know that backstairs office—cheap, plasterboard walls, Rojack's messy desk, flyers from the mimeographs in the storefront downstairs lying all over the place. Pulled out a couple of bottles of rye, they did, which made it interesting at last, and starting passing them around. Then, suddenly, everything gets quiet. I'm standing there looking at Rojack, sipping merrily away, listening to some joke he was telling about wiring the mayor's office, and his innocent bohunk face goes blank—white, excuse clichés, as if he's seen a ghost. Which, given the vote, and what we were doing down there, is pretty nigh the truth. Because that, boss, is what Vlad Paddy had become if you think about it the way you lefties do: history, you know, and specters. Guilt is a horrible thing, buddy. It turns even the most Homeric handsome faces ugly."

"I can do without the half-ass classical comparisons," I said.

"Anyways, I look over my shoulder and who is standing there in the doorway but, surprise, the man himself, Vladmir Padikoff, along with five, six other Commies, the last friends he has in the world. That's it,

I says to meself. That's all there is, all that's left of the once powerful ERMWA…in this town at least. And, brother, you better believe it's silent in that office, except for Bilinski, who's sort of huffing and puffing and turning red in the face over in the corner, getting ready to do to Vlad Paddy and company what he's been doing to Tommy's walls, I guess. Then Vlad Paddy comes into the room, taking that little dance step walk o' his, and everybody—Bilinski included—moves out of his way. If he looked like that back when he was walking toward them company goons when he got shot, I can understand how it was they misfired and hit him in the foot. He looked like Banquo on a bloody night."

"I can especially do without lame literary allusions," I said.

"Um, so I'm getting ready, too—just in case the Comintern has issued a death warrant for Rojack. I keep looking at Vlad Paddy, that wavy black hair and those bushy eyebrows. How old do you figure the guy is—sixty, sixty-five? And hair still black as ebony. I keep waiting for a sign he plans to pop our own sweet bohunk savior for Friend Joe and Mother Russia, then I figure I'll have to grab him by his Wobbly red tie—"

"Oooh, tough guy," said the kid. Hoops frowned at him.

"But he don't do a thing," he said, looking back at me. "Just walks through the crowd there, right up to Tommy, and just stares. Just stares at Rojack, I mean. And, swear to God, I think he's got tears in his eyes. And it gets me, right here."

"That's your wallet, Hoops," I said, "not your heart."

"Then he looks at me, Vlad Paddy does. Looks at me, back at Rojack then at me. He says, 'Where is Red Randall?' 'Home,' I says, 'boozing or snoozing, ha, ha, you know ole Dell.'"

"Yeah, man, right," said Guthrie.

"No, no. Now, listen, kid, I'm serious about this. I mean I am one scared newshound. Here is this local legend just staring at me and asking about our very own legend, and I'm quivering in me Florsheims. I mean, the man has *intensity*. Comprendez? And he's staring at me *intensely* with those *intense* black eyes, a real Rasputin of a stare, and all the black hatred of a thousand years of life on the tundra and working-class deprivation is swarming out at me, *me*, the clarion of decadent boozewah culture and, I tell you, it is almost more than I can take."

"Now you're putting us on, daddy-o."

"I'm not making up a word of it. This old Commie, he's so used to talking in world-historical language, the mumbo jumbo of dialectics, you *dig*, boy, that he thinks this itsy-bitsy local election has some meaning, that it's—ooooh—all Hegelian and everything, the high drama of spectral history, kid. No, no, no, I'm not making it up at all. He goes on like that. Ask Harker here."

"Bullshit," I said, but I could say that any time Hoops talked. "What else?"

"More mumbo jumbo," Hoops said, pretending a reluctance to go on. "'Whose America is this now?' he says, like he's some old owl of wisdom flying at dusk. 'Harker's America.' Now ain't that some shit. Just between us, if *this* is Harker's America, then I am Sidney Greenstreet. Anyway, Vlad Paddy twirls around on his one good foot and two-steps out of the room along with the five folks left in the world who agree with him, ruining the whole goddamned evening. Even Bilinski didn't feel up to smashing walls now."

I closed my eyes…and let things slide. Next thing I knew, I heard Hoops worried voice: "Boss?"

"Sorry," I said. "Sorry. So, what about McKnight?"

"Still working on the soldier-boy angle, right, kid?" he said, turning again to Guthrie who nodded. "Tuckerman's given the story back to me till you're fit to handle it."

"No, no, no," I said. "Bring what you get to me first before you write anything."

"You're the boss," Hoops grumbled. After an awkward pause, with one of the nurses haunting the doorway, he got up to leave. I looked at the kid to keep him in place for a moment. At the door, Hoops stopped. From where I lay, he seemed magically to be entering the bare wall. "That cop, Shaunessy, has been in here a couple of times trying to find out who it was drilled a hole in our ace wordsmith. Had a list a mile long, but we all guessed it was the punk, Wilson?"

"I didn't actually see him," I said. "But I believe it was."

"Yeah, so does Shaunessy. Wilson's disappeared."

I said, "I dreamed that, too."

When Hoops had gone, Guthrie—waving off the nurse for me—came over beside the bed. "How do you feel, really, Jack?"

"How do I look like I feel?"

"Like some old, really old, tough guy," he laughed.

"Sentimental slob. Tell me something—do you know who has been up to see me?"

"No, not all of them, but I can guess. You were off the critical list, they said, like about the time you arrived here. They have you hopped up on dope, so you've been pretty loosey goosey. Dyers said if Wilson could hold a gun steady enough to aim, you wouldn't be such a drain on everybody around you. There was a cadre of characters here the only other time I came to check out the scene—Shaunessy and Tuckerman. Jack Haugen."

"Haugen? What the hell was he doing here? Gloating?"

"More like trolling for copy. You should see his riff in the *Times:* Draft-avoiding pinko editor fires hard-working war veteran. Veteran strikes back. Bip bop boop."

"Find out if Haugen knows this Lefty Mills, or anybody associated with Mills. If we can put Mills and McKnight together in a sentence and back it up, we may actually have something. Check out a guy named Bob Weaver. Paul Toland can put you in touch with him. Convince Weaver you're not on orders from Moscow and ask him for anything more he can give you about the saga of Lefty Mills, or, if not, which of his old East Side pals you *can* talk to about Mills. Those guys are mean and a little crooked, some of them, but mostly they are Democrats. It might take some doing, but if you find yourself tempted to buy Weaver drinks to loosen him up, forget it. You won't be able to afford it and the *News* doesn't have the budget to cover the expense."

"Wilco, Dad."

"And check downstairs somewhere. With the nurses. A doctor. Who knows? Find out if Kathy has been here, how many times. Oh, and find me a telephone somewhere while you are at it."

When I paused, the kid, sharp as ever, said, "What is it, Dad? Go on, man, say it."

"Talk to Sharon for me. Sharon Parks. Her number is in my wallet, and she works at the Emerson. Tell her what's up, whatever she doesn't know from the papers. Tell her for me I think it's okay for her to come visit. But suggest she make it discreet, just to be safe."

He found my pants in the closet, took the wallet, got the number, and left. A doctor wandered in following the nurse while Guthrie was gone. He said, probably for the hundredth time, the kind of shit all doctors say. I had suffered shock and loss of blood, but it wasn't too serious. I could go home in a few days, maybe a week or so; we'd just wait and see. But I'd have to take it easy for a while. Do some rehab. I was a lucky man.

In his wake, in tromped Kid Guthrie. As the nurse tried to shoo him back out, he spoke up, "Kathy has not been here at all, not even once; Sharon said she'd try, maybe tonight."

"When you get a chance," I said, "see if you can find out where Kathy's gone. Probably her folks' place in Ravensport..."

The nurse had blotted out his nodding image.

"And find me a telephone—" I called around her.

Morphia. Blessed sleep. I dreamed I wrote the perfect piece. The puny column and a half I was allowed expanded, as if magically, and—within only that limited space, using only the most common of words—I was able to create the kind of prose all writers have longed for in a language as limpid and precise as poetry, as muscular and fluid as the best fiction. I had no need for long descriptions or heated analysis in that language, only words, the simplest of words, perfectly chosen, and, though ordinary, conveying more meaning than any word we ever really use in our corrupted, frayed, workaday gibberish. These common words laid bare to immediate perception the feelings, the thoughts, the full sense that actual words hold only the trace of, if they do not in fact erase it, the way dry blood erases the flowing, the redness, the very life of fresh blood. And, again as if by magic, the perfect article gave perfect pleasure, the kind of pleasure that is the special gift of the greatest works of the imagination, full of insight and of vision. I was the ultimate traveler, the complete spectator, the absolute observer, the author, whose language is beyond measure and whose words carry not so much meaning as they do value.

In the dream, I had only to write: *Lawrence McKnight was born and raised on a chicken farm in Winnebago County*, to communicate fully the long, lonely years of an uneventful and unnecessary childhood; the single dusty road through rolling farm country and scraggly woods—a road impassable half the year—that grew more and more to mean escape and salvation to the boy whose restless arousal became a parched hunger in the course of his seemingly endless adolescence; the suffocation he felt as he came to hate the postage stamp of earth his father called home, his mother labeled the farm, and he knew as My Prison; the mortal terror he experienced when it seemed to him that his father, his mother, and even he himself were all beginning to take on the natures of the beasts that inhabited the long, low-roofed buildings surrounded by a plot of churned dust and a rickety wire fence and bordered by a sloping lawn and a square-framed white house amid the only trees in sight; the disgust he finally knew for his mother, who seemed no more than a hen herself, with her round, plump body, always clucking at him, scratching at the very days passing as if they were solid things and not tortures invented to teach a desperate boredom; the hatred of his father he hid away like found treasure, his father who swiped at him daily like an angry rooster, who seemed to strut and crow about the farm for more years than he ever wanted to remember, and who could see nothing else as endowed with any significance but his smelly, stupid chickens huddling against the rain and drowning in their own heat, their own shit, their own beastliness.

I had only to write: *After his father died, McKnight sold the chicken farm and moved to Jackson City to become the local John Deere dealer*, to say how he grew to love machinery, the farm equipment he saw on the normal farms of the boys he went to school with, to love its strength, its sleekness, and its efficiency; its material solidity and inorganic breathlessness; how the very name of the equipment he sold seemed daring and how selling it was for him the great adventure, the escape from the dustiness of his father's narrow world, always already defeated; how he felt akin to some pirate, a swashbuckling soldier of fortune, a cavalier; how he longed to become the only thing that everyone he knew, even his father, admired totally and without hesitation—the successful businessman.

I wrote: *He went bankrupt*, and conjured the dizzying horror of defeat, the plunge into the abyss of human failure.

The words: *So he became a United States senator* spawned the sense of his fear and his futility that was the essence of his corruption and the heart of his cynicism and created the full image of the man, a little man expanded beyond recognition and reason by what he knew to be his unbelievable luck and a few other folks' lack of attention.

It was all there. McKnight's face inscribed on a vaulted night sky, looking now like some transparent celestial rooster, appearing now as a huge gaping blankness. Politics glowed there in that sky, beaming pompous vanity and ignoble ambition. Votes, like stars, hung there with a light almost illicit, illuminating a vagueness called human approval. You could feel the lust, the luxurious sense of unearned power in that night, too, like a constellation forming the shape of a whore's body.

And I was like the navigator of a ship, who by means of his chart, his compass, his quadrant knows at any moment his course and position on the sea below and relates it to the uneducated crew who sees only the waves and the sky. My dream language, my perfectly chosen words, was just that chart, that navigator's plan, and it showed whoever read it the truth, the real meaning of the face in the night sky. What before had possessed me completely and moved me intensely appeared in that chart to be cold, colorless, and, for the moment, foreign. I brought back to the crew, my readers, McKnight's life in the abstract, the life a man always lives—if only in the texts that survive and judge him—next to his real life in time where he is abandoned to the storms of reality and the gnawing winds of the ticking seconds, where he struggles, he suffers, he dies like an animal. My chart, my dream language, captured not only the hideousness of McKnight's abstract existence, his public life based on the drunken fear of returning home forever, but also something like complete knowledge of the world in which I lived.

But the morphine began to lose its grip, and I was floating back from No Time. I was beginning to feel once again like any man, any man who realizes he has in any way lost self-control, been struck down by misfortune, grown angry, lost heart, seen how things are different from what he expected—yes, like the young McKnight I had dreamed up. And I knew, then, I had been dreaming; I had been laboring under a mistake. I knew, then, I had not written the perfect piece—I did not know the world enough nor life—I had not inscribed a monster across the firmament for all to see. I had only dreamed a character out of my own past. I had only dreamed myself.

And between dreaming and waking, I knew, too, I coldly accepted, the truth that at every step the will of the individual, my will, was crossed and thwarted by chance, by indifferent nature, by stray bullets, by feckless history, by sterile walls, by contrary aims and intentions, by the malice I seemed to inspire in others. I could no longer find the words, the grammar of my perfect language, the one I had been using such a short time ago to arrive at general knowledge and to chart the exact location of evil. McKnight seemed hideous no longer, just a man who had gotten lucky but who had not been much changed by it, and to me he wasn't even a man now, only a job. Every keen pleasure I had expected to experience once as a writer, even the polluted pleasure of paying the bastards back, appeared now to me to be an error, an illusion, and the perfect piece not worth the work or the pay.

The morphine was going fast now, I knew, and I thought that no wish of mine, even if attained, could truly satisfy me. I lacked the imagination, the words, to form one that would. I lacked the power of judgment, the compass, the easy self-control called grace—I was the one who feared time, not McKnight, because time was consciousness and consciousness was pain. Only the pain was real, now, because it rested on the disappearance of the illusion, the dream. No. No. It would go too, next shot. Both—the pleasure of the perfect language and the pain of losing it—grew somehow from defective knowledge.

I was awake.

7.

Off and on, I would notice things—what flowers which people sent, that the nurses looked as plain as nuns (maybe they were nuns). I asked about food when they seemed more interested in my shots than my meals, and they removed the IV and placed some indifferent tasting mush in front of me. I wanted a drink and a telephone. Guthrie had promised to keep working on that—the phone, I mean—when he departed, eons ago. I wondered if hard time—jail time—was like this hospital time, so freakishly boring, and I wished Tuckerman had spared some expense and gotten me a semiprivate room. Then, at least, I would have had somebody to jawbone with between druggy snoozes. Regardless how I had imagined hell before, I had been wrong. It was this, the here-and-now, the pristine whiteness of these walls a thousand times worse than the white outside made filthy with the coming and going of men and their machines. Maybe it was several days (how the hell would I know?) before I heard Shaunessy's familiar lilt out in the hallway.

"Randy," he beamed, coming into the room. "Reborn, are ye? Back with the rest of us wretches?"

Mike Shaunessy takes some explaining. When people accuse us of being friends, I never know what to say. A third-generation cop, handy with his fists and street smart, he hid carefully inside the clichés of his ethnic heritage and excelled at drinking, bullshit, and easy-going corruption. I was as shocked as anyone that he and I got along. He even called me Randy, something no one else dared do. Not that I could have stopped him—he was no taller than me, but a lot meaner and more determined. I met him years ago, when I wrote a feature for the *News* on the old East Side mob and mentioned his grandfather favorably in print—"Father" Timothy Shaunessy, that is, who had been Capital City's first Irish chief of police and who had been gunned down by the Black Hand on August 15, 1914, for enforcing prohibition and policing local rumrunning out of Canada.

Mike stood now just inside my hospital door topping six foot three with a derby perched over a high forehead. He had bushy red eyebrows. His face, with its T-square chin that probably still never regularly saw a razor and its freckles fading faster each year, was haggard, its flesh constantly wrinkled into blarney smiles. He chose to dress in the garb of urbane Gaelic political success, wearing a white silk scarf and a black wool overcoat. But even if you missed the bulge under his left arm, the insolence of his carefree posture and his dread stare let you know he was more copper than ward heeler. Too much his own man, or nobody's man, to be anything but a pest to Paul and the aging New Dealers currently in city hall, he was a homicide captain, having worked his way up the ranks through nepotism; he belonged to that part of the City PD neither Collette in the '20s nor the New Dealers in the '30s could ever do much about. If the world were 100 percent honest, then he would be too. But even perfect honesty would not touch the rancor that lay at the root of his character underneath all the offhand congeniality and sardonic self-assurance.

Born in the East End on Irish Square—what was once the worst four blocks of Rats Row—Shaunessy became a cop because his father was a cop, just as his father became a cop because *his* father had been a cop. Mike had joined the force before World War II, and I think he joined not because he needed a job or even liked the work but out of a sort of perverse loyalty to the family, some kind of need to keep a Shaunessy around to irritate the politicians. I know he enlisted in the marines during the war so he could fight in the Italian campaign and kill those he called grease balls. I know because he told me so. Even before that, though, back when I was working on the article, he revealed that it was his father—a kid barely in his teens—who had been watching out the window for the old man to come home that day in August when an ill wind blew Father Timothy away.

Mike claimed that just as his grandfather climbed the wooden steps to his front porch, he heard a voice call softly to him from the street behind. He turned and looked back into the gloom. Like his grandfather, Mike's dad saw the man, too, he said, a dark, dumpy little fellow standing on the cobblestones just beyond the gaslight. His grandfather stepped off the porch, and the twilight ripped open with

explosions heard clear across the river. Kids playing up the street on
Cork ran to their houses because they thought it was a storm when
the street lit up as if struck by lightning. But what they—and Mike's
father—had seen were the flashes from a dozen shotguns fired from
the four alleys a block apart on both sides of the street in front
of the house. Not much was left of Chief Shaunessy, hit from all
sides at once, his clothes shredded by the shotgun blasts, lying on
the cobblestones, unrecognizable, bloody, nearly naked. After that
story, inherited in all its gory detail and bitterness, all Mike ever really
wanted from life, he told me, was to get even somehow for the trap
the twilight ambush made of it for his father, Mike senior (and for
junior, too, I figure).

Another neat little package, I thought to myself, watching Shaunessy
stroll around the room, checking the cards on the flowers, carrying a
stack of newspapers he had brought for me to read.

"Pretty popular lad, you are, Harker," he said. "Now would you
mind telling me what in Christ's almighty name this one here means:
'It's your own fault.' And it's signed: 'Plato (student of Socrates)'?"

I laughed.

"That's Paul Toland's idea of a joke."

"A fine sense of humor," Mike said. "And me thinking maybe I
should have gone to school, to the university. Then, I, too, could send
you cards with jokes senseless to common folk. Here, I brought you
a pack o' lies to read."

"Yeah, thanks," I said, listlessly. "You're the only one who thought
I might like to look at the fucking papers—" I said as I gazed out the
blind-scored window.

"Quite interesting," Shaunessy said. He looked at me, mugged a
little concern. "Say, you feel up to this, Randall?"

"Up to what? I'd just as soon not spar with you. Why can't the
nurses be better looking?"

"They're keeping the pretty ones off this floor at my request so you
can concentrate on the healing thing. Up to answering a few questions? I put them to you before, several times now, but you seem to
have a difficulty with weighty matters concerning the villain who did
you decided harm Tuesday last. You keep wandering off, blathering

of the ghostly and the damned and some of spiritual matters. I fear you may be finding religion."

He held one of the newspapers he had brought with him out to me between his forefinger and thumb as if it were smelly underwear.

"The aforementioned lies. Mostly they seem to concern yourself. Scurrilous slanders, no doubt, to do with the shameful manner in which you treat your employees. From the pen of a fellow named Haugen."

I accepted the offering and glanced at the screamer. **EDITOR SHOT.** Below in italic, caps to lower: *Disgruntled Veteran Seeking Revenge a Suspect.* Haugen did not have the art of true hatchery in command, but he was taking a whack at it. I caught a few fairly accomplished phrases. "Rumored fellow traveler." "Associates hinting of ideological rigidity." "Closely connected to the United Electrical Workers union and its burly president Thomas Rojack." I was willing to lay odds Haugen had never met Tommy Rojack.

"Says here Wilson was decorated in the war," I frowned.

"Purple Heart," Mike said. "It means he managed to get in the way of a stray Japanese bullet and bleed on a few boon companions. Our reporter thinks it unfit to mention the young man was given a medical discharge as well. His nerves went bad as the wound got better."

"So I probably owe my life to a Jap private," I said, coughing a chuckle. When Shaunessey frowned, I explained, "Dyers claims he couldn't hold the gun steady."

"Ay, ain't it the truth, now. That's an odd fellow for you. A bleeding patriot out to right the wrongs of the world and he can't even take steady aim. I love the little details of life, Randy. Take f'rinstance the bullets: forty-fives they were. Two of 'em. No doubt from a U.S. Army issued handgun, like the one Wilson happens to own. The first bullet, well, from where you were standing, must have but barely missed your noggin, traveling on through the front window of the downstairs lobby, right over the check-in desk and the receptionists drinking coffee, whizzing between them with a whine (they said they heard the whine) and smack into the wall 'neath an old retouched photograph of the Mr. Tuckerman's granddad and father. Left a neat little hole in the plaster. Now the other, it caught you in the back, scuttled along your insides for just the briefest span, and entered city air from below your left shoulder above the chest, lodging in the roof of the lobby. Missing all vital organs, though I do not imagine it could have done much harm had it hit your liver. A miracle, I swear if it ain't. Was it Wilson?"

So, I am being interrogated, I thought, and I smirked. I had seen Shaunessy do it to others. No bright lights shining in your face. No big-fisted, hateful bastard of a cop threatening you with dire physical damage while another acted polite and concerned. No series of fast questions thrown at you without time to think of an answer. Shaunessy was more Irish than that. He wore you down with talk, blabbing on and on like a cousin at a wake about anything that came into his head, naturally jocular, smiling his wrinkled smile, and then he popped his question. The talk lulled you, and the question at the end seemed just so, well, *right,* I guess, that you answered without blinking. That was the idea, anyway, and maybe it worked as well as most kinds of torture, but once you knew him and understood the trick, it could be irritating. Like a facial tick or a habit of speech, it got on my nerves.

"The bullet?" I said. "No, it never said its name."

Unperturbed, Shaunessy strolled over to the window, lifted one strip of the blinds, and stared at the street below. "My sister died right here. Not in this very room, mind you, but in one looking out on the street as this one does. Paralysis, they whispered, and the family sat around wailing, and I walked over and gazed out the window, watching the fucking traffic lights change. She looked pale as you did when I got there that night, also a Tuesday. A fine lady, Randy, a young lass with her life before her. I guess it matters damn little how it is we go. When I came back the next Friday, I knew there was no hope for her this time: it was the third attack. Night after night on duty I would pass by the hospital and study the little square of lighted window, and every night when I glanced up at it, I said softly to myself the word *paralysis.* Twisted bodies. That's what I thought about when I saw you crawling around in that lobby, Randy boy, like a worm: twisted bodies, paralysis, death. There was a gaping hole above your chest—this is a bit later—when the ambulance attendant had ripped open your shirt. You could smell the alcohol. I said to myself, I said, 'Randy, now he must have been hitting the bottle all day somewhere.' We found out from Hoops you had gone to see Paul Toland about our fine homegrown Irish politician, The McKnight. But they, none of them, knew where you had been the whole of that afternoon. You see Wilson?"

"Not since I fired him," I said.

"Ay, so you did let him go. Irritating little shit, was he?"

"Shaunessy," I said irritably, feeling tired, very tired. "Why don't I just save you a lot of time and beating around the bush? Yes, I fired Wilson. I don't know why I chose that morning to fire him rather than some other. Maybe I had a hangover. Maybe I was in a bad mood because Tuckerman had put me on his pet peeve story and it had backfired the night before. Whatever it was, letting Wilson go had nothing to do with his politics. I had been planning to do it for a long time. Wilson was the kind of reporter who cares more about the way he writes than if what he writes is true. He thinks he can get by on style. In short, he was lazy. But he had to tell himself it was political, I guess, to salve his pampered ego. I fired him and he started boo-hooing and I never saw him again till he pointed a gun at my back and pulled the trigger. I don't know it was him for sure. All I saw was a reflection in a glass door, and the glass was etched, so the reflection was distorted in about a million different directions. But the clothes were right and the general look was right and the method—shooting in the back—seems right. That's all I know other than everyone says he has disappeared."

There was a lull in the conversation. Very slowly now the latest hit of morphine had begun to wear off, and pain was seeping back into my wound. It felt as if someone were calmly, methodically, sadistically inserting a long, razor-sharp, very thin hatpin under the skin up my back. Like the nurses, I began to care more about my shots than my meals, more about dope than I cared about anything in the world.

"So, okay," I said, clenching my teeth. "Yes. I disliked him. His dandified looks and his morose war vet arrogance; his fastidious rich-boy mannerisms and his fucking constipated prose style. And I despised his self-satisfied politics. But that's not why I fired him. I fired him because he's a bad reporter, as bad a reporter as he is evidently a marksman."

"Randy. Randy, my boy." Shaunessy placed his derby on the tray by my bed and sat there smiling and shaking his head. "All this is so unnecessary. You may feel some wee guilt for giving your young man the ax, but it don't matter a tinker's damn to me. That you fired him and he thought unjustly so is enough to suggest motive. All I was trying to discover after my fashion is where you had been all that day a'drinking. You see, we had your boy down at headquarters Tuesday morning. Seems he had been waving his Army forty-five about the office and your Mr. Dyers gave us a call. Wilson was a nervous Nell, I'll confess, refusing to answer questions and wringing his hands in answer to those we put to him. He was a disappointed man, you could see that, but we actually found no gun on him when we got there, so what could we do? What it is I'm trying to discover is when and where he picked up your trail. Whether he just waited there in the cold shadows for you to come back to roost, although nobody at the paper remembers him lurking about, or if he followed you all day, seeking his best chance. It's fairly simple. If I can find out where you were that afternoon, I may find where he happened to be. And if I find where he happened to be, perhaps I may find me a witness. And, blow me away, I might find some little detail useful in tracking him down. We have visited his apartment, and all his fine clothes are still hanging in his closet and all his fine luggage, too, sitting there. Nothing seems missing but the man himself. And we have questioned his mother in Ravensport. You realize he is a good boy? Never got into any trouble? Sure, a little nervous, and he keeps to himself. What he needs, Mum says, is a nice girl."

"I don't think there's much hope on that score," I said while Shaunessy kept talking.

"He has not been home, apparently, here or there, though I admit we have not the infinite resources to keep watch on both places. It's the war, Mum says. The war that made him so sick, so resentful of everyone, so nervous, so sullen. One night, so she says, right after he returned from the Pacific, he smashed her radio. For no reason. Right before her eyes. Without a word. Just to spite her, she says. But, still, he's a good boy. Where did you spend the day?"

This time I simply answered his question. I told him about my visit to Paul's and my second outing later in the day. I tried to lead him around with Bob Weaver and me from bar to bar as best I could remember, though I was still hazy about some of it. And as I told him, as the afternoon came back to me, I began to feel strange, knowing Wilson may have been there, too, in each of those places I described. I tried to imagine the spots where he would have had to sit, the alleys in which he must have stood, and I felt foolish for not noticing him. I saw myself through his eyes. Here was a man I had just given the boot, and he was following me, watching me as I got drunker and drunker, sillier and sillier. I could almost taste the hatred as it grew more intense in him each stop Bill Weaver and I made, and I could almost hear him thinking: So, this is the man who took my livelihood? This is the guy who thinks he's such a great newspaperman? This is how he does the job he tells me I'm no good at? I watched myself—the tall, skinny fellow in the loose-fitting clothes, sitting slouched at angles in chairs and booths, his hat pushed back on his head—toss down his throat drink after drink and laugh his cynical know-it-all laugh, shrugging his shoulders and yapping with the burly, ugly, short-haired bruiser, frumped down onto the table across from him, the hefty fellow holding his face up with the palm of one hand, elbow on surface. And the tall, skinny one smoked cigarette after cigarette till the ashtrays filled to overflowing, and the big ugly one kept pointing to people in the bars. And both of them would look around slyly, and make their conspiratorial nasty laughs. And I began to despise myself the way Wilson must have despised me, dodging back out of sight in his dark corners. And I began to feel the cold grip of fear that always comes when we suddenly see ourselves as clearly and as harshly as everybody else sees us. And I wondered why we always fail to notice when we are wasting our lives.

My back was being hacked to pieces by someone with a large, freshly sharpened, bloody ax, each slash crushing deeper than the last.

"Shaunessy," I said. "Jesus Christ. Get the nurse. Get the fucking nurse. Quick. Tell her to bring her goddamn needle."

She came, and this time she was beautiful, and in a very short time the pain began to throb more slowly, and then it slid away—down some snow-covered hill—and Shaunessy rode it out of the room like it was a sled. He was smiling through his wrinkles, his bitter wrinkles;

at the bottom, once again, I found the warm and wonderful continent of No Time at All.

❧

I confess, I don't know the order of things. I know I lay in that hospital too long, feeling sorry for myself, and not worrying about it because my quack gave it a name: depression. The kid had shown up at some point with his report on Kathy.

"She's gone," he said.

"Did you find her?"

He nodded. "I checked her folks, like you suggested, and called her. She said there was nothing to talk about. She said I was sweet, I was the best friend you had, but it had been coming for a long time. What she didn't say was I should mind my own business."

"Somebody talked to her, kid. Told her about me and Sharon."

"You didn't really make it much of a secret," he said cautiously, not looking at me. "What is it, jack? You told me once she saw what she wanted to see. There were other chicks, too. She must have copped to that."

"Sharon's her excuse. She wants out. She's wanted out, really, for a long time. Sharon simply allowed her to admit it to herself. It's me—my life. I don't know. Times change."

I hoped he would drop it now and leave, before I made an even bigger fool of myself than I already had. Hell, I didn't love her. I probably hadn't for years. But all separation is a kind of suicide. Kathy had been part of something, of some self I hated to let die. After her, there would be only work and sex, I thought.

"I'll say this, her timing was not so cool," Guthrie said.

He was making a noble effort to be sympathetic when he really did not feel sympathetic.

"*She* didn't shoot me."

"The vibe I got, she wished she had."

8.

Afterward, I lay watching the ceiling and making up explanations for Guthrie I would never actually use, phony laments in the depressed first person. A bullet shatters more than your body. You say to yourself you can take it. Whatever you have to take, you can. It's part of the code. But the bullet comes, and it's not true. Kathy left, kid, because she was afraid. She saw that things can just stop with one shot. After all, she was a wife: she watched and she disapproved. She made what I thought I wanted when we got married the measure by which to calculate my fall from grace. She kept it like a faith throughout. I would write the novel, she knew that, despite joining the party. I would write it, despite the *News*. I would write it, despite the booze. I would write it, despite the other women (she was careful never to know about with anything like certainty). She watched. She disapproved. Now and again she offered her comments: You worry too much about the significance of what you write. It doesn't matter. You know that. It's only the writing that counts. You live too fast to think well. That's all this job is, action. You've lost yourself in events, Randall. In things that don't have anything to do with you.

At first what she said made sense to me, but somewhere what she described and what I felt split apart, became attracted to other things, and she blew up (we blew up) from the accumulation of petty details that were not the substance of my life any longer: You let your writing drift. It doesn't have focus. Soon, I stopped even the pretense of writing fiction, and she had nothing on which to comment. For years now, she had only questions: Have you been drinking? What did you do after work? Do you like this dress or not? Should I get a job? Should I go back to school? Can't you talk to some of your big-shot city hall friends about the trash in the street?

And Sharon, maybe she's the real killer here. Sharon Parks. She is tall, kid, with long blonde hair, the figure of a model, and a complexion pure as ice. She works, too, though I don't think she actually has to make a living. Downtown, in the Emerson Museum, doing exhibits and publicity, and she dresses…well, let's just say she dresses. She wears a coat Siberian animals died to account for. And her pale blue eyes, her face—they make you think of satin sheets and real money. She's nice.

She thinks a lot about design, her exhibits—kid, she has exhibits— and current fashion. Maybe she loves slumming. She picked me up one Friday afternoon in the Wharf Waldorf where she had come to get ideas for a display of lake-related paintings, and where I had been waiting every day that week to screw up the courage to talk to her. Don't get me wrong. She's not empty-headed. She's anything but dumb. She doesn't pretend to any innocence, either. She seems to see the world as something aesthetic, a trifle to be enjoyed for a time like everything else. She told me she found me attractive immediately because I was taller than she was. Then she laughed.

She finds my politics a bore and my messy life amusing. I thought, at first, she would be impossible, but once we started seeing each other, she seemed perfectly content with me. Self-contained. Affectionate. Undemanding. Yeah, she's good in bed. She seems to enjoy it. She's open to whatever I suggest as long as it has nothing to do with business. I noticed the first week I knew her she was reading Kerouac and Tolstoy at the same time. She doesn't smoke, she drinks, she tells me she once tried heroin. She likes the toughs I hang out with, or the idea of them anyway, but her crowd lounges in country clubs and hosts lavish dinners on the North Side. I think she assumed from the beginning I would leave Kathy sooner or later. But she never mentioned it. The only embarrassing thing she does, seriously, is to sleep with a stuffed white rabbit her mother gave her when she was a little girl in Rhode Island. The only thing I actually know for sure about her past is that she was once married to an architect in East Lansing. He lacks intensity, she says. She's twenty-eight. Sometimes—when I'm well and I'm drinking—I resent the hell out of her.

Sharon came the first time to the hospital after hours, and she looked the room over carefully as we talked—at the walls, the crucifix, the flowers—not showing the estrangement she told me later she felt.

"Do you hurt?" she asked.

"Kathy knows."

"Oh."

"Somebody called her, I'd guess."

When she did not respond, I thought I better change the subject. "And Charles Wilson's gone missing."

She wrinkled her brow. She shook her head.

"The man who shot me."

"I read about it. Who is he?"

"Some fairy who thinks more about his writing style than the truth."

"Okay," she said, a little impatiently. "Why don't you simply tell me what Kathy said? We'll start from there."

"She didn't say anything."

"Fine. You don't want to tell me. I understand. Should I come back later? Is that it? You did ask me to come see you?"

"No. No. Honestly, she's left. Gone back to Ravensport."

"Oh."

She sat for a spell. She crossed her legs. We looked over the room together. There was another bed, empty (compliments of Tuckerman's largesse), separated from me by a half-drawn white curtain. There was a small metal table where, presumably, I would (and, ultimately, I did) eat my meals when I felt like eating again. There were two filled ashtrays, one still smoldering.

"You even consider quitting smoking?"

I tried to smile and couldn't. I had not expected it to be either awkward or tense. And it was both. I had expected her to know what to say. She always knew what to say.

"You look like you died last week," she joked and smiled. When I could think of nothing typically snappy to respond, and thus said nothing at all, she began to gather up her things to go. "You must be awfully tired, Randall. I'm sorry. I've been thoughtless." She slipped into her coat and lifted her purse with one simple movement, and for just a moment before she reached the doors, the sound of my voice came to me from No Time: Let it go. You don't need it. Kathy will come back.

"Sharon," I said. "It hurts. It hurts badly."

I heard the sweep of her glide around the bed, but I didn't see it. I smelled the faint, sharp whiff of her expensive perfume. I felt her cool cheek press up against my face, her hair touch my neck with the delicacy of a spider.

"I thought you wanted me to go," she said. She kissed me. "I thought you meant it was over."

❧

After that, she came with books in the afternoons. The nurses clucked at us, but my quack was charmed by her. The books were the ones I always wanted to read but hadn't the time for. Now and again she came when others were there, and she met most of the gang at the *News* formally for the first time, and Shaunessy, too, who said after she left, "Now there goes one fine-looking lady, Randy Dell Harker."

The snow, they told me, had stopped before the weekend, but it came back now with a vengeance. And with the snow, the parade of visitors slowed. But Sharon still came, openly now, regularly. We adjusted to the space left by Kathy in our lives during my sojourn in the hospital. But Sharon worked days, and she could not always get away, and when the snow came back, I had again too much time to think. And those times, when Sharon would arrive at night, she let me talk. And talk. Talk the way I had imagined talking to my mythical Guthrie, the one I needed to pull no stops with. And at least she didn't laugh.

"The damn snow," I'd say. "Know what I thought about today? Dust. Dust and my father."

"He committed—"

"Yes," I said.

She sat, watching lighted swirls of snow through dark windows, waiting for me.

"The worst of it began for him in 1934," I said.

"The Depression?"

"Yes. I finished high school that year, and I remember the dust. It was so thick on the pasture that the cattle would not eat. And cows, and calves, and steers wandered around bawling their hunger. He found it hard to believe. Oh, he knew all about the dust storms out West, on the dry plains, but he was a Republican—a moderately well-to-do Republican—and Republicans only think about prosperity. The

Depression for him was a Roosevelt plot, made up by Democrats to create a pretext for canning Hoover. For drought and wind and dust to sweep like a plague over his precious Winnebago County must have seemed to him like a bad dream. Unreal. But it was real, all right."

I stopped talking.

"Do you want to go on?" she asked. "How's your shoulder?"

"He lasted two years," I said. "And some. To be fair about it, the dust got to all of us. Mother stuck papers along the windowsills and rolled rugs against the door, but it still sifted in, dry and fine like talcum powder. It was gritty to the taste, you know? It left this film on the dishes even in the cupboard, on sheets folded in drawers, on every damn chair. In our faces, too, and our hair. Cars used to drive around during the day with their lights on. Drifts of dust piled up against fences like that snow out there, sometimes two, three feet high. I could take you out there now—well, in the spring—and show you the ruts carved by the Big Blow, even though that ground has been plowed and planted twenty times since then."

"Maybe we can do that," she said.

"Yeah, maybe. If he thought the dust was a plague, he found the Farmers' Holiday something even worse, spreading like a wild fire in a fast wind across the state. That summer we saw neighbors dumping milk that ran like water through the ditches along the sides of the roads. We saw the roadblocks they set up, and we heard about the shootings."

"The shootings?" She was suddenly alert, worried about the direction I was taking.

"Yeah. Crazy neighbors shooting each other. One of our old hands, a man named Homer Calkin, had his arm shot to pieces with a shotgun when he tried to deliver milk from Old Man Carter's creamery to make up the wages he lost when my father had to let him go. And this Judge Mason, who had gone to school with my father, was hanged by a gang of Milo Reno's boys after he put all these farms up for penny auctions. Our time came late in the summer, right before I returned to college that year. And there was no help for us from the Farmers Holiday. My father could barely tolerate Collette as governor, then senator, because he was at least a Republican, but he had nothing but

scorn for socialism and he hated Roosevelt with a passion, a venomous passion."

"A venomous passion?" she said, smiling to herself.

"Go ahead," I said. "Smile. It's pretty funny. Not very serious."

"I'm sorry," she said. "Maybe we should just drop it."

"No. No. Look, I'm sorry, too. I just…his first love, and his last
love was land, right? Any land. Especially land he owned. But he
had to sell it off, piece by piece, when prices plummeted after the
First World War, just to keep the farm operating, right? And when
the drought came, he—like every low-down populist he hated in the
state—was mortgaged to the gills. The sheriff—another old friend of
his—brought out the notice of the foreclosure in August 1935. With
apologies, mind you, and this very agonized expression on his face.
Dad had a year to work it off, and I guess we might have made it, I
don't know, maybe if I'd stayed and helped him out, if I hadn't gone
back to school, which cost us money he could've used."

She stood up, walked over to the window, her back to me.

"But I hated him, at least I thought I did then. Hated his crappy
bootstrap rugged individualism that got him nowhere. Like all of us,
you, I learned early how we lived in the best possible times in the best
possible country."

"Randall," she said.

"He was so damn dumb. That's what finally got to me. So stupid
in the face of this great historical moment, this giant dust storm. Me,
I wasn't stupid. I had been to school. I had read a lot of philosophy
and a lot of political science. And I knew more was going on than the
weather, damn it. And I had met Kathy. And I was writing my novel.
And the world was a lot bigger than the old man's plot of earth, his
goddamn land he loved more than us, me, my mother, my brothers.
He lost the farm in the fall of '35. My brothers took off for California. Mother died at her in-laws in the winter of '36, the coldest winter
this state has ever seen, or ever will. He killed himself that spring…
Screw it, can I get some water?"

She brought it back in little hospital Dixie cups and handed one to
me, gently rubbing my arm. I took a sip, smiled, and nodded.

"Why don't you tell me about your novel," she said politely, smiling
too.

"Okay. Okay. First, see, it was going to be a regional masterpiece. About the growth of a writer's mind. Oh yes. A farm boy from Winnebago County discovers the stirrings of genius in his soul. Call it my Thomas Wolfe period. I sent a section of it to kindly old John Frederick at the *Midland*. When I was still in high school, I think. Maybe the summer after. I had read where H. L. Mencken said it was the most important regional magazine in the country in the latest issue of *Smart Set*. Anyway, Frederick—he wrote me a very carefully worded rejection slip, designed to, I think, save me from myself. By the time I met Kathy—in Shakespeare class, no less—I no longer thought of that one as my novel at all. Now, of course, I can see they were all a part of the same novel. The one Kathy waited for year in, year out. Until booze and politics and other women must have made it clear to her, too, that this sophisticated romance she read one year, and the political adventure she read the next, and the social melodrama she read after that, you know, were all the same book, rewritten. No book at all, in other words. Just this kind of twisted diary, an excuse for self-pity—" I took a sip from the Dixie cup. "The last time I saw my father alive, he was covered with dust from his fucking land. Calmly betrayed."

"I think," she said, "maybe I had better give it up for tonight." She put on her coat as she spoke.

"Yeah," I said. "Maybe you should." Then I managed what I hoped was a smile. "For tonight."

But we kept on, night after night, till I reached bottom. I told her about Vlad Paddy, the ease with which his radical politics sucked me up after my father's suicide, and how Padikoff played on my guilt and my anger. When I met him, I told her, he was already a legend and still the strongest voice in organized labor in the state, a party member and a dialectical terror. He showed me what a dupe my father had been to the system, I said. Then he showed me how little that mattered in the great historical scheme of things.

"Padikoff was the man," I said, "who taught me if you want to know about life, real life, you should try to look around the corner of your country. He is taller than I am—you'd like him—with long dark hair and this square handsome face. But delicate, too, you know?

Strange…one of his legs is slightly shorter than the other—he was shot. You don't notice it till you get to know him and start to wonder about his bouncy little walk. He looks like he's always on the verge of dancing, the way Hoops looks always on the verge of sleep—"

She gave a squeal of recognition. "That's right. That's right. Hoops does."

"He—Vlad Paddy, I mean—talked in a world historical language that flew by the nets of normal English. In that language, he showed me the petty bourgeois nature of my desire to write The Novel, with a capital *T* capital *N*. He made me see how much it was like my father's lust for land. It was a need, he'd say, to possess an imaginary world—any imaginary world—rather than our own, the real world. He became one of my closest friends.

"At least for a while," I added. I remembered how he had read everything I wrote then with care, admitting talent where he saw it, criticizing with precision, talking at length about the waste ambition made of American writers. "He showed me," I said sarcastically, "the dignity of the proletariat." And the place in world literature for the poet of the masses, but I did not say that out loud. "I joined the Party in '37. By '38, I was a confirmed Stalinist. The Hitler-Stalin Pact in '39 shook me out of it, but by then writing had already become for me a question of tactics and fiction—fiction was useless in our time. I sang the praises of the United Front; I even helped out this little New Dealer named Paul Toland I had met in school, who was languishing away in the University Chancellor's office, just yearning to plan a city in which we all could really live. I got him a part-time job in the attorney general's office."

"What happened?" she said.

"To Paul? He's still there. Languishing away in the mayor's office, yearning to plan a country we can all really live in."

"No. I meant to you."

"Me? By the time I compromised my politics with Tuckerman to make city editor, I had lost my taste for Stalin and found my taste for scotch. I got elected president of the Newspaper Guild. I had responsibilities. I knew too much to write novels now, of course, which seemed not so much useless as self-indulgent. The world I owned then was the real one, and it not only killed novels, it made Vlad Paddy, with his leg and his language and his damn theories seem stupid to me, too, as much a fiction as anything he attacked. He lashed out at things he no longer appeared to me to understand. He was an anachronism. I purged him from the PAC—that stands for Political Action Committee, a kind of Jesuit arm of the CIO—that stands for—oh, forget it. Somehow, I must have known all along dialectics was a substitute for fiction. Then liquor became a substitute for dialectics. Happens all the time."

"Oh no. Here we go again."

"No, no," I said. "My god, that's the one thing I feel good about."

It got worse my last days in the hospital. I would sit in bed reading during the day and trying to fight the thought that out there, in the world, in time, *something was happening*. People—in the magazines, on the radio—were talking about events and politics, using words like good and evil, and I would see in the *Nation*s and *New Republic*s strewn about the hospital room the phrase "the vital center" over and over, pro and con. I had no vital center. Wilson had blasted it away. The change was taking place outside of me, around me, and I thought I could *feel* it, but I could not make sense of it. It seemed to me I had patched together a life out of compromises and interruptions, that I had spent it doing things of no particular value with people I didn't especially like. The compromises were so many that they blurred together, like my novels, into a totality called *The Mistake*.

I was not much company for those who did visit—Tuckerman, Hoops, the kid, Dyers, Gene Gibson, some workers and union officials, Rojack and the rest (but not Paul, not Paul)—and they caught my temper and kept their stays short. I blamed everybody in turn for bringing me to this miserable pass, tubed to a cell with a cross on the wall and nurses as Catholic as nuns, with only hospital juice to drive away the dust and keep off the snow when I wanted night and Sharon and whiskey.

I remember thinking, in my own personal great depression, that the Chinese attack on Korea was not really an invasion—it was simply spillage, human spillage from the touted end of ideology. Even Bill

Weaver's bespectacled Truman hurling thunderbolts changed for me. I had understood Weaver to mean the political gods would hurl a thunderbolt at me if I caused too much trouble. But in here I would never be able to cause enough trouble even to attract their attention. I felt left out, a discharged shell from an empty gun.

When Sharon got there that night, she sat with me while I whimpered. She suggested I see a shrink when I got out. He would help the depression, she said. It was nothing to be ashamed of, she said. Just expensive. She said she had gone through a nervous collapse, too, when she left the architect, Mr. Parks.

"It isn't exactly pleasant," she said. "But getting shot is as good an excuse as any I can think of for facing up to things."

I told her it wasn't a shrink I needed. I already had one quack, I said.

"What do you mean?" she asked with her faintest, her most...sophisticated smile. She glanced quickly around the room, at the other bed, the crucifix, twice at the doors.

"You know what I mean," I said.

The next time, the next night, she arrived very late in the evening, long after visiting hours, though the nurses were used to her being there late by then.

"Has anyone been to see you?"

"Not forever. They're off fretting—and writing copy—about the great doings in the world."

"Last night...what you said you needed? Do you remember the scene in *A Farewell to Arms,* where—"

"I remember," I said.

She slid one of the visitor's chairs, the only one that didn't fold up, over against the doors. She looked at me, winked, and lifted one shoulder and one leg slightly, imitating a B-girl.

"That won't stop the nurses at this place," I said.

"To hell with it."

She walked over and turned off the lights, leaving only the glow that seeped in through the cracks below and above the door from the hall—and through the window from the streetlights outside—to see by. She reached under her skirt and pulled off her panties, dropped them with a sleek motion to the polished floor, then climbed onto the bed next to me. The rest was easy, if a little awkward at first.

When I moved, it hurt, so she hiked up her skirt and did all the work. I followed the roll of her breasts and reached up under her creamy-colored wool sweater to touch one erect nipple with my free hand. She moved slowly, watching my face through pale eyes, and smiling, touched my lips now and again with a long manicured nail. The ugly scrape of the chair across the tile floor that I worried about never came (not that I heard, anyway), and she never faltered—she rose up and back and up again, like the North Sea (I had never seen the North Sea), oblivious to all that desired to contain it. And, smiling as we finished, she traced my mouth with her finger for silence.

9.

Kid Guthrie did not take my being shot lying down. After leaving the hospital room that first Monday I came back from No Time, he headed straight for Paul's office, walking past Janice and then on through the building toward Bob Weaver, stopping just long enough to charm out of Toland the weather vane's exact location. How the boy ever got Weaver to tell him he was pretty sure Jack Haugen was on Lefty Mills's payroll I'll never figure out, but he did. Now all he needed was some kind of proof.

He said he followed the vibes, whatever that means. The information he culled from Gene Gibson, our crime reporter, convinced him that Lefty Mills was too small-time to throw money around the way the Italians did. If Stefano Calenti, our local Mister Big, was worried about Lefty's friendship with his Sicilian rivals in Chicago, he did not act as if he was worried, Gibson told Guthrie. And why, if Mills was about to move into the big time, was he still working the nickel-and-dime grifts on the docks and with the Teamsters, getting kickbacks from stevedores for a day of work? Maybe he's just finding it hard to break the penny-ante habits of lifelong petty hoodlumry, the kid thought. Whatever Mills paid Jack Haugen would be entered on his books somewhere as a phony expense, the kid decided—on the basis of no information at all as far as I can see, certainly on no knowledge of any kind about how mobsters operate, especially those who are moving up in the underworld, and apparently on no kind of logic.

When Guthrie asked, Gene Gibson made a face that said, Are you nuts? Why would he do something crazy like that? But when the kid kept at him, Gene threw up his hands and told the boy if something unheard of like that were ever to spring into existence in the mob's world, you would probably find it logged in Mills's construction company books or in the ledgers of the dock workers' local, run by his right-hand man, a bone crusher called Frankie Swede. But be careful, Gene warned the kid. Mills has been loan-sharking and floating craps for most of his life, and his instincts are not as refined as the elegant Calenti's; he hits first, Gene said, and asks questions later only if he has to. He's direct and sloppy. Gene told Guthrie he had once seen a college kid who got lucky enough at one of Mills's East End weekend crapshoots to clean house and who was dumb enough to walk back to campus, drunk and alone. They used a baseball bat, Gene said, and the boy's father identified him by the gold watch he had given him for his twenty-first birthday. They probably only left the watch because they had smashed its face, too, but by mistake.

Which sent Kid Guthrie, whistling and smiling, bobbing and weaving his short little body in a peacoat, a fisherman's sweater, denim jeans, and sneakers down to Tommy Rojack's headquarters on Walker Street to talk to some workingmen about how to break into offices after hours. Rojack, the Adonis of the East Side, took one look at our altar boy and broke out laughing. It's illegal, he said. But one of my guys has got a sister who's married to a guy who works for the Mills Construction Company, he said. Yeah, he's foreman on the work crew, added one of the big lugs the kid didn't know, also standing around laughing at him. We'll talk to him. Maybe he'll let you in free late one night. It ain't nice, but it ain't illegal, neither, long as he don't pay much attention to what we do once we're in.

That's right, Bilinski went along with the kid. Bilinski may once have been an electrician, I don't know. When I first met him, he worked for Vlad Paddy. His job description might have read something like: "Being big and Polish—50 percent of overall work time; walking around next to Vlad Paddy—50 percent of overall work time." The nature of his position had not changed much over the years, except now the name "Tommy Rojack" replaced "Vlad Paddy." On this night, Bilinkski was freelancing. Or better yet, moonlighting. And the name had been changed for the evening to read: "Kid Guthrie."

Guthrie said he had never been that far into the East End before, and if the idea was it got worse as you traveled closer and closer to the Atlantic Ocean, he was giving up forever his dream of hanging out in a genuine coffee shop in Greenwich Village. It wasn't the slum, he claimed, since, after all, he lived in a pad on the near Southside in a university-connected pocket ghetto. There, all you had to worry about were a few neighborhood gangs; the two or three Negroes who live in our state, work for the post office, and get drunk on Saturday night looking for nonexistent black women; and the hopheads. In the East End, he said, you worried about your soul first, then your health. On the South Side, people lived in misery, but they lived. In the East End, they just worked; feeling miserable, feeling anything at all, was a luxury. No more talk about alienation for me, the kid said. Out there, I saw it. It was crazy, man, and ready to swallow me up. I'm beginning to dig suits with vests and shoes that lace.

I had never seen the Mills Construction Company, but I could imagine how the place must have appeared to Guthrie—streets barely paved; the wet cobblestones gleaming through cracked asphalt and steaming snow; no light, with block-long buildings casting shadows darker than fear. There would have been a dive or two—nothing you could call a bar, but a doorway next to an alley with neon above it, one rod of the name on the blink, the only sound its buzzing, like some dying blackfly.

What he noticed were the hookers and the loafers staring at him. They knew he didn't belong, he said. He said his hip pals dug smoky undergrounds and the kind of kicks associated with decadence and dissipation and abandonment and sensitivity, getting wasted, smoking weed, fucking a friend's babe—no hang-ups, no guilt. The squares called it alienation; the hipsters, authenticity. But real alienation, he said, was those stares. Alienation was when you weren't a man but a stare. A stare like the ones they gave him. And he laughed and told me he was going to quit watching gangster movies, too.

But down those mean streets went Kid Guthrie and Bilinski, and at midnight on a dark, dreary, snow-cold eve they found Tommy's man's sister's husband—Lefty Mills's foreman—behind the locked garage doors of the Mills Construction Company; he let them in, shushing their knocks and cursing his wife for having a brother she loved in the fucking CIO for chrissakes. Hurry it up would choo and don't turn on no fooking light for chrissakes—wanna get my goddamn fingers broken one-by-goddamn-one? And, no, I ain't got no fooking key to Lefty's office; what the hell you want to get in there for, anyway? Ain't nothing there but fooking pin-ups of all the goddamn whores he's fooked in thirty years; okay, okay, I don't want to know nothing anyway; hey, punk, where the hell did you learn to do that? You see that big fella, how he just popped open that goddamned lock like that? Jesus H. Christ, you wouldn't think it to look at the little jerk—okay, okay mister, don't fooking push me, gaddamn it, I let you in didn't I, didn't I, fooking didn't I?

They found it in the double-entry books on top of one of the filing cabinets first, under something called "marine repairs." Imagine that, Bilinski said to Tommy's man's sister's husband, Lefty Mills's foreman, marine repairs. Hell, the man replied, rubbing his shoulder where Bilinski had slugged him, the only marine repairer fooking Lefty Mills ever had, hell the only one he ever fooking needed, was Frankie Swede, ha ha, and he don't do much repairing, if you know what I mean. There had to be a check, Guthrie told them. A canceled check. Or a stub. Something he could take home. They found it—a canceled check, by God, made out to John Haugen for marine repairs—in the safe, in a batch of canceled checks held together with a rubber band and stuffed in a tin box, after they found the combination to the safe taped to the bottom of the telephone, after they persuaded Tommy's man's sister's husband, Mills's foreman, to tell them where Mills kept the combination to the safe, and that came only after they convinced him he had more to worry about right that moment from Bilinski than he did sometime in the future from Frankie Swede.

Bilinski laughed all the way back to Walker Street. He laughed at Mills and his stupidity, and at Mills's foreman and his fears, and at the kid for being able to pick a lock. And he made the kid stand around with him and Tommy and the boys, drinking rye, while he told the story again and again, adding a little something new he found funny each time. Finally, Guthrie, back in his pad on the near South Side and far from the world of alienated labor, wrote his news story. It appeared two days after Hoops's article on McKnight, under the headline: **MOBSTER "LEFTY" MILLS LINKED TO TIMES ARTICLES**. And marine repairs—accompanied by hoots and hollers, snickers and snide remarks—entered the political lexicon of our state as a new phrase for payoffs and corruption.

༄

"Sounds here, Randy, that you people might be saying Lefty Mills had something to do with the bit of rheumatism you collected in your left shoulder last week?"

Shaunessy, my daylight visitor, sitting in his uncomfortable hospital chair, leaned dangerously away from the bed, with his feet resting on my clean sheets, his derby pushed to the back of his light red head, his wool overcoat slung casually over the footboard, a black cigar waving around in his free hand, the *News* held up in the other. He was smiling and at home, and occasionally he would take a sip of the unnatural tasting tomato juice I had left untouched on my breakfast tray. When any visitor other than Sharon stayed more than five minutes, I found I got bored. Even Guthrie. Especially Shaunessy. He looked at me, smiling.

"Shaunessy," I said. "It seems to me you'd do better off somewhere else, say, out on the streets looking for my would-be killer or picking up your weekly payoffs, or some damn thing, rather than sitting here drinking tomato juice with most of the tomato removed and reading me newspapers I can read for myself."

"Too boring," he said. "I've already looked in every nook and cranny in County Buchanan, and our little outlaw has vanished in the wind. We sent out flyers, Randy boy. Don't worry, some copper will come across him one of these nights now. And if you've taken one payoff, you taken 'em all. No thrill left in the work for me. I'm just putting in me time, waiting on me pension, aye, waiting on my pension. Besides, I pick up more this way, sitting here discussing matters with you and using the old noggin. Never occurred to me, for instance, how damn odd, how out-and-out strange it was, that our boy Haugen simply assumed it was your friend Wilson who went gadding about town with your name on his bullet. Now I haven't talked to him, though he was here several times during your rantin' and ravin' period, asking me what about this here and that there. And how would it be that he even knew you had gone and lost your temper, firing the boy that way, you think?"

"There were a lot of people who saw it," I said. "Some of them didn't like it much. Any number of people at the *News* might have told him."

"Now there's an example of exactly what I mean," he smiled. "All those co-workers of yours so angry about what you had done and worried about what kind of influence Stalin has on the *News* and maybe one of them talked to this Wilson, he was so angry. And maybe he was just so angry because he liked Wilson, you see what I'm getting at? Maybe he—or she—though you say that is rather unlikely—has Wilson stashed away. Now, Randy, I have me something to do for the day: Find out who it was gave this Haugen his information and drop by their home this evening to ask a few questions, just glancing around, looking the place over for tiny Wilson tracks. Of course, we probably questioned most of them already, but maybe we were asking the wrong questions. Now let's get on to Mr. Lefty Mills before I have to be leaving you for the day. I was not aware you knew Mr. Mills."

"I don't," I growled. "And I don't care to."

"Pity," he said. "I do. When I was a youngster, we shot craps together couple times in the East End. He was the kind of man always anxious to get ahead, with the kind of temperament of such a man— the kind of temperament that was the very thing keeping him from getting ahead. No patience. Any time he was the least bit stymied, even small setbacks, would send him off shooting folks or banging heads. If he had lived anywhere but the East End, he'd have spent his life in prison, or be a dead man by now; instead, the boys tended just to stay out of his path. 'Old Lefty,' they'd say, 'you've got to watch out for that one, I tell you. He's the crazy one.' You know, of course, he used to run booze down from Canada for old Giuseppi Calenti. When young Calenti took over from Uncle Joey, he wanted Mills out of the organization, and out he went. Roams the street starting this and that bit of business. Getting ahead. And folks just allow him his space, the way they do the village idiot in someplace like, oh, I don't know, some little town with an Elm Street and Main. Yes, sir, a pity you have never made his acquaintance, because I have this nice little picture frame sitting on my parlor wall, empty, very, very blank, that could easily fit around two mug shots of the man. You positive the fellow who winged you wasn't around fifty, dressed like a cheap clerk in a shoe store, and shouting obscenities?"

"Shaunessy," I said. "I don't know the man."

"You wouldn't be holding out, Randy, would you, now, so you could turn this thing on The McKnight—some hairbrained scheme such as that?"

"Get out of here, Mike. I need my rest."

"Because if you are, Harker my boy, forget it. Mills, he doesn't think exactly straight, not even for a thug. My guys have got express orders not to take the time of day from him or his pals because even cops can't trust them. And you, you would send him to the floor frothing at the mouth just looking at you. You can't be bought and you don't own nothing you care about. All he would have left to do is kill you. And that makes more sense to me than some queer coming up behind you in the dark because you took away his job and insulted his prose style."

"Shaunessy," I said. "You have derailed. I'm telling you the truth. The man behind me was Wilson. I can't swear to it in court, but it was him."

"Pity," Shaunessy said, dropping his feet off the end of the bed, throwing his long coat around his shoulders, still smiling and shaking his head. Bitter wrinkles creased his face as he stamped out the cigar, pulled his scarf tight, his derby down, tipping it to me goodbye, and smiling. "A terrible shame, that it is," he said more to himself than me. "A terrible shame."

When I woke up again from my midmorning druggy snooze, Shaunessy was somehow still standing there, leaning against the door, his derby cocked, his white scarf dangling down over the lapels of his suit, his wool overcoat casually slung across one arm, with a newspaper now pressed under the pit of the other, next to his gun. Yes, sir, I thought, he was open to a little honest graft and he knew who his friends were.

"You are a cliché," I said. "Know that?"

"And you have become a legend," he said. "Overnight."

As he pulled out the newspaper, he went rambling on. "I am making reference to page one of a certain newspaper that happens not to be published right here in our crime-beleaguered city."

I looked at the paper under his arm.

"The *Journal?*"

"None other," he said, plopping it down on the tray next to me.

For the first day since the invasion, Korea did not command a headline. I saw my picture (the one I liked best) and one I recognized as McKnight before I read the lead.

"And how is it," Shaunessy was going on, "might you tell me, that the gentlemen of the rival press seem always to know more about you and the motives of our ghostly Mr. Wilson than does yourself, well-known recipient of his affection?"

"Good question, Shaunessy. Good question." The screamers above my image and McKnight's read: **SENATOR MCKNIGHT RENEWS ATTACK ON RED NEWSMAN HARKER.**

So we had McKnight's response to Guthrie's piece, and our local witch hunt had heated up.

10.

The article in the *Ravensport Journal* Shaunessy offered was composed around a series of questions Senator McKnight said he wanted answered—here, or in Washington before his committee if necessary—and it included some rather vaguely worded charges the *Journal* quoted from a nine-page mimeographed news release sent out by McKnight's Senate office. According to the article, the senator's press release charged that I was a Communist and that the *Capital News* closely followed the party line. McKnight leveled several specific charges. First, he again noted, as he had in his memorial auditorium speech (was it only a week ago?), that Tuckerman himself had once called me "the Communist leader in the capital city." Second, he said a man named Robert Kelly, a former Communist Party member who lived in town, had testified years back under oath that, quote, "The president of the Capital City Communist Council is Randall Harker, a reporter for the *Capital News*, who has been a sympathizer with the party and a fellow traveler since 1936. He joined the party toward the end of 1937."

According to McKnight, the *Journal* wrote, I had also been identified as a Communist by William Murray of Cotter, Ohio—a Young Communist Party member from 1936 through 1939, attending college at the University of Wapsipinicon. I was also supposedly listed as a sponsor of a mass meeting held in June 1938 by the American League for Peace and Democracy, which, McKnight's news release pointed out, had been labeled an "advocate of treason" by the House Un-American Activities Committee. McKnight charged, too, that I had cosponsored with Eugene Dennis, a Communist leader now under federal indictment, a statewide conference on Farm and Labor Legislation in April 1939. HUAC, he claimed, listed this organization as "Communist controlled." McKnight said I had attended a meeting of the Wapsipinicon Conference on Social Legislation, a group listed by the United States attorney general as a Communist organization.

"Who the hell is the attorney general?" I asked Shaunessy. "Not Tom Clark, Truman put him on the Supreme Court last year."

"That guy from Rhode Island," Shaunessy said. "Some Mick. Mc-Grady? *McGrath.*"

I turned back to my reading. According to the *Journal*, McKnight said I was named by HUAC as "being affiliated" with the Communist-inspired Citizens Committee to Free Earl Browder. McKnight, said the *Journal*, claimed I had recently fired an employee of the *Capital News* for espousing anti-Communist views and that my action had been "applauded" by John Tuckerman, "owner of said paper."

"The evidence indicates," the *Journal* quoted McKnight, "that Harker, better known as Red Randall Harker, was at one time a member of the Party and was closely affiliated with a number of Communist-front organizations. Nothing in his subsequent writings would indicate he has in any way changed his attitude toward the Communist Party."

The *Journal* claimed the rest of McKnight's news release went on to "prove that the *Capital News* was the red mouthpiece for the Communist Party in the state and that it never attacked Communists." Evidently, McKnight "proved" all of this by pointing out the many and varied similarities in the views of both the *News* and the *Daily Worker*. Finally, the *Journal* printed the questions McKnight claimed needed answering immediately:

1. Has the Communist Party with the cooperation of the *Capital News* Corporation won a major victory in our state?
2. Is Red Randall Harker, city editor of the *Capital News*, a Communist?
3. What has become of Charles Wilson, the employee fired by Harker for his patriotic American political views?
4. Is the *Capital News* Corporation the Red mouthpiece for the Communist Party in our state?
5. What can be done about this situation?

I had just enough time to finish the article and to look up at Shaunessy and say: "McKnight would make one hell of a biographer," when Hoops and Kid Guthrie pushed past him into the room, Hoops puffing a little.

"Have you—" Guthrie started to say.

"Got it right here, courtesy of the police."

"Now, Randy, my boy," Shaunessy replied, sticking his arms into his wool overcoat and buttoning up. "Don't let's be bringing my good name into this. All a man has, as the bard says, is his reputation. You're okay over a deck o' cards, but I have me livelihood to be thinking on."

"I thought you were a loyal friend," I said with mock surprise.

"Oh, but I am," he said. "I am. You can be most sure of that, Randy Dell. But as me pappy, me wee tiny pappy, who lived a lot longer than he should have on the East End of this damn burg, always said: 'A friend is a man who keeps his mouth shut. Period.'" He crossed one end of his white silk scarf over the other and stuffed them between the lapels of his overcoat, patting it in place and grinning his grim Irish grin.

"We were at the Cove, man," Guthrie said, sticking his nose ten or twelve miles in the air above Captain Shaunessy. "When the news hit the stands. Everybody was talking about it."

"How much of that crap is true?" Hoops, catching his breath, asked in a certain tone. His eyes met mine steadily and without effort.

"None of it would stick in court," I said.

"Yes, sir," Hoops said, his head bobbing up and down in determination. "Yes, sir. But how much of it is *true*?"

I turned to Guthrie. I won't say his mouth was agape, but he was standing there, staring at Hoops, doing his best to hide his surprise and failing more miserably than he suspected.

"Go find my quack for me, would you?" I said to him.

"What?" he asked, distracted, still staring at Hoops.

"I've got to get out of here," I said, patiently. "Before the others show up."

"The others—" he turned his gaze from Hoops for just enough time to ask me the question. "Who?"

"*Who?*" Hoops said. So, he understood. This was between us, the two of us. "Haugen and Jenkins and Miller from the *Journal,* and every pencil pusher who thinks he knows our local Hemingway here. The Wapsipinicon wolf pack will be on the attack. So get going."

The kid left. Indignantly, but he left. And when he had gone, I looked at Hoops.

"Okay, I'd say—except for the dates—two of his assertions are accurate as far as they go—"

"Well, Randy," Shaunessy interrupted, catching on as well. "It's best I be running along now. Got myself a would-be killer to snare and a few lousy rackets to look in on for the weekly dole, you understand. Keep 'em honest."

"I understand," I said. "And you better get a move on it, too. I'd suggest you take the backstairs, not the elevator. The boys won't be long now, and you don't want to have to answer any questions on the way out."

"Randall Harker." He held out his right hand and with his left pushed his derby straight and a little down over his forehead. "You are a man of fine distinctions, a man with a most discriminating sensibility. When you've gotten yourself out of this mess, look me up, and we'll be having a whiskey or two and a good laugh over it. Meantime, I might yet find myself in need of asking you a few more questions about this other business, in which case *I* shall get in touch with *you.* "

I took the proffered hand.

"I'll look forward to it, Captain."

Ersatz formalities finished, Shaunessy, too, left. Hoops, having lost his inertia, was looking for a chair. Then he gave me his undivided attention.

"Two are fairly accurate," I said. "One or two others have some basis in fact. The rest—the rest is pure hokum."

"What do you plan to say?"

Hoops watched his hands. Round cartoon hands, hands that sat still, like dead weight, in his lap.

"Deny everything, flat out. Yes?"

A nurse had just stuck her scrawny, never-kissed neck in the room.

"Telephone," she said cheerfully, mindlessly. "A Mr. Tuckerman."

"Okay. Let's go."

"What's this?"

Hoops, seated now, lethargic, seemed suspicious of all movement. The skinny nurse came into the room, dragging behind her the folded-up wheelchair she had been concealing in the hall. Why quacks and nurses try to add such mystery to their profession I'll never know, but they are forever coming at you with needles and hidden things.

"She's got to wheel me to the telephone," I explained. "No one—no patient—ever walks. It reduces his dependency. Makes them seem superfluous." I waved a hand in her general direction. She smiled her condescending smile and began to jabber her pleasant routine about doctor's orders and how I was not a well man.

I ignored her, telling Hoops: "The Old Man's about to ask me the same questions, in about the same order, but not with the same tone that you just did. Wait here for the others. If you can bring yourself to do it, lie. Tell them I've been transferred to County General for safe keeping."

"Why don't I just tell them you died peacefully in your sleep. It would save the rest of us a lot of grief."

We had to talk to each other around the nurse, who was making a production of unfolding the wheelchair and turning back my sheets. When she reached down to take my arm, I pushed her away, stood up, and looked at Hoops over her head, and—under my own steam—sat down with dignity (always with dignity) in her contraption.

"Suit yourself," I said to him. "I'll be taking the call in a little break room back of the nurses' quarters—the other side of the dressing rooms down the corridor. If Guthrie and my quack get back here before the gang arrives, please direct them there."

He nodded Buddha-like as she wheeled me from the room. Past the elevators, as I was turning into the corridor toward the nurses' quarters, I saw Jack Haugen and that old coot Jenkins step into the foyer from the opening elevator door and make directly for my room and the waiting Hoops. I hoped he would handle it. It had not struck me so much till now how his logorrhea and his wisecracks masked the meaning of his conciliations and his sloth—Hoops was a very cautious man. He had made it at the *News* by simply standing still, like so much neutral ground, between me and Tuckerman.

The nurse stopped in front of the break room and left me unprotected in the corridor for a moment while she went in to chase out, officiously, two or three co-workers who were sitting around with their feet up, drinking coffee. Then she wheeled me toward the phone and told me what to say to the switchboard. I caught her bony arm as she tried to leave.

"Listen. Don't smile at me like I'm your idiot son. Listen. Go back down the hall. Stand by the elevators. Don't talk to anyone, don't look at anyone, and don't answer questions. Stand there and wait. When my quack, Dr...."

"Dr. Johnson," she said, starting to smile again but wiping it off quickly when I glared at her.

"When Dr. Johnson gets off the elevator with an overgrown boy in black loafers and a loose expression tell them to follow you, that his patient is waiting here. Don't use my name. Especially if anyone is standing around or gets off the elevator with them. Got that?"

"Yes, sir." She smiled.

"Ah, ah, ah," I said, waving my finger, and she snapped to attention. "Go."

I picked up the telephone, talked to the operator, and—when she put me through—said in the closest imitation to the nurse's cheerful voice I could muster, "'Lo, boss. How's the weather?"

The quack and Guthrie arrived just as I was explaining to Tuckerman that McKnight really had nothing because all the specifics he used were at least a half-decade old, and that he, Tuckerman, should look on the bright side of things. They had not mentioned Vlad Paddy. I teased him about why: if they had, it would naturally bring up discussions of the *News* policy on labor, Tuckerman's policy, which was well-known and much applauded even by Republicans. He snapped something witless back to my little barb and hung up.

The quack listened attentively to my conversation and tried to get Guthrie to explain to him what was going on at the same time. When I was done, he took on the air of a man in deep, deep thought, then he said what I knew he would say, that considering the circumstances, I would probably get more rest at home, out of the public eye.

"And out of your hospital," I said, smiling. "What's the matter, Doc? Scared of a little publicity?"

He drew himself up to be indignant, but before he could say anything, I turned to Guthrie: "The problem now becomes how to get back to the room and retrieve my clothes without running into some eager-beaver newshound. How bad was it down there?"

"A real drag," Guthrie said. "When we slipped past, Hoops was talking jive, saying nada, at great length as usual, to the crowd (at least it felt like a crowd, maybe a couple—two or three, really) and still keeping the squares' attention. But not for long. Pretty soon they'll be nosing around."

"Doc," I said. "Go down there and announce I've checked out. They won't believe it at first, but just stick to it. Give them a time and tell them that's all you know. Tell them I was much improved so you sent me home. After a while, they will grow bored of asking you and Hoops the same questions, and when they've gone, we'll wait even longer to make sure they've gone, and then I'll check out."

I looked at the scrawny nurse.

"Go downstairs and tell them at the switchboard the same thing. I don't want any more calls."

Out in the hall the two of them whispered about *the nerve*—meaning mine, I suppose—and Guthrie and I smiled at each other.

"You look very hip in hospital flax," he said.

"Women seem to think so." I shrugged.

We waited half an hour. Back in the room we chased out the nurses, and Hoops and Guthrie helped me dress.

"The doctor was good," Hoops said. "He said he was a very busy man. What did the Old Man say?"

"Are you now, or have you ever been—"

"That's not funny, pal."

"Fuck you, fat man."

"I don't have to put up with this tough-guy act, Harker. You know that."

"Then don't."

"Hey, man," Guthrie said, stepping between us. "Hey, cool it. C'mon."

"That's right, Hoops. I'm a wounded man."

"You are a sick puppy, buddy. And what gets me—what gets me right in the ass—is—the rest of us, the rest of us pay—"

"*Hoops!*" Guthrie said. "What's bugging you? Man, oh, man."

"He sees his career flushed down the toilet," I said. "And he's too old to join the circus. Why don't you just try doing your job for a change? Where's the information on McKnight I asked you for a week ago?"

Hoops stepped toward me like he planned to take a swing at me, and I stood up directly in his face, forcing him to step back.

"Falling apart already," Haugen said from the doorway. Today he wore an impeccably tailored camel hair sport coat, wool slacks just the right shade of dark brown, and an expensive print silk tie. His slick yellow hair gleamed green in the hospital's new florescent lights, and his cashmere overcoat was folded neatly on one arm, the other stretched to support his weight on the doorframe. "I thought you might be coming back here," he sneered. "Why else was Hoops hanging around? Certainly not to talk to the press."

"Get him out of here," I said to Guthrie.

The kid, his shoulders sloped, looking as menacing as he could—which was fairly menacing considering he sometimes reminded me of one of the Young Rascals, even if he was kind of cool—headed toward Haugen, who backed judiciously but slowly out of the doors that swung both ways.

"Feels a little different with things turned around, huh, Harker? What'd you say? I didn't hear you, Commie. Lefty Mills sends his love. Says stay out of dark alleys. Oh, I forgot. Do you have any statement to make about the recent allegations—" The doors closed on him.

I looked at Hoops, who was still red in the face.

"Look," I said. "I'm sorry."

"Drop it," he said. "I'll get you the shit you asked for."

"Bring it to the apartment," I said. "I'd better get started on the next installment of the *Rise and Fall of Turd McKnight* tonight, if I can manage to sit up straight for more than twenty minutes." Hoops managed to grimace what was supposed to be a smile. He is trying at least, I thought.

As Hoops took off, my quack and Guthrie returned. The quack had some second-thought instructions about how to take care of the wound, asking if I had anyone at home, and—in response to the silence from both Guthrie and me— making me promise to call if it started to bleed freely again.

"We'd better take the back stairs," I said to the kid. "And make sure no one follows us." Guthrie laughed, dismissively enough, I guess, but I could see he was nervous.

Outside, clearly, winter had struck. No longer was it just a question of snow, though there was still plenty of that. Now it had turned cold. Cold, in the way only the Midwest can turn cold. But despite the sharp stab at my unprotected skin and another sudden flare of pain in my shoulder, I felt oddly elated. As Guthrie helped me into his car, I sucked in the air, fulsomely. Breathed it right in, that cold, cold draught of freedom.

Part 3: DARK ALLEYS

Truly, alas, we are strangers in the alleys of a sad city,
where in the fake calm of a constant clamor,
some molded shape cast from emptiness swaggers out—
the gilded racket, the bursting memorial.

—Rainier Maria Rilke, *Tenth Duino Elegy*

11.

When we got to the apartment, Hoops was waiting outside in the cold, holding a bunch of bulging manila folders tightly against his chest like a child on the first day of school. He took the hospital debris from Guthrie and dumped the folders into the kid's hands. Inside the two of them helped me settle in, and we sent the kid back to work. As the door closed behind him, Hoops reached for one of the folders and grinned.

"What? *What?*"

"You ought to look at this," he said, handing me the folder. "From Guthrie," he laughed. "Too bad he left; he'd have enjoyed telling you all about it. It's a copy of McKnight's MOS and a bad mimeograph of something called a unit history of the Army Air Force bunch Mc-Knight belonged to. The kid somehow got them dispatched up from Maxwell Air Force Base in Montgomery, Alabama, which keeps a load of Air Force shit—records, histories, orders, battlefield communiqués, awards, medals, whatever. Some old college honey of his down there got her mitts on a copy and snuck it out for us, I guess." Reaching for another folder, Hoops said, "And here's the story Haugen did for the *Stars & Stripes*." With the next folder, he added, "Here's all the local newspaper stories about that amazing hero of our times, Tail Gunner Larry." Then, holding on to one final folder, Hoops stopped to watch as I read.

The *Stars & Stripes* piece was so clearly a joke I was surprised the military broadsheet had printed it. Every achievement of any flight crew hero on a B-17 to win a medal during the war, Tail Gunner Larry seemed to have achieved, too, on that single outing—shooting down maybe a dozen Messerschmitts, tossing out by hand a burning phosphorous bomb that had blown back up into the bomb bay, crawling the length of a smoke-filled fuselage to take control of the flight from a badly wounded pilot and co-pilot. Had McKnight actually done any of the things described, he would have been: a) dead or disabled; b) awarded the Medal of Honor several times over. The whole thing was an inside joke, tongue-in-cheek, and typically disagreeable. In other words, flyboy humor, and every airman who read it would have immediately understood the nasty parody. The next folder held several 1946 news clippings from the *Winnebago Gazette* and a few of the state's other backwater rags with stories featuring such headlines as **TAILGUNNER LARRY SETS SIGHTS ON SENATE**. Each recounted a version of the *Stars & Stripes* piece, treating the gist of it—that he was a hero—as gospel, either intentionally ignoring or missing altogether its obvious broad humor and irony.

I looked at Hoops and held up the *Stars & Stripes*. "Did they know out here it's supposed to be funny or did they just not get the joke?"

"Cynical or stupid, hmmm," Hoops grunted. "Keep reading."

In the next folder lay McKnight's service orders.

"Jesus," I said after I read them. "A supply clerk?"

"You got it, boss. A corporal, never an officer. Just a paper pusher. Man never set foot on an Eighth Air Force tarmac, much less a Flying Fortress, except that one night. It was a reconnaissance run, a press flight. Filled with newshounds from all over. McKnight talked his way along as an observer, a favor to one of the army press guys. I wonder who?"

"Haugen," I said.

Hoops nodded. "That'd be my guess."

I picked up the next folder, the one that held the faintly legible mimeo of the unit history for McKnight's outfit. It took some time, but I read it through, then I looked up again at the smiling Hoops. "No McKnight," I said.

"Not even an honorable mention," Hoops confirmed, "except to list his name along with the names of the other unit members in his squad. And this is the stuff they use to document what happened. He'd need to be in there, for example, if he had been awarded any kind of medal. So I told Guthrie to call both the offices of the secretaries of the Army and the Air Force to see if he could find out something about McKnight's Purple Heart or his Distinguished Flying Cross. Both made him request it in writing, then they passed him off to the National Archives, who sent him back to the commander of Maxwell to check the records they held on Army Air Force sergeants and enlisted men.

"And this," he said, smiling and handing me the last folder, "this we got Monday, yesterday, when they finally delivered the mail from last week, before the storm hit. This is the *pièce de résistance*."

The letter was from Major Lamar MacDuff, Chief Air Force Historian, and it was addressed to Dear Mr. Guthrie:

> Per request of the Secretary of the Air Force and others, I am responding to your enquiry regarding Corporal Lawrence McKnight. I am authorized to inform you that the National Archives of the United States of America, the Department of the Army of the United States of America, and the Department of the Air Force of the United States of America have no record of the Distinguished Flying Cross having been awarded to Corporal Lawrence McKnight. I am also authorized to inform you that the National Archives, the U.S. Army, and the U.S. Air Force have no record of the Purple Heart being awarded to Corporal McKnight. If you have any further questions regarding this matter, please forward them to me in writing, and I will attempt to answer them for you as expeditiously as time permits.

When I shook my head in wonder, Hoops said, "By the end of the war they were handing out Purple Hearts like Hershey bars, so it might be more scandalous that McKnight did not get one than that he lied about it. Before it was all over in some theaters, they even dished out the DFC left and right. For finishing twenty-five missions, for example, though that was dangerous enough, I guess, if you talk to any real flyboys. The odds were against you living through the standard number of combat missions, but back in the '46 election that's exactly what McKnight claimed he did. Flew thirty-two missions, he said. So that, too, was a big lie just like bragging he won the medals. Best I can tell, the only missions he actually went on were training exercises. Those, and that one piss-ant milk run over the ruins of Germany at the end of the war."

"And the medals—I mean the physical objects—pinned to his chest?"

"Boss," Hoops said. "The war was over. Lot of guys didn't care about that crap anymore. Yeah, a medal might make you feel okay for a little while about what you did, and you might maybe say to the folks back home and in public that it made you feel proud, but it could also remind you how worthless your life was during the war, something you couldn't tell anybody—not civilians, I mean—even if you admitted it to yourself. I know GIs who pawned them—or tossed them in the trash. Right this minute, I got no idea where my Purple Heart is. McKnight could of picked them up anywhere, cheap."

"We need to get a piece—"

Hoops handed me copy. "Been working on it."

TAIL GUNNER LARRY LIED ABOUT WAR RECORD
In his 1946 campaign for the United States Senate, Lawrence McKnight may have lied about his military career when he claimed he won a Purple Heart and the Distinguished Flying Cross for his service in the Army Air Forces during World War II. According to U.S. Air Force Major Lamar MacDuff, McKnight received neither medal, nor did he fly the thirty-two combat missions he claimed earned him the awards.

Hoops's copy went on to rework a lot of the information he had summarized for me last week at the Cove, and I told him to cut it, that I planned to narrate all that again with my editorial column (we had been calling it "OUR MAN IN D.C."), which would run with his piece.

"What about McKnight himself?" I asked. "Did you call his office, try to get a response?"

"I tried, like always. But, Harker, we been ragging his ass so often, his office don't bother to return calls from us, much less react to anything we plan to run."

"Take the opener," I said, "and give Hickenlooper another call. Schultz, too. Get quotes, even if it's a 'no comment' from the SMA. Put some of that jazz in there you just told me about how easy it was to get medals, only say it respectfully. You know: 'Our boys were so routinely brave that the medal count went way up by war's end.' You'd know better what to say than me."

"So imply McKnight betrayed them, too," Hoops nodded, "when he lied about winning both. Just like he betrayed the voters of this state."

"Lead them to it," I said. "Show them, but don't spell it out. I'll make that point explicitly in my piece."

After Hoops went back to the office to finish his piece, I spent time mulling over what I would write. I tried to imagine how McKnight felt when Haugen's story appeared in *Stars & Stripes*. Jokes zipping around the enlisted airmen's mess, the rough, derisive, brutal humor of the flyboys and the ground crews as they slapped their supply clerk on his back and called him Old Tail Gunner Larry. Did McKnight grin through it all? Did he shuffle away, humiliated? How does the butt of such a joke, maybe the laughingstock of a theater of operations, look at himself in the mirror the next morning? And what does he see when he does? Then something about it struck me as very strange, and I called Hoops at his desk. As we talked, I could hear him pecking at his typewriter.

"Last week, Guthrie told me *McKnight* talked Haugen into writing the piece," I said.

"Yap," Hoops said. "Haugen told him McKnight suggested they do it to lighten things up. Little bit of fun for the old unit. What ho."

I looked at the *Winnebago Gazette*. Then I said to Hoops: "He planned it from the beginning. McKnight's a supply clerk. He's never going to see action. So he fixes it over there to have the *Stars & Stripes* story for the campaign he's planning when he gets back here. Didn't matter if it was supposed to be a joke or how humiliating it was, just so long as he had something in print he could use in his postwar campaign. Who knows what he had to trade with Jack Haugen, who probably outranked him, to get the story planted? And he took the calculated risk nobody would bother to check it out before he was elected even if they could." I shook my head. "What gets me, he actually knew how the folks upstate would read the piece. He guessed the boobs back home would not see what the flyboys saw instantly. He figured he'd get away with it, with using it in his campaign. He gambled it would work."

"See what I been telling you," Hoops said. "He's a dangerous man. Wallows in shit, comes up smelling like a rose. Take him seriously."

"No, Hoops," I said, amazed that McKnight's ambition could make him so utterly complicit in his own debasement, "not dangerous, just even more slimy than other politicians."

"Have it your way, boss," Hoops said, and I caught a whiff of the anger and resentment I had heard in his voice back at the hospital.

As I walked around, I noticed how clean and vacant the apartment appeared. Kathy always kept house especially well when she was upset, and I was surprised to remember the care with which I had picked up the place the night she left. I made myself a scotch, touching nothing, and skulked back to the second bedroom, the one I had reworked to resemble some combination of library and office. Homemade bookshelves lined the walls around a secondhand desk I had picked up from a bankruptcy sale and a settee we'd bought when we got married. On the way, I checked our bedroom, where Kathy would normally have been hiding out, but it, too, was spotless and empty.

I spread the notes I had made about McKnight and the material I'd gotten from Hoops and Guthrie in a semicircle on the desktop. I took off my shirt and shoes, dropping them over and under the office's meager furnishings (a habit that had irritated Kathy almost as much as my drinking and my line of work). I pulled the typing table with the old Underwood I had liberated from the *News* up to the desk. I sipped a little scotch and tried to think my way into a hard-boiled mood.

These days, when I worked at home, I no longer ever considered the original reason we had set up this room, but Kathy's absence set off memories of the great American novels I had once promised her and instead killed dead with staccato blows from a stolen machine. No surprise, I guess, since Kathy had always been more enthralled with the room and the typewriter than I was. She always insisted on calling the place my study rather than my office. And, until I became well known locally as a hack for Tuckerman's rag, she had always introduced me as a writer rather than a reporter. In fact, our first real clash had taken place here, one night when she found me working against a deadline.

There had been other arguments, other articles. During this one or that, I told her she had so sanctified the place, had made it such a shrine to artistic truth, it was hard to produce anything at all on the spot. After the week I'd just gone through, maybe I felt remorse for the unfinished fiction and the inescapable fights, because, as I banged out the title of the series as the header: OUR MAN IN D.C., I found myself calling up a memory of her in bed in Chicago before we were married.

"When my grandfather announced he was going to run for mayor of Ravensport," Kathy had said that night, "grandmother took to her room. She never fought him on anything, but she knew too many politicians, she said, and she would not marry one. She said she was not getting up again until he quit the race. That afternoon, he announced he was dropping out because of ill health. He always joked afterward that he meant to say ill temper—grandmother's ill temper... He would have won, too."

Tonight, below the header I typed the description of the piece we always ran in ten-point italics:

> The latest in a series of articles by veteran political reporter and *Capital News* city editor Randall Harker on United States Senator Lawrence McKnight.

"Oh?" I had responded to Kathy in Chicago.

"I'm serious," she said. "This newspaper job you took, it's temporary?"

"Until we get settled," I said.

"I'm marrying a writer not a reporter," she said.

"Just till the novel's done," I said.

Now, I finished my drink and mixed another before I exorcised the demons in the study and ran a few sheets of union bond through the Underwood. It's the machine's fault, I thought. Tuckerman put a hex on it before I sneaked it out of the office. It won't type fiction, only facts.

> When Albert Collette, Sr., the late, renowned leader of the Progressive movement in America, was first elected to the United States Senate in 1928 after an unprecedented three terms as governor of Wapsipinicon, he reminded the press that the voters always got the politicians they deserved.
>
> "The voters of this state," he said behind his famous poker face, "are obviously very deserving."

"Prince" Albert's witticism was duly entered into the annals of the state's political lore where it took on the weight of an eternal verity. For years, writers on the editorial pages of local newspapers have found occasion to quote Collette's comment as absolute truth. But it is time we take his witticism off the shelf and examine it again in the light of contemporary events. For the question arises: Do we deserve Larry McKnight?

In a sense, Albert Collette is as responsible for the need to ask the question as he is for giving us the form the question takes. It was with Albert Collette's blessing that Lawrence McKnight, a bankrupt chicken farmer, first ran for public office. It was through Albert Collette's sufferance that Lawrence McKnight, embezzling state treasurer, continued to hold office. And so it was, too, after Albert Collette's sudden death—and the failure of his son to live up to his father's legacy—that Lawrence McKnight, bogus war hero, was still around to win a Republican seat in the U.S. Senate in 1946.

I could have sworn I heard the front door of the apartment gently close and I stopped typing, waiting for Kathy to call out. When she didn't, I went back to the typewriter.

The facts of Lawrence McKnight's political biography are known to readers of the *Capital News*.

The last night I had seen Kathy, she stood in the doorway to this room and said, "Drinking and working late again?" She was dressed for shopping in her tweed skirt and her wool coat and her nylon hose. She had her high heels in her hands because she'd just stepped out of her boots. She had had her hair done. It was shiny black and came down in curls almost to her shoulders from its part on the side. She wore more makeup than usual to cover the circles under her eyes and hide their puffiness, but it also concealed her freckles and made her look pale, washed-out—the ghost-woman our marriage had made of the colleen I met in college. She was still very attractive in a willful sort of way. Green eyes refused to meet mine.

"Deadline," I said apologetically. "How are you?"

"Me? Oh, I'm just fine."

She left. I guessed I was supposed to sigh, pull the page out of the typewriter, pick up my glass, and follow her into the living room. Instead, I had kept writing, as I did now.

> In 1928, as Collette first took the oath of office for the Senate, Larry McKnight dropped out of college to take over his father's chicken farm, a business he sold the next year to invest in the sale of farm implements. By 1930, he was on the edge of bankruptcy.

Back then, Kathy had reappeared at the door for a moment, then she left again. In between, she had said: "I need to talk to you." And I had sighed, pulled the page I was working on out of the typewriter, picked up my glass, and followed her into the living room. Once there, I had headed on through to the kitchenette and began mixing a scotch.

"Want something?" When she did not answer, I had continued with my elaborate concoction (two cubes of ice and a twist of water from the kitchen faucet) and with the writing of the article in my head.

Now, as I made my way in this current piece through McKnight's biography toward his campaign for the Senate, I could almost hear her say again, as she had then: "I went down to the university today and I enrolled for next semester. I'm going back, I'm going to finish my degree."

"In what," I had asked, standing across the room from her, "English literature?"

"I knew you would think that," she had said, looking at me for the first time since I answered her summons. "That you'd think it was like Mother. That's the way you think. You summarize things up, put them in neat little packets, little boxes. It's the newspaper training."

And me: "Everything is the newspaper training. If I take a drink, it's the *News* getting to me. If I join the party, it's the *News*. If I don't finish a novel, it's the *News*. If I fart in public, it's the *News*."

And her: "Oh, shut up. Not tonight. I'm not going to fight tonight. I just want to explain this. Why I'm doing it. And then I just want to go to bed. I'm going after a degree in literature. I talked to my father."

And me: "Well, well, well, this is an event. This calls for a celebration. I think I'll have another drink."

And her: "He didn't even mention you." Talking off into the distance, into the eons below the coffee table. "After all this time...he didn't even mention you. He acted as if it hadn't been years since we talked. I borrowed Jenny Hutchins's car. I drove all the way down there and back despite the weather and the roads, and he didn't say a word, not like he was surprised to see me…nothing. It was as if I was just twenty-three and had gotten my BA and come to him for advice about school. Like a scene we had missed when we were right for the parts and got together now to play at last after all this time—you know what I'm saying?"

She had looked up at me again, and I saw she was scared. Lately, she had talked about going back to school often, but always rhetorically, as some kind of threat. She had taken the first step.

And me: "It means you're leaving."

And her: "I don't know, Dell. I don't think it means that. Do you want me to leave?"

My *no* was automatic, and it was enough.

And her: "That's not how I thought about it. I am just tired of always bickering. Of waiting for you, waiting for you to do something."

And me: "I am doing something."

And then she was crying.

"At first, I thought it was the *News*," she had said—or something very much like that. By that point in our marriage she was always saying the same thing more or less. "You are right. That's what I thought. You were such a fine writer. When did we stop talking about it? About all the things you were going to do? Oh, God, you can waste so much time waiting for somebody. Waste. All those days I would think: if the little things would change, if you would stop drinking, or dropping your clothes on the floor, anything, then I could stand it. Then I could stand having made a mistake; I could stand the not having children. I didn't pay any attention to the women. I didn't care about the women. I didn't care about my father, my family. If you could just write, just do something. And then I thought it was your friends. That Vlad Paddy. Or the union work. And then I thought it was me, and I should leave you alone, and then you would work. But you lied to me. Oh, you never came out and said you planned to keep writing, not after the first few years you didn't. But you made me think you did. You made me think you were going to somehow. Don't ask me when, I don't know when, you just made me think that, that's all. I thought that was the only thing that held us together. Because, despite all the fights, and the other women, and the lies—how long can you keep going telling yourself you plan to write someday? When, when, when? Despite all that, I thought my faith in you kept us together, and maybe it did, because I love you, I still love you."

She had talked on for a span, moving about the apartment, picking up after me, putting away the clothes I had dropped in the study, the glasses I had dirtied in the kitchenette, drowning me in a flood of words I had heard before in other sentences on other nights. The new thing had been her plan to go back to school. That, and her talk with her father. Now, of course, I know it should have seemed significant to me, but then I thought it was only her attempt to up the ante. So I had played along. I asked her how we would pay for the school, and we spent time working out a half-ass budget we both knew we would never use. "This way," she had said, "if things don't work out. Between us. I can—"

And me: "Things will work out. They always have."

And her: "For you."

I shook off the memory and finished off the familiar litany of mean truths about McKnight's career that Hoops and I had rehearsed so often. It was late in the day by then, so I looked for a quick ending, a way out of the article and the apartment.

But one fact in Senator McKnight's political biography is not known to readers of the *News*. Lawrence McKnight misled voters about his war record in his first campaign for the U.S. Senate. Never a "hero" as he claimed in his speeches and his campaign literature, he had one of his pals pen a story of false bravery to publish in the *Stars & Stripes* as a joke.

It seems McKnight was so well known in Germany for remaining safely behind Allied lines that all the European Theater flyboys and many of its with-it GIs found the made-up story a perfect satire of the kind of reporting done in army publications about real, honest-to-God heroes. But what was funny in the ranks during wartime became something like fraud when McKnight used the article again and again in his campaign for national office. The army is not known for its love of truth, and to expose McKnight at that point might have caused embarrassment, if anyone in the military was even aware of McKnight's misuses of history. But making sure that the story was not unmasked before his home state audience, McKnight, after the war, put the fellow airman who wrote the *Stars & Stripes* piece in charge of publicity for his Senate bid.

And, as the *Capital News* reports here for the first time in a related news story, not only did Lawrence McKnight never receive a medal of any kind for his service during the Second World War, he was never a captain in the Army Air Forces. Instead, he was a corporal. He seldom flew, and he was never called "Tail Gunner Larry." Instead, he was a ground-bound supply clerk.

What do these facts show us about the man who represents us in Washington? They show us a failure at business who turned his hand to the one profession where sycophancy and hypocrisy are often rewarded as if they were honesty and ability. They show us a liar and a moral bankrupt who has managed to use the accidents of history and the tumultuous screen of current events to elevate himself to a position of power normally beyond the reach of the average citizen. But more important than what these facts show us about Senator McKnight himself is what they show us about ourselves when we consider them in the light of the question taught to us by Albert Collette.

Do we deserve such a man?

Only when we elect him.

I looked over what I had written before heading downtown with it and decided I felt better for some reason than I had a right to feel. I finished my scotch and phoned Sharon at the Emerson from the living room.

"Me," I said.

"Randall Harker! Where have—"

"Listen, Sharon, I've got to run an article downtown to the office and talk to a couple of people there. I thought maybe I'd come over afterward."

"You thought you'd come over afterward? Do you know how—"

She said she had read the paper and tried to call the hospital but they told her I had checked out. Then she tried calling the apartment, and there was no answer. Then she tried the *News.*

"Which is what I wanted to ask you about," I said. "I'm at the apartment now, but I just can't stand the ghosts, and I think I might need help with dressing my wounds. Okay if I stay with you a couple of days? I know it's not really proper and all that, but, like Guthrie would say, nobody's going to go looking for me at some rich chick's pad."

"Ooo, you're so persuasive," she said. "Sure, as my wealthy father would say, the horse is already saddled, we ought to give it a ride."

There was a long pause, then she laughed at the surprise in my silence. "What? You thought I might turn you down?"

"What do I say?" I laughed back. "That's my girl."

"C'mon," she said before she hung up. "I risk my reputation and all you've got is *atta gal?*"

"I know. I'll explain when I get there. Okay?"

"When you get here?" She managed to make the question sound incredulous, and she was laughing at me when I hung up the phone.

I was thinking about taking a quick bath, but then I saw how late it was.

I went back to the study, took the flask from the bottom drawer and stuffed it in my back pocket, pulled down my hat and overcoat, put on my shoes, and headed for the bedroom to grab a pressed shirt and a sport coat. Then I called a taxi.

When I got to the *News* building, the streets were deserted just as they'd been the night I got shot, and I had the sudden, frightening flash of memory combat vets sometimes talk about. So I soldiered on, past the surprised receptionists and up the stairs.

By this time, most of the city room was deserted too, and dark, but for the circle of card players at a table near my office, caught in the spotlight of the overhead, filtered through the smoke rising from half a dozen filled ashtrays they had gathered from the ends of the building. During the day, we used the table for copy editing, and women and cubs sat around it, pooling their knowledge of grammar and syntax, chopping away at our prose with sharp little twists; at night, it was transformed into a pretty good poker table, and a few nights a week you might find four or five of the crew flopping down jacks and queens amid stacks of green as they gulped booze from the mugs they used for coffee the rest of the time.

Bill Dyers sat at the table with Guthrie, Hoops, and a couple of Dyers's kids from downstairs in composition. Dyers being there meant they had put the paper to bed except for my column on McKnight. He should have been home hours ago, but he was more hooked on the place than I was.

A big man with a crew cut and a clean shirt open at the collar, Dyers lived on the East Side with his mother and his daughter. Someone told me his wife had died in 1932 of acute hepatitis from a dirty needle, but I had never asked him about it. It was the kind of thing you didn't talk about to co-workers (unless, maybe, you were Kid Guthrie), even over poker. Generally, though, the conversation, like the liquid in the coffee mugs, seemed somehow better at night. Guthrie, my hipster understudy, sat next to Dyers, robbing the table blind, as usual, while Hoops, watching his money vanish with his indolent mandarin air, was, as usual, talking.

"Yes, my friends, it was a sad sight to see. Old Vlad Paddy standing there, surrounded by ex-comrades, pulling the heartstrings of even the most calloused picketeer with his near-English. Ever notice how fucking sentimental an old Bolshevik gets when he slips from power? Like a funeral, I tell you, and I was in a panic because I'd forgot to bring me hanky."

"Call," said one of the boys.

"Fuck," said another.

"Shit," said Dyers. "Harker. You finally made it. We thought maybe the creampuff had popped you another lead pill in some dark alley."

"That's right," Hoops said. "The kid here was just about to ring the city morgue."

"Whose deal is it?" someone asked.

"Guthrie's, I think," came the answer.

"Boys," I said. "Which one of you wants this?" I offered the folder with the McKnight article as a sacrifice to the table.

"Too late, Harker," another of the composition wits—Jonson, I think—replied. "The world will just have to wait some other day for your message. We was sure you had finally expired from Wilson's drilling. We loaded the paper onto delivery trucks an hour ago. Was an hour, about, right?"

"Shut up, Jonson. Just look at your cards," said someone else.

"Don't need to. Guthrie dealt them. Might as well fold now, save some money," said Jonson.

"Ante up, Hoops," said Dyers.

"Kiss my ass," I said to Jonson.

"And that's just what it's going to be," Dyers said, tapping the deck with one hand and running the other over the top of his perfectly flat skull, "Your ass. Next time you hold my crew up like this. My contract with the Old Man dudn't say nuddin about having to coddle the local prima donna all hours of the night."

"Dyers," I said, grabbing a chair from one of the nearby desks and rolling it over to the table. "You never worked an extra second for someone else in your life. My ass is right, if you didn't get here five minutes before me because Guthrie called you up at home and said Hoops was down here wanting to play some poker."

Everybody laughed. Hoops had never won a card game. Any card game. But he kept right on trying, throwing good money after bad.

"Ten," Hoops said. "Ten minutes, I mean. Dyers got here ten minutes ago. First, he had to go downstairs and play Satan to his minions on the presses. Working evil, late into the night, that kind of thing."

"Not me," Dyers said. "I'm only a second-class demon. Jonson..." Dyers motioned, deck in hand, to the wit on his right. "Take the master's sermon there and run it downstairs. Page two, editorial, column one, 36-point head."

The boy took the folder from me and handed it to Dyers, who looked over the copy, pulled the blue pencil from behind his ear, deleted the words ~~liar and a moral bankrupt~~, scribbled *dishonest and unscrupulous politician* in their place, then raised his eyebrows when Jonson showed me the change. After my shrug in response and Dyers's nod, Jonson disappeared into the darkness beyond the floating haze of smoke. I pulled the flask from my back pocket, set it down next to Hoops's coffee mug, and said, "Let's play some cards. Hoops keep talking. Have a drink. Break out what's left of your paycheck."

12.

We got no immediate response from the McKnight camp on our latest charges, but come the evening of my second day free of the hospital, Tommy Rojack called and asked Sharon if he could speak to me. (So much for hiding out.)

"You ought to see this," he said when I picked up the phone. He sounded very serious. I had had about as much as I could take, I thought, for one week. I was at Sharon's; it was after sundown; I was busy.

"Tommy, how did you get this number?"

"From a friend. At the phone company. What the hell does it matter? Harker, I mean it, goddamn it. You, *you* better see this."

"Who?" I asked. "Not Gilda." Gilda was an old flame who worked for Ma Bell and gave me unlisted numbers whenever I asked. "And what had I better see?"

"What?" Tommy said. "Yeah, yeah, Gilda. Goddamn it, Harker, for once, Jesus, just once, can you cut the crap? *This. This. This.*"

He must have been pointing at things...or throwing them. I heard noises in the background, as if something was falling. I had never heard Tommy hysterical before, and I had been with him at strikes and floor fights and long, wild drunks and feverish convention battles, dozens of them, dozens of proletarian nights, when your nerves are shot and an hour's sleep seems the closest you'll ever come to salvation. Whatever caused this response must be something, I thought.

"Okay," I said. "Okay. Where are you?"

"My wife, Harker. She wasn't here. But it could have been my wife. That may not mean much to you, goddamn it, but it does to me."

It sounded as if he had kicked something else over.

"Tommy. Where...are...you?"

"Fuckin' assholes, they—"

"Tommy. Tell me where you are."

"The local...headquarters. They—"

"I'll be there in fifteen minutes," I said and hung up.

Sharon pulled her blonde hair back from her face and looked at me. Bare shoulders, banded by freckles, promised what seemed to me luxurious beauty sheathed in dark blue sheets.

"Something's happened," I said, lighting a Camel. "That was Tommy—Tommy Rojack."

"He said."

She waited.

"He's the big bohunk you met at the hospital."

"The really good-looking one?"

I frowned. "Yeah. The really good-looking one. Little short, though, don't you think?" She laughed. "He sounded," I said, smiling and blowing smoke away from her face, "Jesus, I don't know, *hurt*. Will you give me a ride down there?"

"Now?" she asked. "We're not finished."

"Now," I said. "He's a friend, and I told him fifteen minutes. Besides, all this is no good for my convalescence."

She flung the sheets back and lay nude for a second, ushering up the strength to get out of bed, then stood and grabbed her silk underwear on the way to the bathroom. It was all so new, having this time with her, time I did not have to account for, time to watch her—the way she moved, the way she responded to anything, anything that happened to happen—and I could not keep back a painful sort of longing admiration for the light-traced curves of her body when she stopped in the bathroom doorway.

"I wish I had a trench coat," she said. "So I could dress for the occasion."

She drove an Aston Martin, and the way she drove it, it took us less than fifteen minutes. The union's headquarters sat on Walker Street just the other side of the river, so she took Eighteenth to Ashton. As we came down the bluffs toward the river, I noticed the Wharf Waldorf was packed, and I could not help thinking I ought to stay away from any crowded bar where I was well known.

An old Glenn Miller tune was on the radio, which worked about as well as a radio ever does in a sports car, and it reminded me of the end of the war and the way the GIs looked when they came home to their jobs hauling crate off the lakes or laying concrete on new highways or slitting the throats of fattened pigs in our very own little stockyards. A light snow had swirled up, adding white on white and sealing the silence in which I could hear only the odd squeak of the Aston's wire wheels over packed slush and the too-loud mesh of the gears when Sharon downshifted.

Inside the car it was cold, and the canvas top did not do much for the interior windshield. Frosted by our breathing, on the outside it was beaded with moisture that the short, silly excuses for wipers would smear almost clear in their choppy, arrhythmic swings. I saw the red slash of a fire engine first, the only one lingering at the scene, evidently, its lazy top light rotating as it pulled out and headed slowly down Walker. I saw the crowd in front of the building on Walker more as a series of stills, larger each time the wipers swept across the glass—these long slashes of black down beyond the road's dip and swerve across the bridge to the left at hill's bottom. By the time the muted plaids and leather-brown shades of working-class garb began to turn the colors into a crowd of people, I could see the rubble.

"Drive past," I said.

Below the top of the glass picture pane of the storefront, the building was gone like a missing jaw. Bricks lay piled on the sidewalk and out into the old cobblestones of Walker Street—piles that radiated outward from the jagged frame of the broken glass left in the window. Now and again—as we drove past, for instance—a sharp piece of the frame would come loose and disappear in the slush at the corners of the glass and crack to bits with a delicate plink on the sidewalk. Directly below, where once there had been the office facade, there was now only space, and snow had been blown clear of the ground in front and out in the street, making by its absence a silhouette of the forward thrust of the bomb.

"Good Lord," Sharon said.

Faces watched us as we drove by, and a few of the men recognized me, elbowing those who stood next to them and pointing cautiously with their heads, the way I had seen crowds of strikers warn themselves the scabs had arrived. They had been calling each other since the bombing, one or two at a time, each new arrival phoning his pals to come down and see the damage. I picked out Bilinski, Tony Martin, some others I knew.

"Slow," I said. "Look out for your tires. Those things are expensive. Okay, here. Let me out."

I was about a block from the explosion. Once free of the car, I could make out more debris along the sidewalk. Sheets of typing paper with smeared lettering or charred edges, broken pieces of burned wood, chips of brick, even the long, black twisting of a typewriter ribbon or two. Before I closed the door, I bent down on my haunches and said, "Congratulations. You win the Kid Guthrie driving award of the week."

"Thanks," Sharon said, leaning across the passenger seat for her goodbye kiss. "How long will you be? Long? Why don't you just give me a call when you're finished and I'll come back to pick you up?"

"I will."

She had some trouble pulling away. Her tires spun, but she rocked the small car back and forth in first and second until she managed to spin off. A wife, dropping hubby off at the office, I mused, thinking I have to get control of this self-loathing.

The men let me through to look at the window. Inside what had once been the first-floor offices of the United Electrical Workers, Local 455, three or four desks (it was hard to tell) lay in various degrees of destruction; one or two, maybe more, had been reduced to splinters; another—toward the back—was in perfect shape but for a black charring along the edges and down one side. The rest was mayhem. Paper, shattered wood frames, bits of clocks, typewriters, mimeograph machines, and broken glass—glass strewn everywhere. The bottom half of a water cooler raised its shorn head, with ice dropping like a stalactite from its base. On one of the half-destroyed desks, a huge pool of black ink had spread, oozing down its mutilated side to form patterns like veins below the skin of an anemic arm. Another sharp piece of glass fell from the window top with a soft chink into the slush at my feet.

"Was anybody—" I said.

"Nobody got hurt," a couple of the men said together, trailing off as they interrupted each other.

"Empty," a few more mumbled.

"Harker," Tony Martin said into my ear. "Tommy's inside. He wants to see you."

"Okay." I moved toward the blackened doorframe.

"Maybe you guys ought to go home, too, or something," I said. "Get out of the cold." They had all been standing there long before I arrived, and after a couple of minutes of it, I was freezing. "At least come inside."

"The coppers chased us out, Harker," Bilinski said. "When the bomb squad and the fire inspector showed up."

"Yeah," Martin added. "Then they took a quick gander and split. They the ones wanted to get out of the cold."

"We're waiting for Tommy," explained a third man I didn't know. "We gotta fucking *do* something, man."

"What's matter, Harker, can't you take the weather?" Bilinski laughed.

"Naw. Naw. You seen them other press boys," said the third man.

"Yeah. Stood around maybe a whole five minutes." This from Martin.

"Five minutes, my ass, five questions, maybe," Bilinski sneered before turning to me and explaining. "They left when the assholes from the bomb squad and the fire department left—after they done their so-called investigation of the incident."

"Okay, okay," I said. "Freeze your asses off, see if I give a shit."

"Up yours, Harker," said Martin.

The charred smell was much worse inside the narrow stairwell that led up to the second-floor office. Acrid and heavy, it got down into your throat and lungs. The smell was uglier than the sheer confusion of objects inside the bombed-out downstairs. It gave you more the feeling that something had been damaged, more the sense of outrage felt by the men in the crowd.

A squat-faced cop in uniform blocked the top of the stairs.

"Can't go in there."

"My name's Randall Harker, from the *Capital News*."

"I know who you are, Mack. We sent all you hounds home. *You* can't go in there."

"Tommy Rojack called me. He—"

"I don't care if Harry Truman called you, newsy. You don't go in there."

He seemed to think he was funny, grinning a Neanderthal smile that was hard to distinguish from a snarl.

"Get out of my way, cop," I answered with the same kind of wit.

The cop unsnapped the flap over his .38 and stepped in front of the door. He had plunged to the depths with his last comment and exhausted his linguistic resources. Behind him the door into Rojack's office stood slightly ajar, and I waited for somebody who had heard our repartee to come end the tomfoolery. They did not, and my cop's eyes were a little too wild, a little too reminiscent of our common ancestral home, the cave.

"Try me, you fucking Commie," he said.

"Oh," I said. "I see you decided to pick up the conversation again."

"C'mon, smart ass. Just try to get past me."

"Okay. Okay," I said, shrugging. I turned to go. "When did they start putting you fanatics on the bomb squad?"

"Fuck you, Harker," he said to my back. I could hear the petty victory in his voice. Oh yeah, he could relax now since he had mouthed the magic phrase.

I hoped if I used my right shoulder, I wouldn't feel much pain. But I was wrong: it shot down my back along the spine, feeling again like the swipe of a live wire across my kidney. I bumped him chest high with my shoulder, pushing him back out of the way, and—catching him by surprise—stepping through the door. I stopped short just inside the room and saw a detective or two I did not know and Tommy Rojack looking my way. Meanwhile, my copper had drawn his Special.

"It ain't going to be no shoulder wound this time, Commie," he said. The gun was pointed at my head. Tommy, relaxed as a preacher at Sunday dinner, stepped over and casually slapped down the gun.

"Hi, Tommy," I said, smiling. "What'd you want to see me about?"

"Our friends here were just leaving," he said. He stared at one of the detectives long enough to make even a cop feel uncomfortable. "Thank you, Captain, for all you've done."

"Glad to be of service, Rojack," the captain said sarcastically. "'Day to you. 'Day to you, too, Harker."

I paid little or no attention to Alley Oop's glare and the gun he was still waving around like a kid playing cops and robbers, and I smiled politely at the captain. After the door closed, I walked over and sat next to Rojack on the desk. Even Adonises have their bad days. Even Gabriels get tired of all the shucking and jiving for the Lord. Rojack was not so much blond today as washed-out. He was not so much handsome and even featured as he was pasty and chisel faced. The cops gone, he dropped the casual attitude. But the tension, the hysterical edge I had heard on the phone, had vanished, and he seemed listless, lethargic, almost in shock. He reminded me of Hoops, of Paul Toland. It's a new disease, I thought, striking swiftly everyone I know.

"Not much interested, were they?" I said, indicating the retreating policemen with my head. "I need a drink."

"They're on the take like the rest of their breed," he said, looking at the door the way Kathy had stared at the space below our coffee table. "I don't much blame them. The whole East Side has exploded. Calenti disappeared last night—you hear?"

He produced a bottle of rye from his top desk drawer and handed it over.

"No," I said and sucked the bottle and rubbed my shoulder. "I've been kind of tied up."

"Yeah…right, right. Calenti's vanished. Poof!" He was deadpan, watching the door behind me. "Didn't show up to work this morning, wherever he's supposed to show up to work. In his limo and his fancy eyetie clothes. Where do guys like that go, when they are supposed to show up for work?"

"Search me," I said. "Poof, huh?"

He, too, took a drink now. Offhand, he said, "Yeah, poof. In a big black new Cadillac, so says somebody's sister's husband."

"Lefty Mills own a new Caddy?" I asked.

"I guess," he said. "Or whichever Guido now owns Lefty Mills owns a new Caddy. I can't follow this shit, Harker." He shook his gaze loose of the door. "Who's killing who from what picayune village in Sicily or outside Naples this week. Got enough on my hands making sure the ones we get in the union are clean. Anyway, something's up, and I have this feeling you oughta be the person explaining it to me. All that shit about you in the paper, and then this, this—" He swept his hand downward, toward the floor, toward the mess below, and some of the edge came back into his voice.

Tommy dropped down off the front of his desk and walked around to his chair. He rummaged through a couple of piles of messy papers and pulled out a sheet with the unmistakable blue ink of the mimeograph all over it. "Here." He handed me the flyer. "Teamsters been handing out these. All around town, wherever we got people in city jobs. And that AF of L outfit—Brotherhood of Electricians—they been passing them out right here, right here under our fucking noses. Some of the guys tell me—they tell me there's s'posed to be more wops go like Calenti, several more."

I could hear the men outside on their way up the steps. The two groups, the cops and the crowd on Walker Street, had finished trading insults. I tried to filter what Rojack was telling me through what I already knew from Bob Weaver. It was going down pretty much as he said it would, only faster and better timed. I made a mental note to tell Gene Gibson, our crime reporter, that Calenti, Capital City's Mr. Big, had finally had his rendezvous with destiny and that we were probably in for a small-scale gang war, Chicago-style. Calenti was always East Side, which meant his juice, for what it had been worth, was with the Democrats. I just could not imagine petty hoods—a special-interest group in the Democratic Party the way the SMA was in the Republican—going over to the other side. Tony Martin, Rojack's secretary-treasurer, stuck his head through the door.

"What's up, boss?"

Rojack raised his washed-out, round, innocent-looking bohunk face, shaved clean, with a halo of blond curls, from the desk. It was that look of innocence Phil Murray had half counted on last year to help at the national convention, when, finally convinced, Tommy had split with Vlad Paddy's ERMWA and joined the newly formed (on the spot, you might say) UEW. A clean union, I said then, needs clean hands. Rojack looked at me instead of responding to Martin's question.

"Yeah," I said. "Tell 'em to get in here, out of the cold."

"Harker's going to give us another lecture," Rojack said flatly, dully. It was a small shock to realize he must have been thinking of the convention, too.

As they crowded into the office, I read the flyer.

DID YOU KNOW?
Tommy Rojack was a Communist Dupe? Rojack, the president of United Electrical Workers, Local 455—the ONE union that since 1949 is supposed to represent YOU—is a friend and supporter of RED RANDALL HARKER, the Communist reporter who works for the RED MOUTHPIECE of the State's Communist Party, the CAPITOL (so-called) NEWS.

DID YOU KNOW?
Hundreds of loyal union buddies were purged from YOUR union at the COMMAND of RED RANDALL HARKER? In the twisted world of COMMUNIST thinking, where loyalty and friendship are mere words, RED RANDALL HARKER is supreme. At every breath from Moscow, at every whim of "Friend" JOE STALIN, Communist policy changes, and men and their livelihoods—and the bread-and-butter concerns of all good, loyal, hard-working union members are SACRIFICED to PARTY TACTICS. Recently, such PARTY TACTICS have called for all true COMMUNISTS to go underground, after purging from their ranks the poor dupes they tricked into speaking out OPENLY and HONESTLY for the "old" PARTY LINE. This is what lies behind RED RANDALL HARKER'S resignation from the Congress of Industrial Organizations all-powerful Political Action Committee in our city after he convinced the unsuspecting and the innocent to help him PURGE his former best buddy and ADMITTED COMMUNIST Vlad Paddy from the local labor scene. Under the guise of ridding the city of the RED INFESTED Electrical, Radio, and Machine Workers of America, RED RANDALL HARKER has managed to gain influence over

the new UEW—the ONE Union in this city officially recognized to represent YOU. RED RANDALL HARKER led this
purge with the knowledge and the backing of the CAPITOL
(socalled) NEWS, the organization that PAYS HIS SALARY.

DID YOU KNOW?
That the recent city-wide strike by the ERMWA and the
UEW went on weeks longer than necessary at great costs
to the average rank-and-file dues-paying member because
JOE STALIN, our "friend," wants to cripple the American
economy? Our Mayor himself has stated OFFICIALLY that
he was PERSONALLY willing to grant the unions all they
asked for weeks before the final contract was signed, but
that the ERMWA and the UEW—the two COMMUNIST
CONTROLLED unions for electrical workers in this country
—were more interested in fighting among themselves over
the fine points of FOREIGN IDEOLOGY than in securing
good wages for the American working man. All this happened
because Tommy Rojack listens only to RED RANDALL
HARKER and RED RANDALL HARKER listens only to
his friend JOSEPH STALIN.

DO YOU WANT?
Your hard-earned dollars paid in union dues by mandatory
dues check-off to go DIRECTLY to the aid and comfort of
our ENEMIES at home and abroad?

DO YOU KNOW?
What you can do about it? We do.
Come to the Wharf Waldorf tonight at 10:30 p.m. and we will
tell you.

We are the Representatives of the only unions in this city not under the DOMINATION of the RED MENACE from Moscow.

Here it is, I thought, the Red baiting. This was a little balder than anything Tuckerman tried against me back in the '30s to keep control of his paper, maybe not as rabid as the Red Scare of the early '20s, though I would guess it was a little more devious, using the very things I would try to use to defend myself—my public stands against the party line, my resignation from the PAC, the "purging" of Vlad Paddy—to condemn me. In a bleak enough irony, it was sort of Bolshevik in its deviousness, and for a moment I wondered absurdly if Vlad Paddy had written it. Then I pulled myself together. Bob Weaver's paranoia was catching. In any case, the timing was truly unsettling. Obviously Mills had his takeover of the East End and his move on the CIO's membership planned to dovetail with McKnight's attack on me. True, Weaver had implied as much, and he was on the money. The right-wingers were all banking heavily on the politics of fear, on that very thing we, even the radicals, thought FDR had banished once and for all. No wonder Socrates had crossed himself. If I believed in anything, I would too. Now everybody and his mother would be taking potshots at me.

"I don't have a lecture prepared," I said to the crowd in Tommy's office. "But it seems clear enough what's happening. Lefty Mills and his gang are using Senator McKnight's attack on me as a smoke screen to take over the East End, and the unions, if he can. Senator McKnight has made me some kind of reverse stalking horse."

"Yeah?" one of the men toward the back of the room said. "That's what I read in the *News*."

The sullenness from standing in the cold of Walker Street had returned. They were packed into the office now, standing along the walls, leaning against the exposed support posts, sitting over on Tony Martin's and Bilinski's desks or on the long worktable, and they were silent. None of them was smiling. They avoided my eyes, as if they were embarrassed for me or, even worse, ashamed of me.

"Hey," I said. "What is this? These guys, these hoods, Senator McKnight, they think they can use what I said, or what you said, too, for that matter, or what we did ten years ago to get at us. So? They think they can force-feed this shit to the public because the public has gotten tired of hearing about labor's trouble. They think the public will take quiet corrupt small unions over loud militant big ones any day, and all they have to do to get rid of the militants is scream Commie this and Commie that. A guy in the Democratic Party told me last week this would happen. I didn't believe him exactly, but he told me. It ain't that big a surprise."

They continued to stare, still silent. Then Bilinski, whose job description put him at my height and whose size let him say what was on all their minds, spoke up. And despite the job description, he was one of Tommy's best organizers, and you shouldn't let his grammar fool you—he was smart, very smart.

"Seems to me," he said, "you was talking not too long ago about this thing—what was it? Effectiveness? Yeah, that's it. That's what you called it last summer at the CIO convention—effectiveness. Remember?"

"I remember," I said, taking the rye in hand from Tommy.

"You was saying how Vlad Paddy and his boys," Bilinski continued, "had lost their effectiveness. 'Cause the whole entire direction, you said, of labor just had to change now't the war was over. Remember that? Don't get me wrong, Harker…I ain't saying that piece o' shit, that flyer, you got in your hand is true—nothin' like that. It says the ERMWA and the UEW is Commie. *I* ain't no Commie." He looked me in the eye very carefully, very obviously. "And I ain't *never been* no Communist. Not when I worked for Vlad Paddy. Not now. I just don't give a fuck what a man calls himself, or what anybody else calls him, as long as he gets the job done. But how is what McKnight and Lefty Mills and whoever the hell else it is—how's what they *supposed* to be doing any different 'n what you and your Political Action big wigs did to Vlad Paddy and the ERMWA?"

"Phil Murray didn't throw any fucking bombs."

"The point is, *Harker*…" Tony Martin said in his near-nasal voice. Short and squat, he was from dark Balkan stock. His father had been a coal miner, they say, and the family left Bloody Harlan when the old man was killed in a collapsed shaft.

"Yeah, what's the point, *Martin*?"

"Oh, man," he said. "Don't come at me like that. I'll bust you a good one, bum shoulder or no bum shoulder. You ain't been around for a while, Harker. You wudn't here at the celebration, and you wudn't here the night Vlad Paddy and his boys came over, and most of all, you wudn't out on the streets today, Fuckwad. In fact, man, you ain't been out on the streets in a long, long time."

I realized I had better tred lightly. These people were probably the only friends I would have left on down the line, except Guthrie, Shaunessy after his fashion, and maybe Sharon. They weren't out to get me. They had just been bombed. They were in shock. But something else was going on, too. Something odd. They seemed to act as if they felt they almost deserved it. As if they felt guilty. Because of the purging of Vlad Paddy, I supposed—Old Valdimir Padikoff, who would laugh at them, or would have once, for the very way they were behaving.

"Tony, I'm sorry. A lot of people have been taking swipes at me. I'm kind of edgy, I guess. What's the point?"

"The point is," he said, relaxing a little, "Mills's men—if they are Lefty Mills's men—been out there all day pushing us around and shoving us around, and nothing happened to them. Guys, working men, electricians, just stood there. And watched. And it's not that they're afraid, man. I mean a lot of the rank and file are listening to those thugs. A lot of people, not just electrical workers, but guys from other locals, you know, related industries, plan to show up tonight. And it's because of you. What Bilinski was trying to say was maybe you just got caught in your own trap, you know, throwing out the most radical people in the union, which left you and your CIO execs the only people left to attack. Maybe you better back off, let us try to handle this. You ain't on the PAC no more, anyway, and the Newspaper Guild's got nothing to do with this."

They were angry, I thought. And felt guilty. And frustrated. And they wanted to do something. So they were aiming it all at me. As if I had written the fucking flyer. Threw the goddamn bomb. Maybe they were right. Maybe I did act like I ran their union and it was none of my fucking business. Why should I care what the hell happened to them?

Tommy had been sitting, still and quiet behind his desk, since the guys had come in. His mouth was set in a thin, tense line, and his eyes stared off beyond the room somewhere, the way they had been when I was first talking to him alone.

"Where does it end?" he said.

A dozen of us said *What?* together

"Listen to me." He got up, walked around the front of the desk, and took the rye. "I don't know what's going on. This right-wing politics…I don't know." He took a long swig. "But I know—look, I was just a rank-and-filer, just a guy putting in his time and paying his union dues, like the rest of them going to that meeting tonight, like some of you here now, till Harker talked me into taking this fucking job. He could have gone to some international organizer in Vlad Paddy's old union, some mucky-muck official, when Murray's troubleshooters came here looking for a man. But he didn't. He came to me. A worker. Like most of the guys in the union. So I figure I owe him, and you can take what I say from that. Except maybe what I owe him is a punch in the mouth. I mean, it's just a fucking job. I don't have to keep it. I don't."

He put himself between me and the rest of them, so I couldn't see his face. He probably thought I would be tempted to crack wise or laugh out loud at his show. I could see the tilt of his head when he raised the bottle. "I didn't like it two years ago when he came to me neither, when he said Vlad Paddy had to go. I didn't like it at all. Maybe, though, even if I didn't like it, I agreed with him about the old ERMWA. Maybe I knew Vlad Paddy was a Commie, maybe we all knew that. He didn't make no secret of it, and we all knew that. But he was an okay guy. Okay to me. To everybody." He looked back at me and smiled. "He really did talk up a storm. World politics and doing this and that to educate the proletariat. Teach them their class-historical role, all that shit. And some of it didn't make no sense to nobody but him and his Commie pals, those dudes with the beards. Remember them? Hey, Bilinski, remember them?"

Some of the others besides Tommy were smiling now.

"But Harker said Vlad Paddy had to go. And so he goes."

He turned back to me again, wrenched the flyer out of my hand, crumpled it, and slung it to the floor; and I felt a little light-headed with the notion that maybe he wasn't just speechifying.

"Real shit," he said. "More shit than Vlad Paddy and the Bolsheviks ever talked. Oh, yeah, sure, the city was ready to settle early. Sure they were. With the fucking Teamsters, man. For next to nothing. Those guys would sell their own fucking mothers to fill up their goddamn rolls. What the hell are the Teamsters doing organizing electricians just because they work for the fucking city? And then that Brotherhood bunch, just as bad. They offered to cut off their dicks if GE gave them the privilege of representing us. Personally, I'd rather hang on to my balls."

"Better than hanging onto Harker's balls," somebody whispered too loud, and everyone laughed. Tommy, too.

"And this time," he said. "This time the city wouldn't even talk to Vlad Paddy. Everything that happened, they said, was the ERMWA's fault. And anything the ERMWA asked for was not a legitimate demand, they said. Because it wasn't a real union. Because it was, oh my god," he put his hand on top of his head and whispered, "*Communist.*" Bilinski laughed out loud. "When really," Tommy said. "Really it just wasn't effective anymore. Harker was right about that. And then the city decided it would talk to us, like GE had been doing all along since we chased off those Brotherhood assholes. And Harker was right about that, too. He was right. Maybe you don't like it. Maybe I don't like it, I don't know. But he was right."

He paused, thinking some, and then walked back to his desk, absently dropping the bottle back in the drawer, before looking up.

"Now, *he's* getting it. And you say we ought to dump *him*. To be more effective. But think about it. Think about it a minute. *Harker ain't a Communist. Vlad Paddy is a Communist.* See it? Do you see it? Maybe Harker was a Communist. Ten years ago, maybe. I don't really know. And if I do, I ain't saying. But he's not one *now*. See it? The reason we did one thing last year, this summer, yesterday, was because it was *true*—true, Vlad Paddy is Red. True, Reds ain't no good for us no more. The reason you say to do this now is because somebody's *lying*—somebody's saying Harker is a Red, but it's not the truth. That's the point, *it's not the truth,*" he said, then added with surprisingly perfect diction: "It does not accurately describe the situation."

Again, he paused and came back around front, closer to the men.

"All Vlad Paddy's talk—it taught me one thing. It taught me to think things through. To look at who is doing what and why they are doing it. To see what is true *now*, not the way some management PR man wants you to think will be true tomorrow or the next day. McKnight is a fucking right-wing reactionary Republican, man. He does not have our interest at heart, and anybody that uses his lies does not have our interest at heart. Everything Harker's ever done—including giving Vlad Paddy the ax and quitting the PAC because of it—says that is exactly it for him. He has our interest at heart. Plus, it proves he's got a fucking heart. Hard to believe, I know."

They looked at each other. Bilinski was smiling.

"You're good, Tommy," he said.

Before he could go on, Rojack cut him off. "Something else." He turned and looked at me for the first time since he had started. "Harker, what's your connection with this Weaver guy the Democrats got out here keeping an eye on things? He the one who told you about Lefty Mills?"

If I looked surprised—and I must have because Tommy went on as if I looked surprised—it was because I was surprised.

"He called me today. He says I got to drop you, Harker. Like that." He snapped his fingers "He says if I'm a real Democrat I got to stay the fuck as far way from you as I can. For my own good, he says."

Some of the men in the room, Tony Martin, for one, looked at me now, too, only they looked more embarrassed themselves than embarrassed for me.

"And I kept thinking," Tommy went on. "I kept thinking. If some puny, drunk, brainless asshole like McKnight can scare these Democrats, they ain't got a prayer. Not in the '52 election, not in helping us stand up to management, not nowhere. Next week Truman will be turning around, snapping his fingers, and saying: Drop the whole CIO; Drop the pussy AF of L; Drop labor. Who needs 'em—the war's over. We need jobs, new industry, productivity, yeah, baby. For the new fucking war. For Korea. To fight the Commies."

He had turned back to face the room.

"So I'm not dropping Harker. And neither are you. Vlad Paddy taught us to fight for what was true *now*, and he taught us how to fight by fighting us himself. So we are going to that meeting *now*. And we are going to show that bunch of thugs that bombs don't scare us and sleazy U.S. senators don't scare us and kill-crazy hoods don't scare us and scared Democrats don't scare us."

It was quite a performance, and it worked. Vlad Paddy would have appreciated it, and I certainly did. They had something to do now—we all had something to do—and I grabbed the bottle of rye out of the desk drawer and followed Tony Martin out the door and down the stairs behind the others. On the way down Walker, while they gabbed about whether to take cars or walk over to Ashton, I got Tony to hold back.

"Tony," I said. "You said nobody was hurt?"

"Right. Nobody was here when it happened."

"Yeah. Well, Tommy—when he called me—he kept talking about his wife."

"Yeah," he said. "That's right. Somebody said she was here. Earlier. But—oh, ten minutes before—see, she was working late, I guess, typing up our own flyers. We were going to post them over those others, man. And Tommy and me, we were off talking to the guys out working the street, you know, and she was typing downstairs—"

"Right. Right. So she was there."

"Yeah. And about ten minutes before the bomb went off, she gets this call. Some lug tells her Tommy is in trouble up at the GE plant with a bunch of guys, and the cops are coming, and he wants her to get over there; he needs the car, see. Only Tommy ain't nowhere near the plant, he's down dealing with some railroad electricians coming up for a grievance hearing and—"

"A warning?" I asked.

"What?"

"A warning. Mills was giving him a warning."

"Yeah," Martin said, seeing it now. "That son of a bitch. That's what he was doing all right. You got it. A fucking warning, man."

Bilinski, Rojack, and I took Bilinski's Ford. Bilinski drove. Tommy and I sat up front, huddled in our overcoats against the cold, and we passed the bottle till it was empty.

"Thanks," I said to Tommy.

He kept looking straight out the window, down Ashton, along the frozen river.

"I didn't do nothing," he said.

"Don't believe none of that shit, no way, Harker," Bilinski said. "Tommy don't like you, man. He was just getting us boys motivated." Bilinski laughed. "Motivated. That's it. Fucking motivated."

"Harker," Tommy said a block before the Waldorf. "What's with you and Hoops?"

"Nothing," I said. "Why?"

"He was up here earlier tonight. At headquarters. Covering the bombing. Him and that kid with the whiskers, along with some other newshounds. Is there any of that rot-gut left? Fucking cold, know it? I tried to get *him* to call you. Instead of me. Wouldn't do it. Flat no. Him and the hipster was having words—you know?"

Bilinski was snickering again. "They don't like you none, neither, Harker," he said.

"Bilinski," Tommy said. "Why don't you just shut up and drive."

"Whatever you say, boss man. I just thought Harker, he should know, I'm the only guy left down here even likes him a little bit."

Bilinski smiled sweetly at me over Tommy's shoulder, taking his eyes off the road. I fought my panic successfully because Bilinski was the most accomplished driver I had been with in a month.

I smiled back, just as sincerely. "Yeah, Bilinski. That's what I need. Friends like you."

Bilinski pulled in next to the Snow Castle Diner, a half-block up from the Waldorf on the Wharf and on the opposite side of the street. We could see something of the crowd through the lighted bay windows of the bar. More men came, in groups of two or three, while we sat with the motor idling.

"We better wait for them other guys," Bilinski said.

"It wasn't just that," Rojack said. "It wasn't just him refusing to call. Hoops seemed as edgy as you. He said something like, Call him yourself. He's not the only man who knows about labor in this town. Or politics. And the kid got pissed off. I was too busy to listen, with everybody asking questions, and the cops, of course, doing nothing— then, Susie called. She was out at the GE—"

"Martin told me," I said.

I did not want to talk about my troubles with Hoops, so I let it drop. Tommy had enough worries. Mills had shown him how easy it is to get to you, to anybody. Sometime Susie might not receive a saving phone call. And that made me think, despite Tommy's little speech, maybe Martin was right about me. I was a liability—and expendable. Had Tommy actually been under Red domination as the flyer claimed, he would dump me in a flash, unless we could figure out some way to turn the attack into a propaganda advantage, the way I had back in the '30s when as Tuckerman painted me more and more radical I became more and more popular in the guild.

"There they are," Tommy said.

We saw Martin and the rest of them coming up in a group the other side of Ashton. I checked my watch. 10:45. Bilinski started to get out.

"Wait," Tommy said. "Give 'em a chance to get warmed up in there. We don't want to listen to all the early shit."

"Why did Jerry let them use his place?" I asked to pass the time.

Tommy looked at me. "Calenti owned him," he said, bitterly. "Gambling debts. That's one way you can figure Mr. Big is dead. Mills would never have the clout to stage a play like this at the Wharf before tonight—not the Brotherhood or the Teamsters neither. But Jerry's a large fella himself. Make a good target. He probably figures if he didn't have such a pleasing personality somebody might want to shoot him, too."

"Cut the gab," Bilinski said. "I need me a drink."

"Okay. Okay. Let's go."

The Wharf Waldorf was a converted warehouse that sold relatively cheap drinks and good food. You can't find places like that anymore. It had one huge room downstairs, under exposed rafters, a bit rotted, hung with nets and old whaling equipment—though the closest I had ever come to an ocean was Lake Superior, and I was a native. Along the walls, men sat in rude wooden booths, and the center floor was filled with crude park benches and picnic tables—anything Jerry could get for people to sit on and drink at. Barrels served as barstools along the long, low, nothing-fancy bar that ran the length of the south wall.

The second floor was a loft—an old storage area, just wide enough for two rows of smaller tables that hung out over the booths along the north wall—from which you could look down and see the people sitting in the center tables and the people serving them from behind the bar. Jerry had knocked out the east wall and put in bay windows. But not much light made it into the place despite the newer windows, and there was no—absolutely no—ventilation. The old-fashioned ceiling fan twirled above hopelessly and unnoticed.

The place was packed with bodies and smoke. A couple of pot-bellied lugs in cheap three-piece suits and clip-on ties stood atop a table in the center of the room downstairs. At their feet stood a few thugs, no doubt more expensively dressed under their unremoved overcoats than the two union suits.

Martin and the boys had made enough of a stir coming in that we slipped over to the bar without attracting too much attention.

"J and B, Jerry," I said.

"Now I recognize that voice..." Jerry was bald and bulging with muscles under an apron-like getup and a white short-sleeve shirt that looked decidedly strange having just come in from the cold winter night. There was a scar along the base of one side of his jaw. No eyebrows to speak of. Little Orphan Annie eyes. "Harker! I thought you'd be dead by now, pal. They tell me your own staff's blowing lead your way."

"Naw," I said. "The guy was trying to hit the side of a barn and missed. I just happened along."

"Make mine rye," Bilinski said.

"Tommy?" Jerry asked.

"Nothing," he said contemptuously. "Not from you."

Jerry laughed. "You mean those lugs?" He pointed with his head toward the center of the room. He was using his huge arms to squirt and mix. "Nothing personal, Tommy. I gotta eat and live, especially live. Same as you."

"Then, nothing personal but I don't want no drink."

Jerry's smile got thinner. "Suit yourself, Rojack." When he brought my drink, he said close to my ear: "This ain't the place for you, Harker. Not tonight. Those guys in the overcoats, they never shoot at the side of a barn, and they never miss what they shoot at."

"To your health," I said. "You never told me you liked to gamble."

His smile completely vanished. "Not you, too. You, I won't take it from."

I smiled even bigger and shrugged. "Naw, I like to drink too much."

He laughed. "Calenti was a man didn't like his name in the paper. The last time I looked, you worked for a paper. Mills don't like it any more than Calenti did. Seriously, Harker, I was you, I'd go home and climb in the sack with that blonde you ran to ground here not long ago."

"Rojack won't let me. Can't stand the idea of me having fun."

The potbelly standing on the table and doing the talking was saying: "Now you all heard the difference between trade unionism and socialism. And you all heard how we trade unions be pussy unions. You all heard how we walk arm in arm with management. Maybe you even heard we climbed in bed with them. Yeah, you all heard a lot.

"You heard about the Teamsters, too, I don't doubt it. Bunch of gangsters, they say. Taking orders from the Mob. Hell, man, is that any worse 'n taking orders from Moscow? From Mr. Joe Stalin?

"The CIO is finished. Even if you ain't Red, and don't get me wrong—I ain't saying you are Red—but even if you, personally, ain't Red, you got to carry that suspicion with you each and every time you walk up to and sit down at the bargaining table. The suspicion, brothers, is that you are Red. And Walter Reuther, he can purge the Reds all he wants, and Mr. CIO himself, President Phillip Murray, he can purge the Reds all he wants, you can purge the hell out of the CIO till there ain't nobody left but one man, and him, he'll still have that reputation. Look at it for a second the way management looks at—"

The low mumbling in the bar turned into loud booing, then a few hisses, a few shouts, and even a loud laugh or two. Somebody upstairs threw an empty beer bottle onto the table at potbelly's feet. But the speechmaker waited it out.

"Just listen," he went on when the crowd had simmered to a low roar. "I'm on your side, brothers. But you are being used. You are being used"—By you! the shout came from the back—"and you can't see it. What do you think you are doing here, tonight if—"

"We're getting bombed!" Tommy shouted, and there was some

laughter, some catcalls, and then the crowd picked it up—We're getting bombed! We're getting bombed! We're getting bombed. . .

"Who's that?" the speaker shouted. "Who's that? That Tommy Rojack?"

Upstairs they started chanting—Rojack! Rojack! Rojack... and I could hear Tony Martin's voice and a few others I recognized from the office. It looked as if the bombing may have turned the tide, as if the Teamsters and the Brotherhood (backed by Mills?) may have overplayed their hand, tried to move in too early. Gangsters and politicians always underestimate the solidarity of the members. They get bored—like Vlad Paddy's Communists used to—with the daily shit that takes up the life of the rank and file. But the Communists had always made up for it with organizing ability. All the Mob had in the way of organizing were a few tommy guns and a couple of baseball bats.

Still, this speaker was pretty good. "Tommy Rojack! I'm *glad* you're here tonight! I want to talk to you. I want you to come up here so we can talk this out in front of the men."

They were still chanting Rojack's name in the place, but the overcoat boys had cleared a path from the table to where we were standing at the bar, and everybody was watching us—watching Tommy, I mean.

"I don't talk to thugs," Tommy said.

The gang of shouters, led by Martin, started up a new chant—*Throw 'em out! Throw 'em out! Throw out the thugs!*

I should have seen it coming, but I didn't. Tommy had taken the hostility of his gang back at the office, at UEW headquarters, toward me and turned that hostility toward the AF of L organizers. Now they needed to turn the hostility toward them back again. The man standing beside the speaker, let's call him Potbelly # 2, silent till now, shouted out:

"Who's that with him! Red Randall Harker! That's who! Red Randall Harker!"

The crowd slowly fell silent to the latest name being shouted. The two men up on the table seemed a little afraid of the tenseness they had suddenly created. In the silence, they knew they had to move very carefully.

"I want to talk to *you*, Tommy," Potbelly #1 said, softly. "Not to him. Not to him."

"What union does *he* belong to?" Potbelly #2 said, more to the crowd than to Tommy.

"Okay!" Tommy said. "Okay. I'll talk to you. I'll come up there." He started toward the table, along the path cleared, followed by Bilinski, behind whom the path closed.

"Not while *he's* here!" shouted Potbelly #1. The crowd exploded, shouting all sorts of things at once, but none of it coherent, none of it a chant, just noise, simple shouting.

I shoved a few men out of the way, grabbed Bilinski's shoulder, and said loudly into his ear: "Tell Tommy I'll meet him when this is over. At the Snow Castle. By the car."

And I left.

Outside the streets were deserted except for the row of heaps parked along both sides near the Wharf. Vlad Paddy would not have left, I thought. He would have leaped up on the bar in the middle of the speeches and begun lecturing, smiling and talking in a loud monotone, ignoring the hubbub, ignoring whatever the potbellies did, till one of the thugs pulled him down, and then the crowd would have sprung to his aid. But my shoulder still ached from tackling the cop. And those were the old days. And I was not Vlad Paddy. And he had no secret desire to write the perfect news piece.

The white silence was uncanny compared to the roar and buzz inside the Wharf. All the shops and offices were closed along Ashton, and there were not many bars or restaurants on this street that could compete with the Wharf Waldorf. The only real light came from the slow, rhythmic flashing of neon behind me, across the street above the entrance to the Snow Castle Diner. The streetlights along the corners, the ones that worked, were pale spotlights on a deserted stage, little orbs of brighter white. Except one. A man in an overcoat and fedora, smoking a cigarette, leaned against the pole making harsh shadows a block off. He saw me, dropped the cigarette in the snow, and started my way.

When I stepped into Ashton Street toward the diner, he picked up his pace. So did I, though I did not run. Must maintain my dignity, I thought.

Then I saw the other one. He was standing near the alley next to the diner. A car door opened, and the third man got out, directly between me and the green swatch of light cast by the diner's neon signs. I could hear the crunch their steps made on the snow, coming at me from three directions. The one from beneath the street lamp got to me first, and I turned to face him, only to have the alley-spewed one grab my shoulder, the bandaged side. He twisted his free fist into it.

"Lefty Mills wants to meet you, pinko," he said.

The pain jabbed deep at first, then became peristaltic, and I could feel the wound crack open like a picked scab, and warm liquid trickled down my back inside my shirt. I thought clearly: That would be the blood. There was not much use fighting, so I allowed them to drag me as loosely as I possibly could toward the Cadillac the third man had gotten out of—yes, a new black Cadillac.

They walked me past the automobile and shoved me up against the cold brick of the building next to the diner. The one who had my shoulder from behind kept a steady and painful pressure on the reopened wound, while the one from beneath the streetlight stood next to me on the right. I heard the crunching walk of the third and looked over my shoulder to see him open the car's passenger door.

Lefty Mills was not what you would expect of even a small-time hood. He looked like a cross between a high school teacher and a news-stand operator, with all the worry lines of the small business-man concerned about the direction in which America was headed. He wore cheap, bargain-basement clothes—a worn, lined raincoat for an overcoat, a frayed white shirt collar and string tie barely visible at the opening of the raincoat, a cord-weave sports jacket to judge by the lapel showing, checkered pants, and no hat. I was willing to bet his shoes weren't shined. Maybe not even leather. He must have been in his mid- to late-fifties, with a flat face, false teeth—even but dull-colored—a five-o'clock shadow, no lips to speak of, and heavy, black-rimmed glasses. His hair—oily, stringy, and too long—was combed straight back from a widow's peak. He didn't *look* dangerous. You wouldn't have called him dangerous.

But he walked around constantly and quickly as if he were in a cage he did not own and wanted out of, jerking this way and that for no real reason, twisting one hand over the other. He talked fast, too, spitting out each word as if he hated the sound of his own voice and resented the language he had learned from birth. I got the impression that a normal tone was too much for him, and though he spoke low and swift, he seemed almost to shout. It was the tone we use for swearing.

"Let's get this goddamn straight right off, you fucking loser," he said. "I don't fucking like you one goddamn bit, asshole. I don't like the shitty lies you been printing in that motherfucking rag of yours, and I don't want to see another damn lie about me there again, you goddamn fuckwad. Hurt him, Frankie, for God's sake."

Frankie did.

"That's a whole hell of a lot better, you two-bit goddamned yellow fucking journalist. And you can bet, asshole, you can just fucking bet there's a hell of a lot worse you're going to fucking get, cocksucker, if you don't lay the fuck off, you hear me—"

In one of his turns, he knocked off my hat and grabbed my hair with his knobby hands. Staring right into my face, his eyes seemed swollen to huge dimensions behind the thick glasses, and I honestly found it hard to keep from laughing. But then I remembered what Gene Gibson had told Guthrie about the baseball bats, and I noticed the spittle Mills created when he talked.

"Jesus fucking mother of God, I got more important shit to fucking do than babysit you for some goddamn drunken sot asshole of a shit-faced senator, and I mean it, you fucking pipsqueak. Give him one in the goddamned gut, Frankie."

Frankie did.

"I hope the hell we fucking understand each other, you shit heel. Next time I'll have 'em cut your fucking balls off."

Down the street I heard the sound of breaking glass.

The hood standing to my left, now they had turned me around, said, "Hey, Lefty, it's started."

"I got ears, stupid. Okay, goddamn it, drop the fucker and let's get the christ-almighty hell out of here."

Frankie stepped away from me and shoved me back against the wall.

It felt as if some punk was playing pinball with a razor-sharp, jagged steel ball along my back. The four of them climbed into the new Cadillac and roared off, slinging slush up over the curb across my legs.

I could see, far off, the black shapes of the men pouring out of the Wharf in front of the broken bay windows, fighting. Then, though it must have been there before, I heard the shouting, the firecracker pop of a gun. The meeting—of course, of course—had turned into a brawl. I remember thinking that Tommy Rojack would be lucky to come out of it alive, since that was obviously what the whole set-up had been about from the beginning—to get Tommy, accidentally, an anonymous victim of a labor free-for-all.

I managed to crawl, then limp, toward the Snow Castle Diner. Without dignity, I clamored across the room to the pay phone on the opposite wall and called the paper. Bill Dyers was there, of course, piddling around, and promised me after some pushback that he would stop the delivery trucks already firing up their engines out back so we could tear up his goddamn already-printed paper to run a new fucking page one and that he would call up Guthrie, too, yes, and get him out of bed, yes, and get him down there, yes, as fast as he could.

When I got back outside, I headed for Bilinski's car, figuring if Tommy did manage to get out, that's where he would go. I was leaning against the hood when Bilinski came dragging Tommy up the street from the crowd, and I limped over to help him.

"Looks like you got some of it too," Bilinski said.

"Later. How is he?"

"Could be worse," Bilinski said. "The fat lug sapped him from behind, that's all. The fuck won't use his arm again, ever."

"Good," I said. "Still, you should get him to a hospital."

"They shot Tony," he said.

"Tony Martin?"

"Yeah, Harker. You should'a been there. You could of took a picture or two. They blew his goddamned face off."

13.

Labor violence hardly made for front-page news any longer, but in fact all the rags in Wapsipinicon, save us, carried a piece somewhere in section one that implied I led Tommy Rojack and his men down to the Wharf Waldorf to disrupt an organizing meeting of the peace-loving American Federation of Labor. I got thrown out—so the boys all scribbled—and Tommy's union toughs responded with a brawl that left one man dead, one badly hurt. At work the next morning, I lasted about an hour before I stopped pretending it was just another normal working day, and I decided to attend to the other disaster in my life I had left dangling. I asked Bill Dyers to borrow his heap till tomorrow and told Tuckerman I was taking more time off. He did not especially appreciate it, not least because he was expecting a new column on McKnight from me soon. He insisted I should be on hand to help answer the blasts in the other papers sure to follow last night's performance. I tried to convince him it would be better for us if, today at least, I was "on assignment and unavailable for comment," making quote marks with my fingers as I spoke.

"We can pick it up tomorrow," I said. "By then you and Dyers will have our strategy worked out."

"It sounds awfully irresponsible to me, Randall," he said. "First, you get this paper in a whale of a lot of trouble—"

"Hang on, pal," I said. "This was *your* idea, *your* assignment. *Get McKnight.* Remember?"

"Still," he said, "you are deserting under fire to run off and spend the day with that woman."

I rose from my chair. He knew he was pushing it. He pulled his pipe from his tailored suit and stuck it between his remorseless lips and stared directly at me with all the white intensity he could muster. A dead giveaway—Tuckerman became direct only when he knew he had made a mistake.

"My resignation will be on your desk this afternoon," I said.

"You can't do that." He glared more theatrically. "That would be the worst thing you could do. It would be tantamount to admitting we thought there was some substance to McKnight's charges. It would look as if I had let you go—as if I were afraid, personally and professionally, for the paper."

"My resignation will be—"

"Okay, damn it. I'm sorry. You have the day. Take tomorrow, too. Hell, take the entire week. We are only in the middle of the biggest political challenge we've faced since Albert Collette died. What do we need you for? If it pleases your fancy, though, would you kindly tell me your plans? Just so I have something to say to anyone who questions on which assignment I supposedly have you working."

"I'm going down to Ravensport," I said.

"Oh…"

He looked away from me then and fidgeted for matches. So he knows about Kathy, I thought. And he doesn't care to hear any more about my trip.

"Say I've gone down to interview Wilson's mother about the shooting, if you want. She lives in the same neighborhood."

"I will," he said, watching the coals in his bowl begin their glow.

He waited till I got to the door before he said, "Come to think of it, that's not such a bad idea: victim interviews assailant's mother. Take the time while you are there to see her. That way you get the day with pay."

"I'll put in for travel, too," I said, and closed him back into his quotidian cage.

❧

The clutch on Dyers's bomb, a secondhand Willys, slipped. I did the bump-and-grind over to my quarters to grab my best wool duds, one set of clothes I had yet to transfer to Sharon's for the simple reason I so seldom wore the suit. I called Sharon at the Emerson from my apartment to tell her I was leaving and would see her later tonight or, at worst, tomorrow after work. I took a couple of knickknacks of Kathy's to use as an excuse for dropping down. I swallowed my pride and tried to call her once or twice, but her mother was running telephone interference. Ravensport was only an hour or so away, but if I went down after work, her father would be at home—though he was retired now, he still fooled around days on the boards of various cultural organizations and hung out at his club—and I stood a much better chance with Mom. I headed down Firman, making my last stop at the liquor store for the wet courage I had exhausted at home.

U.S. 218 South takes you straight to Ravensport from the capital through the state's, and maybe the country's, and maybe the world's best farmland. Vladimir Padikoff, the émigré's son, had once asked me, the farmer's boy, on a cold winter's night during a union picket, why anyone in his right mind had ever stopped here as he headed West. It was so Siberian, so bleak, so harsh. And I said to the city boy: Look at your feet. You are standing on pure gold. Earth. Soil. The land, Vlad Paddy, the land. Even an old Bolshevik like you, I said, maybe especially an old Bolshevik like you, should understand that. And he had looked at me oddly for a time, vapor rising from our nostrils in puffs as we jumped up and down to keep warm, our hands in our pockets.

But I was a stranger to the country now, a creature of man-made horizons. And maybe because I was, I could only see what we had done to the land, not what it had given us. Out there, below the uniformity of the snow, it was gentle, sloping prairie land, a prairie that had once covered the southern half of the state and much of the Midwest with wild grass higher than a man's head. We had lopped it off for the dirt down below. The prairie had given us back an upside-down image of ourselves, gazing up at us as we gazed down at it. They had called it the Looking-Glass Prairie, because it stood under water that never completely drained from the flat terrain, creating a natural—and the world's largest—mirror. Then someone discovered even better, richer dirt below that, and we cracked the mirror with underground tile, drawing off our own reflection as we drew off the water. When I was still a boy, I had often heard of the looking glass and I longed to see it, knowing even then that it had vanished for all time.

Now it was winter, and there was no native prairie underneath the snow. Chopped into greedy little quarter sections almost a century ago, it had been pillaged by men like my father. They calculated its worth right down to the number of dollars lost per foot of arable land when, say, the state wanted to build a highway across it. They rode the land the way they rode their women, taking every ounce they were good for as long as they lasted. But that, my father would say, was city boy talk, crying for a lost Eden. Besides, he would have said, the farmer does not *use* the land, he *becomes* it. It gets down into his bones, and he knows it as a *living* thing that can be cultivated, yes, and nurtured, too, the way a child is nurtured and taught to become productive. That was what he called *farming*, he would say, and no government could tell him differently. No government could say it was a matter of possession, distribution, economics, mortgages. It was not a business at all, he said, but a *life*. That's why, I thought, when he lost the farm, he shot himself in the head.

And somewhere I almost agreed with him, in that part of me I left behind when I grew up and moved into town. I could imagine in the plowed-under fields on either side of U.S. 218, unified now by the whiteness, a living thing. But it was no ancient, rolling prairie, nor the hidden heart of America, nor the earth goddess my father married, though it had been each of those things once upon a time. Even the time-haze of scotch and the jerky movement of a second-hand heap, the legacy of city life, could not keep me from thinking clearly through the matter. The land, too, was something historical, something that grew and changed and became a different thing in a changed world, just the way men did. No, I thought, the land is no more or less mutable than human nature, which my father insisted never changed, and I knew changed all the time.

And thinking that led me right back to McKnight, because his attack denied exactly that I had changed in a decade. And to the people who lived in the square-framed houses between the clumps of trees that dotted my trip down to Ravensport, that kind of argument would make sense. Like my father, they believed in land, not history, and McKnight would be able to fix me for them like a character in a novel, who develops maybe but does not fundamentally change. The irony was not so much that Tuckerman's dictum had backfired, that instead of us getting McKnight, he was getting us. No, the irony was that he was a better narrator than I was, that he was creating a more believable villain for his audience than I was for mine. I was his boogeyman whose evil ways explained to these people what had gone wrong with their modern world.

I took another sip of scotch and laughed at Tuckerman. He should get out of the city, I thought, and look at this. The way these people made nature itself so uniform, their formidable fucking strength. Because they were going to buy the used car McKnight was selling. They understood the true threat I posed to them when I deserted my father and came to believe in a different reality from their family-owned plots. I was indeed a stranger in my father's world, an alien, and McKnight had found a scary new name for my condition. And these people, even more than the gang at the memorial auditorium last week, made up the choir to which our politicians preached. To use the clichés of the campaigners, they were the backbone of our state, the salt of the earth. Truth to tell, they made me more nervous than the senator ever would.

❧

"It's you," he said.

I had been inside James Spencer's house once, years ago when I drove Kathy home over Christmas break, sophomore year at Wapsipinicon U. I had stayed only a day, and he was away at some business conference. I'll say this for him, he had taste. The thing I remembered most was the huge sweep of the living room. It had a high ceiling, with exposed dark-wood beams trailing nicely above a mahogany mantel over a large fireplace, a good half-day's journey from the expensive golden sofa, high-backed wooden chairs, and mahogany coffee table. It had been intimidating to a farm boy from Winnebago County, and I told Kathy while I was there that I thought "taste" was the weakest word in the English language.

"It's me," I said.

He looked as distinguished now as he ever had, with dark gray hair turning pure white at the sides, a hawkish kisser (righteously indignant at the moment), and Kathy's perfect teeth. But he was short, shorter even than McKnight. Kathy was probably in the living room behind him, sitting on that dark gold couch of his, looking into the fireplace beyond the flames toward eternity.

"What do you want?"

He asked it with difficulty. Anger had joined the indignation in his face and he was turning very red. I hoped, perversely, he'd have a stroke.

"I want to see Kathy, naturally."

"She doesn't want to see you."

"I thought you still pretended to work days."

"You have thirty seconds to get off my land," he said. "I'm closing this door, walking over to the phone, and calling the police."

"It won't be difficult if I've got thirty seconds," I said. "It's not much land, when you look at it. Just a little suburban plot with—"

The door had slammed so there was no use continuing. That was it then. What had I expected? For Kathy to hear my voice and come rushing past him to the swell of violins? As I turned back toward the drive where I had parked Dyers's Willys, I could hear him shouting at Dr. Spencer. Kathy said he never raised his voice to anyone but her mother.

"He's done quite enough to her! And to me, if you want to know the truth! To me! And to this state! And to this country, yes, to this country!"

I got off his porch, then, before he could get to the world, the solar system, the universe, God. I didn't like his nasty old land, anyway. I took a kick at the well-tended lawn I knew had to be there underneath the snow. Wind caught the spray and blew it, glistening and icy cold, into my face.

I heard the garage door open as I climbed into the Willys. I had two impulses: first, to dive down on the front seat to avoid the bullet, and, second, to smile and rush over to Kathy as she came rushing out. Instead, I was standing there, head above the open door, half in, half out, and it was Kathy's mother who issued forth from the gap in the bottom right of the house. She was striding out into the cold, sun-shot, late-morning air in her determined little way, arms folded across each other, gloveless hands buried in her wool sweater, the red highlights in her hair gleaming in the sun through the gray, and her white breath streaming behind her from her nose.

"You shouldn't have come, son," she said. "I told you that on the telephone."

"Where's Kathy?"

She stood level with my chest, looking up fixedly. As she talked, she stamped one foot to keep warm, but it made her appear schoolmarm-ish, as if she were tapping it impatiently.

"She's not here. *He* could have told you that, but he wanted you to understand she refuses to see you. And she does, Randall. It won't al-ways be like that, son. Give it some time. You have hurt her, somehow, hurt her badly, though I don't know how, since she won't talk about it, even to me. Fifteen years is a long time to put up with someone and then leave and then have nothing to say about it. Has it anything to do with all that bosh in the news about you?"

"Where is she, Dr. Spencer?"

"Now? She's playing tennis. But if I tell you where, you will go find her, and I don't want that. She doesn't want that. You can probably find her anyway, now, but I honestly hope you won't try to, Randall, until she is ready. Do you think all this in the news, do you think she is frightened by it, somehow? That she has been…well, scared away by your tribulations?"

I could see she was troubled by the possibility. She did not enjoy the idea that Kathy might be made of less sterner stock than she herself.

"No," I lied. "It's not that."

"Because I would hate to think that was it," she said. "I told her so. I told her no matter how she felt, I did not think it right for her to go off and leave you that way, Randall, right now. Then what was it? I know enough about you, you know? I hear about you at the caucuses; and at the conventions, I would see you. You were not much of a husband. Drinking and womanizing. And a woman has to make up her mind about that. Whether she will put up with it or not. But it seems to me she had made up her mind, long before this. Was there somebody else, somebody important?"

Once again, the pain was evident on her weathered face. She liked me, I knew, but I did not realize how much she liked me till now, when despite the fact she thought I was a poor husband, she was hurt by the idea that I would give up her daughter, yes, and her, too, for another woman.

"No," I lied. "Not anyone, not anyone I would have—"

"I understand," she said, looking now out across her front lawn, a little blue about the lips from the cold. She must be freezing, I thought, without a coat. I looked back toward the house. James Spencer had come out into the garage now. He was standing just inside, staring angrily at her. She followed my gaze. "But there *could* be someone?"

"I don't know," I said. "I just don't know. That's one of the reasons I wanted to talk to her. To explain."

"Don't worry about him," she said. "He didn't call the police. He hates you." She looked straight at me again with her level, honest old woman's eyes. "And so do I, son, in a way. So do I. Do you think children would have made a difference?"

"No," I said. "No, Dr. Spencer, I don't."

Rose, he called from the garage.

"Don't be so sure," she said, ignoring him.

"I think she left, Dr. Spencer, because she came home one night and realized I was someone else. Not just someone different from the man she had married, not something so, well, *direct* as that. But somebody different from who she was sure I had been all along. That I was really the way I acted. That there was not somebody she loved hidden underneath the way I acted. Do you understand?"

Rose.

"I think so," she said. "But—but that happens to all of us, sooner or later. We become like we do. That's no reason to leave someone. You don't give up your life, or your marriage, for something like that. You give up your marriage because a man is cruel and mean souled. Because he beats you. Because he comes home and he says he is in love with another woman. Not because he is different from what you thought he was or what you want him to be. That's nonsense, son, nonsense."

Rose!

This time he was coming. He moved out of the garage so quickly that he slipped some and almost fell on the icy drive, which only made him angrier, and he reached us in a near run. His hair was a little disheveled from the jolt of the slip and his face was a little wild. He hit the car door with all his weight, jarring me back against the jamb on my shoulder.

"You son of a bitch!" He was screaming very loudly now, having lost all dignity, and he was shoving the door up against me over and over. I held the door with my good arm until he seemed almost out of breath. "You son of a bitch! You son of a bitch! You son of a bitch!"

She pulled him off and pushed him back toward the garage. He allowed it with surprising listlessness. She came away ashamed and angry herself. He stood back there staring and fuming and impotent.

"You better leave now," she said. "I'm sure Kathy will talk to you when she's ready." Suddenly her face twisted into a million wrinkles, a shocking expression of worry and doubt. "What are they doing to you, Randall?" she said. "What are they doing to all of us?" She stopped till she caught hold. "Please. Just go. Leave now."

I drove around Westgate writing the names of streets in my notebook until I came to a market called The Quick Supply with a public telephone, and I looked up Wilson in the directory. There was only one of the thirty or so Wilsons in the Ravensport phonebook who lived on a street listed in my notes: Mrs. C. L. Wilson, 260 Portsmouth. I wheeled around Westgate till I found the street again and then found the house. It was an oversize mock Tudor that sat square on the plunge of Portsmouth down the bluffs toward the river. It was larger than the Spencers' and in the spring the lawn would be shaded by full-grown elms. Now, it made a perfect winter scene, a faux chalet among bare trees trimmed with snow, the last word in respectability.

Having found the house, I took a long break from work. I backtracked to the Westgate Country Club, the first word in respectability, and looked for the Spencer Buick Mom always drove to caucuses and state conventions that had been missing from the garage this morning. I still had those knickknacks to deliver, and I could taste victory when I saw the family wheels parked near the empty outdoor tennis courts. Kathy would, of course, be playing inside on the field house courts just beyond these. I parked Dyers's dumpy wagon and waited, hoping no one noticed the heap that stood out like a sore thumb among the new and the polished. She appeared half an hour later with a broad-shouldered, clean-shaven type. She had on a new camel hair overcoat I'd never seen, and she was smiling. When she left him for her car, she tossed her black hair back, free of her hooded collar, and touched his forearm. She was flushed and healthy looking and she had no need of knickknacks, so I waited until she pulled away and then I headed out of Westgate downtown, toward the giant, ugly industrial core that made up the real city. I knew a good bar called the Substation just the other side of the tracks.

∾

The butler—if that's what he was—vanished. Mrs. Wilson appeared.

"Hello. My name is Randall Harker. I work for the *Capital News* in Capital City. I believe you know Mr. Tuckerman?"

"I know who you are."

"Well, Mr. Tuckerman thought it might be a good idea if I came down to talk to you—not for the paper, you understand—but, well, because we are so…ah, *involved* in your son's problems, and we would like to find out if there is something we could do to help—"

"John called me," she said. "Earlier today. He said you wanted an interview."

"He wants an interview," I said. "I simply want to talk about Charles. I fired the guy, and he…ah, *attacked* me, and I just want to know what makes the man tick."

"Mr. Harker, have you been drinking?"

"No," I said, solemnly. "Oh, well, I may have had a beer or two with my respectably late lunch…"

She remembered herself and invited me in. After all, I was wearing my best wool duds. The sun, poor ghost of itself, hung low in the sky, nearly ready to dip farewell in the frozen waters at the foot of Portsmouth Street, and with dusk coming on, the air was turning even colder. Inside, the place was elegant and warmly lit, a perfect haven from the long, growing shadows of the barren elms outside. I followed her gaunt, demurely clad figure into a sitting room of some sort.

"Allow me to offer you a drink," she said.

She was nothing like her son. I thought she had to be at least forty, forty-five—she may well have been older, but if anything, she looked younger. She had the lean, nearly wrinkle-free face and the tight skin of a woman who had recently had her face lifted. Her black hair, dramatically streaked with gray, was combed away from that face and cut short. She was rather severe-looking and attractive in a black widow way.

"I am afraid I won't offer you any more than a drink. If John Tuckerman weren't so dear a friend—he knew my husband well—I wouldn't offer you even that." She had gestured toward a photograph on the table by the far lamp. A handsome man in khaki looked out from behind a rather pathetically dead water buffalo. "He died in the Spanish Civil War. Lincoln Brigade. A true hero," she said. I revised my estimate of her age upward by half a decade.

"Unlike your son," I completed her thought.

She stared at me. "I don't know that you need a drink," she said. "I am not one of the new generation who mistakes rudeness for honesty, Mr. Harker."

"Or vice versa?"

A younger, dark-clad woman appeared in the doorway in answer to a summons I had not seen Mrs. Wilson make. The girl and the bald, butlerish fellow who had answered my knock at the door were emblems of the several blocks closer Mrs. Wilson lived to the river than the Spencers. She left off staring at me when the girl arrived and ordered us both drinks, hers a sherry. On the way out, the girl lifted my overcoat and my hat off the chair where I had tossed them and took them with her.

Mrs. Wilson was nothing like I'd imagined her from listening to Shaunessy. Had to be that the local cops questioned her for Mike. If he'd done it himself, he'd have made some remark to me about money and servants and rich, domineering broads. Instead he'd painted the picture of a fretting and maternal worrier, the typical gray motherhood we associate with mom and apple pie.

This woman did not fret; she ruled. Wilson never had a chance.

"Just what is it you want to know, Mr. Harker?"

"Why your son shot me in the back."

"Did he?"

"I think so."

"Then he must not have liked you very much."

"You got that right, lady."

"He did not like very many people. It's not surprising."

"You talk about him as if he were dead."

"Do I? I certainly do not intend to do so. I suspect he is very much alive."

"Where?"

"I have no earthly idea. Just as I told the police."

"I'm not the police."

"No. You are the man who fired my son from his newspaper job because you disagreed with him politically."

"I fired him because he wouldn't do his job."

"He writes well. He always has. He takes after his father in that way."

"Pretty sentences," I said. "Very bad news stories."

"He writes well. You don't deny that."

The arrival of the drinks sounded the bell for round one. I took a sip of scotch and decided to try another tactic. "This is getting us nowhere."

"I agree."

"What say we try a different approach, you and me? I'll ask you what I want to know and you tell me in as few words as possible."

We both laughed.

"You have a peculiar kind of charm, Mr. Harker, even dead drunk," she said. "But I am afraid it won't work, any more than your act of contrition at the front door worked. You don't want to find out anything about my son—not even for a news story, as John wants me to believe. You wish only to discover his whereabouts so that you can have him arrested before he shoots you again."

"You *do* understand," I said, mugging gratitude and relief. She laughed again, more freely this time. "No one ever called me charming before," I said, laughing too.

She almost gagged on her drink. "Now that—" she said, stopping to suppress another fit. "That, I don't find in the least difficult to believe."

She got up from her chair and went back over to the doorway to the den and pushed the button to call her maid-like creature, or maybe the butlerish boyo. Anyway, end of round two.

"So that's how it's done," I said. "I was looking, you know, for one of those ropes that dangled from the ceiling."

"Two more, Betty," she said when the girl showed up. "And bring the bottles."

"You may not believe this, Mrs. Wilson—"

"I shan't even try."

"But you should. You really should. It wasn't all an act at the door. I do want to know more about your son. Where I come from, it is not all that common to shoot a man for letting you go from a job."

"Charles is a disturbed boy," she said, suddenly serious. "I had him in analysis for a while when he got back from the war but I grew weary with the voodoo theories of the doctors—and with their bills, too, which were all out of proportion to their services. I decided what Charles needed was a profession to practice. So I talked to John."

"Disturbed? Did you tell the police this?"

"No, of course not. I told them he was a little moody. I told them that it was just like him to disappear after losing his job because he would be ashamed to face me. I told them I did not think he was capable of shooting anyone, and neither did his doctors if they wished to check."

"That's not the story I got from the police, Mrs. Wilson."

"Oh?" she said, taking the tray from Betty and handing me my drink.

"I was told that he was violent at home. That he had destroyed a radio set for no reason. Senselessly. That you thought the war had made him that way."

She looked away, out the wall of doors way in the back of the study that adjoined the sort of sitting room. She sipped her sherry.

"The police," she said. "They must have questioned the—help. Gossip, that's all."

"Is it?"

"What?"

"Gossip?"

"Do you print gossip?"

"No."

"Then it's gossip."

"And if we agreed not to print it?"

"Mr. Harker, I think the time has come for you to leave."

I waited her out for a minute or so while I finished my drink. She did not turn around. She did not speak. I got up to go. End of round three.

"Don't ring for Betty," I said. "I saw where she hung my coat."

"No," she said. "Don't go. Sit down please."

I did, and she continued, "Do you know you are infamous these days? If you had knocked on any other door in Westgate, the response would not have been to invite you in for a drink but to call the police. You have become a monster, Mr. Harker—Red Randall Harker—and most of my neighbors hint to me they think you *deserve* to be shot. That *whoever did it* should be given a medal. Special emphasis on *whoever did it.*"

"He already has one medal, I'm told," I said. "A Purple Heart."

"But my neighbors don't know me very well," she said. "They did not know Charles, Sr., at all. He was not their kind. Not their kind at all. All this, all this, you see, my parents left to me. My first husband died in World War I, in a training exercise. He was a pilot, and he was training boys to fly for the Air Service. He was quite a bit older than I. Oh, I know all this sounds as if I am rambling. As if I am some empty-headed old lady. But I want to explain why I allowed you in my house, when after the stories in the paper these days any other person with good sense would have sent you packing."

"I know why you let me in," I said.

"Do you always pretend to be drunk when you are taking advantage of a woman?"

"Only when it's necessary," I said, not paying her the compliment she fished for.

"Well, I did not allow you in because John Tuckerman called me. John Tuckerman is a friend, but he is not enough of a friend to trick me into helping hurt my boy. But let me finish my tale, please. I was an airplane spotter. Back in those days, you know, they did not have radar, so they hired young women to stand in towers and watch for airplanes. My husband, my first husband, got the job for me. I was just a girl, barely out of school. But I was watching his plane—I knew it was his plane because he used to buzz the tower when I was working. I was watching his plane the day it crashed. He was killed immediately, and the young pilot he was training got hurt terribly. They saved his life, but they put him on the critical list. That young pilot's name was Charles Wilson. He was a young soldier, wounded and far away from home—we were on the coast of North Carolina, then, for the war training, you understand—and I was now a young widow, lonely and far away from home, and I used to visit him in the hospital. We fell in love, Mr. Harker—"

"Just call me Red," I said. She frowned, and as she continued to talk, I went over and made us both another drink.

"Terribly in love. We got married when—against the odds—he got better. At first my parents did not know what to think, but when they met Charlie—"

"Ah, Charlie," I said.

"Please, Mr. Harker. There really is no reason for you to be rude. This does concern you. You would have liked Charlie, don't laugh, you would have. He believed…as you do. He loved two things besides me. He loved people, common folk, and he loved danger. I know it sounds romantic. It was. It was very romantic. He would not stay out of what he called the good fight. When the civil war in Spain broke out, he was one of the first Americans to join the Republican cause. And he was one of the first to be killed. I used to say he thrived on death, and he said if it had not been for death, he would never have met me, that death was the world's great redeemer, that there was no way to a free future except through—"

"Mrs. Wilson," I said. "It's getting late. I think, I should be—"

"He would have defended you," she said. "He would have stood up for you. That's why I let you in tonight." She sighed. "If he were around, maybe Charles would have been different. Maybe Charles would have been on your side, too. His father used to make fun of all this." Her eye movement and a slight twist of the wrist indicated she meant the mansion in which she lived and the kind of life it housed. "He used to tell Charles that he must fight very hard to keep from becoming a sissy or a snob with all he had been given in life."

"And, of course," I said, "he became both."

For a moment, very briefly, I saw a flicker in her eyes of something other than determination and glib self-assurance behind the artificial mask of the face her money bought her, something like the worried expression I had seen on Dr. Spencer earlier that day. One of my blows had opened an old cut from a previous fight.

"Charles was born in 1926. He was not yet a teenager when his father died, just fifteen when the Japanese attacked Pearl Harbor. He tried to live up to his image of his father, I suppose, and attempted somewhat foolishly to enlist in the Marines. I wouldn't hear of it. When I informed them of his age, they rejected him. But the day he graduated from high school, he signed up again, not needing my consent, and that week he shipped out for the war in the Pacific. I knew it was a mistake. He was not his father. He was a frail child. He suffered tremendous ego problems, and he was very self-conscious about his acne. He had periodic trouble with his lungs, chronic bronchitis, which he hid from the recruiting officer and somehow, despite that, survived basic training. And after the war he did come back changed. He said the war was not at all as he had imagined, not at all what Charlie had made him think it would be. You were right. His nerves went bad. He seemed shell-shocked, I believe they call it, or is it battle fatigue these days? Yes, and he had nightmares, terrible dreams, and fits of violence, when he seemed to think things were crawling on him. He had no interest in girls, in work, in life. He was not at all like Charlie, not like his father. He did not have Charlie's looks, Charlie's backbone. He was…"

I supplied the word she was looking for: "Weak."

"Yes. Weak. But you are not weak, Mr. Harker. You are very much like his father in that way. I simply want you to understand what you represent to him. He hated you. He said you talked like Charlie, but you were much worse. Oh, yes, he talked about you sometimes—often—whenever he was home. His doctors had told me that he resented even me for—well, I simply want you to understand that he was unbalanced, and that you were someone who could push him over the edge."

"When did you see him?" I asked, looking directly at her.

"What do you mean?"

"After he shot me, when did you see him?"

"I'm afraid I don't know what you are talking about."

We were back to the verbal sparring.

"Come off it, lady. You didn't let me in here tonight because of your husband, dear old Charlie. You asked me in, and you argued with me, and you fed me a few drinks, traded a few insults, and told me this nice little fairy tale your lawyers probably cooked up. You are worried maybe we've found him, that maybe that's why we want an interview. You know he shot me because he told you himself he did. Did you think you could persuade me to back off or something, not to press charges? Is that it? Because your dear old dead Charlie was a fellow traveler? Oh, you've seen your son, all right, and you know where he's hiding, and you want to know if I know, too. And that makes you an accessory after the fact to attempted murder, Mrs. Wilson."

"It makes me his mother."

Bingo, I thought. She had seen him.

"No, it makes you a sometimes snob worried for your reputation and hiding behind a fairy tale about your husband. Hell, you don't even like the boy. He's weak."

"Get out," she said.

"Not till you tell me where he is."

"I don't know where he is."

"Lady, you've let the cat out of the bag. Now it's me or the police. And this time they won't talk to the—help."

The trouble with sparring with women is they sometimes go soft on you, even the rich ones. Mrs. Wilson went soft. Behind the purchased youth, the aging woman she was covering up—or staving off—collapsed. Underneath the unwrinkled face and the swept-back hairdo, the woman she was doomed to become—Shaunessy's gray-haired American mother—folded up tent and bolted for high ground.

"The night it happened," she said, slumped down boneless in her overstuffed chair, "he came here with another man—a good-looking boy, too good-looking, with blond hair and expensive clothes. They avoided telling me his name. Charles said he had come for some of his 'stuff.' He said he couldn't go back to his apartment up there. He said he had done something, at last. And he laughed. Like Charlie, he said. He laughed at me. He said he was going to see it through, no matter what, and his friend was going to help him. They wouldn't tell me where they were going, what they were going to do. He acted, well, he acted—"

Now she really did gag—and not with laughter. I suppose if she had had anything on her stomach besides sherry, she would have tossed it up right there on her Persian rug. She seemed too beat down to move.

"He acted as if he was *in love* with this other man. Oh, my god, as if he was *in love* with him. It was sickening. He seemed to be fawning over him, and the man ignored him, that slick, handsome man, I don't know who he was."

"I do," I said, getting up this time and actually intending to leave. "His name is Jack Haugen. He works for the *Wapsipinicon Times.*"

TKO, Round Four, I thought.

"You are going to print it," she said. She sat dumb, leaden, talking to a monster in a nightmare.

"Yes, I am," said Red Randall Harker.

There were two of us in Dyers's heap on the way back to Capital City. The land, featureless now in the dark, swooped toward the horizon on all sides, conspiring with the night sky to swallow us up, we aliens—both Harkers in the Willys. There was the infamous one, Red Randall, who wrote for the *News,* wrecked people's lives, and badgered old women, mothers, and mothers-in-law—a mythic creature with no heart, backstabbing his old mentors, scorning his enemies, and frightening the hoi polloi. Villain. Tough guy. Man of history.

And then there was me. I was driving the car. Occasionally, I would get his bills, and I always paid them. The costs were extravagant—a bullet hole in the back shoulder, an estranged wife and over-anxious friends, some public humiliation and a lot of self-loathing—but I met the price to keep him alive, this artificial monster I had stumbled through my life creating. He was the one who had threatened the nice lady with his cop friend if she tried to stop him from using her pal's paper to accuse her only son of attempted murder. Him. He did it. But it was me who had carefully explained to her the danger her son was in if Red Randall did not print the story. It was me who told her how the handsome man who promised to help her son was the man who had been writing the *Times* stories that virtually pegged him as the would-be killer. He was no friend of Charles's, I told her, but he had friends, very dangerous friends. And the longer this went on, the longer her son remained at large, the more dangerous life became for him.

The first Harker, Red Randall, sided with Mother Wilson in her scorn for her pansy progeny, but the second one, much to my surprise, had begun to empathize with the boy. Charles Wilson had fought a war I was too cynical to fight even though he was afraid to fight it. And it had cost him. So what if he was really only trying to prove something to his dead dad? I, too, knew what it was like to lose a father violently and prematurely, how it weighed on your soul and made you want to change things. And finally, we both, evidently, preferred blondes. I just liked mine with breasts instead of balls.

Yes, there were two of us Randall Harkers, and one of us was laughing in triumph as usual and the other was writhing in guilt as usual, and we were both drinking the dregs of my morning bottle on the way back up U.S. 218. Pain and sorrow, that's what we, the two of us, offered mothers worried about their children. I did not know which of the two I hated most, the one with the tough, cynical hide, living by the column inch, or the human one, the one rotting away in time, the one with the wound.

We headlined the story **SHOOTING SUSPECT CONNECTED TO TIMES REPORTER.** Tuckerman showed no more feeling for his old friend Mrs. Wilson (and good old Charlie) than he had when I fired her son in the first place. It was not his doing, he said, he didn't dig up the story, I did. After all, he said, she will endure regardless, which I took as proof he knew her better than he let on. Still I wrote the piece carefully, saying nothing that could cause her more trouble from the police than she already faced. I didn't like her much, but I don't particularly care for little kids either and yet I try not to stomp on them when they get underfoot at the checkout counter in the five-and-dime. The Ravensport papers interviewed her and she told them she was worried about her son and very confused and she simply did not know what to believe and, yes, I had badgered her and intimidated her till she gave me some information and they should henceforth speak to her lawyer.

Haugen told his bold lie and stuck to it. He had not withheld anything from the authorities. All he had was speculation. He met Wilson last year sometime at some veterans' get-together. They became acquaintances and shared a beer or two now and then. On the night of the shooting, Wilson had called Haugen up and asked for a ride to Ravensport. He sounded desperate. But he would tell Haugen nothing. Haugen had taken Wilson to his family home, where he had picked up a few clothes and said goodbye to his mother. Haugen dropped him at the Ravensport bus station. Later, when he saw the news about the shooting, he put two and two together—on the drive down to Ravensport, Wilson had told him I had booted him off the paper—and he wrote his articles. That was all there was to it. Johnny-on-the-spot. Meanwhile, no Wilson, no arrest, no connection to McKnight, and we fought on alone against the senator.

To the constant questions about McKnight's attacks, we stuck to our party line. I had always worked for the *News,* we said, not any political party, and I was just trying to do my job. I argued for challenging McKnight—for admitting publicly I was once a party member and then using my recent writing and labor union work to prove I was no longer even a sympathizer. But Tuckerman said no. He was afraid they might drag me to Washington to grill me about my past. What we needed was less, not more publicity on this thing, he said. We were beginning to obscure the real objective, he said, which was, as everybody in the city room listening to the argument could repeat in their sleep, to get McKnight.

I asked him how being defensive would help us get McKnight, but as usual when he did not want to face something, he puffed on his pipe and went about his business. He issued the—for me—embarrassing statement: "Randall Harker has repeatedly assured the management of the *Capital News* that he is not a member of the Communist Party." An intelligent reader of the paper, if there were any readers left at all by now, might have asked why, if McKnight was lying, did I need to reassure John Tuckerman of anything?

The Old Man made me write an anonymous article quoting myself denying McKnight's various charges, at least those I could deny. I admitted in print that I had sponsored the American League for Peace and Democracy, but I said I couldn't find anything subversive in that, since many good Americans were members. I used the phrase *many good Americans* often that first week out of the hospital. So much, in fact, that I began to wonder if it had any meaning at all. I denied connection with the Earl Browder committee. I said I doubted that I had sponsored the Farm Labor Legislation Conference because I hated farms and farmers, but I had sponsored so many things the first year as president of the Newspaper Guild that I might have. (Tuckerman cut the line about farms and farmers.) I said I had never met Eugene Dennis and did not want to. I said if I had attended the Conference on Social Legislation, it was only as a reporter, and I was too drunk to remember. (Tuckerman cut the too-drunk-to-remember line.) Tuckerman added to the story a long list of anti-Communist credentials for the paper, which I tried to point out would only be used against us as an attempt to cover up our real ideology. In a rage, he called the "alcoholic senator's" charges the "delirium tremens of a reactionary Republican whose standard defense mechanism was to place the label of Communism on anyone who opposed him, from the highest public servant to one's own wife when she complains about the late hours, the messy rooms, the loud mouth, and the constant staggering."

"Good stuff," I said. "This is the kind of thing we should be doing. Attacking full front." His response was to cut everything after *him*.

The real thrust behind Tuckerman's defense, however, became clear to me the next day, when the second article signed by him in as many weeks appeared on the editorial page. Somehow, the article got past my desk not only without my okay but also without my even having seen it. That meant that he and Dennis Sterne, editor-in-chief (and editorial page editor) (and Tuckerman toad), plotted behind my back with Bill Dyers. The editorial claimed confidently that years ago, when I had first been elected president of the Newspaper Guild, I had signed a non-Communist affidavit and filed it with the National Labor Relations Board. I hated to tell Tuckerman, but he should have cleared it with me first. Instead, he printed a lie, and McKnight, who before had nothing but the half-lies of his own creative efforts, was ready with a devastating reply. In another speech, a cut-and-paste job by Freeman, this time before the Chamber of Commerce in the Ritz downtown, the senator pulled from his briefcase (he had gotten to like that effect, I noted) a letter from G. Spivak, affidavit compliance officer for the NLRB, and he read: "This office has no such record of a non-Communist affidavit being filed by a Randall Harker."

"My god," I said to Tuckerman in mock horror, "I lack credentials."

"Oh, shut up," he said.

The worst of it all, though, was an attempt Hoops made to clear my name. Tuckerman should have known better than to let him try it. Hoops and I had been squabbling all week, and he kept joking, not so tactfully, about the subtle way I dug up news by threatening old ladies. But Tuckerman saw what he wanted to see and he heard what his prissy little heart could bear to let him hear, so he ignored the spats and assigned the apologia to the fat man. Hoops tried to explain the remarks Tuckerman had made to me in 1941 that McKnight had quoted in his memorial auditorium speech.

> Harker made a speech at the State University in which he called John Tuckerman a "war monger" and a "red baiter." At the time, Harker was a reporter for the *Capital News* and an influential leader in the city's CIO. Sometimes [and this was the killer, I thought] the policies followed by Harker at the time were the policies advocated by the Communists. Tuckerman called Harker a Communist because Harker's view that the coming war was imperialistic happened to be the view held by the Communists at the time.

This one did come across my desk, and I tried to keep the entire article out of the paper. It was well within my authority. Tuckerman objected.

"Is Hoops after my job?" I asked him.

"Why?" he said, looking for matches.

"Because this thing is obviously an attempt to clear you and the paper while damning me with faint denial. I figure, if I go, he gets city desk."

"Can it, Randall," he said. "I thought you were the one who wanted to admit you used to be a Commie, like some martyr."

"Yes," I said. "Admit it. Right out. Not softly, ever so quietly explain why maybe somebody might think I was a Communist once back when because everything was, oh my gosh, *so* confusing in those days.

We ain't saying I was and we ain't saying I wasn't. You are letting us be hamstrung by the truth, because you are afraid of it. McKnight's writing a horror story, mixing up fact and fiction. He thinks that all he's got to do is say it first, before anyone else, because it's a good story and it scares the hell out of folks. You can't fight that halfway. The only thing you've got is the truth."

Of course, the real problem was that McKnight's charge against Tuckerman was true. In 1941, Tuckerman had just begun to shake off the Progressive mantle of Prince Albert. I was still in the party, hanging on to a failing god though I had done my about-face from Vlad Paddy and the hardline Stalinists. Neither of us had yet gotten caught up in the New Deal the way we would once the war was underway and the United Front eventually masked our differences. Back then you could hate each other's politics and, now and then, still share a beer after work. Hell, we were all somewhere on the left, even the president. There was no vital center.

Early that year, Tuckerman—who has a temper—became embroiled with the CIO leadership at the Axelrod Machine Company on the East Side. He demanded that the union members at Axelrod categorically repudiate communism. On the PAC, we objected publicly to his "dictating" to us. When we got the workers at Axelrod to pass an innocuous little resolution opposing Communism, Nazism, and Fascism, he blasted the city's CIO leaders in a public letter to Richard Barton, the secretary of the Steel Workers Organizing Committee.

> I wonder [he wrote then] why you are so afraid of taking dictation from the owner of the *Capital News* and why you so readily accept dictation from the hands of Red Randall Harker, the Communist leader in the city.... Let's get down to cases. Mr. Harker is a Communist and I defy him to publicly deny that statement.

We had had the argument out at the paper that year several times already before he wrote the damn letter, and he knew I wouldn't respond to it. Later, he told me if I had been a little less headstrong over the Axelrod business I might have made city desk a lot sooner. Regardless, Tuckerman was sure I was a Communist in 1941, despite what he was saying now.

"I don't need a lecture on how to run this paper from you," he said now. "Or about how to handle Larry McKnight for that matter. Why don't you just get your column finished, for a change, and let me handle this. We are as much on the line as you are."

Part 4: FELLOW TRAVELERS

CLARENCE: In God's name, what art thou?
FIRST MURDERER: A man, as you are.

—William Shakespeare *Richard III*

14.

"Samuel Endicott wants to meet you," Sharon said.

Endicott built the Emerson. He was well-off, well-spoken, well-dressed. Some said dashing. Some said he had a real eye for beauty, and he certainly had a passion for art. Sharon had been having an affair with him when she moved to Capital City and took the job as his public relations manager. Not quite five years later, she was still trying to break it off, with only sporadic success. Both of us hoped she had managed finally to do it, if maybe for different reasons.

"How interesting," I said.

Sharon swore she had not slept with him since she starting sleeping with me, but I took it for granted she was lying. Part of the story she was trying to peddle—we all have our little fictions—was that for a couple of months now, Endicott had been after her to tell him what was wrong. He even promised again to leave his long-entrenched wife. When Sharon laughed at him, he demanded to know the name of the other man.

I told her to tell him. I told her that to reach the end of an affair, you had to create the sense of an ending. I didn't know what the hell I was talking about, but it sounded good. Whenever I had wanted to finish off one of my little flings, I had simply stopped talking to the lover in question and walked away. Clean, done, and out—brutal maybe—but *over*. Sharon didn't know about that, though, and she listened to me, and she told Endicott my name. So now, for almost a month, he had been trying to pry information out of her about me. Oh yeah. He wanted to meet me. He wanted to discuss matters with me. He wanted to make sure of my intentions. Right.

"He sounds like your father," I said. "He's old enough to be."

She rolled away from me under blue sheets. I clicked on the lamp by the bed and lit a Camel.

"It's not what you are implying," she said. "It was that, once, I admit. He wanted to look you over and see how you measured up. He wanted to know what chance there was that you were like the others."

"Oh," I said blankly. "The others…"

She looked at me, mugged disgust, and went on to make her point.

"But I think it's more than that now, Randall. He's not a bad man. Sometimes he *is* fatherly. There were some men at the museum today asking questions about you and me. Sam got very angry. He brought them to my office and made them ask me their questions directly. Questions about you—us. Afterward, he wouldn't tell me who they were. I think he got confused about whether he was angrier at them or at me."

"What did they ask?"

"How well I knew you. If you were really a Communist."

"Hold it," I said, sitting up against my pillow, crushing out one smoke and pulling out another. "You mean they interrogated you? Threatened you?"

"No," she said. "In fact, they were rather pleasant about the whole thing. I think they were surprised I didn't deny…going with you. Sam wanted to know if you were a Communist, too, after they left. And if I had told them the truth. I told him that I thought you had been once, but not anymore. I told them I had no idea. Then I asked him who they were, and that's when he said he wanted to meet you. To talk to you about it. Who do you think they were?"

"The FBI," I said. "That's what I would guess. What are Endicott's politics?"

"How should I know? He runs the Emerson. That's all the politics he has, I think. He once said something nice about Adlai Stevenson. Maybe he knows him?"

"A fucking liberal," I said, making a face at my latest puff of cigarette.

"Oh, I don't know," she said, smiling and then laughing out loud. "He's no longer so fucking liberal with me."

"You like that kind of talk, huh?"

I took a lazy swipe at her with the hand I had just used to mash out the smoke, and she ducked her head dramatically.

"Oh yes. It makes me feel slutty, you know, like all your other women. So free. Risqué."

"Foolish," I said.

She moved over to my side of the bed and peeled the sheets back clear off our bodies. She let her hand glide by its nails across my belly to the inside of my thigh, while she softly kissed my neck and the lobe of my ear. We were very careful with my left shoulder, bandaged and in need of periodic dressing and cleaning, because once or twice it had bled. She placed an arm out on either side of me and lifted herself up over my chest, turning down her head and allowing her hair to brush lightly the length of my abdomen. She slipped pale, full lips over the tip of my erection and rolled her head round, playing with her kiss along the ridge, and when she tilted her face, she looked at me with her nearly colorless, knowing blue eyes that held the hint of her slightly crooked smile.

We had begun to know each other's bodies well, timing the sex better these days. As she lay at an angle from me, her breasts sloping back against her frame, one knee placed against my side and one of her long legs stretched out away from them, I touched her and made her lift her body in waves, and she grew damp, waiting for me. She swung around on top and took her time, moving slowly at first while I worked my fingers, then faster, till she let go and leaned backward, supporting herself with an outstretched arm on the bed behind her, moving only the lower half of her body like a belly dancer.

There had been times I couldn't manage to hold off, and she would have to give up her orgasm at the worst possible moment in answer to a helpless, whimpering twist or two from me. And there had been times I just managed to make her come, pounding upward harder and harder as she rolled in light abandonment, before I, too, lost it. And there had been times like this one, the best times for me, when I would hold out, and she would gasp, collapsing forward onto my chest, and hang there, limp, relaxed, trying to bury herself in me, while I finished leisurely, moving rhythmically and steadily and lifting her slightly off the bed.

We weren't at the stage yet where we talked freely about fucking, telling each other how good we were and what we enjoyed best and what we wanted to try next, but we were getting there. For now, we lay scrunched up together after sex, she in the curve of my arm, her leg resting over my stomach, and I smoked, and we talked about the day, and us, and what we might do come spring, when all this was over.

Tonight she said, "Randall, why didn't you talk to Kathy when you were down there? You could have waited till that man she was with—you didn't know him?—you could have waited till he left and talked to her. Maybe, you could have gotten some of the dead wood cleared away, you know…something."

"Sharon, it's over. Finished. I'm not the one who walked out."

"But it's not finished. It's so obvious what she wants you to do—make some effort."

"I made an effort."

"Not much of one."

"It was an effort. Why are we talking about this? Why are you taking up for her all of a sudden?"

"I'm not. I'm taking up for me. You were the one talking about a sense of an ending. This trip to Ravensport—it was no ending. You're more, I don't know, *hers* right now than you ever were when you two were together and we were doing afternoon quickies and fooling around a few odd nights."

"Now I'm supposed to talk to her for your sake? Not mine? Call her up and what do I say to her? Hi, Kath. Just thought I'd ask you why you left me bleeding to death in the damn hospital. Nothing vital, you know, just sort of curious."

"No, of course not," she said. "But it's not over till you lose your pride about being left."

"You'd know all about that."

"Lord. *Yes.* I know all about it. Good night."

She slept, and I smoked. If the point was we both had other… entanglements—hey, okay, I decided. That was a fair point. No one ever came to these things without history. But I was the one who had to do the talking in both cases. And I didn't want to talk to Endicott for any reason. The way I felt now, I might kill the man for saying something about Sharon being a good lay or, I don't know, *anything* about her. I tried not to think about it, so I, too, could sleep. Didn't work, of course.

Finally, I left her there, naked, her face on the pillow, her rich golden hair spread out across her shoulders, her perfect body with its perfect ass as still as some Dutch masterpiece. Left her for another cigarette, another splash of scotch, another sleepless night.

Things had not been that easy for us in the last few days. You'd have thought they would be, with Kathy gone, but no. For one, I couldn't leave anything alone. When Sharon was at work and I was still trying to finish the next column on McKnight—writing at Sharon's the way I used to in my apartment—I found all things could distract me from my work. I moved around, poked into things, gathered information about Sharon from her home, picked up the small details of her life that I half-consciously hoped to use in constructing the real Sharon, the actual woman I knew was there somewhere behind the glow of my infatuation that hid her from sight. Okay, say it was a professional habit. Of course, normal people would call it prying.

I found the diary the first day. It was more a combined "events" list and a "readings" notebook than a diary. Otherwise, I would never, ever have read the whole thing, each entry, start to finish. She listed under the date what book she was reading, the page she was on, and a line or two of her impressions. She was a pretty impressive reader. *War and Peace, Notes from the Underground,* a little Hemingway, a little Fitzgerald, some poetry—Baudelaire. The last thing she read seemed to be *Lady Chatterly's Lover.* She wrote it had a foreign imprint. End-icott had gotten it for her on one of his trips to Paris. The last note fascinated me (and I thought he was so American), so I decided to read the thing, but I hadn't been able to find it on the little wall-hanging bookshelf in her bedroom.

After the book titles, she noted occasional plays—all we ever had in Capital City were occasional plays—and movies. Then there were the names of people she met or the places she had gone on a particular day. Sometimes a man's name would have a lightly written plus mark beside it. Sometimes a minus sign. At first, I thought they indicated a buy for the museum or some business matter, but when I found my name listed on the day I first spoke to her at the Wharf (You don't belong here... I suppose you do?) without any mark, and then a few days later, on the night we first slept together, with a plus mark beside it, I knew. That's when I found out, too, about the others, the previous attempts she had made to break free of Endicott. Always, the "-" would appear for the last time by a name two or three days after Endicott had reappeared with a "+." She had tried as recently as early fall to break away with some guy she labeled "Dr. Logan +."

I made myself a drink, lit a fag, and sat out in the Tropics, waiting for something to happen, for events or fatigue to catch up to me so I could go to bed and join Sharon, but I knew I was in for another long night.

Anywhere, I thought, puffing my cigarette—holding it the way I imagined a French *flâneur* might when he took his turtle out for a walk—heaven or hell. Anyplace, just out of this world.

Sharon was too private. That was the problem. Five years of a clandestine affair with a prominent man had gotten her used to keeping her own counsel, to going her own way, tactfully, unnoticed, out of the public eye, to reading her nights away in her hermetically sealed aesthetic world. She was not in the habit of revealing herself or her life. She opened up to no one, not even the few pluses and minuses in her calendar, not even this last plus—me—the important one. And I told her everything, whether she listened or not. Everything. These days, I couldn't seem to keep my mouth shut.

The imbalance made me feel exposed, the way events happening outside the Tropics, out there in the cold, made me feel. She could get at me, and no woman had ever gotten at me. I was really out there in it, and I had nothing to go on with her, no way of protecting myself from the bad weather except what little I could garner from the notebook and, my God, I couldn't use that, she would know I was a sneak. I would have welcomed her reticence in some of the women I had known, but not in her. With her, I wanted the details.

And why? I knew I felt out of control, that without Kathy around, without my marriage as a stumbling block, something serious might develop between us, and maybe I wasn't sure I could handle that. Nothing had ever developed with the women I slept with casually around town and at conferences and conventions, because I had always had Kathy, and no matter how bad the marriage, she was the real woman, not these…others.

Not that I didn't care for the others, I guess. There was Mia, who
lived on my father's farm for a while, the daughter of hired help, a
virgin the afternoon we first went to bed together, who kept trying
out new things, hungry for getting it all done now that she had given
herself to me, saying oh-so-politely, Kiss me, no not like that, there…
Skinny Mia, with toothpick legs. And there was Connie, short and
cute, my freshman year, wide and moist and hungry, who liked me to
use my hand, rubbing in and out very hard, almost roughly; Connie,
with the bloody sheets the day she was on her period that we had to
wash before her roommate came back; Connie and the rubber we lost
inside her and couldn't find till she took a piss. And Antonides, the
first affair after I was married, who I called only by her last name, tall
and dark, with a full body like Sharon's, and long legs, too; a Greek she
was, the daughter of a CIO official, and she used to keep me waiting,
hard and desperate, in the afternoons while she put in her diaphragm,
and then I would come immediately and remain inside her while she
wriggled me back to excitement; always playing games, that girl, trying
to entice me to stay with her instead of going back to work or home to
my wife, rubbing her long legs and looking at me with dark, luxurious
eyes. And there was the one whose name I couldn't remember with
the permanent wave and a dead boyfriend, killed in the war, the one
who kept going dry in the middle of the fucking and talking about
her kaput soldier boy afterward. And Elaine, Chinese from Chicago,
very small, very tight, who wrapped herself close around my body and
pulled herself off the bed, twisting and turning and talking and moan-
ing midair, who called me sarcastically her "happy interrude," though
she was born American and spoke English better than I did. And little
Martha from work, who gave me head in the back room during break
one day, who kept wanting it more and more often, climaxing quicker
and quicker each time, who was always talking about coming even
more often until she frightened me half out of my mind. And Gilda,
from the phone company, who insisted on fucking by candlelight and
keeping me outside her till she was, as she said, *satisfied*—and sometimes it took hours—and it was never worth the wait. Others floated
to mind: Nancy; Linda; Barbara; the other Kathy; Alsatia; Candace;
Claire, who cried for a month and had never had an orgasm until she

relaxed with me, and then I started having problems with her, too, and she never wanted to stop even when I couldn't get it up, threatening to tell Kathy about the two of us, to kill herself, to do anything she needed to keep me, to make me hers, till one day she just up and moved to Boston, and I found that, hell, I *missed* her. They all returned to me now, in bits of bodies and stretches of skin, in scars and moles, in navels and nipples, in shapes of lips and shades of hair, in a variety of expressions, and in eyes, watchful eyes, staring at me, seeking me out, asking me why I am the way I am. None of them bad people, all worth something to someone, but not to me, because I would let nothing come of our coupling but some wasted hours and a few wet spots on the sheets.

As if I had to prove to myself that the various bodies, the utter unavoidable specificity of sex that makes it different from anything else, was nothing to me, nothing but the occasional clack of bones together, covered with the lie of time, yielding flesh, and the corruption of an easy intimacy, that *they* were nothing to me but momentary escapes of a night, and that Kathy, my wife, was real. But thinking like this made one harder than one should be, I decided; it led to blindness not to insight. Because I was not at all indifferent to the memory of them; in fact, I relished my memories of them; I loved them precisely to the extent they were memories—my counterweights to married life.

Sharon was different. She was simply too stunning even for me to sleep with and walk away from. Maybe the truth was that only the rich, like Samuel Endicott—or the Old Man—with their arrogance and their sense of entitlement, felt comfortable possessing real beauty. The rest of us bums, I thought, just suffer the longing it creates. For having a thing, owning it, drains the owner, sucks him into the being of the thing possessed, and beauty sucks hardest, faster than any other possession, till you're depleted beyond replenishment, lost beyond rescue. In truth, I was worried by my need for Sharon. I was worried by the way I found myself on these sleepless nights sitting in her perfectly decorated apartment, each room done tastefully, lying in my bathrobe amid the ferns and the fruit bowls on her bright green-and-white sofa, languidly thinking about her through the time-haze of scotch and nicotine.

When she told me, in answer to a carefully put question, that part of her reason for taking the job at the Emerson had been she had fallen in love with Endicott's collection of native abstractionists, I had looked at the large black-and-white monstrosity in her living room (I thought it resembled more a giant check mark than a painting), signed by an obscure artist listed in her calendar with his plus and minus, and I had said, He should call it "One Down." She had not known then that I had read her events diary, but she got the point anyway. She laughed, and she said, No, he should call it "Easy Living."

I was worried about her easy living, about the shadow Endicott cast over her life. I was afraid that he was real for her the way Kathy had always been for me, and so nothing could ever come of this, of the two of us together. But it was more than Endicott. She spoke the flawless English of a finishing school. Her laugh was a clarion of good breeding and its utter insularity. She never argued, she joked. She smiled her disapproval. Most women would have been scarred somewhere by the kind of life she had lived the last five years. Most women would have trembled the insecurity of the mistress's shadowy existence through their gestures. I had seen it—the hesitation in, say, the lift of a spoon as eyes cut worriedly at some perhaps nasty re-mark—often, in the women I took and dropped as the mood struck. But even Sharon's apparent dependency on Endicott during those five years seemed willful instead of sordid, and she had become only unhappy with, not devastated by, half a decade as the other woman. She did not even feel the need to talk about it, now that she claimed it was over. She stated it once or twice as a curious fact.

So she was different for me from the others, though we had started out so much like the others (You don't belong here... And I suppose you do?... Right. But you belong in a dream I once had... Lord, mis-ter, with a line like that, you do belong here, among the other antiques ... This stuff, you mean? It's not antique, it's junk... Okay, have it your way, you belong here among the other junk.... May a piece of junk take you to dinner?... Can a piece of junk *afford it?*) that I hadn't no-ticed at first. But now I could not watch her walk into a room without feeling good about us, and, feeling good about us, feeling trapped.

God, I thought. I'm in love. It's almost...demeaning.

Besides, there was no time for it. Not now. No time among the events outside. Larry McKnight, Lefty Mills, Charles Wilson, my wife Kathy, maybe even J. Edgar Hoover were all out to get me in different ways, there was no time for Sharon to be getting me in hers. Especially when my glass is empty of scotch like this, I thought, trying to bring myself via irony back down to earth, and I have to get up, go back in the kitchen, and find a refill. When I returned, I eschewed the green-flower couch and plopped down on the wicker lounge, trying out another perspective on the Tropics.

I may have had my drink, but I had lost my compass, and with the slow, sinking fear of a defenseless navigator at sea in a storm, it occurred to me I might well miss landfall. I was lost. But then came the flash in the dark and the sudden pitch of a huge wave and, with a kind of sick horror, I realized all I really wanted, right now, this minute, Jesus Christ, was for Sharon to say she loved me. She had never said it. But if she said it, I could say it, too. And I was stupid enough to believe that professing it, that the expression alone, would give me my bearings. Then I could stop sitting up here all night, drinking and smoking and worrying my course through the trouble I was having with the column on McKnight, my uneasiness about Kathy, my fears about Endicott, my sense of growing vulnerability. If she would say it, I could say it, and, saying it, banish the general sense that things had gone wrong. But how could she? All we ever did was banter and screw. She never got the chance.

Kathy would hate her. She would hate her easy sensuality. These last few years, Kathy and I had had to work at it, work at it too hard. The freshness of our first weekend in Chicago vanished pretty early on. It wasn't that my estranged wife wasn't sexy. She was—sculpted breasts and well-shaped legs and, once upon a time, a darkly passionate nature. But the second year we were married, she had gotten pregnant and there had been some trouble—some pain or the other—and a miscarriage. Then she had gone through something close to frigidity, not repulsion, exactly, but a kind of dispirited anxiety. We had waited it out, discovering after a while that we did okay when Kathy could concentrate completely on the sex and nothing else. I could not breathe heavily, nor sigh in pleasure; I could only move, slowly, quietly, smoothly; otherwise the sex became dry and painful. We tried, half-heartedly, to laugh it off. We called me the "silent lover." But after a time, the struggle grew disquieting, almost spiteful, and we fought. Oddly, when we fought, the fucking got easier, and the last few months had been better sexually, more passionate, than any time since Chicago. Still, I was sometimes surprised when Sharon would whisper to me while I was inside her, and I felt awkward talking back, as if it was somehow even more a betrayal of Kathy than falling in love.

Sharon seemed to slip so easily out of her clothes. It was exciting and disconcerting, like everything about her. Once or twice she had come home during lunch, and we had made love on the living-room couch and in this lounge with pure lust. We spent the long weekend mornings in bed, and then all evening, too, breaking up the conversation in between with dinner out, brandy in. We made love and took leisurely baths and made love again. Food got better and so, too, conversation about nothing. I found it wrenching to think we would inevitably lose all that one day.

Some of the burn, in fact, cooled when I started going into the office all day each day again, but enough remained still that nights, like tonight, I would sit here and fantasize about her body. It was crazy, crazy. I would start with worries and woes and wind up once again with the flush on her pale cheeks as she pulled her dress back on over her smooth, just-damp skin; or the two sharp bones jutting from either side of her abdomen far enough, almost, to grab hold; or the long, even curve from her rump to her thigh I could not help but trace with my open palm; or the triangle of pubic hair hiding the wet crease between her legs. Hers was not just an everyday body, with its parts and places; she was not like the others. There was nothing frail, nothing tentative, nothing defeated about her body—she was in all of it. It was animated with her simmering and her sensuousness. Lying pressed naked against her at night, I felt not only the pleasure of stolen time, of smooth, warm flesh, but the ecstasy of knowledge, of intimate truth.

There is no time for this, I thought, drinking my drink. No time at all.

❧

The time was two a.m., and I know just how far gone I was because I was remarking that even Sharon's messiness was better than the messiness of other people; it was the temporary and casual mess of a busy woman who offhandedly dropped her days onto the solid world she had carefully established—a messiness not like my messiness, which was simply the abandonment of all order. It was two a.m., I mean, when Sharon came into the Tropics from her bedroom. She screwed up her cosmetic-free face against the brightness of the living room. She stood there openly disrobed, desirable, unselfconscious, lush.

"What's wrong?" she asked. She stopped blinking, found me amid the cloud of exhaled smoke, smiled, and said, "I miss you now when I wake up nights and you're not there."

"Hi," I said. "Welcome to Harker's all-night symposium. I've been thinking."

"About me, I hope."

"About you."

She walked over to the wicker lounge in that flat-footed plop sleepy women use, took me by my hands, and dragged me over to the sofa. She pushed me down till I lay straight with my feet suspended over the far armrest, then she opened my bathrobe, climbed onto the couch and squeezed herself beside me with her back to my chest, wrapping the robe around both of us.

"I'm cold," she said.

"*Cold?* It must be eighty degrees in here. This is the Tropics, lady."

"The Tropics? Oh, right. Ha. Ha. I'm cold."

I let her get my arms placed around her. She was comfortable to hold. Relaxed, she perched on the edge of sleep, wanting only to be hugged.

"I've been thinking," I said. "Times change."

"I know," she yawned. "You keep saying that." She squirmed her shoulders back and forth, lightly, against my chest, preparing for another plunge into sleep.

"About your maid," I laughed. "That's what I've been thinking about."

"Vera?" she said, half awake. "You think about the strangest things. An odd beast you are, know that?" Another yawn.

"Time was," I said. "I'd have given you a lecture about your maid. I'd have asked you why she should pretty up your mess for less money than it takes to feed her family."

"Yeah, yeah. Which is something like giving me the lecture, without giving me the lecture, it'n it? I work, too. And in the morning, no less."

"You dress well each morning and leave the house."

"What do you suggest, dear? That I fire her? Okay. First thing next week, she goes."

She flung her arm out majestically, then let it drop and dangle along the floor. I laughed.

"I don't know. Kathy used to do all the cleaning, which is worse. Maybe we should just not clean up until it's so bad we do it ourselves. Which in my case would be never. Up. Up, I say. Time for more booze."

"No," she sleepily protested. "No. It's so warm."

I rolled her off the couch and got up. In the kitchen making a drink, I watched her through the open door climb back on the sofa and try to curl into a corner. I wondered if we would make love again now. I said, "Sharon? Just how serious is this—us—and Endicott?"

"Oh, he wants to meet you. I told you. You know more what it's about than I do. Politics. Hurry up, please. Get back in here with your long warm body."

"No. I meant *us*. I mean, was that quack, that Dr. Logan-plus sign you slept with last month, was that like us?"

"What?" She sat up straight on the couch. She looked at me. I stood in the doorway of the kitchen. We stared. She crossed her legs as if she were fully dressed. She sat, demure, poised, awake, naked. Then she started to laugh as I walked over to sit by her. She threw her head back and bounced her body against the sofa, lifting up her knees, hugging them, laughing.

"Oh, no," she laughed. "You *didn't*. No. No. Oh, my lord, you did! I mean, really, Randall. I know you are supposed to be a newspaper reporter and are paid to snoop, but that? My notebook? And you figured out my secret code, you clever devil. Lord."

"I don't think it's so funny."

She laughed.

"You should see your face. You look so serious. Tousled hair. Thin little moustache. You'd think you had just accused me of murder. I confess, Randall. You've got the goods on me, Harker."

"Was Dr. Logan-plus sign married, too?"

She laughed. "Yes. God, yes. He was married, too."

"You like us married, don't you?"

"You are outraged," she howled. "You really are outraged! Old love 'em and leave 'em Harker! Listen, honey." She tried to control herself. "Listen, now. You know you had no right to do that, oh Lord, I've been *investigated*!" She started laughing again.

"When does my minus get added to my name?"

Suddenly, she was serious. I could see the real anger underlying her laughter. It made me feel good, too good.

"Maybe we should put it in right now. No. Better yet. Next time you open my diary just add in the minus sign yourself and close the door behind you on your way out. Or next time you steam the flap on one of my letters or listen in on one of my phone calls. I really ought to throw you out. You know that, don't you?"

We both stared at each other over my scotch.

"Oh, go to hell," she said and suddenly smiled again. "I don't care. Give me your bathrobe. I'm freezing. Hand it over and we'll call it even."

It took me a second to get her point.

"Oh. You mean we'll both be exposed."

Sharon's smile grew wider. I gave her the robe. I went back to the bedroom for a pair of pants. I felt mean, small, ratlike.

"You're so blasé," I said, coming back into the living room.

"Yes, Randall. Only most people call me 'even tempered.' And some of the nastier ones say 'smug.' Make me a bourbon, will you, now that you're up. This really is unfair, you know. I can count the number of men I have slept with on one hand. Just open up my diary, count the number of pluses, then add my husband—ex-husband—and you've got it. Go ahead, count them."

I ignored her as I passed her on the way to the kitchen for water for her bourbon. She was twisting her small mouth up in a half pout, half smile, with sparkling good humor. Sometimes she did seem complaisant; yes, almost smug.

"No," I said. "I won't. Then I started to laugh, too. "I already have," I said.

"Oh no," she squealed. "It's just like you. Just like you. Don't you trust anyone? If you had asked me, I would have told you the truth."

"What's trust?" I said, handing her the drink.

"Thanks, snoop."

"Can't help it. And you can only count them on one hand including your husband—ex-husband—if you don't count me."

"Mathematics," she said. "Bet you can't do that with the women you've slept with in the past year. Besides, you are the only one who counts."

"Me and Endicott," I said.

"Okay," she said sarcastically. "Have it your way. You and Endicott."

We sipped our drinks. We kissed. Sharon pushed me down on the couch again. She unzipped me, sitting on her knees and tugging at my pant legs. She pulled the bathrobe down over her shoulders, leaning through my legs onto my chest and slipping it off the rest of the way. As we kissed, she trailed her nails along the inside of my thigh. She held me lightly in her hand, waiting for me to stiffen, then ran her closed fist up and down, until I was ready. She placed me between her breasts, playing with her hand along the underside, kissing me from my navel down. I held the back of her head while she took me in her mouth, and I watched her as she pulled her knees up under her body to get a better angle. After a while, I sat up a little, and pulled her away, toward me.

"Now," I said. "Before it's too late."

"Okay."

I started to slide back down, so she could straddle my waist, the way we had been doing it, but she shook her head.

"No. Why don't you do it…back there?"

We rolled over, and she sat up facing the back of the couch, and I placed myself up against her ass, pushing steady and hard till there was no resistance, one of my knees resting on the couch, the other foot on the floor. I heard her moan, then felt her just let go, breaking out in a sheen of sweat, her body shivering with a new flutter of excitement with each stroke I took.

"Feel good?" she whispered.

"Yes," I said. "Yes. It feels good."

"Yes. It feels good," she said.

I was aware of the brightness of the light and of the plush excessiveness of the plants and of the heat and of her pale skin. Her body dropped away from me on the couch, her brow furrowed, her mouth open, her eyes closed.

"Yes," she said. "Do it a little harder."

She made a long hissing sound, taking in air, just before I finished. She rolled over. I looked at her. She was watching me, too.

I sat on the floor afterward, my back against the couch, and smoked. She lay, staring at the ceiling, and playing with her fingers in my hair.

"I'm glad we did that again," she said.

"So am I," I said. "I'm sorry about the diary, Sharon. I should not have read it."

"No, you shouldn't have. But, honey, I want you to understand this. I'm not ashamed of myself. And no matter what you do, I won't be. I'm not ashamed of anything I've done. Not of Sam. Not of the others. Not you. I did not end it with Sam because I was ashamed or felt he had done me wrong or anything like that."

"Why did you? It was never over before. Five years is a long time to put up with a situation and then—poof."

"Oh. Circumstances. I finally realized the circumstances made it unhealthy. And I had found you."

"But I was just another affair. Not now, I know. But then. I was married, too. It seems you were just repeating the circumstances, the sickness."

"No," she said. "I was immunized against them, it. I'm losing the thread of the metaphor here."

"Marriage as disease," I mused. "Makes Kathy a germ—and you the wonder drug."

"I knew you were curable." I looked back to see her smile.

"You knew? How could you? I didn't even know."

"From Sam. I could see the difference. He always talked about his wife, about leaving her, but he never intended to. You never said a word about Kathy, till it was over. One person, one disease, prepares you for the next."

"Sharon," I said. "I am ashamed. Ashamed about Kathy. Of the failure."

"I know."

I turned around to face her on the couch. She had pulled the bathrobe over herself like a blanket. Its dark blue contrasted harshly with the bright tropical motif of the room.

"The reason I snoop," I said. "The reason I read your notes. I need to know about you. I need you to open up. To tell me things, the way I tell you."

"But I've told you what's important. I—"

"No. I mean all of it. The why, too. Why Endicott, not just the fact that it is Endicott."

"Was Endicott."

"Was, is, what's the difference?"

"I told you about Ted, about Daddy."

"Oh, yes. Sharon Parks has a past. Like me, like the rest of us, yes, you've told me. Your maiden name was Coffin. You were born in Rhode Island. In a little town outside Providence named Coffinsville, after your grandfather. Daddy, Robert Coffin, Jr., owns Coffin Textile. He sent you to school in Europe for polish. You went to Brown where you met Central Parks, the architect—"

"Edward," she said, laughing.

"Edward Parks. More important, Daddy approved of him. You married. Moved to Lansing, stayed with his family during the war, after he was drafted. Took a course in art history because you were bored. Met Endicott at an art show, admired him, but didn't sleep with him because you were married. Ted came back from the war thinking more about the firebombing of Dresden than about transforming Lansing. He had lost his intensity. So you took the job Endicott offered. He more or less forced himself on you one night during a business trip. You liked the work. You fucked him. Job security."

"Enough, Randall. Stop."

"You divorced Teddy. Daddy approved. Paid for analysis. Your analyst said the affair with Endicott was good for you. But his wife walked up to you at a cocktail party after a year and said she had always wanted to meet the woman destroying her marriage. So you stopped going out. You read a lot. You—"

"You make it sound like a story."

She reached over and took what was left of her drink off the wicker coffee table and sipped it.

"*You* make it sound that way," I said. "When you tell it. Like a job *resume.*"

"It's the analysis," she said.

"I'm not interested in psychoanalyzing you," I said. "I just want to get to know you. What you think about. How you feel."

"About what?"

"Your father, for instance. Don't tell me you are secretly in love with him and Endicott is a father substitute—or bullshit like that. Just tell me what he's like, the things you did together growing up. That would be enough. I can draw my own conclusions."

"He owns things."

"*Sharon.*"

"I don't know how to do what you want, how to tell you what you want to hear. I'm not a writer, I don't have the words."

"You can learn," I said. "All you need are the right words and enough time. And that's what we have. Words and time."

"Okay," she said. She looked at me. She leaned down from the couch and kissed me. "I think about you. And I feel good."

I laughed to myself. I shrugged.

"I give up," I said. "I think maybe you are right. I should talk to Endicott; I'd probably learn more about you from him. Let's go to bed."

False dawn insinuated itself into the bedroom from the night outside as we climbed back under the sheets. We moved together instinctively against its chill. I looked at the stuffed toy animals, lumps in the dark against the far wall. I had banished them from her bed when I moved in. She had said they were good lovers because they were warm and they did not talk about themselves. That was all I did, I thought, talk about myself. The worst thing about McKnight and his slanders were that they made me even more self-conscious, even more morbidly introspective. Christ, now I was even feeling guilty about feeling guilty.

"All right, Randall," she said. "I'll tell you how I feel. What I think."

So she was still awake, too, still thinking, too.

"I think about you. You make me feel alive again, sometimes silly and shallow, but alive. You don't try to own things. You try to understand me, not own me. Even tonight, with the diary, you were trying more to get me to tell you about them, the others, than to make me feel wrong for sleeping with them. You seem to think nothing belongs to you by rights, and I like that. I feel good about that. I feel free with you. It makes me a little dizzy. I'm tired of people who think things belong to them by rights—like my father, and Sam, too, of course. He thinks that buying paintings and sculpture means he loves them, when he just owns them, and his passion for art is really sort of shallow because of that, sort of awkward, if you know what I mean. I admired his tastes, and what he was doing for American art, at first, and I wanted to be a part of that. But, no, wait. I'm talking about *you* not him. You don't hide things. You, I don't really know what to call it—you don't want anything, not for yourself. And you don't ask me to change. You allow people to be what they are. Even if you don't like it, you allow it."

"That's not true," I said. "You should talk to my friend Vlad Paddy. Or to Kathy. And I do want something. I want you."

"I'm talking about the way you make me feel. Not the way you are. Besides, you are very different from the way you act. You try to make people think you are virtually illiterate, but you are smart. Smarter than people who think they are brilliant and let you know it all the time."

"Like Endicott?"

"Yes. And you act tough, even vulgar. But you aren't. Just look at the women you get seriously involved with. Your buddies would say they aren't your type. Kathy. Me. But we are exactly your type. Maybe you do want us, but you don't need us. That's what makes me feel so good. You do it out of choice. And you are not hard, the way they say you are, the way you think you are when you drink and you work, you know? You are—I can't say this—"

"What?"

"Tender."

"Now I am embarrassed," I said.

"And I need you," she said.

"You've never met me. You've met him."

"Him?"

"Red Randall."

"Are you cracking up again?"

I laughed.

"No. No. It's just something I started thinking about on the drive back from Ravensport. A man goes along, trying to fit himself to his circumstances, as you call them—his job, his marriage, whatever, lying a little here and there to make himself look good, acting a way he doesn't feel, just like you said, and he creates this *thing*—this shell, you see, made up out of bits and pieces of what people say about him, what they find attractive about him, what they think he is good at. And, like some handyman, he takes whatever he's given, whatever's at hand, and then he uses it, creates this device and makes it sift out all the crap he gets thrown at him every day, protects himself with it. He keeps himself to himself, and lets the device do the talking. Then one day *he* disappears, and there is only the device, acting the way it's supposed to act, moving through his life for him, smooth and serene. It forgets it's just a device and begins to mistake itself for him, and he forgets to correct it until he, too, can no longer remember what is device, what is real."

"My analyst would call that dissociated personality, honey. He would diagnose you as schizoid."

"No. No. It's not psychological. It's technical. An invention. He knows that when the device begins to fuck up. He discovers he hasn't disappeared at all, he hasn't even changed much. Red Randall is the shell, the device. And I've spent too much time creating him to trade him in on a new model, but it doesn't matter much what happens to him, because it's not happening to me. I don't care if Tuckerman admits Red Randall was a Communist, because he was. I'm not. I don't care if McKnight ruins his life. He's not worth that much to me, now, anyway."

"But I was talking about you," she said. "Not him. And I have met you, you know. Every time you touch me."

"I love you," I said. "And that's me talking. Red Randall could never say that."

She moved closer to me.

"I think I love you, too," she said. "I hope I do. Oh, God. I want to. I really want to."

She was pressed up against me. I could feel her heaving. She was crying.

"Sharon, what is it? What's wrong?"

She didn't answer. She buried her face against my shoulder. She cried. She did not talk. We lay there together, without words, with only time. Real dawn assaulted the room, surrounding the stuffed animals and both of us. The new light snared us, our spent bodies twisted round each other, caught by circumstances and cleaved by will, on a cold morning in the middle of the country.

15.

Nothing was as urgent as the clanging demanded. Hell. I rolled over from the bed, trying to find the telephone, to silence it. Sharon was gone. It must be after nine. I found the thing under her pillow on the floor.

"Hello?"

"Harker? Hoops. What's up?"

"Didn't Sharon call?"

"No. This morning you mean?"

"Damn. She was supposed to," I lied. "The wound started up again last night. I was coming in around eleven."

"It's ten now. Tuckerman is pissed. There's a guy from *Time* in with him."

"*Time* magazine?"

"Right. He wanted to talk to you. They are doing a piece on the Old Man and McKnight and you. He had a lot of trouble explaining where you were."

"Lying is good for his soul," I said. "I'm staying out of it. You going to be there most of the day?"

"Should be."

"I'll give you a call every couple of hours. When our man is gone, I'll come on in. If you leave, tell Gene about it, and I'll talk to him. *Time,* for chrissakes."

"I don't know, Dell. Maybe I should check it with the Old Man."

"You do that, Fatso. You march right into his office and say I'm playing hooky till this jerk sitting there next to him leaves. He'll love it."

"Right, chief," Hoops said sarcastically and hung up. He was becoming objectionable.

I climbed back into bed and smoked a cigarette and waited. I must have slept, because the next thing I was aware of was the noonday sun, busy old fool, worrying away at my eyelids. I had a shit, shower, and shave, and I called Sharon. She said she hadn't wanted to wake me when she left. She said she was just about to phone me.

Janice smiled when I walked into Paul Toland's office as if she had been waiting for me. The taxi ride crosstown had been harrowing. I thought Toland should be told the FBI was mucking about his burg. It never occurred to me he might know already, until I saw Janice. The bun was gone, and so were the glasses, and so were the muted clothes. Her long brunette hair cascaded around her shoulders, and a band of freckles had appeared across her nose. She was painting her lips now, and they were full and sensuous. Without a jacket, her breasts swelled out her blouse, and you couldn't help but follow on down to her legs. Sans her office uniform, she no longer looked like a secretary, but like the woman Paul had been making love to all these years—she looked virtually naked, I mean. She was a compact little knockout, and she was enjoying my surprise and my once-over.

"Paul's not in," she said.

"What happened to 'Mr. Toland?'" I asked.

She smiled all the brighter. She radiated well-being. No wonder she had hidden her charms underneath the business dress all these years. I kept thinking only about one thing as I looked at her, and it had nothing to do with Paul or the FBI. I needed a drink; instead, I found a chair.

"Okay," she said. "Mr. Toland is not in. I'm sorry. He's with the mayor."

"He's always with the mayor," I said, "when he doesn't want to see someone."

She flushed again, the way she used to, only now it seemed anything but demure. Sharon, forgive me, I thought. Paul, too.

"But that's okay," I said. "What are you doing for dinner?"

Finally, unable to hold it in any longer, she blurted, "We're getting married."

"You and Paul? Incredible."

"That's right," she said, smiling. "After Christmas. He made me promise not to tell anyone but you. He said it was all right to tell you. Because you already know about…us."

So Paul Toland is a Senate candidate at last, I thought. Weaver had convinced him to run. Yes, he'd need a Mrs. Toland looking this good standing beside him on a platform while next to McKnight stood a twice-empty space.

"You don't have to tell anyone," I laughed. "It's written all over you. Best wishes."

"It's the new me," she said. She walked out from behind the desk. "Mrs. Paul Toland." She spun on her heel, like a model.

"I like it," I said. "What are you doing for dinner?"

"I'm afraid, Mr. Harker—"

"Call me Dell. We're practically family."

"Dell, I have a previous engagement. With my fiancé. Oh, that sounds nice."

She was ebullient. I still needed a drink.

"Speaking of your fiancé, I really do have to talk to him."

She stopped prancing and returned to her desk. She was holding it all in again, trying by sheer willpower to return to the world of shorthand and letter filing, but failing miserably, wonderfully, busting out all over.

"Dell, I'm sorry. He really isn't here. And he, please understand, he doesn't want to see you. Bob Weaver—I don't like that man, do you?"

I thought about telling her that it was Mr. Weaver who had proposed to her; Paul was just Weaver's Cyrano. Only in this version of the story Toland was the one who got to climb into her bed at night.

"He's okay over a drink," I said.

"Bob Weaver has convinced Paul he should not, well, you know what I mean, be friends, or something, with you, until after the election, because of your reputation—and because of all that trouble you are in. It makes me angry."

Paul knew, I realized then, that the FBI was in town. Of course. Such things did not happen in this city without Toland knowing about them. He knew, and he hadn't told me. Janice was right. I was in trouble.

"You look stunning when you're mad," I laughed. "All right, so Paul won't see me. And you are getting married. When does he plan to announce his candidacy?"

"Oh no," she said. "I wasn't supposed to say anything about that. Paul will be furious."

"Calm down," I said. "Calm down. I'll make a deal with you. I won't breathe a word of this to anybody. But you've got to find me a drink. I know Paul keeps a stash here somewhere. Find me a drink, we'll celebrate your engagement, unofficially of course, and we'll forget the rest."

She was smiling again. She skipped into Toland's office. She brought back the bottle. We toasted her engagement. We had a couple of drinks. She indiscreetly told me Paul would not be back till late in the afternoon. He was actually off with Weaver, talking to Democrats. He was always talking to Democrats, these days, she said. We had another drink. She was alive, and breathless, and happy, and sexy, and she told me all about herself, her family, the farm in Kansas, but before I left, I promised her I would not repeat any of it. Paul Toland, I had decided, was one lucky man.

I got to the office late. Tuckerman had fled homeward, frustrated and angry with me, so said Gene Gibson, our crime guy. He had talked about firing me, Gibson said cheerily, but that was nothing new. He had heard Tuckerman complaining to Dyers that there were other things to do, other stories to cover. I was using McKnight as an excuse to slack off, the Old Man told Gibson, and besides, I still hadn't gotten my next piece on the senator finished. I asked him where Hoops had gone off to and he said unconvincingly he didn't know but Bill probably did.

Dyers told me the Old Man was really pissed at me. He told me Hoops had rushed off to talk to Carol Cole.

"The second Dame McKnight?"

Dyers nodded.

"She kept trying to call you all afternoon. She wanted to talk to you specifically. Each time, Hoops would keep her on the line a little while longer. Finally, he got her to meet him. We were all joking about Hoops stealing your story. That's why Gene wouldn't tell you where he was. Some of the others round here, Dell, are pretty pissed off, too. About your high-and-mighty attitude. They see you dangling on a thread."

"Where is he meeting her?"

"Where else? The one place you are avoiding."

"The Cove," I said. "Thanks."

"Yeah. Just don't say I told you."

Sharon did not answer her phone when I called to tell her I'd be late. We had no set routine, but we had been meeting pretty regularly around dinnertime at her place. The after-work crowd had thinned out by the time I got to the Cove. Hoops sat there, all right, next to a woman I'd guess to be still in her twenties, the two of them hunched close in one of the back booths. I did not see anyone I could imagine worked for *Time,* but then what does the ordinary look like? Lonny Vosteen, the joint's owner, bartender, and head cook, was lounging near the cash register and the front entrance.

"Who's Hoops's new lady?" he asked.

"That's a lady?"

"I'd say she was a knockout."

"Some guys," I smiled at him. "She's okay, I guess, if you go for the Betty Boop look."

"They been boozing it all afternoon. Say, Harker, a fella was in here asking for you. I can't remember exactly what *he* looked like."

"Yeah, when was this?"

"Lunch rush. Then later. Couple, nah, maybe an hour ago. Said he was a friend of yours."

Vosteen was leaning up against the cash register, behind his counter, arms folded into one another. I shook my head.

"No. He was no friend of mine."

He watched me watch Hoops and Carol Cole for a while. Hoops was enjoying himself. Sitting back, immobile, talking away, and deigning to give her his most charming smile, the same smile he gave everyone, the only smile he had. She was half listening, watching the parts of the restaurant and bar she could see.

"Well," Lonny said. "You going to muscle in on him or not?"

I laughed. "Yeah, I guess I am," I said.

"Some guys," he said. He grinned idiotically. He raised back from his money machine to reveal the glass of scotch he had hidden below. He held it out to me, laughing.

"Oh, funny," I said.

"We had a bet." He pointed to the door that led back into the kitchen. "Any time Hoops comes in here with a good looker, I said, Harker ain't far behind. One of the guys got the idea from Hoops you was dodging this other fella looking for you. I win."

If Carol Cole had ever been on the wagon, she was off it now. Indeed, she seemed on a binge, which would explain why she had not been working away on the typewriter at her law office. Short dark hair, done in curls. Dark, moody eyes. Pouty lips, loose at the corners, but that would have been the booze. Petite. Pug nose. Cute. Her features seemed squeezed together in the center of her face. Yeah, some guys would have called her a looker. But I had spent last night with Sharon and this afternoon I had drunk away with Janice soon-to-be Toland née something else.

"May I join you?"

She glared at me.

"This is Harker," Hoops said.

She recognized me as he was saying it, and her glare changed to a kind of open invitation; it was an expression a drunk might think was sensual and inviting, but it was actually only licentious.

"So this is the bozo everybody's talking about," she said.

"Carol is celebrating," Hoops said. He was obviously not happy to see me. "Aren't you, sweetie?"

She bristled.

He gave her one bold stare.

"That's right," she said. "And, oh, looky here. My glass is empty. Be a dear, and go get me another."

"Hoops moves for no one," he said. "Not even you, love of my life."

"Fuck you, Fatso," she hissed.

Only in the silence afterward did she realize she had been unladylike and seemed to find it vaguely embarrassing.

"I—I think it's time for a visit to the powder room."

"I'll order you a drink," I said.

She was standing, unsurely, but standing. She touched my face with her palm. Hoops looked at his beer.

"You're sweet."

"*You're sweet*," he said when she staggered toward the restrooms. I waved down a waitress, Charlotte, and ordered a round. I had rarely seen Hoops smashed.

"Why didn't you tell me you were boffing her?" I asked him.

"Didn't seem like any of your business, Harker. And besides, that was a long time ago. Right after I started on McKnight. Ain't seen much of her lately."

"What's all this?" I asked, indicating the situation in the Cove.

"The reason I ain't seen much of her lately."

"I want subtlety, Hoops, I'll catch a play."

"She was doing good, you know. Off the booze. Working. Took a little pride in herself. McKnight wasn't the kind of husband good for a lady's pride."

"You liked her?"

"Felt sorry for her," he said. "It was a part-time thing. I'd see her off and on. We'd laugh about the stuff I wrote on Larry. She'd tell me stories about him. I ain't much of a lover, Harker. But it was a good time, once, twice a month. Then she started seeing somebody else. I'd notice a bruise here and there, know what I mean? At first, I thought maybe it was McKnight again, whenever he came back to town. When I started asking questions, she cut me off. No more good times. She was in love, she said."

"Haugen?" I asked. "It was Jack Haugen."

"Jesus," he said, flatly. "That's what I hate about you, Harker. One can't *tell* you a goddamned thing. You always know what's going on."

"There had to be some reason she didn't want to talk to us," I explained.

"I been busting my balls off just to get her to admit it. I got suspicious, like you say, when she wouldn't talk to me. Not a word. I suspect he was there, with her. That's where he probably stashed Wilson. They were most likely banging away in the bedroom when Wilson was out dusting you, then he ran to find his old army buddy. She was scared to talk about it."

"And now?"

"Now, he's hit her one time too many. They've split up, she says. She says the one thing he kept saying was, Stay away from Harker. He'd kill her if she went near you. So, of course, that's the one thing she's gotta do. I don't think it's to get at him, see; I think it's a question of pride. I don't know. What the fuck do I know about women? All I know is she called all afternoon for you, and I had to convince her you were just short of being a corpse, convalescing in some rest home, before she'd even meet me again. She's been needling me all the fucking afternoon about you. How good-looking you are in your photos. Bunch of other crap."

"Sorry, Hoops," I said.

"Can it. You are always in the catbird seat. Always. She's the one you oughta feel sorry for. She feels like a fucking hand-me-down and she's acting like a fucking whore. Strange creatures, us humans. Don't talk. Here she comes."

She almost swerved into Charlotte, who was bringing our drinks. They arrived at the table at the same time. She made a ceremony of taking the drinks off the tray for us, while Charlotte stood by, not amused, just indifferent.

"One for long, tall, and handsome," she said. "And one for—"

"Hoops," I said.

Laughing, she took the last drink off the tray and drained it, still standing.

"And one for me. Take me home," she said to me, gulping booze. "Or just take me, I don't mind."

I looked at Hoops.

"Somebody has to," he said. "Obviously." He looked at her. "And it ain't going to be me. Have fun."

She took an inordinate amount of time gathering together her things. Hoops avoided my eyes, watched the room behind us. When we left, he was still sitting there, filling the booth, watching the fizzle of his beer, and tearing at the label. Beyond the kitchen door, Lonny Vosteen, no doubt, was busy collecting another bet. On the way out, I made her wait while I called Sharon again but got no answer.

"My car," Carol Cole said as I pulled her toward the cab I had hailed.

"Forget it. You can pick it up tomorrow. When you're sober."

The cabbie drove us to her place as badly as she would have, and he was sober. But during the ride, she was all over me, distracting his attention. Her kisses were wet and sloppy, though she probably thought they were passionate. Her roving hand, meant to be exciting, was clumsy, and when it found what it wanted, brutal. I didn't fight her off in front of the cabbie, but I managed, carefully, slowly, to get her settled down into the crick of my arm, and I became suddenly aware again of the still aching wound under the wrinklings of my shirt.

"You ever made love to a fat person?" she asked.

"Tell me about Jack Haugen," I said.

"He's not a fat person. He's a bastard. Hoops is a fat person. He's a bastard, too. Hell, you're all bastards. Hoops, he used to be funny. Never did like to fuck him. I suppose he told you all about it. Kinda disgusting. Close my eyes, picture somebody else. Or even him, some- times, with his clothes on, talking. You know, being funny. But then, I would open my eyes, and see he was fat, fat, fat."

"Shhhh," I said. "Let's talk about something else."

"Fatty Arbuckle squished a girl to death, know that? Plop, plop, squash!" She laughed. "Bet you aren't disgusting."

"Let's talk about—"

"Let's talk about us," she said. "I like your moustache. Like William Powell. Kind of tickles when you do this…"

"Eightieth, bub," the driver said.

I got her out of the cab and pointed in the direction of her porch. I turned back to the taxi driver.

"Keep the motor running," I said.

He looked at me in surprise.

"I like 'em to be able to remember my name in the morning," I said.

He laughed, nodded. "I know what you mean, bub."

The harsh shadows her porch light cast did nothing for Carol Cole's looks. I was becoming painfully aware of the avalanche of seconds rolling over me as I slouched toward death. She was obviously upset, seeing that I had asked the taxi to wait. She reached up, kissing at my face, and as she did, rubbing her leg in between mine, swaying with her hips against me. The trouble always begins in the imagination, I thought.

"Don't you want to come in for a while?"

"No."

"But you—you feel like you do."

"I won't," I said.

"You don't find me attractive? Is that it?"

"No," I said. "I don't."

She had collapsed up against the outside wall. Her features screwed into each other in the center of her face. Crying is such an ugly thing. I will never understand why it has its pull, its own special kind of sensuality.

"I can't do anything right," she said.

"I don't think drunks are attractive," I explained. "It's not good like this. Some other time, maybe."

"No," she said. "I don't have other time. Please." She pulled herself up from the wall. "Just a drink. And some talk. I'll tell you, I—I'll tell you what it is you want to know. About Jack."

"One drink?" I said.

She managed to smile. She nodded. "One drink," she said.

"What's the matter, bub," the driver said after I told him to keep the five. "She remember your name?"

"Something like that."

"Hey, no offense, bub. May be a sin, but there's not many that'd walk away from a broad that hot, married or no. Not a looker like her."

"Yeah. She's the 'It' girl."

"Come to think of it, yeah," he said. "Looks like her. Besides, bub, I thought you Commies believed in free love."

I stared at him.

"Unlike the broad, I don't forget names. You don't even have to fuck me, Harker. I seen your picture in the paper."

"What of it?"

"Man. Cool it. I'm a fan of John Reed's, too."

I gave him a couple more bucks.

"Someday," I said.

"Yeah, comrade," he laughed. "Someday."

She had left the front door ajar, the door to her apartment unlocked, her street clothes lying where she had dropped them. She was wearing a loose-fitting robe, barely tied at the waist, her legs, sans hose, very white below. She had my drink in her hand.

"Something more comfortable," she said.

"I thought we agreed, one drink."

"That's it," she said. "One drink, and then…"

On the divan were piled nylon hose, slippers, camisoles, and bra. The rest of the place, too, was a mess, the wreck a binge makes in a typist's life.

"They say you Commies fuck good," she said. "Real good."

That night I came up with a new rule: Never make love out of pity. You might find yourself hating yourself instead of the other. Oh, she had been around. She probably knew how to treat you when it got soft and flaccid after the first time and how to stretch it out for herself the second time, like someone who understood ballet. But it would have been just fucking. She was insulted at first when I refused to do her, as she called it, and she talked about how she had laid awake nights thinking about me shot like that while Wilson and Haugen talked about me in her living room. I was so, so handsome, she said; she thought, what a waste, what a waste.

As she sulked, she watched the night out her window, the night that revealed a thousand sordid images of men, men like me, who had passed her amongst themselves like so much folded cash, the images of fucking that I imagined constituted her soul. Looking at her, still roughly attractive, I had a vision of the street outside, that the street would hardly understand in its cold, hard, asphalt blackness below a thick layer of ice. Ultimately, she talked, as she had promised, about what I wanted to hear, sitting along the bed's edge, clasping the yellow soles of her feet in the palms of both soiled hands.

"Yes, that little faggot came here the night you got shot. Larry was real mad at Jack for telling you boys that story about the war and the newspaper, so Jack just scooped Charlie up, run him home to Mommy when he started whining, then brought him back here for me to hide. And that pissed off Larry even more.

"Larry, he forgets things. He tells so many lies, you know, trying to make himself look good to people, he forgets he's not really a war hero or anything like that. But you have to know Larry, you know, not like a public figure or whatever, like a person, I guess, to see it doesn't matter that much. It's like he wants to be what he is and everything, but kinda off and on. Mostly he doesn't care that much about it as long as things are going okay right then. He sort of doesn't see tomorrow, you know? How things will work out, even when it's as plain as the nose on his face. After he left me, he wanted me to come back—this was a long time after he left—but he just wanted me to come back so he would have a wife to stand on platforms with him. No. That's not it. No, I mean, that's the reason. Not that he thought it would be good for a politician or whatever to have a wife—that takes too much planning. It was just that he couldn't picture himself standing up there without a wife. That's the way he had always seen other people do it, so it had to be like that. One day, it just hit him. He was thinking about it and he realized, hey, some woman has got to stand up there with me. Carol, maybe. Maybe she'll do it. After I said no, he even went back and asked his first wife. And the only reason he asked me first, probably, was that I looked more like the women he had pictured standing on platforms with their husbands than she did. It's funny: he's so dumb about things—about life, you know—that you don't even hold it against him.

"But not Jack. Jack is a bastard. Jack was real pissed at you for causing him trouble with Larry. He does not like Larry, but he needs him. You know that kind of person? It's very important who he knows and what people think about him? So, he blew his stack when you found out about him and that gangster. Jack was trying to keep that really secret. Jack is the kind that needs his clothes, you know. He kinda primps around, taking poses in the mirror, stuff like that. And let me tell you, he's okay in the sack, like most guys, I guess, but he's not anywhere near as good as he thinks he is. You got to tell him, though, how good he is, all the time, or he gets real moody. That's when he'd hit me, mostly, when I'd be pissed at him, and I wouldn't tell him that stuff, he'd get moody and smack me.

"He hated you because you were a quote 'stupid fucking Communist and a bad damn newspaperman who thought you were such hot shit' unquote. Then, I don't see him for a couple of days, but I have to keep feeding and babying good old Charlie while Jack was off wherever he was off at. And then when I do see him, all he can do is talk about how he's got you now and how everything is coming up roses and we're not going to have anything to worry about any more. And at some point, I see your picture in the paper and tell him, kind of teasing, kind of casual, you know, that I think you are pretty good-looking. Just teasing him, you know? And he hits the ceiling. He starts yelling at me that I had better not have a thing to do with you. If I ever talk to you, or anything, he'll kill me. He kept checking to make sure I don't plan to spill my guts about it all—him, Charlie, Larry—though I don't know what he thought I'd say. I don't know anything except Larry drinks a lot and doesn't think too much about what he says or does and wasn't much of a husband, when you get right down to it, though he's no worse than some, I guess, and he can be a great drinking pal.

"Charlie was still hiding out in here that day that Hoops came by and tried to talk to me when you were in the hospital. And when he tells Jack about it, Jack hits the ceiling again, especially when they figure out I used to make it sometimes with Hoops, and he starts calling me a whore and smacking me around. Then Charlie took off."

Very carefully, I asked, "Where did he go?"

"How should I know," she said. "Maybe down to Denise's in Iowa."

"The first Mrs. McKnight?"

"I think they said something about hiding him out on the farm, I don't know."

"So, the senator was in on it? On hiding him?"

She looked at me so blankly I felt guilty for asking her. Then she simply picked up her narrative. "Jack and me, we just been drinking together for a while, you know? Well, I was drinking, anyway. Jack does not drink much. A beer to be polite, you know? With him it's… Anyway, the times started getting longer we'd spend in here, just us.

I'd miss work. But he didn't like it when I left. He was afraid I'd meet people. Talk to them. Something like that. Then after Charlie took off, Jack just up and says it's over. Finished. He doesn't want to have anything to do with me. I'm just Larry's castoff cunt, he says. And I better realize that. And keep my mouth shut, if I knew what was good for me. He had friends. He must of said that a hundred times. He had friends. *Friends.* Hell. People who use him, that's all. The bastard. I been drinking ever since."

I did not sleep with her, I thought, but I am about to fuck her. Thanks to her, I might soon be able to put Wilson, Haugen, and McKnight together in a single sentence. So, I was using her, which made me like all the others who had fucked her. I got away by midnight. I reached Sharon's by half past. The trouble with just fucking of any kind is the toll it takes—the cost in words and time.

"Where have you been?" a worried Sharon asked when she saw the look on my face.

"You sound just like Kathy."

"Don't attack me, Randall. It was a simple question."

"Fucking somebody. What about you? I called all afternoon."

"Sometimes I can't tell when you're joking."

"I never joke."

I made us a couple of drinks.

"And where were you?" I asked.

"I had dinner with Sam. He wanted to tell me he thought I was in some danger being with you. I ought to stop seeing you, he said, at least for a while, before I hurt my reputation, and the museum's—"

"And let me guess, you should go back to him."

We sipped our drinks.

"I thought maybe you were in trouble again, that something had happened to you, when I didn't hear from you."

We sipped our drinks.

"They are trying to build a case," I said.

"A case for what"

"Subversion."

"Subversion?"

"Yes, Sharon. It means I notice things. I notice things like—

"Like what?"

"Like Endicott's got a lot of money."

"What's that supposed to mean?"

"It means you don't have to go drinking your life away in bars and fucking fat men for fun. It means you can enjoy your work and feel safe falling in love with relative strangers. It means you can turn to psychoanalysis rather than the bottle when a guy dumps you."

"That's unfair. You've been out with some... some... *woman*. And then you come back here and attack me for having dinner with Sam. It's unfair." Sharon refilled our empty glasses. "You don't know what I was like when Sam met me. You don't know. I was completely neurotic. I could hardly let a man touch me. Especially my face. The idea made me sick. I felt like an alien from some other world. And I was. Edward, when he came back from the war. He would—well, he tormented me, tormented me and told me to go run home to Daddy. And Daddy had approved of Edward to start with, so he was not going to change his mind now. If something was wrong, it had to be my fault. I was so confused I hardly left the house. In Lansing, I mean. Except to attend the art lectures."

"And Endicott helped?"

"More than Daddy's therapist. Sam gave me a job. He showed me I could do something on my own. He let me run the museum even when I made mistakes."

"So I fell for Sam Endicott's masterpiece, a woman who sleeps with stuffed animals, can't talk about herself, and cries when she thinks she's in love. All he gave you, honey, was an expensive shellacking."

"And you, of course, offer so much more."

I gave up the fight, went back to her den, sat down with the typewriter, and started pecking.

"Are you working?"

"I've got to have this done by tomorrow or Tuckerman's going to fire me."

"Randall. Please try to understand this and don't make more of it than it is. I—I need to be alone. Tonight. For a while—"

"Okay," I said. "But I'm sorry. Honestly, I did not sleep with anyone."

"Please, that doesn't change a thing. I—I've got to think things through. Please."

Morning came to consciousness as I sloshed across wet streets to work from my own apartment, the faint, stale smell of scotch pushing me on at five, almost six o'clock. My body ached, as if stretched tight across the slate gray skies fading behind city blocks. At eight, I turned in my next piece about McKnight for Tuckerman, who I imagined picking it up as he stuffed his pipe with short square fingers, his eyes assured of certain certainties, impatient to assume the world. On my way over, I had thought it looked like snow, again, and when I got the chance, I headed back home for a few hours' sleep.

16.

Before I got back to the office, Tuckerman—more or less avoiding me—left early. On my desk lay a written invitation, cold and formal, to his place for drinks and dinner. It was never good when the boss wanted to explain something, at length, over brandy in his study. It probably meant he had not liked the new McKnight piece, which came as no surprise, since I had written pretty much what Tuckerman had been telling me not to write—admitting I had once been a party member in preparation for documenting McKnight's twisting of the truth, just as he'd twisted the truth about his war record. I figured it was my one shot at pinning down reality before I got hauled off to Washington and paraded before Congress, or, worse, some federal court. I tried calling Sharon a few times at the Emerson, but the receptionist told me patiently each time Miss Parks was unavailable and asked over and over if I wished to leave a message. Hoops avoided me, too, keeping our talk trivial whenever our paths crossed.

I took a taxi to the far North Side, where the Old Man lived in the gentlemanly luxury becoming a Progressive publisher. His Italianate villa had been built in the 1830s on bluffs overlooking the river by one of the lumber barons who originally platted Capital City. For a time, before his grandfather bought the place, it had served as an elegant and discreet whorehouse run by a Madame Chouteau for the rivertrade moneymen. Dinner was well prepared, conversation with the family pleasant, Mrs. Tuckerman stridently charming. Afterward, he sent her and his daughters and their boyfriends and one husband all on their way in fine cars to a wonderful evening's entertainment at the symphony. We retired to the library, not to his study, for brandy and a smoke and for the moment of truth that was the point of his Olympian summons.

Tuckerman's library, like libraries everywhere, was filled with books. The difference, though, between the Old Man's library and mine was that his books—exquisite in their Moroccan-leather binding with gold-leaf lettering and tiny crimson tassels for bookmarks—sat on dark, wood shelves in specially built cases lining the wall. The Persian had a deep plush. The French doors opened onto a small patio looking down the bluffs. The scotch was sequestered in a Waterford decanter below an antique mahogany table adorned with a Tiffany lamp. I drank Chivas Regal. He drank Martel.

A large fireplace with a marble mantel neatly broke the line of books and shelves. Hanging above it, Tuckerman's grandfather, painted by a frontier artist in some atrocious shade of purple the textbooks might call mauve, looked hopelessly out of place and startled. Around about, here and there, were all those photographs and tabletop cigarette lighters and jade trinkets with which the rich love to clutter their lives. One of the pictures, I was surprised to discover, was an old sepia-toned oval rotogravure of Prince Albert Collette. Tuckerman saw me look at it and motioned with the wave of claw.

"Yes, Father took that," he said. "He became something of a goddamned good photographer in his days at the *News*."

"Don't tell me," I said. "You keep his darkroom intact. Just the way it was. Down in the cellar, the other end of the wine caskets."

He chose not to take offense. "You shouldn't resent someone's inheritance, Randall. It's unbecoming. I don't fool myself that any of this is essential to the good life, and certainly not a decent one, any more than you do."

"I don't think about it much."

"Jesus Christ, man. I met your father once or twice. You simply cannot pull that poor boy from the farm rubbish with me. He was a well-to-do Republican stockman, and you had things not unlike all this most of your life."

"He was a land-rich, cash-poor, middle-class suicide," I said descriptively and, I hoped, without either rancor or malice.

"Care for another drink?"

"Do you need to ask?"

When he finished the ritual of pouring, returning my glass, setting his down, looking for the lighter (in plain sight on the side table), lighting his pipe, and checking his watch, he picked up the photograph of Prince Albert and launched himself on his meandering journey toward the point.

"He was an admirable man," Tuckerman said. "He and my father worked together, like brothers, reforming the old Standpat Republican Party. It was dangerous then, too, Dell, to talk responsible social reform, with the anarchists and the ignorant immigrants, all those revolution-crying lunatics. But they did it. They did. And for thirty years we had responsible reform and clean government in this state. Good government. Progressive government. Socially constructive government. Intelligent government. Until—"

"I know," I said. "Power corrupts. Absolute power corrupts absolutely. I've heard it all. Want to get to the point? How about another?"

"You go ahead. I've had just about my quota." And when I had filled my glass, he said, "Come here. Sit down a minute. I'm an old man, Randall. And I'm not prepared to give up the *News*, not at my age. But I don't want you to jump ship on me, and I'm afraid you will when I tell you what I have to tell you. You are one goddamned fine newspaperman and a good city editor, regardless of your politics, but this has gotten beyond all that."

"What are you talking about?"

"Advertising, Randall. Money. Even my paper runs on money. The radio station, too, it runs on money. And I don't have the kind of money, personally, I need to keep it strictly a family concern anymore, I'm afraid. Someday, and someday soon, I'm going to have to go public to survive. You Communists—forgive me, Dell—you labor people have always had a very shaky notion of finance. How does Marx treat money?"

"As a commodity," I said, blankly.

"Well, I don't know about that. Maybe a *symbol* for the rest, for all commodities," Tuckerman said. "That's what he would have said, if he wasn't so damn afraid of idealism. This McKnight thing. It's starting to hurt us—in the pocketbook, I mean."

"You can't be serious."

"If it was just that, Randall … I don't know, I might fight it, despite the fact I feel old right now, too old to *really* fight change. The attorney general's office has dropped the proceedings against the senator. We are losing credibility with them."

"Damn Paul Toland," I said.

"It's not him. Not *only* him. And then there's this. I want you to look at this. They sent us galleys. It hits the stands next week."

He handed me galley proofs of *Time* magazine, folded to the "Press" section, and kept quiet as I read about the seventy-year-old firebrand muckraking owner of the *Capital News* in Capital City, Wapsipinicon, and his crack-reporter-cum-left-wing-ideolog city editor slinging mud at the state's incumbent junior senator and anti-Communist champion before this former war hero turned the tables on them.

When I sighed and set the pages down, Tuckerman said, "You've become an event, Randall. It's the worst thing that can happen to a reporter."

"Please, boss, just tell me what you are going to tell me. Let's get it over with. Stop it. No, don't go looking for a light. The lighter is right here. Now, tell me."

"I'm not going to run your piece on McKnight."

"I figured as much this morning when I saw your note."

"I'm not going to run any more articles on McKnight at all."

I stood and headed directly for the scotch. When I poured the drink, I poured him one, too. I handed him the glass.

"You've got to be out of your mind," I said.

"Listen to me, Dell. Listen to me. Before all this started, McKnight had only a slim chance of being renominated by his own party, and an even slimmer chance of being reelected. Now you can't walk into a shop in the city without hearing people talk about him. Because he has found an issue. Because he has made himself newsworthy. And every word we print, every denial we make, every time we run that egg-sucker's name in *my* paper, he gets more publicity."

"I—"

"No, don't interrupt me, Dell. I don't like it. I hate his ass. I hated him when he came sniffing around Prince Albert's camp back in the '30s. I told the Prince that little shits like McKnight were going to ruin the Republican Party he and my father built. And I've hated the man ever since."

"So," I said, "you had to go and pound him flat with your very own sledgehammer. And you made him famous instead."

"You think?" the Old Man said sarcastically. "Well, no more. Not another goddamned word, do you hear me?"

I waited until he had calmed down before I told him I was leaving, picked up the galleys, and headed for the front door and my coat and hat. When I got there, he stopped me, asked me what I planned to do. I said I planned to call a taxi. That's what I planned to do. And I planned to go home and write him that letter of resignation I had been promising off and on for years. Only this time I really planned to write it. And I planned to give it to him in the morning. And I planned to grant interviews to the press, any newspaper but the *News*. And I planned to tell them everything, everything I could think of at the moment. Just as I had always wanted to do, I said. I planned to fight this thing out my way, with the truth.

"Why?" he asked, looking at his pipe as if it were a gun he might use on himself after I left. "What's the use?"

"Because I don't like suicides," I said.

So I didn't write the resignation I promised him that night any more than I had written those I promised in the past, so what? Any idiot would have recognized the gig was up, and unless I did something very clever and did it fast, McKnight's attack would mean more than just my job.

I bought some Johnny Walker noir on the way home, and when I reached the apartment I noticed the silence that was always there these days amid the dust accumulating in Kathy's absence. I noticed again the dust becoming general all over the apartment, gently falling on each piece of furniture, falling gently on what was there and what was missing, drifting into my life. I could calculate the time by the number of concentric circles my drinking glass left in the dust on the table as I waited for Sharon to return my calls. I poured myself another shot of scotch, lit up a smoke, spread out the galley proofs Tuckerman had handed me, and read a little *Time*.

MUD FOR THE MUDSLINGERS

John Matthew Tuckerman, 70, the firebrand, muckraking owner of the successful (circ. 40,181) *Capital News* of Capital City, Wapsipinicon, likes tough, independent reporters who are not afraid to talk back to him. Reporter Randall Harker, 35, had measured up to the boss's standard almost too well. In his fifteen years on Tuckerman's staff, Harker had earned a reputation as a crack reporter by such stunts as storming into tough gambling joints one jump ahead of raiding policemen. Reckless, hard-drinking Reporter Harker had also earned a left-wing reputation as a local CIO official who had faithfully followed the Communist Party line.

In 1940, when "Crazy John" Tuckerman was an interventionist and Communists were not, "Red Randall" Harker publicly denounced his boss as a warmonger. Editor Tuckerman denounced back, and later in an open letter to the CIO, he called Reporter Harker "the Communist leader in Capital City," and added, "I defy him to publicly deny it." Though Harker did not deny it, Tuckerman did not fire him. In 1948, he promoted him to city editor.

Finished with the drink, I placed it carefully over a circle I had already made in the dust, put down the typeset pages, and decided to scramble a couple of eggs. I mixed another scotch with the eggs.

Rubbed noses. Both Editor Tuckerman and Rebel Harker saw eye to eye on one thing. They had no use for Wapsipinicon's Senator Lawrence McKnight, an ex-army captain who, in 1946, had followed Tuckerman's good friend, Senator Albert J. Collette, into office after the "Prince," as he was known to the state's pundits, died in late 1945.

In 1947 Harker dug up, and Tuckerman delightedly splashed across his front page, the fact that McKnight had been compelled to fork over $3,500 in back income taxes on stock market profits when the Treasury disallowed some of his deductions.

More recently, and more potentially damaging to the senator's political fortunes, the dynamic duo accused him of misleading voters about his war record, a charge Senator McKnight's bright young chief aid, Daniel ("Slick") Freeman, categorically rejects. "Senator McKnight's bravery under fire

during the Second World War is a well-established fact, beyond dispute," states Freeman.

As usual, *Time* sort of had the facts and almost had them right. They
still had McKnight a captain instead of the corporal we knew him to
be. It was Collette's son, of course, McKnight defeated, not the Prince
himself. He had kicked the bucket between the wars, and his son was
first appointed by the legislature to replace him. I took a breather to
get a new pack of Camels and thought about calling Sharon before I
fired the fag, but I went back to magazine.

> **Skinned knuckles.** Last week, it was Senator McKnight's
> turn to rub Tuckerman and Harker's noses in some old muck
> of their own raking. To 400 editors of Wapsipinicon daily and
> weekly newspapers, McKnight sent a blistering letter charging
> Tuckerman's paper with continuously parroting the *Daily
> Worker* and asking whether it was not "the Red Mouthpiece
> for the Communist Party" in Wapsipinicon. He cited Tuck-
> erman's own 1941 accusation that Harker, now city editor for
> the paper, was a Communist and added: "There is nothing in
> his writing [to] indicate he has in any way changed his atti-
> tude."
>
> Harker denied last week that he was any longer a Communist
> and threatened to sue McKnight. Editor-in-Chief Tuckerman
> snorted that McKnight was simply getting ready for his 1952
> reelection campaign by attacking his No. 1 newspaper critic.
> Commented Wapsipinicon's biggest daily, the conservative
> *Ravensport Journal* (circ. 319,126): "We have a feeling that no
> one will take Senator McKnight's question very seriously. Po-
> litically, he'd probably do a lot better charging Mr. Tuckerman
> with being what he is—a capitalist. It would probably make
> Mr. Tuckerman a lot madder."

Funny guys, this is great fun.

> **Save a few.** But there are indeed a few people who are tak-
> ing Senator McKnight's charges seriously. J. Edgar Hoover,
> director of the FBI, expressed an interest in the case and

is rumored to have dispatched an agent or two to the Mid-western state to investigate the allegations. Members of the House Un-American Activities Committee (HUAC) admitted to reporters they would like to have the chance to discuss the senator's charges with either Mr. Tuckerman or "Red Randall" himself.

In a series of wild countercharges, the *Capital News* has attempted to embroil the senator in a local scandal with a Capital City mobster. Senator McKnight's office dismisses Tuckerman and Harker's new accusation as well. But others, who point to Harker's key role in the recent and violent labor unrest in the city, are not so nonchalant. Says "Slick" Freeman: "We knew when we started there was a certain amount of risk involved in dealing with an unsavory character like Randall Harker. If it comes down to threats on the senator's person, we will not flinch from our duty as Americans."

That's when I noticed the package. Sitting on the small lamp table behind the old loveseat, just inside the door, it was bright blue, about the size of a book, and wrapped in gold ribbon. There was a note attached to the top with tape. I had not noticed it when I came in. I tried to remember if I had turned on the lights then or later, when I started to read. Had I left the door unlocked? Could somebody have put it there while I was in the kitchen? I was suddenly cold sober. I imagined I could hear the ticking halfway across the room, but I probably rushed to put it there, the way you do in a dream, because I heard it when I picked the package off the table. Depending on the charge they used, I thought grimly—with an odd detachment—it could take the whole apartment with it. Gingerly, I pulled the white note free of the wrapping. It read:

Randall,
If I were to write all day I could never express myself as well as Henry James can for me, "Why, why have I made this evening such a point... There comes a day when something snaps, when the full cup, filled to the very brim, begins to flow over. That's what has happened to my need for you—the cup,

all day, has been too full to carry. So here I am with it, spilling over you—and just for that reason that is the reason of my life. After all, I've scarcely to explain that there are some hours which I know when they come because they almost frighten me that show me I'm even more so."

Every hour I spend with you, Randall, is such an hour. Today, something snapped, and I have so much I want to tell you, no more holding back.

I meant to give this to you at Christmas, but now, the way things have happened, sometimes I'm afraid there will not even be a Christmas. So, take it now and let it mark the time till "this is over" and you can be with me. Just me.

I love you,

Sharon

P.S. I quit my job today. Please call me when you open this.

Inside the package, stuffed with paper, I found a gold watch on a chain. I thought about Paul Toland and Janet and his three-piece suits, but it comes too late for me to try for distinguished. More than that, I was alive and my palms had stopped sweating, and I knew why she had not phoned this evening—she was waiting for me to call her.

I checked the time on my brand-new gold watch: 11:30. I felt on top of the world as I dialed Sharon's number.

"First off, I love you," I said.

"That's nice, honey," she said. "That's very nice. I love you, too."

"I got your package."

"Your landlord let me in. He seemed very pleasant."

"You walked out on Endicott?"

"Half walked out, half got pushed out," she said. "He kept going on about those men, the ones I told you about, the FBI agents. When he threatened me with my job, I quit on the spot. He's been calling all afternoon, and a couple of times earlier this evening, but I hung up on him. I knew this was you. It's too late for him to call. He's with his wife."

And as she talked, I realized what was wrong with my little meeting at Tuckerman's, why he was suddenly so eager to kill my copy. It wasn't just the *Time* piece. That was only the tip of the spear. Hoover's boys had talked to the Old Man, too.

"Did Mr. Shaunessy reach you?" Sharon asked

"Who?"

"Mr. Shaunessy. That's his name, isn't it? The big Irish policeman you introduced me to at the hospital? Captain Shaunessy?"

"Wait, wait," I said. "I'll be right back."

"*Randall.*"

I stuck my head under cold tap water in the kitchen sink. Never believe anything like that does you any good. It only causes more discomfort. Now I felt drunk *and* cold.

"Let's take it from the top," I said, "Shaunessy called you, too?"

"Yes. Because he couldn't reach you. He telephoned twice. He said it was very important. I told him I thought you might still be at Mr. Tuckerman's, that you had left a message for me you were having dinner with him."

"What did Shaunessy want?"

"He wouldn't say. Randall, what is going on?"

I could hear the worry in her voice, and why not? She was alone at twenty-eight and unemployed, and her new boyfriend was both an un-happily married man and a social outcast. Tuckerman was right. This had become a story about me. Why didn't Shaunessy call again? Then I realized I had been back for only half an hour, maybe forty-five minutes.

"Sharon," I said, "I have to get off. I don't want to. We have a lot to talk about, you and I, but right now I need to free up the line in case Shaunessy is still trying to reach me. After I see what he wants, I'll call you back."

"I thought something had happened to you," she said.

"Nothing has happened that I can't handle," I lied. "Just relax. Find something to read. Relax. Read. Read some more James."

"Henry James?"

"Right. Read that. Relax. I'll call you back."

"Who can read Henry James on a night like this?"

A quarter hour later the telephone rang, and I heard Shaunessy's familiar lilt. "Home from your wanderings at last?" he asked.

Only no faithful Penelope awaited my return, I thought. "This had better be good, Shaunessy," I said.

"Good may be a stretch, Randy Dell. Interesting, more like. You see, I have got my man."

"Wilson, you've found Wilson."

"Better, I'm sitting next to young Charlie. At the bar in a dump called the Spotted Horse Inn—"

"I know the place," I said.

"Capital," he said, "because you need to amble on down here. The bonny lad wants to talk to you, and I think you should attend."

I told him I'd be there, changed my clothes, washed my face again, and brushed my teeth. On my way out, the telephone began ringing. I figured it was my Circe calling me back, but I could not bring myself to answer the call just yet.

17.

For some reason, I associated Kid Guthrie and his hipster pals with the old prewar Weimar Republic's smoky underground excesses, and I hadn't truly registered just how strange our town had grown since the days I had trolled its dives and dark alleys during college. Take the Spotted Horse Inn. It began life in a featureless, turn-of-the-century, two-story yellow-brick office building also housing a car dealership and a couple of shysters and stuck in the middle of downtown, up the street from the *News* and not far from campus. Catering initially to parents checking out their kids' progress at school, it proved too tasteless even for these old homebodies. Already in my day, it had become a joint where we drank and—if we had enough cash and a little charm—rented one of its second-floor rooms for weekend sex with willing girls. Now, the inn remained, but the automobile showroom was gone and the lawyers, too, replaced by a lounge for locals full of beats like Guthrie and queers like Wilson, all of them wearing black and looking dreary. In the lounge, a jazz trio played blue notes, and Wilson sat at the bar next to Shaunessy.

"His mother called," Shaunessy said as I sat down. "Said he was giving himself up but he wanted to talk to you. I told her I did not answer to rich old broads with expensive mouthpieces and troublesome offspring. Few hours later, I get a call from upstairs letting me who it was, in fact, I truly worked for—"

I started to interrupt, but he held up his finger. "Let me finish, Randy Dell. I should have figured I was done for when I realized she knew to call me, the local constabulary messenger boy." He took a bitter pause, then he continued, "Here's the deal. You listen to what he's got to say, and you decide. If you want me to pursue it, my pal, fuck 'em all, I'll plunk this piece of shit in a cold cell and let hell begin to howl. We're here because this is where he wanted to meet you. I had him on ice most of the night at the precinct and he's said nary a word, the smart little bugger. Now I'm heading to the diner across

229

the street—this place gives me the fucking heebie-jeebies—and, when you've finished your palaver with junior here, bring him along and we'll see where we all stand."

Not a man in the place other than me watched Shaunessy walk out, though every one of them knew he had left, and the drinkers' din immediately grew louder. I looked at Wilson, who had been fidgeting on his barstool as Shaunessy talked, but now seemed to have settled down some. Still, he wouldn't look me in the eye. He gestured toward my shoulder with his head. "Is it … damaged?"

"Not permanently," I said. "The quacks say it may always ache in bad weather."

"Since Okinawa," he said, "I get these rages."

"Your momma told me."

"Come on like thunderstorms. Most last a few minutes, some of them hours, one or two a few days. Then the vertigo hits and I get sick, like I have the flu. The VA doctors say it was the head wound as much as my nerves, sort of a spasm, a vasso-spasm, like a migraine, they said."

"Okay," I said, sarcastically enough. "I get it. You couldn't help yourself. Let's move on with it."

He sighed, looked away. "C-could we take a booth? I don't like sitting at the bar like this." When I just looked at him, he added, "You can't see it because you're not one of us, but people are watching everything we do."

I grabbed up my coat. As we made our way back to a booth away from the band and the bar, a young man casually dressed in a seaman's sweater and blue jeans stopped Wilson with a touch to his arm and asked, "Are you all right, Charlie?"

"I'm fine," Wilson replied. "It's okay. Really."

Wilson tossed his double-breasted empire coat up against the side of the booth and sat down across from me. Maybe it was the light or the hour, but the thing no longer looked so pretentious to me, just big and warm. Something about the interchange between Wilson and his friend sparked my reporter's itch, and I found myself instinctively and irresistibly asking Wilson a background question. "Okinawa?"

"Yeah, Harker," he said, and for the first time tonight I saw the kind of anger—all aggressive arrogance and condescension—that had made me dislike him when he reported to me. "Us pansies actually become soldiers, too, sometimes, like everybody else. Shoot people. Get shot." Then he remembered who he was talking to and shut up.

"I'm not making fun of you," I said.

"It'd be the first time," he said.

"What happened over there?"

"To make me the way I am?" he mocked. When I didn't say anything, he calmed down some. "War happened," he said. "Jungle rot and tropical fever and the island shits and fucking snakes dropping from the trees."

"Snakes?"

"Yeah. Big brown ones. Five feet long. Jump the length of their body and more. Japs called them Habu or Kufau, I never could get it straight. Very poisonous. Deadly. Nights when I wake up spinning, I'm mostly dreaming about the snakes leaping down on my shoulders and I'm turning and jerking, trying to throw them off."

For the first time since I met him three or four years ago, Charles Wilson did not seem to be either whining or complaining. He seemed indifferent, abstracted. And oddly, his pitted face no longer looked petulant, like the acne-ridden teenager his mother had described, but rugged, the way his dad seemed to have struck folks.

"What's your tie to Jack Haugen?"

He looked at me for a while before he replied. "I fell in love with him. I met him the first time after the war at the VA hospital in Chicago. I was there for combat fatigue, which is what they thought was wrong with me back then, and he was there trying to go cold turkey from a heroin habit he'd picked up in Berlin. We clicked, I thought, and when I discovered he was coming out here to work, I had hopes, especially after Mother found me the job with Old Man Tuckerman. But Jack broke my heart."

I was alone in a crowd of aliens. It was late, and the trio packed up its gear while the atmosphere in the joint, filled now as far as I could tell solely with men, was changing. The talk in the booths and around the tables and at the bar grew more intense, and I noticed shoulders being touched, and faces. One fellow leaned over and kissed the guy sitting next to him. The scene resembled exactly every bar I had ever been in near last call, except there was nobody here I could imagine taking home with me. I suddenly realized why Wilson chose this place to meet. It was a place where he felt more at ease, a place where he felt he might belong, a place where he felt less a stranger.

"You mean with Carol Cole," I said, and he laughed out loud.

"You," he said. "You…guys. You always think women threaten us, or something. Carol Cole is the warm spot where he parks his dick some winter nights." It struck me as probably the most demeaning thing I'd ever heard anybody say about a woman but, God forgive me, I understood it. "No," he went on. "In fact, we were there, together, at her place. I was in a bad way, enraged and twitchy, you know, like I am, and Jack was trying to calm me down. Afterward…Jack hustled me out of there, down to Mother's, set things up."

"Took you to Iowa."

He looked surprised. "What—?"

"Carol Cole said she thought they took you down there to Mrs. McKnight's."

"When did you talk to her?"

"Yesterday."

Wilson laughed again. "That's a good one. Shows you what she knows. She has quite the imagination. They—McKnight and Jack parked me with the FBI, Harker."

"FBI?"

"Yeah," he laughed. "They were going to deliver me to testify in D.C. about how you are such a Red, and always have been, when they dragged you before McKnight's subcommittee. That's how this whole thing got started. Me and Jack used to swap info, you know, like reporters do. I'd give him an insider's look at Tuckerman's rag, he'd tell me about the senator's political plans and his doings with the unions. All that stuff about you McKnight said in his speech? That came from me—shit I picked up around the office, stories I heard people tell. Everybody talks about you, you know, you and the Old Man, all the bickering over the years, you busting up that poker game, your being such a pal of Vlad Paddy. Bunch of them at the *News* dislike you even more than I do. Makes me sick, sometimes, thinking how a jerk like you stayed home, bad-mouthing the war effort all the time me and my buddies were fighting the Germans and the Japs." Once again, Wilson visibly took control of himself, fighting back a burst of anger. "But I was learning the business from you," he said. "That's what I told myself. And, to tell the truth, sometimes I even admired you, you know, the way I hated and admired my father. No question, I wanted your approval."

"That why you are here?" I asked quietly. When he shot me another of his flashes of ire, I quickly added, "How did Jack break your heart?"

"He betrayed me. He led me to believe our time, you know, *our time* had come. Soon as I testified and got myself out of this mess, he promised, there'd be time for us. Then, well—then, I talked to Mother long distance. And she said you had been to see her. And she started reading me the shit Jack had been writing in the *Times*, stuff they'd been careful to keep me from seeing. I flipped out—big rage this time—and took off back home, despite the mess the special agents said I was making for myself."

"So what are you peddling?" I asked. He looked at me. "Oh, give me a break," I said. "You wouldn't be here if you weren't selling out somebody."

"Last call," the bartender said, picking up Wilson's beer and wiping down the table. It was then I realized I hadn't even ordered a drink.

"Another of these," Wilson said.

"Nothing for me," I added.

When the bartender was gone, Wilson said, "I want free altogether. Not only did you not see me when you got shot, you know for a fact it wasn't me. That's what you tell your Mick cop pal."

I thought about it, then I nodded.

"Freeman," he said. "Slick. McKnight's aide?"

I nodded my head again.

"He's one of us."

I looked at the bar, at the five or six guys gulping their last drink, all of them more and more openly eyeing our booth.

"I have been a newspaperman a lot longer than I was ever a Commie, Wilson. I'm going to need sources, proof, something."

He smiled at me, I swear, coyly. He reached over and grabbed his coat and fooled around in its double-breasted folds and pulled out an eight-by-ten glossy creased in half and spread it out on the table between us. "I used to work for you, remember," he said. "I always get art." The picture was of Freeman and a young kid, late teens, maybe older, sitting in one of the booths here, his arm resting on the boy. Nothing dirty, really, that you could point to, but you knew just looking at the photo what was up between them.

"There's more," he said, plopping down a proof sheet and a half-dozen strips of 35mm negatives in glassine envelopes. Some of these were much more salacious images, shot inside what looked like a motel room in weak light.

"Where—"

"Upstairs," he said.

"Who's the kid?"

"A hustler. Passing through. Already gone."

"Who's the photographer?"

"I don't think I'm going to tell you that."

"They will come after you, you know," I said.

"And do what?" he said. "Expose me? Shoot me? It'd just make it worse for them. Besides, how will they even know where you got these unless you tell them?" He glanced at the boys at the bar, then asked impatiently, "So?"

As I looked down at the glossy, then across at him again, the lights in the place came up full blast, and the bartender set Wilson's beer down. I instinctively turned the photo face down, and he said, "Drink up. Time to go, Charlie."

I folded the photo again and put it inside my coat, sticking the negatives in one side pocket and the proofs in the other.

"You heard the man," I said. "Charlie."

We found Shaunessy with a patrolman waiting dutifully at the diner, a place called Packey's. Mike looked up at me, then at Wilson, and asked, "Well?"

"Cut him loose," I said

Sitting by the window, Shaunessy shoved aside an empty cup of coffee and an ashtray filled with cigar butts and said to the patrolman,

"Take him back to the precinct and process the paper. Make sure he signs a waiver we didn't smack him around." Then, looking at Wilson, he added, "Now get this piece of shit out of here."

When the policeman stood up, Shaunessy said, "This is our man, Harker. Harker, Patrolman Doolin."

"Mr. Harker."

"Nice to meet you."

I filled his space in the booth, and when they had gone, Mike said to me, "You sure about this Randy Dell? We got the little fairy's great big gun, and the ballistics are gonna match its bullets to the one we dug out of the lobby wall."

"I'm sure," I said.

"So who'd he finger as queer—McKnight?"

I did my best to keep a poker face. Of course, Mike would figure it out. He was a corrupt enough cop, but a good detective. "Naw," I said. "Freeman, the slick sidekick." And I showed him the pictures. I watched him catalogue the information in the rogue's gallery he kept inside his noggin.

"You'll print these?" he asked.

I shrugged. "Tuckerman says we're finished with attacking Mc-Knight, but that was before we had anything like this."

"Okay," he said. "I'm out of it as of right now." He thought about it some more and said, "If they get tough, though, or if Lefty Mills comes after you, anything like that, let me know, I'll see what I can do." Then, after another pause, he asked, "The little poof took these?"

I laughed. "I was wrong about him," I said with some admiration. "He may be light in the loafers, but he could make one hell of a newspaper man one day. He's smarter than he looks, he's dogged, and he's got grit."

Captain Shaunessy stared at me as if I'd lost my mind.

18.

The city room was dark, a matter of empty desks and piled papers. One of the office boys moved about picking up, removing, and returning things in the silent gloom. I hooked my mug from its place in the neat row of cups fronting the coffee urn, waved back to the kid when he lifted his hand to me on the way into the elevator, trash can in tow, and I grabbed the bottle of scotch in the bottom drawer of my desk. I poured a splash, invaded Tuckerman's vacant office and raided his icebox for a few cubes. I knew I should have invited Shaunessy up for a nip, street courtesy, but I was weary from the effort it took to control my hands, which shook badly enough to make lighting a Camel a chore. Drink complete, I sought my rude office along the far wall, ferreted out some typing paper, checked the time on the end of my chain, and dialed Sharon's number.

She, too, had spent the night sleepless.

She felt fine about quitting her job.

She was worried when I didn't call back, and she was curious where I had been and what I had done.

I told her.

I promised to meet her later this evening.

Around five-thirty, Dyers would be the first to arrive. I wanted to talk to him, before I faced the Old Man, but luck might need to flow my way for it to happen. I typed a short, concise resignation letter, did not date it, Hancocked the bottom, stowed it in a clean white envelope, scribbled the Old Man's moniker across it, and tucked it away in the wool jacket I draped over the back of my chair.

The fire-exit door swung open. Dyers, sleeves already rolled for work, strolled in. He always used the stairs, never the elevator, thoroughly unmodern Bill. He peered through the gloom, smiled, grabbed his cup on his way over, extending it toward me as he reached my desk.

"What we celebrating?" he asked. "The Old Man killing your piece on McKnight?"

I poured him some watered scotch from my mug. He held up his forefinger and thumb, close together, then showed me his palm.

"You look beat. What we celebrating?"

Leaning back in my chair, I rested wet shoes atop my desk and sipped my morning pick-me-up. "Now, that, William, is precisely the thing I wish to discuss with you."

By six-thirty, after a bit of haggling, he had the front page to me. He refused to run the dummy on the web because of the costs, but he made it up on a handbill letterpress we used for makeready ads and special features we could run any time we could slip them in. He warned me that if Tuckerman ever—ever—caught wind of it, he'd kill me himself. The head on the fake front page screamed: **SENATOR'S AIDE CAUGHT IN LOVE NEST WITH TEENAGE BOY.**

We washed out our cups and filled them again, this time with coffee.

"To Charles Wilson," Dyers said, lifting his cup.

"To Charles Wilson," I said. "Fellow reporter."

The lights came on. Lillian, good old dependable Lillian, who answered my phones and weeded my mail—and, when I was especially nice to her for more than two days in a row in any given year, did my income tax returns for free—hung up her coat, patted her white bunned hair into place, looked at us, and said, "I see you've decided to start keeping regular hours again."

Dyers laughed. Before he left to go back downstairs, Bill waited out Lillian's scrutiny, and, when she moved far enough away, he said, "I don't know what you're pulling, Dell, and I don't wanna know, but I take it I keep my mouth shut?"

"Buttoned tight."

He contemplated the dregs of his coffee cup. Our office pot always left grinds in the bottom. "I know you didn't like him, Wilson, but I never saw that much…wrong with him, you know?" I shrugged. "The Old Man," Dyers went on, "he acts like he never heard of Wilson, like he was not sure how or why he hired him, but he—well, he told me he felt kind of responsible for the boy, even though he knew there was nothing you could do for sick people. He thought it wasn't worth taking up with you when you fired him. Now maybe he should know."

"Not now," I said. "Maybe in a day or two. Not now."

"I don't like it. I don't like it at all. This is wrong. No matter what they are saying about you, Dell, we can't print this kind of stuff, and you know it. I don't want this coming back to haunt me, understand."

"It won't," I promised.

"Remember that, Dell. Be sure you remember that."

At eight o'clock the line of cups had disappeared from in front of the coffee pot. Typewriters clacked. Phones rang. People buzzed in and out. Tuckerman, dapper and spry, dragged me with him into his office as he passed by my desk at five past eight.

"What's going on?" he demanded. "Close the door."

"Larry McKnight's making his bid for reelection," I said. "He's a slithering no-good bastard. Worse than that, he never does a god-damned thing."

"You've got a perverse sense of humor, you know that, Randall."

"Yeah," I said. "Lunatic right-wingers put me into stitches."

"Stop it. Damn it, man. You know very well what I am talking about. Why am I being called at all hours of the night by detectives from the homicide squad and questioned about the whereabouts of my infamous city editor?"

"Oh, that," I said. I laughed as effectively as I could for five seconds or so. "That's a funny one. Sorry, just my perverse sense of humor. Seems Shaunessy found young Charles Wilson. The FBI were babysitting him for McKnight."

"The FBI?"

"But you know the FBI," I said. "They won't tell us anything about it unless it involves gunning down a couple of country boys for the glory of it. But what am I thinking? You know exactly how the FBI are."

"What do you mean?"

"Sorry," I said. "Maybe I'm wrong." I looked at him.

He glared back then began searching for matches. So I was right. John Matthew Tuckerman, firebrand socialist editor and mighty muckraker, had found the vital center of old age with a bit of help from the moralizing agents of the only Hoover who mattered these days.

"Harker, I…damn it. I told you. No more McKnight. Now, do you work for this paper or don't you? Are you planning to be at the staff meeting today for a change?"

❧

When Hoops came in, I dragged him into the restroom for a private chat.

"Where is McKnight staying?" I said. "Does he own a place here? Stay with friends? Or did he take a room in a hotel, what? There's no mention of it anywhere, and no one at his official digs is talking."

"Freeman likes to control the press. I thought the Old Man ordered you off McKnight? I'm sure he doesn't want me—"

"Hoops, it won't work. Standing between us—me and the Old Man—anymore. When you were pretending to like me, it wasn't so obvious, but if you want to make city editor, you'll only get there if I decide not to come down too hard on you before the opportunity you've so patiently awaited arises—know what I mean?"

"He's staying at the Ritz," Hoops said. "Under Freeman's name. They are careful. They have to be, the way they run high-class hookers in and out. The Hamilton, McKnight's official 'digs' as you so colorfully put it, is more like campaign headquarters. I doubt you even tried them there, but if you did, and if they gave you the political vagaries, like you say, that's why. Now, anything else, Massah? Shoeshine? Towel?"

"No. Staff meeting at ten. Tuckerman plans to stick you on Toland. Paul doesn't know it yet, but he's about to tell us earlier than he wants to tell us of his soon-to-be-announced candidacy for the senate. Just to keep things even steven between us, I'll tell you where he'll be if he tries to duck you. Him and his new political manager, Bob Weaver. You can catch them both eventually at a place called the Lewis and Clark. It's not Paul's kind of joint, but Weaver likes it, and that makes it perfect for dodging fat, lazy, ambitious reporters like you. If you have to do any arm twisting to get them to admit it, you can mention Janice told us, but it would be better for everyone if it didn't come to that."

"Janice?"

"Paul's daytime secretary, nighttime teddy bear, and newly intend-ed."

"You have a way with the ladies, don't you, Randy?"

"Aw, shut up, Hoops."

"Especially the women who run with your pals."

"From now on, Fatty, talk to me only when it's absolutely necessary. Otherwise, don't event grunt in my direction."

"Fine," he rasped. "Fucking fine with me."

"And I don't want to hear you've been running me down to the people I know ever again—like with Tommy Rojack. Now, get out of here before I belt your doughboy pug." He glared at me. He turned away toward the door. The toilets lay behind us. "Don't worry," I said. "You'll be city editor one day soon. You were born to the job."

He made ironic porcine grunting noises.

"Things will be getting back to normal around here," Tuckerman said. "From now on city editors will act like city editors and sit at their desks, city editing. Not running around the streets getting shot in the back or hiding out avoiding reporters from national magazines or driving prominent citizens crazy. Crime reporters will act like crime reporters, reporting crime. Not sitting around at their desks, acting like city editors. Managing editors will manage production and make sure the paper hits the stands. Political reporters will report politics. Is that perfectly clear?"

These meetings, with all of us spread out uncomfortably around Tuckerman's office, were usually informal, necessary, and boring. This one was tense, necessary, and boring. No one said anything when the Old Man paused. We all felt a little like children.

"Where do we put the FBI?" Dyers piped up at last.

"In the restrooms flushing toilets," Gene Gibson said.

We all laughed, Tuckerman included.

"I realize," Tuckerman said, flipping off his smile, a mechanical thing at best. "I realize I am partly to blame for what has been going on here. My dislike of Senator McKnight, no secret to any of you, has blinded me to the essentials of putting out a newspaper—printing the news, as it happens, when it happens, not before, not after it happens. We'll leave that kind of thing for the secret novelists on our staff to work on in their spare time, if they have any."

Nobody knows where to set his eyes when one of his own kind is being humiliated, so no one in the room noticed I was smiling at Tuckerman and wearing my sports jacket as if I planned to leave right after the meeting.

"For right now," Tuckerman said, "we have a couple of new stories working that require us to do a little shuffling. Hoops, you're headed for city hall."

Hoops listened while Tuckerman explained the assignment I had already told him about in the bathroom. Then Tuckerman turned the details over to me. I told Hoops a version of what I had already told him earlier, cleaned up for public consumption.

"Now," Tuckerman said. "We get to this wave of labor trouble that may or may not be connected to McKnight and to Mr. Harker, here. From now on the senator is a senator. If there is something newsworthy about him, we print it. If not, we don't."

I caught myself half-consciously patting the letter I had written that morning through my jacket and thinking, Well, if it has to be now, it has to be now, when Tuckerman looked at me, paused, and took a long draw on his pipe. We seemed to know, both of us, exactly what each was thinking.

"But things are not completely back to normal, whatever I say," he said, "and, as I said, that's my fault, not any of yours, not Dell's for sure. Dell knows a couple of the major players, Vlad Paddy and Tommy Rojack, in this recent labor strife very well, and there is the chance they will talk to him when they might not talk to others. So, for one more day we are going to do without our city editor and hope that the story he comes back with is worth the disruption—that it is something substantial, that it is a scoop." So Tuckerman had bought my excuse, the one I had given him so I could do what I had to do today. "That's all on that," he said. "Dell, you better get started. The rest of you, let's finish the meeting and get back to the business at hand. Tell me what you've got, Jones…"

19.

I caught a taxi to the Ritz. The too-plush lobby was filled with the desultory midday lounge lizards who smoked, leered, yawned, played chess, gossiped, and read under overwrought capitals topping marble columns. I used some hotel stationery, salmon pink, to scribble a note: "Tomorrow's front page. We should talk. I'm in the lobby and dying for a drink. Comrade Harker." I folded it inside the bogus spread I got Dyers to print up for me, put it all in a cute square envelope, and wrote across the outside: *Senator McKnight.* I found a cocky bellboy and gave him the package.

"Deliver it," I said. "To the right room. Freeman."

"We don't have a McKnight staying here, Dad," he said. "Hell, buddy, we don't even have a senator staying here. Mr. Freeman is a young executive for Spalding." I gave him cash. "Well," he said. "He's not much of a senator. Do I wait for an answer or drift after delivery?"

"Don't waste time hanging around being haughty to them," I said. "Find some place to spend your windfall profits."

"I'm already in bed with the girl, friend."

I tried to lounge, but I looked all wrong for the spot. Hardly was the randy hotel hop out of sight when I found myself face to face with another Ritz employee, this one in civilian clothes, struggling through life with a pugnacious mug and eyes that would never make love to anyone. All he needed was a small printed tag clipped to his shirt that read *Hotel Dick* to satisfy even the staunchest phenomenologist that everything was as it seems. "Wrong mode, pal," he said.

"Let me guess," I said. "You're a musician."

"You want the Starlite Motel. Edge of town."

"I've got business with one of the guests."

"And I drive a Rolls Bentley. Scoot. Or buy a tux and a ticket to the opera."

I gave him the money. "I see you saw me jawing with Rudolph Valentino's kid brother," I said.

242

"Everything costs in this world, pal. Even just occupying space. Hell, try taking a leak here, see what happens to your expense account."

"I'll hold it," I said. I would have continued our philosophical investigation of the Tough Guy's New Economic Policy, but just then the elevator doors slid open and Slick Danny Freeman stepped out. He had the eyes of a poet and a voice that competed with his silk tie for smoothness. His teeth were the last perfect expressions of beauty in postwar America, and the smile he laced around them was the phoniest attempt to do good since Prohibition.

"The famous Red Randall," he said. "We met formally the other night at the memorial auditorium. Let's put it this way, we were both introduced."

"Yes," I said. "I'm afraid we didn't have much time to chat then; I was rather in a hurry. Also, I didn't have as much to say."

He laughed, damn it, genuinely. "The senator awaits," he said. "Let's say he's a'tremble with expectation."

"But not you," I said.

"No," he smiled. "Not me. I always look on the bright side. The fact that your front page comes to us through a bellhop rather than a newspaper delivery boy seems to me a good sign. It seems to me a sign that we might have something constructive to talk about. Shall we join His Nibs?"

"You're good," I said on the way to the elevator. "If I had a limp-wristed kid brother instead of a sexy little sister, I'd certainly want to introduce the two of you."

He laughed genuinely again, and with good humor, let me step into the elevator first. "To save us all a lot of time," he said, still chuckling some, "I'll simply tell you straightforwardly. The senator knows all about my interest in…promising young men. It's not a problem for him."

"Oh?" I said. "I didn't realize our talk was going to be about sex and our private lives. I thought our meeting was about publicity and elections."

He never broke stride from elevator to second-floor suite, and his smile, lighting the hall, never even flickered.

❧

McKnight was wrapped in a wine-colored silk smoking jacket; naked underneath, he had surprisingly scrawny, dark-haired legs sticking out below a rotund and pasty body. More than one string of greasy black hair dangled in front of his eyes, eyes red-rimmed from drinking around green centers made intense by contrast. His face was bloated by alcohol and he held an absurdly tall glass filled with scotch cut the color of piss. Sitting there in an overstuffed, royal-blue-and-bone-white chair, leg over leg, he was more frightening than I wanted to admit. You saw the high school ring among the pudgy fingers around the tall glass, like some apology by the boy he once was for the man he had become, and you felt sorry for him because he still wore it. And then you saw the eyes again, and the falling flesh robed in elegance again, and you felt disgust for his weariness and his indifference. The combination of the emotions he invoked in you, of pity and disgust and fear, made him a monster. He was the only man I had ever met I could imagine actually pressing the button that would send us all to perdition.

He saw me looking him over, and he smiled wetly.

"'Twas a rough night?" I said.

"I don't think we need any introductions," Freeman said. He stepped back a step toward McKnight,

"You wanted to talk?" McKnight asked.

He drank down the yellow liquid in a gulp and handed the glass back to Freeman, still looking at me. As the scotch took effect, the face came together some, and I could see the handsome Irish boyo he had once been inside the jowls and the puffiness of his malaise. He blinked, and I noticed his long, almost feminine eyelashes and, once again, the dramatic arch of his brows.

"Slick," he slurred. "Make Mr. Harker a drink. We, the two of us, we are going to have a drink together." He looked at me, heightening the arched brows. "You wanted to talk?"

McKnight fit the place, a two-room suite, with the door to the second room closed. This was the office and receiving end of the thing, done like the chair—blue walls, white patterned flowers; white doors, blue trim; white tables, blue drapes. At one end of the room sat a desk, standard size, clean, empty, ignored. At the other was a portable bar, behind which Slick Freeman happily attended to his important work. Behind me squatted a white sofa. The floor was of some well-polished dark wood with a thick white area rug. Just this side of the closed white door to room number two, on the burnished chocolate floor, lay in plain sight a pair of woman's red silk panties.

"The bed's in the other room?" I asked.

Freeman's laugh came from the bar. "You want to get a piece of ass from us as well as a drink?" he said. "Can do. My, but you drive a hard bargain, Comrade Harker."

"Shut up, Slick," McKnight growled. When I had my drink in hand and had plopped down on the sofa, and when McKnight had taken his extra tall one from Freeman's dark, long-fingered, well-groomed hand, the senator growled: "Get rid of the girl."

Freeman disappeared behind the white door, but before he did, he made his first mistake of the day. He glanced quickly back at the two of us, and I caught him. He was more worried than he let on. And he was nervous about leaving the senator alone with me.

"Freeman," I said. "That's not his real name, is it? He's too dark. Jewish, maybe?"

McKnight managed to smile wetly again. Like all despots ruled by their subalterns, he sort of despised his second-in-command. "Fried-man, F-R-I-E-D," McKnight nodded. "New York, originally. Worked for an advertising agency when I met him. His biggest account was a Yid company made, I don't know, toilet paper or something, owned by his damn uncle. Now, he studies law nights at Georgetown University when he's not kissing my ass."

"Him being a Jew a problem out here?"

"Jew, not so much. Fag, yeah."

Then McKnight remembered himself and took another huge gulp of booze. He tried to shake it off, his ennui, and to get down to business, but he seemed worried and couldn't start without Freeman there. Then the politician in him automatically took control. "We're from the same place, you and me," he said. "Winnebago County. Why we so different?"

He said *Winnebago County* in the lost and abstracted way I had heard Vlad Paddy's seventy-year-old father once say "Russia," and the question he asked seemed pleading rather than confused.

"We're not," I said. "We just left for different places."

"But we both left," he said.

"I didn't go as far," I said.

"Not in miles maybe." Suddenly his eyes changed. He was still look-ing at me, but he seemed to have lost focus. Odd. "But I think you know what it's like to dream about getting out altogether—am I right? And then you do, you know, and, somehow, it's not enough. You miss it. And you know there is nothing there to miss. But you miss it, some-how. What you don't know—what you don't know is what it's like to work for Albert J. Collette for twenty years. I mean he treated me like dirt. Like mud. Everybody thought he was wonderful. So gentlemanly, so kind, so concerned. But I *knew* him. He was just like you and me. Only he hid behind his high ideals rather than—this stuff."

He rattled the ice in his glass.

"I want you to know, Harker. It's just politics. I mean, this left-wing, right-wing crap between me and you. It's just politics. It don't mean shit. And it was never you we were after. Hell, you're a guy. I'm a guy. You know how it is. But that Tuckerman—he acts exactly like Collette. Like he's a prince, not a guy. Like they want nothing for themselves. High ideals. They started out rich, that's all. They thought that meant they were born to rule."

I waited as he took a long draft from his drink.

"We had to use you to get to him," he said bluntly. "He wouldn't leave me alone. From the start, he wouldn't leave me alone. They were already ahead—the damn Collettes and the damn Roosevelts and the damn Tuckermans—and they acted like all they wanted to do was to help out the little guy, but what they really wanted was to keep us from catching up with them, that's all. And that was just politics, too."

"I'm not sure they think so," I said.

"But you and me," he said, ignoring my interruption. "You and me. We weren't fooled by them, the way they fooled all the others with their talk about public service and helping mankind and fulfilling a destiny. Am I right? You—you know—you with this ideology crap. Me, just fighting. Just fighting tooth and nail, toe to toe, right in the ring, on their own terms. But it was just politics. Underneath, we are both the same. We don't like them. Not a bit. We like fucking. Drinking. Being somebody folks know, respect or hate, it doesn't matter. What's the difference?"

It took a while to realize he had no idea to whom he was talking. He knew who I was, for sure, but he did not actually know why I was there or what my being there meant to him. He wasn't even sure how I had gotten there. All he knew was that I was there, and he had to get along with me. He had to connect with me by any means possible. He honestly expected me to forget, and worse, to forgive, what he had been doing to me and my life for the past month, because he had only been using me to get at Tuckerman, because he bore me, personally, no ill will.

My God, I thought. He wants me to like him.

I remembered what Carol Cole had said about him. About his being a child. That he was unable to understand anything beyond what he happened to be doing at the moment. I took her to mean it figuratively, but McKnight—for him only the present existed, because he so hated the past. He went on talking fast, drunk, and intimate, and oblivious to anything but his own will. No wonder Freeman had been leery of leaving him alone with me.

"—I mean people admire you, Harker, and what have you ever done but throw it back in their faces? Hell. Even I admire you. You don't take shit off nobody, you let nothing stand in your way, you don't care about what people think about you, you just don't give a fuck—and people, still, they like you. Some of them, they hate you, that's true, but they still respect you, and it's not because of your opinions, because you change your opinions, and it's not because you stick by your friends because you don't stick by your friends—you see, we know all about you. Freeman, in there, he did all this research on you, and he talked to all these people about you, and he told me all of it. And it's not because you lead a clean, upright life, because you don't lead a clean, upright life ..."

He downed the rest of the scotch in his glass and paused, waiting, not knowing what to do next without Freeman there, and in the silence, we could hear faintly the haggling going on next door between Slick and McKnight's midmorning twist. I got up, took the drink from his hand, and went over to buy us both some more liquid time.

"Thanks," he said. "I told Slick you were all right. I told him you were Winnebago County to the core underneath all that international Soviet bullshit—or whatever it is your opinions are right now. *Strong opinions.* That's what I thought you had. I told Slick, go out and get me some strong opinions. Like Harker. Opinions I could act on. Opinions I could feel good—inside—about. Hell, I said, I don't have to believe none of that shit, I just need me some strong opinions I can feel proud to hold. I told him, I understand you; he didn't. I told him drinking men understood each other. But he just smiled that damn Doris Day smile of his and said, *No*—"

I put the filled drink back in his hand.

"—At first, I thought the way was to have no opinions at all, you know? That was my mistake with Prince Albert. I thought he despised me because I was from Winnebago County and a hick and a bankrupt who had dreams of becoming something and the way to get along with him was to have no opinions at all. But now I can see that that was why he could use me the way he did—he called me the Weasel. The Weasel. Get the Weasel to do that, he'd say. That's the Weasel's job. When I ran for the Senate right after the war—hell, I didn't have any opinions then and people elected me. I thought they recognized what I knew all along, that I didn't need opinions, because—I don't know if I should tell you…" He dropped his voice to a whisper. He glanced at the closed white door. He leaned forward, arching his brows. "I have greatness of soul."

The scotch tasted sweet. Whenever scotch tastes sweet, you know something's wrong. Reality had lost its contours. I felt as if I had entered another dimension, and I was anxious for Freeman to return and cage the beast. Freeman was slick all right, and dangerous enough, but he was sane.

"But greatness of soul, alone, that's not enough. You could see that, Harker, if you had it. It's inside you, like something alive, and it grows and grows, trying to get out, trying to force its way through your pores—and—"

He gulped scotch.

"But even after I got strong opinions, you know, not the kind Prince Albert had, but the kind his enemies in the party had. Even after

I got them, people still despised me. My own friends, my old army pals, they sleep with my wives, and they despise me. And my wives, they despise me. And Freeman, he says the Republicans, even the old and new anti-Collette-type Republicans, they despise me, despite my strong opinions I got to match yours now. And the voters—the people who voted for me last time? Freeman says they despise me, now, because they're not so confused by the war any more about the kind of guy I am.

"When all this started, we talked about you. I always liked to think about you, because we were both from Winnebago County, and we turned out so different. We talked about you all the time. And I said I don't live any worse than Harker does. And my strong opinions are a lot more popular than Harker's are. We both got nicknames. So what is it? What is it about Harker? What's he got, I don't? You know what he said?"

For the last three or four minutes my eye had been riveted to the closed bone-white door and away from madness, so it took me a moment to hear the silence, and to remember what McKnight had actually asked me and to realize not only that was he talking to me, but that he expected me to answer.

"No," I said quietly. "I don't know what he said."

"He said you had authority. That's what he said."

"Authority?"

"He said you were writing the goddamned book in this state, and that's why you were untouchable, that's why you were always in control, why nobody could get to you, because you had authority in Capital City, and we were letting you write the goddamned book for the whole of Wapsipinicon. He said what we had to do, we had to take it away from you. We had to write it ourselves, undermine your authority, not let you always know what was going on. And that's all we did, Harker. We just did what you did. If you used ten-year-old trumped-up charges against me, we used them against you. If you called me Lazy Larry, we called you Comrade Harker. You and me, we're just the same. We, me and Freeman, we didn't do nothing to hurt anybody. It was just politics, that's all. We were just trying to get some authority. Get reelected. I don't know how it got to be like this—all out of hand like this. Out of control."

"Maybe Freeman was wrong," I said.

"Wrong about what?" Freeman asked. He was closing the door behind him. "The last time I was wrong was, I forget, maybe 1944 on a high school history exam." He was smiling.

"Maybe I don't have authority," I said.

"Maybe not," he said, walking across the room to the coffee table between me and McKnight. The fake front page I sent them lay spread out next to the hotel's salmon-pink stationary.

"But you," he said, "and you alone, wrote this."

McKnight was ignoring us, gulping down the last of his drink. Many more like it, gasped down that way, and he would not be with us for the negotiations, though I was beginning to understand it did not matter much if he were there or not. Freeman took the empty glass from hand to bar.

"Thanks," McKnight said. He focused on me for the first time in a while. "You got the boy's name?" he asked, pathetically. I nodded, bluffing with my bobbing noggin. "You said you wanted to talk," he said, waving an unsteady finger at the coffee table. "In that note there." He stopped. His eyes were gone again. "At least your friends aren't assholes," he said. "Like mine. They don't go off with your wives and—"

"Here you are, Senator," Freeman said.

"Thanks, Slick."

"I take it," I said to Freeman, "you're the one I'm to talk to about this."

"I'm the only one here," he smiled. "To talk to, I mean."

"Does he even know what kind of trouble he's in?" I asked. "What this can do to his—your—campaign hopes?"

"I don't think so," Freeman said, laughing short and quick.

"I know I don't have authority," McKnight said. He lifted his glass and took a drink before it slipped from his hands and dropped to the floor. It broke on the gleaming hardwood. "And greatness of soul dudn't matter."

"Come on, Senator," Freeman said. "Time for your after-lunch constitutional."

He helped McKnight up from the chair. The wine robe came loose, and McKnight held it closed against his nakedness with a stubby, unclean hand. Freeman walked him to the closed door, and as he opened it, McKnight said, "Don't like Jews much. Sneaky people. That's why they are rich. Brains instead of souls. And they got long schlongs, they call 'em."

20.

I waited while Freeman got McKnight bedded and sleeping in the second room. When he came back, he did not smile as much, but he was more relaxed, and, paradoxically, more businesslike.

"Assuming what you say about having the boy's name is true," he said on his way to the bar. "Assuming you could actually get this page on the stands." This time, he made himself a drink, too, a dry martini. "What do you want from us? To drop this silly Red baiting, is that it?"

"How often does he get like that?"

Freeman took off his suit coat, from a blue three-piece number, and dropped it over the chair McKnight had been sitting in. Then he came around the coffee table and sat down on the sofa next to me, spreading out the front page our way so we both could read the bogus head. "Does it matter?" he said.

"Some," I said. "He's a sick man. He should be attended to professionally."

"He probably doesn't drink any more than I do, certainly no more than you, if you average it out over, say, a year. Besides, he's right, he has greatness of soul."

It was my turn to laugh, and I did. "How do you get him to stand up on a platform steady and speak without slurring? I knew he was drunk at the memorial auditorium, but that was nothing like this."

"It hits him differently at different times. These kinds of bouts are rarer than the others. The others seem to help him. And don't think I'm being ironic when I praise him. You've seen him at his worst. I've seen him at his best, his most brilliant."

"You're as crazy as he is," I said.

"Maybe. But he's going to be our president one day, so you might as well get used to it."

"Not like that he's not," I said. It seemed to me almost insane even to talk seriously about it. But here we were. "No matter how far right the country swings. He won't make it through the next campaign like that. And that's not even taking Paul Toland into consideration."

252

Freeman smiled. He wasn't condescending. He was assured. "I didn't know we were going to discuss metro politics. Paul Toland will lose."

"Let me guess," I said. "He doesn't have greatness of soul."

"No," Freeman said, "he doesn't. But, as the senator said, that doesn't matter. The other thing he doesn't have is exposure. You know Toland. You sense that aura of innocence about him. If he got exposure, that aura could be devastating. But he won't get it. Without it, all he has are rumors to define his image. He isn't seen for what he is. He's seen as a kind of old-style ward heeler and a pal of the Commies. Now, let's get down to it. What do you want to kill the story about me picking up little boys in local bars?"

"I want my life back. Right here in Capital City."

"That I don't have to give you."

"Then I want you to drop me from McKnight's reelection plans. I want to be able to live and work without having my past always thrown up in my face. If not here, then wherever else I go from here."

"That I can do. And I will do. But I can't help you here in town, it's just too late."

"Rhode Island?"

"Oh," he laughed. "That state you can have." Slick Freeman sipped his martini and gave me the gimlet eye. "You think you two can actually find happiness together somewhere, is that it? Put all this behind you? You think she can both run home to Daddy and take you with her. I don't know, Harker, I'd think about going back to the wife if I were you. Move down to Ravensport. Have some kids. Lead a decent, respectable life."

It's the only thing, I thought bitterly, he and Bob Weaver agree about. "Just what I need," I said. "Matrimonial advice from a queer political hack who works for a madman with delusions of grandeur. Look, do we have a deal, or are you staring at tomorrow's headline?"

Slick made us another drink while he thought it over. He came back to the couch, and he handed me my glass, and he folded up the newsprint carefully and slipped it in his front shirt pocket under his blue vest. "It's not that I think you could pull it off. I doubt even John Tuckerman would run the risk of using such salacious copy. I want you to understand that—"

"Oh, you have no idea how much he hates McKnight," I said.

"—you were just our market test to see if we could sell our message here in Wapsipinicon. Now we know, and we don't need to keep attacking you in particular. Any old Commie will do. So, deal?"

Why not, I thought. I had no intention of trying to get the article run anyway, not to the glory of and in the newspaper owned by the man who wouldn't think twice about selling me down the river to protect his family's investments. The Old Man could stuff his bottom line, I was moving on.

"If this crap about me starts up again anywhere, anytime," I warned, "I'll turn the pictures—not just that one of you two holding hands and about to play kissy face, but all of them—over to some Democrat."

"Believe me, it won't start up again for you. And even if you did give them to some Democrat, maybe by that time, it won't matter if I'm ... the way I am," Slick said. So he, too, I thought, was a dreamer, indeed as crazy as his boss. He extended a hand. "But you have a deal. The senator and I will be leaving town tonight. A pleasure. Here's hoping we never meet again."

Part 5: UBI SUNT

Where are last night's tears?
Where is last year's snow?

—Bertolt Brecht and Kurt Weil, *Nana's Song*

21.

"Maybe *I'll* take over the East End," Bilinski laughed. His huge feet sat on the edge of Rojack's hospital bed. He had unbuttoned his jacket. He leaned back in his chair. He was relaxed. A big man, Bilinski. "There seems to be a real definite shortage of hoods applying for the job. I'm as mean as any of 'em. Have to practice on my corruption, though. You betcha, I need some work in that area. Harker, they say you sold out."

"They'll say anything," I said. I looked at the object of my visit. "How long has he been like this?"

"Comes in and out," Bilinski said. "Sometimes he's the old Tommy. Other times, zilch. The quacks keep saying to the sisters who keep saying to us, We don't wanna operate, we don't wanna operate, we don't want no operation 'round here. Truth is, Harker, they don't know overmuch about the damn brain of a working man, not having much fucking contact with common folk. How about it, is you is or is you ain't one of us no more?"

—*The reason I'm going,* Sharon said, *it's got nothing to do with this, I promise you.*

—*You don't have to promise—or explain—anything to me.*

—*Stop it.*

"Now that's a job to have in this burg at the moment," said one of the four UEW organizers in the room, turning toward us some article he was reading from an old magazine he'd picked up in the waiting room. "Undertaker. A man could make a killing."

Snickers filled my silence, the one I created when I did not answer Bilinski. Tommy Rojack lay in the bed at Mercy, slack under stiff sheets, his head wrapped in bandages, his eyes, unseeing, open, his mouth, unspeaking, nearly closed, tubes running out his nose and arms. He was a bruised reprove, bleached with sick-room swaddling.

"Maybe we ought to get out there and organize them fellers," another of the four said. "You know. The ones what plant the remains come spring?"

"Gravediggers?" I said offhandedly.

"Check," he said, looking at me. "Gravediggers. Need a classier title, them boys—make that one of our demands. Call them eternal relocation experts."

"They sure gonna be overworked when the warm weather hits," said the first.

"To start," the third one said, "we oughta go downtown, organize the employees at the city morgue. Bet they bellyaching all over the place 'bout the workload."

"Yeah," said the last. "Got to roll them dead bodies out ever time some damn relative wants to make a identification or some news-hound buddy of Harker's wants to snap hisself another photo."

They were ragging me about the death of Tony Martin, and I knew better than to respond to their grim humor.

—I simply want to get back there and think things through, take stock, you know? Away from this damn place. Spend Christmas with my family. Go down to the ocean and walk along the beach the way I did when I was a girl—until things become clear. And I don't want to live in this place, this apartment, anymore. That's why I'm taking everything I can with me. It has nothing to do with you. Not directly.

—I'll keep the place. I can't stomach my flat.

—Good. Oh, good. Then I won't have to worry about storing the furniture. I'd probably try to sell it, anyway. But, Randall, when I come back ... when I come back, I want to live somewhere else. Together, maybe. I don't know, yet. I just don't know.

"Automation," said the one who had spoken first. "That's what we oughta talk to them about. Automating the fucking slabs. Then, ever time some clown wants to gape at his future, the guy just pushes a button, and whirrrrr—out comes a stiff."

"That's good," said number two. "Creates more jobs for us electrical workers."

Again, everybody laughed.

"Hell," Bilinski said. "We'll make that one of our demands. Non-negotiable."

"He's comatose?" I asked quietly.

—You're leaving for good. I know the signs.

—Oh, bosh. I wish you were coming with me. Then you'd see. Why don't you? Come with me, I mean.

—Maybe later, when you don't come back—

—I'm coming back.

—I'm just not ready yet. Too many loose ends.

—Yes. I forgot about her.

—Sharon, stop it.

"That's what they call it, Harker," Bilinski said. "The boss quack, he told me it ain't that unusual, nothing to worry about. Doc, I said to him, Tommy, he sure don't look *usual* to me. But, hell, he's only been under for less 'n a week. Doc says some of 'em stay that way for months. First time he come outta it, they noticed by him wiggling his toes. Nurse looked down, and there was the sheet moving in this weird way, and she pulled it back—holy smokes, he's wiggling his goddamned big toe. Then they look at him and he says, 'Susie. Get Susie.' Sorry, Harker, he just didn't go calling your name right off the bat like. His wife, she come first. They got her, but by then—by then, he's under again ... Now, you gonna answer my question?"

"I really don't know, Bilinski," I said. "You tell me."

The five men looked at me.

—Daddy won't like you much. But mother. Mother, she'll adore you.

—Hurrah. I'm hell on old ladies.

"You sure one handsome sucker, know that Harker?" said number three.

"Yeah," the fourth said. "Give me the name of your bee-yew-tician. I need me a mug like that."

"He wants to get pretty like you, Harker; give his old lady the hots for him again," said number one. "Add to the pack o' brats she's dropped already."

"Yeah, Harker, you grow pretty like that hanging 'round the city desk?" asked number three. "Now why don't you be a good pretty boy and just go ahead and answer the man's question?"

"Nah," Bilinski said. "Nah. Let him alone, boys. He's here to check on Tommy. I'm happy with that."

—See Kathy. Talk to her. I mean it. For me. Do it for me.

—You'll come back then?

—While I'm gone, Randall. Do it, please.

"You should not go ahead so easy on him, Stephan," said an antique voice from my past. "Mr. Harker, here, now he is a man who feeds on adversity. It is part of his so-called character, as they once say in the novels of the eighteenth century, which happens to be approximately the period of time in which he would doubtless for sure feel most comfortable, enlightened as he is—the period, I am meaning, of bourgeois ascendancy."

The voice's owner stood there in the doorway to the hospital room, my old pal Vladimir Padikoff, intense and dark, his wavy hair brushed away from his ancient, craggy face, black eyes gleaming with spitefulness, and he wore, as always, his dark gray suit and bright red tie, a matriculated Wobbly, unchanged by time, by history, by anything I had done to him in our town.

"Is that supposed to be some kind of rarified insult, Vladimir?" I said. "A bit of obscurantism, perhaps?"

"I was merely and humbly pointing out the objective truth," he said. "The discomfort you feel so obviously in this place of yours here that you have, since shutting me out and shunning me, tried so diligently to build and create. You act as if you had a soul, my old friend, a soul which has been damaged and which someone—me, perhaps?—might be concerned about. You have no such soul, Mr. Harker, you have only the words you use in abundance to hide your true thinking, the true intent of your, I admit, confusing actions. You are flat, my friend—notice I still do not call you comrade—a bit player in a big history. Yes, flat. Flat as the paper you once long ago rolled off your typing machine, a machine, if I remember correctly, you stole."

—Don't look like that. It's not forever. You'll see. Randall, you'll see. I'll be back. In no time, no time at all, I'll be back.

—No, it's not that.

—What is it?

—I don't feel as upset as I act. It's not wrenching. I thought it would be wrenching—your leaving—and it's not. I'm back to being like I was before. I see about as far as the next drink. I failed to realize you were what kept me going.

The five others had fallen silent now, Tommy's boys, the way children at play do when an adult enters the room. And Vlad Paddy entered

Tommy's room, dancing toward the seat offered him deferentially by one of the now-mute wits from the UEW. They had heard so much about him, maybe seen him in action a time or two, this legend, and now here he was, close and actual, a man like them, only older, aging flesh in need of a place to rest its bones.

"You boys notice a chill?" I asked them. "Just now?"

I looked around at each of them individually, and they all seemed to disapprove of what I'd said; but they were no happier to see Vlad Paddy than I was, less so, because I was inexplicably excited, but they—it was as if they felt guilty, as if they had just got caught playing hooky or stealing apples off a garden tree. When my survey of faces came back to Vlad Paddy, I was surprised to see his sparkling eyes looked hurt—he had understood what I meant, and there was still enough feeling between us, despite it all, for what I said to hit him. I was sorry for the jab, sorry he and I had ever come to this, and a little shocked by the way I felt at seeing him again. I never knew the sentiment a mature son felt for his father. My own father ended it too soon, too abruptly, too dismissively, for me to work my way back through the petty adolescent distaste for him—a distaste his suicide had made timeless—to that calm, abiding respect for one another I imagined existed between older fathers and their grown sons. This, the way Vlad Paddy affected me, must be something like that. I was too proud and too sure of the truth myself ever to believe in Vlad Paddy's patter again; I was too close to and too influenced by him to ever stop listening. I could not hate, and I tried, or dismiss, and I tried, the man with the arrogant black mane and the steel-cast countenance.

—*You don't believe me when I say I'm coming back, do you? And you won't, will you, ever? Until I do.*

—*No. I don't believe you. It worries me that I don't even want to believe you.*

"We've come a long way, indeed," he said petulantly, crossing his legs like a European. "If leftist doctrine now constitutes for you the orthodoxy of an evil. If an old, discredited, harmless fellow such as I strike you as Satanic."

"You mentioned my soul," I said. "I just thought maybe you had come to collect."

"In that case, I would be a fool. A fool to look for something that does not in fact exist. No, no, no, no. Besides, Randall, have you not heard the good news I put that all aside? I shun now the party? I say now to Satan, Get thee behind me. Once again, I am the good American organizer—a sage, even, of sorts, advising my younger com—colleagues—"

"I heard," I said. "Which will last until Stalin gets his next round of colic and decides boring within is merely boring."

"Still playing with words, I observe. You have yourself only to blame for providing the objective historical circumstances within which I am allowed once more to practice that profession I have made my life. Wherever else they may hunt us out and prosecute us in this country of yours, Red Randall, they are not at all likely to do it here in Capital City again. Not soon. And beyond that—Comrade Stalin will not always be with us."

"Yes, he will," I said. "Despite the grave. Like a vampire."

"At any rate, I did not come here to participate in a refreshing dialectical exercise with you. You have not the intellect, and you are not my concern. I came to visit with one of your victims."

"My victim?"

"What would you call him?" Vlad Paddy asked. He turned his palm up toward the figure on the hospital bed. "One of your characters, perhaps? In the badly mismanaged creation of yours, the new, the fabulous UEW? That would be quite appropriate, I suppose. He is the perfect Dell Harker character. He does not move, he does not speak, he does not see, he does not act, he merely lies there as he was created."

"I didn't do this to him, Padikoff."

"How sanctimonious you sound. Oh, but you did do this to him. With the poverty of your language and the limits of your imagination. You thought so much had changed, the struggle of the oppressed as such was over, within limits, here in this country. But there is no such thing as within limits. You have always been like that, Red Randall. Too undisciplined a thinker to truly create and at the same time control the situation around you. Reality is, after all, merely a matter of how one organizes the details of everyday life to reflect the objective truth. I have been following your recent writings on Senator McKnight.

You, I fear, simply have not the language with which to surround and control him. You have only your American code language, some criminal argot, and the ideology of a sleazy private detective. We don't search our pasts for a few damning facts and bring them to light, into unconcealment, like the solution to some paperback mystery—that is not effective reporting, certainly not effective action. McKnight is more right than you, in this case. We are what we have been, do you not agree? Till we clearly state what we have been and repudiate it. Otherwise we embrace chaos and the result—well, look at our friend here."

"Maybe the details are too much, Vladimir, too cheap, too tawdry," I said, sounding more bitter than I had intended. "Maybe reality is a question of ignoring unimportant details and taking action on important ones."

"And what is this action you talk about?" he asked, smiling now, warm and interested, talking without pause, without need to think over, to consider, my point, my position. "But just another form of words for you, another way of expressing yourself? No, Red Randall, look at your existence. It is battered and damaged. You have no control of your actions any more. No one with any authority would allow himself to be bashed about like that."

"Vlad Paddy—" Bilinski said.

"Do not interrupt me, please, Stephan. You would pat Mr. Harker here on the back when he created the situation in the first place. Nothing has changed. McKnight still crows in Washington, and Red Randall has merely caused the death of a man like himself, confused and uncontrolled. No, Mr. Harker, you make the mistake, the big mistake of all writers—mistaking your language, a certain form, for reality, devoid of its contents. You purged me from your world, you thought, from your world as you thought you had created it, because you imagined you had learned from experience that a man like me was hurtful to your cause. But you had no cause, only the form of a cause, this UEW, this foul-sounding, vowel-ridden fiction by you and Phil Murray. To start with, there are certain factors that prevent one like you from learning, from becoming any cleverer from experience. For instance, there are changes in the situation which take place too gradually—imperceptibly, we might say. Or if one's attention is distracted by other incidents happening at the same time—the arrival, let us say, on the scene of a beautiful woman. Or if one looks for causes in events that were not causes, as the aesthete does who concerns himself only with the similarity in the contours of events. Or if the person undergoing the event has a strong bias. All of this, Red Randall, would describe you."

—*I'm not going to cry.*

—*I'm not trying to make you.*

—*I'm going to cry.*

—*No. No tears. You are coming back, remember? Now go. And drive this thing right for a change.*

"You look back at what has happened and you think you can make certain calculations—estimates of your position at the time. You only dimly realize how dependent you are in every way on all your decisions, because you never actually initiate these calculations as you think, you simply deduce, looking back, from your own action at the time, as if that were some miraculously clever thing to do. No, sir, people may experience real events and still go astray in this way I have described to you. You, Red Randall, you have learned the wrong lessons. Instead of fighting humbly again on the side of the oppressed because of what has happened to you, you are resigned, and you try to cover it with your tough-guy patter and your newspaper claptrap. You suggest such dubious motives as greed, ambition, anger, jealousy, cowardice, even love, and it's all so very vague. I am here, you see, with Tommy because my motives are historical, not personal. You, however. You are here out of guilt. Pah, you will forever be the failed novelist."

"What you don't see," I said. "And what you never see, is that I can use the form against the form. A printing press prints what you choose, not what it will. And language, certainly any written language, is also just a block of type. It's the intent, where you set it and why, that counts. To hell with your self-satisfied analysis. You don't know enough, you are *ignorant* of what is really true in this particular situation and of what has happened. You can't judge, you just spout your revolutionary pap to justify your actions in dark alleys."

"Pah," he said, almost standing. "The petty bourgeoisie press. The middle class still reacts to revolution as if it were simply a matter of getting its windows broken."

"And to hell with your revolution."

"What an expressive range you have developed, Red Randall."

"Yeah, at least I'm no old, washed-up, hypocritical windbag."

"As long as you think like that, you can go on believing you have won the game and that is enough."

"I know what has happened, at least. And that's more than you know."

"I do not need to know," he said. "I am not the one sitting here thinking there exists some distant linkage between it all, and, not knowing what it is, telling myself I do not care. That is why you think of things like working, your job—or, even, forgive please, the suicide of your father—certainly McKnight's attempt to defame you—probably the invasion so-called of Korea—all of those things there as if they were perhaps some phenomena of nature—an earthquake, a flood, bad weather. They seem to you to affect only certain sections of humanity, our city for example, or to affect one individual, you, of course, or maybe only certain of your habits—it does not matter. Because much later it will occur to you, perhaps, that normal, everyday life turns out to have become abnormal, in a way that affects us all, not just you alone—you will know you have forgot something, something has gone wrong. And what that is will be the same thing it has always been, what I have tried to tell you time and time again it is, Randall. Because of you, whole classes will have their interests threatened without those classes ever having banded together to protect those things they have in common. That is why I say your violent language is impoverished, corrupt, and, worse, inadequate, Red Randall, and why you are responsible for this man lying here, this man you call your friend."

"You are still at it," I said. I stood up angrily, walking toward him. Bilinski moved over a bit in the proud old man's direction. "You still try to make me feel as if I alone am responsible for what happens here, as if I alone could have changed all this."

"You are the writer," he chuckled to himself. "I am merely your bad conscience."

The four workers from the UEW had shifted slightly in their stance. Vlad Paddy occupied the other chair in the room and they were positioned so as to protect him from me. If it had come to a showdown, Vlad Paddy would indeed have won. I was no longer the man to deal with in Capital City labor politics. Tommy Rojack, if he lived, would be calling the shots now. Vlad Paddy smiled and waved his hand at me.

"Oh, sit you down, please," he said. "We may as well stop 'all of this,' as you call it. I cannot change you; we have seen that. And you cannot change me, though you have tried. You cannot even get rid of me. And you I am not alike. I do not resign myself. And still, all my grandiose analyses of the world-historical moment and your individual predicament, all my bold predictions—I suppose I really should say, all my once-bold predictions—about ascending revolutionary classes and doomed assimilated classes will not make me triumph in your book, will they, Red Randall? They leave unaltered the facts. The fact that writing itself is a middle-class activity, and you, Red Randall, will always long to write. And despite your little formula—oh, yes, I heard you. I listen to what you say occasionally—despite your little formula of form against form—genre against genre, we might say—this will always be true. You see, between the creative writer, if you ever truly become that, and the classes you choose to represent, there is always the gap. Pah. Between book and world. Between what you, Red Randall, do today, tomorrow, last year, whenever. Between your work, Red Randall, and your novels. That is why they have always failed. And I am glad they do, to tell you the truth. We do not need one more fellow traveler confusing the whole issue. I think you will never overcome the gap, my friend. You are too resigned. And the gap is big—between that superfluous, middle-class game, literature, and those necessary things you do to stay alive, the concrete reality, activity; you, I think, will always choose activity. The wrong activity, true, but activity."

"Was that an apology?" I asked, looking at the others in the room, confused. Vlad Paddy laughed out loud. He had always loved to befuddle me. It was his game.

"I suppose so," he said. "Perhaps so. Well, well. What is this?"

The figure underneath the sheets had begun to move. It twisted, rocked, bumped, a thing possessed, and we all moved quickly up to it, sending one of the four organizers out to find a doctor or a nurse, and we leaned over Tommy. He shifted his eyes, looking first at me, then at Vlad Paddy.

"Stop it," he said, very slowly. "Stop it, both of you." Then he managed, barely, to smile. And again he spoke, carefully, almost painfully, as if he had forgotten words and had to search for them, choose them from a group that did not contain the ones he wanted. "Yes," he smiled. "I'm alive. I am."

—*I love you*, she said.

—*I know, I know, I love you, too*, I said. But I thought, *It doesn't matter, it doesn't matter.*

22.

Turned out the difficult thing was not the saying goodbye, not spending a final night together, not the farewell kiss I feared would be our last kiss. The difficult thing was packing her car and leaving it parked. The Aston sat out there all night that last night, filled with her clothes, with her jewelry, with her makeup, with a few books. Her things waited in the cold night for her to wake up and take them away with her. I watched her drive away in it, and I knew, if I wanted her, eventually I would have to go to her.

After she had gone, I sent Kathy a note down in Ravensport explaining I had vacated our place and she could move back in for school next semester if she wanted. I expected no response, got none, and let it go. Late one afternoon, I went by the old apartment to pick up a volume of Beard's history and I saw a light shining from the living-room window. I watched for a while till I saw her shadow moving about and then I went back to Sharon's.

The Tropics, without its creator, was not even empty. It was comfortable, if a little lifeless—a pleasantly decorated room, done by a woman with taste. And taste was weak consolation. Each morning, I showed up at work, and each afternoon I rushed back to Sharon's afterward to check the mail. With her gone, life seemed to me simpler and sadder. Days, I worked at the *News*; nights, I drank, sometimes at home, sometimes at this bar or that.

Guthrie spent a lot of time with me the first week she was gone. We would sit in the Tropics and drink and talk about literature, the war, old and new, the silly antics of the fools we worked with. I told him more stories about our city than I ever suspected I knew. Sometimes we would mention the at-odds sensation we both felt now that McKnight had returned to Washington, Paul Toland had announced his bid for office, and the holidays were bearing down on us. I never mentioned I had talked to Charles Wilson. Though, of course, I thought about it.

Guthrie said his family lived in Michigan now, but he didn't plan to spend Christmas there. Since his father had retired, he said, he hated going home. The old man did nothing but mope about the house and complain. I wondered if there wasn't considerably more to it than that. We decided to spend Christmas Eve together drinking, and we wasted hours planning how we would do it. Occasionally he would try to ask me about the sudden apparent end to McKnight's attacks, but I steered clear of telling him too much.

❧

Sharon's letter came before Christmas.

Dell,

I don't know how I can write this after all the things I said before I left. It helps that you knew all along. I'm grateful you insisted on telling me you knew. So, since you know, I may as well simply say it straight away: I'm not coming back.

I found a job. Teaching art history. At both Brown College and the Rhode Island School of Design. My father knew the president of the college, and he is the one who arranged for the interview and moved things along so quickly. I was not at all sure that was what I wanted to do—oh, Dell, how could I be?—especially since it was what he (my father, I mean) wanted. Not until I was actually offered the job.

I start next fall, but I can't come back there in the meantime. The hardest part of all this is I still feel the same way about you I always have, I love you, but I know I cannot ask you to leave Capital City and come here. You won't ever leave. It hurts, it hurts more than I can write, so I will not even try. The way I feel now, if I came out there for even a short visit, I couldn't leave you again, and I want this job, I don't want to live out there any longer.

For the rest, I don't know what this means. I hope, I truly hope, you will write me and tell me what this means for the rest. I'm not talking about the furniture and my things. You would think that out of bitterness. I don't care about the fur-niture and things. I'm talking about Kathy. And about you.

And whether this means you will try again with her, or if you might not come to visit me in the spring.

I know how all this must sound to you, spoiled and selfish. You must think me just like her. I'm not. If you write me and tell me to come, you know I will, no matter what I say, but I don't want you to write me and tell me to do that, but if you do, I will.

I don't know what I imagine can happen. I daydream about you coming out here, but I know that is silly. We could not live here the way we live out there. You once said you *might* come. Please come. If just for a visit.

I love you,

Sharon

The two other important missives I got that week did not come through the mail. One I picked up at the office and the other was tacked to the door of Sharon's apartment. The one on the door was a notice to appear in court on the twenty-ninth of December to show cause why Kathy Spencer Harker's petition for divorce and certain property claims should not be honored. The other one surprised me—it was an invitation to attend a Christmas fundraiser for the Democratic nominee to the U.S. Senate, Paul Toland, to be held at the home of the prominent and wealthy Samuel Endicott, director of the Emerson Museum.

23.

I was drunk. Drunk, dressed, and ready to go. My pal, the pint-sized Kid Guthrie, came by Sharon's at eight. We shared a cab to the far North Side. Downtown, Christmas lights, strung along street lamps, gave off faint, pulsating illumination through falling snow and gusts of wind. It took a while to get to Endicott's. The Great Man's house was one of those tasteless monstrosities built in the twenties, thoroughly un-American, resembling some sandcastle children with vivid imaginations might construct along a seashore. Out of place. Awkward. A thing of turrets and stucco walls and sweeping arches. Huge rooms inside. Faux pillars and foreign carpets. All of it screaming to be noticed. At least the servants wore tuxedos instead of turbans.

"I feel like I just walked into the Arabian Nights," I said to Guthrie.

"Don't let Mrs. Endicott hear you say that," he warned. "They tell me she files her teeth."

"She's proud of this place?"

He shook his head. "It always wipes me out you don't really read the *News* much. We've run two interviews on the babe in the society section. All she jabbers about are the famous people, the big cats, who've slept here."

Globs of folks had formed here and there about the place, drinks in hand, poised, carrying on stilted conversation, watching to be sure they were seen. A fat-faced woman with a dramatically waved, not-quite gray perm, wearing cat eyes, red lips, and a silk evening gown most women would sell their souls for, slithered toward us, smiling her fake hostess smile pinned between round cheeks. Her body, though, was a little younger than her years, and the dress made sure we noticed.

"Welcome," she said. "Dinner is almost served. Why don't you join the crowd, have a drink, and we'll be calling for you in a few minutes. I'm sorry, I don't recognize you."

"Andrew Guthrie," the kid said.

"Randall Harker."

271

"Oh," she said. Her smile popped closed for a fraction of a second, too fast to be absolutely certain it had vanished at all. "It's a pleasure to meet you. Did you come alone, the two of you, I mean?"

"Sharon Parks moved back to Rhode Island," I said.

"Sharon Parks? Should I know her?"

"She worked under your husband," I said.

"Oh, yes, yes, he did mention something about her leaving her... um...position. She was a close friend of yours?"

"About as close as she was to Sam," I said.

Guthrie quickly pulled me away to a crowd that included Tuckerman, some state senator or the other and his pleasant, friendly wife, and Janice, who looked better, if possible, in tonight's black silk dress than she had the last time I saw her. She turned to me, smiling and a bit flushed.

"You mean to tell me," she said, "that you have not sobered up? I understand, I understand. It took me two whole days, and I only drank a fraction of what you did."

"We'll have to do it again," I said.

"Shhh. After I'm married. Then it will be harder for Paul to toss me out. He wants to talk to you, by the way."

I snagged a drink from a passing penguin. "Paul? That's novel. Where is he?"

"Off with his manager, Bob Weaver, of course. They are in some smoke-filled room making kissy-face at a rich dairy farmer. You know, Randall, I see less of him now that we're engaged than I did when I was a lowly secretary."

"He's a fool," I said.

"And I love him," she said.

"I'm sorry," I said. "You know what I mean."

She touched my cheek with her hand and laughed. "I've never seen you embarrassed before."

"I've never been embarrassed before."

We were both laughing when Tuckerman managed to maneuver Guthrie into his spot in front of the state senator and himself, between me and Janice.

"Did I miss something?" he asked, smiling politely.

"We were just discussing the decor," I said. Janice hooted.

"It is ghastly, isn't it?" Tuckerman smiled.

"Have you seen the beast who inhabits the place?" Janice said, arch and catty and loving it.

"She took a bite out of me at the door," I said. Then, looking at Tuckerman, I added, "She wanted to know—she didn't ask—but she wanted to know about *that* woman. You remember *that* woman?"

"Yes," he said uncomfortably. Janice watched him with bright, intelligent eyes, as he wriggled and felt about in his vest pockets. "Did Miss—?" He looked at Janice in a panic, having obviously forgotten her last name. I could have helped him, but I didn't.

"I told him," she said, ruefully.

"Paul Toland and I would like to speak to you after dinner, Randall. About this McKnight thing."

"What McKnight thing?" I asked blankly. I saw Hoops, dressed in a tux, an absurd-looking animal, headed our way. "Look, John," I said. "If you want to avoid an embarrassing scene, keep the fat man away from me." Immediately Tuckerman moved off to intercept the steady approach of his most loyal employee.

"My, that's some chip there," Janice said.

"I suppose you're right," I said, shrugging. "But I can't seem to do much about it."

"*That* woman?" she asked.

"No," I said. "It doesn't have anything to do with her, really. Except she's gone, and I can't get used to it. Sharon Parks, that's her name."

"Your blonde?" she smiled

I laughed. "Yes. My blonde."

"One hears all about her," she explained. "If I weren't a soon-to-be-married woman, I'd be jealous."

"If Paul hadn't decided to start speaking to me again, I'd be glad you were." We broke away from each other's eyes to find another drink. "Look," I said. "You are about the only person here I don't want to strangle slowly with my bare hands, you and the kid, and I've been talking to him straight for a solid week. How about arranging to sit together at dinner? We can avoid listening to any speeches or talk about politics."

"I'd love it," she said.

I suppose you would call Endicott's dining room magnificent. It certainly was large. Twenty-five or so of us sat around the table and listened to the rumors about the number of people who had been invited for after dinner. The Endicott's had made some concession to the holidays, and if you looked very closely you could discover small arrangements of holly and evergreen along the cherrywood paneling. The service was, of course, flawless, and the speechifying, of course, dull. Most of the Democratic Party bigwigs were there, and the Mayor, and our senior U.S. senator, Bill Thompson. Weaver was not much better dressed than he had been the afternoon we spent drinking together, but he sat, ugly and calm, near the head of the table, next to Paul. When Toland came in, Janice went over to talk to him, and she stayed a while, but finally she came back before the stout, loud woman next to me sealed her fate.

"He wanted me to sit up front with them," Janice said. "But I told him there would be plenty of time for that after the wedding."

"You're being polite," I said.

"I know. But he can be so ugly sometimes. He used to be your friend."

"It happens," I said.

"The view is better from back here, anyway."

I bumped her knee with mine, hard.

"I'm going to do that," I said, "every time you tell a polite lie."

"Please," she said. "I've got to get in practice."

Toland was not wearing the white armor in which Weaver had promised to dress him, but he may as well have been. The aura of integrity seeped away from his distinguished face and filled the room with its glow as he gave his speech; his perfectly bland, innocuous speech, short, without issues and full of promises, which lasted about as long as it should last. I would like to say I listened to it, but I didn't. Throughout the whole thing, Janice squeezed my hand under the table in her excitement, and I was happy for her and also worried. I had seen the crack in their facade, and I thought about Kathy, and I hoped Paul would not put Janice through what I had put Kathy through. I squeezed her hand back. She noticed, pulled hers out of mine, and for the first time, took her eyes off the prospective U.S. senator and looked at me. The question disappeared from her eyes as soon as it formed itself. She turned back to Paul, less enrapt, less unselfconscious, less sure.

Over coffee, while Toland dawdled with Weaver and Senator Thompson, she looked me over carefully and said, "Let's go get drunk."

"Surprisingly good idea," I said.

"They said the crowd arriving late, the after-dinner bunch, is back in the back wing. That's where the party is. Come on."

She went to tell Toland where we were going. He nodded his head curtly and turned again to Bill Thompson. Weaver caught my eye, shook his weathered face back and forth, slightly. I raised my shoulders and looked resigned. He laughed quietly to himself and reentered the conversation with Toland and Thompson. Janice was angry when she swept me away to the back wing. Two or three drinks later, and three or four brush-offs to those who tried to talk to us, she grabbed me by the arm and moved closer to say, "You don't think he's going to win, do you?"

We stood under a pair of nineteenth-century portraits, man and woman, a couple I took to be Samuel Endicott's grandparents. They had the stern look American painters seemed to favor when painting on the frontier, and they had been drawn so that no matter how they were hung, they appeared to be turning their backs to one another. Somebody else, like me, I thought, didn't care for the family.

"Can you stand it if he doesn't?" I asked her.

"I'd rather he did. Not because I care one way or the other about being a senator's wife, but because I care about being Paul's wife. I can take it. But I'd rather he won."

"Then it doesn't matter what I think."

"You bastard," she said. She stepped away from me. She was no longer smiling. She walked off and joined another group of guests. I saw Weaver working the crowd now, a fairly substantial crowd, and stuffing envelopes of cash and checks into his coat pockets. I leaned against the wall and grabbed a fresh glass of bubbly as it passed. Janice returned. "I'm sorry," she said.

"So am I," I said. "No, I don't think he'll win. But who knows? Two years is a long time; a lot can happen."

"They want something from you?"

"That's right," I said.

"They think it'll make a difference. Will it?"

"It could," I said.

"That much of one?"

"It could."

"But you're not going to give it to them?"

"No," I said. "I'm not."

"I'm a little infatuated with you, you know," she said. "That's why—"

"I know," I said. "But I'm still not going to give it to them."

"No, I didn't mean it that way. Honestly. I'm glad you aren't going to give it to them. Did I tell you that I was married before?"

"No, you didn't."

"Yes. To a preacher in Kansas. He went to seminary and I attended college there, not at seminary but at the university. For a year. I fell in love with my English teacher. He was the first man I—well, I went to bed with him once before I met the preacher and got married. The honeymoon was really awful, and I left the preacher pretty quick. And school, too. He still calls me sometimes."

"The English teacher or your ex-husband?"

"My ex-husband. He hasn't changed. Would you kiss me?"

"Not here," I said.

"I don't care."

"I do."

"We're both too drunk to be talking to each other," she said, wistfully.

"Or not drunk enough."

"I had the marriage annulled. Nobody knows, not even Paul."

I was relieved when Weaver interrupted us.

"Well, how you hanging, Clawgun? How would you like to join Paul and me and some others for a little talk?"

"Talk's free," I said.

"Nothing's free," he said. "Not even you."

"He's busy," Janice said, pointedly.

"Excuse us, Janice," Weaver responded, with exaggerated politeness.

"Oh, stick it, Bobby," she said.

"You get used to that kind of thing," he told me confidentially as we headed down the hall. "None of them skirts like a man devoted to his work."

"Right, Socrates," I said. I made him wait a moment while I ran down another servant bearing drinks.

The few others Weaver mentioned waited in a cavernous room with huge French doors, high windows, dark, oversize furniture, a desk, a liquor cabinet, and a safe. The few were, left to right: Tuckerman, Guthrie, Paul, Hoops. Guthrie was the surprise. He had decided to stab me in the back after all.

"Randall," Tuckerman said. "Let's get right to the point. Some things Guthrie here has told me indicates we might have a story with substantial impact on next year's senate campaign, a story that would severely damage Senator McKnight's chances for re-election. But he thinks that you are withholding information because to use it could make the situation here very uncomfortable for you. It might even leave you open to criminal prosecution. Is this true?"

"If Guthrie has a story," I said, "let him write it."

"There's no need to take that tone, Dell," Paul said. "If there is any worry on your part about, I don't know, your personal safety or your criminal liability, anything like that at all, I'm prepared to assure you that I will protect you with all the considerable power I have at hand. Trust me. I need the information you have. John has agreed, if you think it best, not to print the story in the *News* at all, but to allow me to release the information under the auspices of my campaign after I announce. That should take the onus off you. And, if you want to handle it the other way, write the story yourself, leaving out whatever you think would incriminate you, then we can work that out, too. Just give us something solid. Trust me. If you are worried about a charge of withholding evidence, obstruction of justice, anything like that, we can clear that simply enough by letting it be known you were working with the DA's office."

They waited. Tuckerman looked irate. Toland appeared to be deeply concerned, but that was an act. Hoops, over to the side, out of my line of vision, would be trying for sardonic. Weaver was behind me. And Kid Guthrie, to his credit, met my glare straightforwardly, unashamed, resolute. I had trained him well.

"Aw," I said, "and it was such a *nice* party." I walked casually over to the liquor cabinet, downed my champagne, and nonchalantly filled the glass with scotch.

"Oh, for god's sake," Hoops said.

"Get the fat man out of here," I said, smiling. "Get him out before we even start."

"I've had it," Hoops said. "Fuck the prima donna act, Harker. You are never as drunk as you pretend. We are talking about professional ethics."

"Get him out," I said.

"He's right, Randall," Tuckerman spoke up, coming toward me, looking sanctimonious now.

"Tell it to the FBI, old man."

Tuckerman stopped. He fidgeted. He didn't know where to go. Paul motioned to Weaver with a slight movement of his hand, and Weaver headed over toward Hoops's corner near the high window to talk him quietly out of the room. While they discussed it, I looked at the kid, smiled, and said softly, "A reporter is always selling out somebody, eh, kid?"

He relapsed into charm. "It's too big a thing, jack. But you dig that already."

As Weaver closed the door on Hoops, I poured another scotch, and I sauntered toward the desk, reaching into my coat pocket as I went, pulling out the envelope with Tuckerman's name scrawled across it, handing it to him without looking, and hoisting myself up on the edge of the desk, saying, "It's a little battered. Like me. I've been carrying it around for a while. It'll save you all sorts of effort. You won't have to get red in the face and prance around like a lost peacock, threatening me with the loss of my job."

Tuckerman gave me his most judgmental expression.

"He's resigned the *News*," he said to the others.

"Don't think this lets you out, Dell," Paul said immediately.

Weaver translated, "Look, Harker. We know you and your buddy Shaunessy are in this thing up to your goddamned necks, get me? Now, Paul, he's made you a nice, polite offer. I was you, I'd think about it. The DA ain't going to take kindly to his homicide captain burying evidence. So, what is it you got on McKnight to make him call off his dogs, and how do we pin it on him?"

"Oh, good," I said, drunkenly. "An oral exam. If I get that one right can I go to the head of the class? This mean I'll get a better job?"

"Funny guy," Weaver said. "Funny guy."

"Dell," Toland said. "It doesn't have to be like this. I know you don't trust me. I know why. But, you, of all people, should understand my position. You aren't naive. You know it had nothing to do with you. It's simply politics. Now the political situation has changed. If nothing else, the way it has changed should convince you you can, at least, trust me. Trust me."

"McKnight said the same thing," I said.

"Trust me?" Toland asked incredulously.

"No. That it was just politics."

"So you *did* talk to him," Weaver said.

I ignored him. I spoke to Paul. "It's not that I don't think I can trust you. It's that you don't get it, you still don't get it. McKnight's mounting a national campaign. This attack on me? It was just test marketing; I don't even count. And McKnight's going to treat you, too, like a local phenomenon. He'll paint you as a penny ante hometown political boss. I've been so carefully wrapped up that, even if I had something, you couldn't use it or you'd look even dumber, even more small time. McKnight's name will be a household word by summer; you'll come off like a couple of backroom boys trying to exploit his all-but-forgotten past, while he's out saving the country from people like me, people *you,* too, clearly treat as suspect. All I can do is give you some advice. Get a lot of money. Get your face spread all around. But don't say anything. Be even blander than you were tonight. And leave the rest the hell alone. If you don't, believe me, you'll be in worse shape than you are."

Weaver and Toland spoke together: "We don't need your advice!" Weaver said. "What was all that supposed to mean?" Toland asked.

Tuckerman had gotten red in the face and begun to sputter some kind of protest.

"Shut up, old man. I don't work for you anymore."

"This?" he said, disdainfully holding up my resignation letter. "This is a piece of paper."

"That's all I have ever been for you, John," I said. "Just a piece of paper." I looked at the group of them, staring blankly at me. "Does this mean I failed?" I laughed. No one answered. I left Endicott's grand study to find what remained of the party.

I followed the noise down the hallway. I did not pay much attention to the couple standing back in the door to one of the bedrooms, until she spoke. It was Mrs. E., her cat eyes red and wild, her painted lips twisted in mockery between round sallow cheeks. "So he's the one," she said to the man in the shadow of the doorway. There was hatred in her eyes as we looked at one another. She was the blink of an eye away from spitting and hissing. "He's the one who stole your harlot," she said. A beautifully manicured hand, nestled by French cuffs with silver cuff links, came out of the shadows and struck her once, soundly, authoritatively, across the mouth, before pulling her back into the room and closing the door.

When I rejoined Janice, I asked, "How about that kiss?"

"Too late," she said. "I lost the mood."

I found us both another drink, but before we could do them any damage, Toland showed up. He looked desperate when he came into the room, but, after he saw her, integrity flooded back over his face, and by the time he reached us it had grown into something akin to Tuckerman's best expression of righteous indignation. "Get away from him," he said. "I don't want you talking to him."

"Paul," she said. "Stop it."

"Right, Toland. You know you don't want to make a scene," I said, perversely.

"Stay away from my woman, you goddamned satyr!"

Paul Toland said it much louder than a politician should ever say anything. I paid no attention to the globules of people that split apart like mercury and reformed around us until after it was all over. I grabbed him by his pressed white shirt.

"Don't go holy on me, Paul," I growled. "This is your town, too, so don't go holy on me. You were going to make it better, remember? You were going to plan it all out so it was decent, remember? And what kind of town is it, you son of a bitch? What kind of town is it? I'll tell you. It's a town full of dark alleys, Paul. A place where nobody cares, do you hear me, where blood dries up on the streets and nobody pays any attention. So just don't go holy on me. It's your fucking nightmare, too."

When I finished, I flung him backward into the crowd, and he fell, like a loose-legged, two-bit comedian nobody laughed at any more. That did it. I had run the gamut, done everything but fall down on my face and spit blood. It was time to leave. You have to hand it to Endicott's servants. They were tops. The butler was waiting for me at the door, my coat and hat in hand, and he helped me on with them and out through the foyer, giving me his "Good night, sir," without even a hint of servile snobbishness—bland, polite, well paid. A happy, contented man.

24.

I had vaguely planned to walk to the nearest drugstore and call a taxi, but this far out on the North Side the houses were miles apart themselves, and the closest thing to a commercial establishment was a new shopping center midway home. The snow was coming down fast now, and I kept telling myself it would be absurd to die of exposure after all this, frozen and curled under by the side of the road. I had just about made up my mind that I would have to suffer the indignity of flagging down someone from the party who decided to leave early when a big black-and-red Mercury pulled up behind me and honked.

"Climb in?" Janice asked. I did, and before she pulled away, she got a fit of giggles. "You made a fool of yourself, you know," she said. I didn't laugh. "No, no," she said. "It was very poetic, really." She laughed some more. "What you said, I mean."

"Take me home," I moaned, almost smiling.

"Where's home?" She laughed, spinning drunkenly from the curb.

"Won't Toland be upset?" I asked.

"He won't even notice," she said, with that sharp edge of hers I'd noticed earlier in the evening. "He's got Bobby. Everybody is talking about you, and I got bored. Paul's too busy repairing his image. By the time he notices I left, it'll be too late to seem odd. I'll tell him tomorrow to pay more attention to me."

When we reached Sharon's, I got out and came around to her side of the car and leaned in when she rolled down the window and gave her the kiss we had talked about all night.

"I shouldn't do this," I said. "I don't exactly know how to say it. I've been dead drunk for almost a week. I don't know what I'm doing any more. I'm angry at Paul. So are you. And that's no good, no good for either of us. I miss Sharon, and I can't go to sleep nights for thinking about her. All that, all that," I hung my head down by the side of the car a moment. "All that means I shouldn't ask you to come up. But will you come up?"

"I said I was a little infatuated with you," she said, watching the dials on her dashboard. "I didn't say I wanted to sleep with you. And I know I don't want to wreck my life over it, do you understand?"

"I know," I said. "It's silly. Stupid. I shouldn't have asked."

She cut the engine. She opened the door. She took hold of my arm. "Anyway," she said, looking away. "I owe this one to myself. This once."

"This once," I echoed, stumbling along beside her into the Tropics.

Inside, she said, "Nice. This must be hers."

"I'm sorry," I said.

"Stop apologizing. It's nice."

"Sit down," I said. "I'll make us a drink."

When I handed it to her a few minutes later, I said, "Let me ask you, you still plan to marry Toland?"

"Yes," she said and shrugged. Looking around the room, she added, "I think we are only going to get along because we both know we're not going anywhere together."

Then we went into Sharon's bedroom together.

Things I thought:

Does she make love better than Sharon? She seems so small, so compact, her skin so dark, much darker than Sharon's. Why did I ask her to come up? After Sharon's letter, technically am I cheating? Some men might find her better-looking than Sharon. We do not fit together like Sharon and I did. Is she thinking about Toland? Did she mean that about doing this only once? Does she think I'm too tall? The way her dress, black silk, drifted to the floor; the simple surrender of her small, neat, elegant body; her lips (fuller than Sharon's); her breasts (rounder, larger actually, given how small she is, than Sharon's); her gem-deep navel; her thin ankles as she steps away from the free fall of her dress after she slipped off her shoes; the curve of her back into boyish hips; the thatch of pubic hair, so much darker than Sharon's. I'm uneasy because I find her so exciting. Sharon would be whispering to me now. Why do some women make only sounds, others use words? Does my wound worry her? Why does this feel as good as it does? Why don't I feel bad about it? Does she think it's good?

❧

Things she said:

Did anyone ever tell you, you make love so much more gently than they thought you would? It's nice, it's very, very nice. I like it. A lot. It might even have been wonderful, if your heart had been in it, too. It's nice to sleep with someone who is as worried about it as I am. Is it always a little awkward the first time for everyone? Did you ever want something badly, and then when you got it, not want it anymore? No, not *not* want it exactly, but not be sure you wanted it? I mean, you want it so badly for so long, and suddenly you have it, and having it, well, frightens you? It makes you think, is this it, then? Is this all there is? Don't look at me like that. I'm not talking about you. About us doing this. This is nice. I'm trying to explain the way I feel tonight about getting married ... again. Not to Paul, especially. Simply getting married. I suppose I mean getting married to Paul in particular as well or I wouldn't be here, would I? I think it might be hard to stick with the just-this-once thing. I don't know what it is about you. You're good-looking, but it's not that. Maybe the bandaged shoulder helps. You strike people, women I guess, as available, like you don't care about any of it. And that's exciting, I think. How about Thursdays? Maybe I can see you Thursdays. Paul's always tied up on Thursdays. He meets with the mayor. I don't know. Maybe not. Maybe I shouldn't. I think you should think seriously about running off to Sharon. It's funny. I don't know her. But I wish I did. I admire her. For you to feel the way you do about her, she must be some woman. I like her for that. Isn't that odd? Maybe it's because the only time I've seen you express anything, I don't know, honest, well at least, uncalculated, was tonight when you told me her name and said she was gone and you did not know what to do about it. You looked almost surprised, like you were being honest and that shocked you. Do you—do you want to see me again? After we're married, maybe I ought to tell Paul about you. I want to be honest with him. Maybe not. What I meant when I said I was a little infatuated with you was that, maybe, I was a little in love with you. I wonder if they are still talking about you at the party? I wonder if Paul even noticed I left? I don't care. See, I go to bed with you once and already I'm beginning to sound like you. That's nice.

That's very nice. This time, hey, this time? Try to put a little heart into it, okay, baby?

ॐ

Before morning, we had taken our measure of each other. Twisting her compact, supple body like a serpent on a grill, she let me know her lips would always be wet for me. With her smooth arms and her hard-biting lust, she could bury what traces remained of my antique conscience in the bedding we shared. On those days we would find time for each other before I deserted her, she would strip me of my clothes and my soul, replacing on mattresses sagging in ecstasy the notion of myself I lost tonight in the cascade of silk.

But when I went to kiss her before she slid from blue sheets to black dress, the light of a surprise dawn caught her thin, ribbed body in a certain way, and I imagined I saw her skeleton underneath the skin, and the marrow froze in me from the thought of *it* lying there under me, working to a frenetic and dry climax, clacking, bone on bone. It vanished as it came, and there was Janice again, fully fleshed, engaged to another man, confused and giving, exuberantly—almost childishly—sinning.

It was time to leave, I knew. Flee the city. Now. Here, for me, there was not even love and work any longer. Now, here, there was nothing.

25.

The January thaw, with its hint of spring, made water gush in the gullies of the street again and the lifeless brown grass beneath the vanishing snow spongy to the step. I stood behind a group of youngsters on the portico of Longfellow Hall and watched her climb out of a car driven by the broad-shouldered bozo I'd seen her with last month down in Ravensport. She pecked his cheek and tromped off toward the campus administration building. She watched as she walked, dancing lightly once or twice to avoid the mud. She saw me coming long before I reached her, and she slowed her walk to keep pace with mine.

"The lawyer warned me you might try to get in touch," she said.

"Professional caution," I said. "The more I agreed to everything, the more suspicious he became."

"You always have a smooth explanation," she said. She stopped, pushed her near-black hair out of her face and behind her ears, and put her hands in the pockets of her open camel hair coat. The sweater underneath I remembered from some other Christmas, but the somber wool skirt was new. She wore a lot less makeup these days. The intent written in her walk as she crossed the quadrangle, and, now, the long range of her green eyes, reminded me why I first fell for her.

"You look the same," she said politely. "Is it true you quit your job?"

"Yes," I said.

"Still drinking?"

"Yes," I said.

"How do you eat? You didn't have that much in savings. The lawyer said he had never met a man your age and with your financial history who had accumulated so little. He refused to believe I wasn't demanding alimony. I'm not, so don't worry."

"I'm not worried, Kathy," I said. "When a man stops working, he becomes a consultant. Tommy Rojack pays me some out of union funds for advice I never give him—I hardly even see him. I did a quick magazine piece on the last legislative assembly. That's getting me through the month."

"I have to register," she said. She seemed dazed, amazed at the sheer physical coincidence of our meeting, the location of our bodies in relation in space. "Do you want to talk, is that it?"

"Yes," I said.

"Funny. I thought you would be bitter."

"Yes," I said.

"Down on this end of Eightieth there's a small place called the Submarine. The kids like it, but this time of morning it shouldn't be too crowded. You could get breakfast there, and I—I'll join you when I've finished."

As she talked, a group of coeds strolled by us, and one—a bit taller than the others, with bouncing yellow hair—looked back at me as I watched her.

"Sounds good," I said.

Kathy had noticed the girl, too. She hooked her head to one side as she looked, and she seemed thoughtful. She said, bitterly, "I had forgotten about all that..."

"I'll meet you down there," I said. "Will it be long?"

"However long it is," she responded, now impatient and half-attentive, "you'll be sitting there, wiggling your legs, looking at the door, and longing to leave." She pulled her hands from her pockets, dismissed me with a slight twist toward the buildings behind me, and said in a tone dripping with sarcasm, "Unless, of course, you've changed."

"I haven't changed," I said quickly, almost nastily.

I waited half an hour at the Submarine. The joint was too small to be comfortable, but the students were used to being crammed in together. The puny tables were rickety. The old wood chairs wobbled. A sign on the fake-wood panel walls read: *Move Your BUTT So Others Can Sit.* When Kathy walked in, one of the cooks behind the cashier chatted with her as she paid. A local hipster bid her good morning on her way over to the table I occupied like a Russian in Berlin.

"What did you want to talk about?" She was uneasy, sitting cautiously across from me and gazing around at the cool and the callow.

"To say goodbye, I guess. I'm moving on."

"From Capital City? I don't believe it!"

"Couple months," I said. "Soon as I have enough dough to buy a secondhand heap."

She sat, quiet, watching her coffee. Her face was flat, expressionless, and the expanded seconds ticked tediously by, weighing us down with their passing. I felt as if we were taking part in some unwelcomed ritual, only a fraction of each of us present, the way you are when as a child you attend church with your parents.

"It's her, isn't it, that woman?" she sneered.

"*That* woman," I said. "Her name's Sharon Parks."

"I don't care what her name is."

"I saw you with your pal this morning," I said to head her off. "I saw you before, too, in Ravensport at the Country Club."

"That's creepy," she said. "You spying on me."

"I wasn't spying."

"Then why didn't you speak to me?"

"You had made it abundantly clear you did not want me to speak to you. And your mother asked me not to."

She tumbled back into silence. We sat, not speaking. She sighed. Clacked her polished nails against the ceramic cup. Then she said, as if it were pointless but required, "I heard about you looking for me at Christmas. I suppose it must have been bad for you, but I wasn't thinking about you, I was thinking about me. I'm sorry, I didn't actually know how to handle it, and I don't think I could have dealt with it any other way, *then. Now* ... it's different. I don't care, so I think maybe I could have done it some other way. But I guess we never really know how to handle things, even when we think we do."

"I suppose not," I said. Kathy made a sour face and drank her coffee.

"Look," she said, exasperated. "I know I did a lot of stupid things. But one gets confused, you know? It's hard, sometimes, to tell the difference between your own life and—well, whoever you happen to be with. Like ripping up your manuscripts. That was dumb. They just weren't worth all the grief I was going through."

"Don't worry about it," I said petulantly. "I haven't missed them."

"Neither have I," she snapped. "Just the same, it was a stupid thing to do... Excuse me a minute."

A couple of girls, years younger than Kathy, had come into the place and taken a table near the window. Kathy joined them. They seemed genuinely pleased to see her, dropping into the conspiratorial crouch of female friendships. The week I spent finding the courage to see her again, I had imagined I would feel all kinds of things at this moment, especially the self-serving hatred for her that had gotten me through the nights when I thought more about the past than about Sharon. But actually seeing Kathy, I felt nothing so complicated, nothing intense or unbearable, only a peculiar, almost relaxed regret. The fact that she seemed indifferent and acted put out by our meeting helped. I did not fully believe in her mask, but I was willing, for convenience, to accept it, if we could manage to make the mask permanent, final. It was true, as folks have always said, most things become flattened by time, and like them I was willing to phrase it more comfortingly and to call it healed instead of flattened. Before she came back over, the two girls began to sneak glances my way, looks both curious and cold. I was, after all, an outsider.

"Tell me about your classes," I said, hoping to ease the tension. She bought it. She said she was reading philosophy as well as literature and had signed up for a class in Existentialism. She had gotten interested in the existentialists over the winter in Ravensport (an absurd notion) after some friend of her mother's mentioned at a party that Nietzsche had really been a godsend, a true lifesaver, when she (her mother's friend) had split up with *her* husband. Kathy knew so little about philosophy, she said, that she thought Nietzsche was an existentialist still living in Paris. She had come up to Capital City a few days at the end of last semester specifically to sit in on some classes by a professor she had heard a lot about who taught a course in Existentialism. She liked him, she said. He was smarter than I was, she said. Finding a man she thought was smarter than me, she said, helped as much as anything, even more than her "friendship" with "Dave," who I assumed was her buff tennis partner and gallant chauffeur.

I asked her abruptly, "Why did you leave like that?"

"Why do we have to talk about it?" she said. "Get the truth out, is that the idea? Get to the bottom of things? It's what you do for a living, right? So you can justify your cheating and your lies."

"It's better than pretentious academic babble," I said.

She reddened instantly, like her father. "What is it you want?" she spat each word.

"I want to know about the phone call," I said.

"That? It wasn't that! I can assure you. Oh, the hell with it! The man said he was a friend of yours, and he thought I should know about *her*. I told him I did know about *her*. That's all there was to it."

"What was his voice like? High-pitched? Whiney?"

"No. Why? What difference does it make?"

"I'm asking that's all."

"Oh, all right. Okay. It was sharp. Savvy. A fast-talking boy from the big city. New York, I'd guess."

"Slick Freeman," I said to myself, matter of factly.

"He didn't leave a name," she said, sarcastically.

"He's a troubleshooter for McKnight. He once suggested that you and I move to Ravensport and have children."

"Now that's the Randall Harker I know," she said. "The bitter one. Don't go flattering yourself that that phone call made any difference. That it caused something to snap or anything like that. He told me some things I didn't know about *that* woman—that she was the mistress of some millionaire—and he said you were wasting your time— but I told him none of that mattered. And it didn't. By that time, I just didn't give a damn."

"What then? What was it?"

She huffed. She frowned. She sipped her coffee. She clattered her fingernails on the cup. She acted as if she carried the tiresome burden of all knowledge on her shoulders, making sure I noticed. She was world-weary, disaffected with all conversation, all facts, all truth.

"If you simply have to know," she said, pausing to think. Then she said, "When you got shot the day after this fellow had called me on the phone about your latest lover, someone from the hospital reached me at Mother's, I don't know how they knew to call me there. The two calls, back to back, seemed to settle it, I guess, to—what?—to *underline* the way I felt about you. But that I should actually leave you because I felt that way hit me that night, that night the man called—otherwise, despite his call, really just another night you didn't come home.

Everything suddenly seemed, well … *seedy* is the word I come up with. Decadent. It simply struck me, the way a curious fact in a magazine piece strikes you. It struck me why you would never be a real writer. You were decadent, corrupt. I'm sorry, I don't especially want to hurt you—I'm happy and I'd just as soon you be, too, though I don't care *that* much. But that's how I felt. Like the little blonde this morning. They are all fascinated by the pretty face of corruption."

When I laughed, she said, "Go ahead, shrug it off like always. During the war I always thought of you as hard-nosed and bitter but basically honest. That's why I didn't leave you when you joined the party and turned your back on our marriage. I was intellectually weak, I thought, and you were tough minded. Eventually, the war would end, I told myself, and things would get back to normal. In this country. In this city. Between us. Even after the war, I thought sooner or later I'd find the energy to work things out with you. Maybe we'd even buy a house. Maybe now we'd have kids. Then, somewhere along the line, I realized it was you, not me, who needed to change. When you were—what?—*exposed* by the senator, I suppose it simply allowed me the freedom to admit openly that you had given up even trying to be the man I thought I married a long time ago, and I realized that I had known for years you had been—what?—dishonest, foul, sullied, *polluted,* and that for years I had simply refused to face it." She gulped her coffee and set it back on the table with finality, looking at me with the blank mask she had used throughout her explanation. Then her face twisted up into a half-sneer. "Are you in love with *that* woman?"

"Yes," I said. "Well, was, maybe. But it seems unreal now that she's gone."

"Where is she?"

"She's not here."

"Are you seeing someone else?" she asked, knowingly. "Now. Here, I mean."

"Yes."

"I feel sorry for her," she said. She gathered up her things to go. She gave me her unyielding face. "For this Sharon Parks, I mean. She doesn't know yet you will always betray her. That's what corruption means, Dell, for you. You just can't help betraying the people you care about. And still lots of them just adore you. Amazing. I did. Despite everything. For far too long. And now I'm finished. With this conversation. With you. With the whole thing. I hope this is final enough for you: You are dead to me." She looked away. "And that's the truth," she said.

ॐ

My last days in Capital City, as my wound turned into just another scar, I spent some time playing pool with Bill Dyers and listening to him gossip about a few of the people we both knew. Thursdays, I saw Janice, but mostly, I drank and sat home, collecting a consultant's fee from Tommy and the union and writing a few articles for hire here and there. Slowly money began to build up in my new bank account, and I got Dyers to help me find a used car, a Studebaker that was due any day to die on the street, victim to a badly creaking universal joint.

Meanwhile, I corresponded with Sharon, and after a month or so, I finally convinced her I truly planned to move near her. We never talked about marriage in our letters, but when my divorce decree arrived in the mail, granting me "all the rights and privileges of single persons," I folded it into an envelope and mailed it to her without comment. She looked around for work for me locally, and she wrote she had found a good possibility with the Rhode Island Historical Society in Providence. She knew the director, she said, who was looking for an assistant he could trust, someone who knew how to think, understood research, and could write, because he planned to retire in a year or two. Since she had told him all about me, he was anxious to discuss the position of editor of the society's publications. We set the interview for late August.

On the last Thursday night I spent in Capital City, Janice rolled over, across my chest, holding her face in front of mine with unaccustomed seriousness, and asked, "Do you think you'll marry her?"

"I don't know," I said. "We haven't *corresponded* about it."

"I think you'll marry her," she said sullenly. She and Toland had tied the knot in the early spring, and I had not been invited to the wedding. Married life became her. She slid into it, despite her doubts, with enviable grace and assurance, and we never talked about Paul again—or love for that matter.

"I think," I said, "that you don't marry a woman. Or a man, in your case. You go to bed with her; you make love to her; but you don't marry her. You marry the circumstances she finds herself in, the situation that contains both of you. If the situation is right, I'll marry her."

It was bullshit, of course, but it seemed to console Janice. Me, I could not stop thinking about how Charles Wilson described the warm spot where Jack Haugen parked his dick on winter nights.

It was summer—and hot—when I left Capital City for good. It would be autumn before I settled out east. Maybe I was corrupt; I accepted the possibility. But I had come to believe, I had convinced myself, that corruption was just a nasty word some people used for the choices they saw other people make.

The water off Nantucket was true blue. There was no ice here, no dark alleys, only sand and some stubborn folk who spoke a strange brand of English. Sharon's father owned an impressive getaway cottage bordering Nantucket Harbor, and after I spent a month finding a place to live and a new set of clothes, Sharon and I were celebrating our reunion by hiding out on the island for a week.

She came in from a late afternoon swim and left her bathing suit on the patio as she showered behind the wall fencing us off from the outside. Tanned a coppery red, she was even better-looking than I remembered those nights back home I'd longed for her. We sat on lounge chairs, drinking Pimms, and watched the sun go down across the harbor.

"How did we ever stand it," she said. "In that awful city?"

"Don't be too hard on the place," I answered. "I grew up with the people who live there. They can't help it if the weather's bad."

"Don't you like it here?"

"It's a dream," I mumbled.

She stretched her body, languorous, sensual. "You do seem happy," she laughed. "And that's odd. I never imagined you happy."

"It's the final corruption," I smiled. I sounded cynical, I guess, but I felt uneasy. "Happiness. Against it, all other sins pale. You'll never—never—meet a happy revolutionary."

Slowly she sank into a sweaty slumber. She drifted in and out, but when she finally woke, it was almost dark, and the mosquitoes were biting. She seemed much more serious now for some reason. She knitted her brow. She looked at me.

"Randall," she said, almost angrily. "*Will* we be happy?"

I glanced at the sun, red-eyed from its work, drowning itself off the west side of the island in the harbor waters. I looked at her body, traced by the sun's redness, an image of pure pleasure. I watched her eyes, colorless now that the light was going. Maybe I could have said yes. I suspected the language to say yes was growing inside me like the surprising wish for the child Sharon may already have been carrying, but I feared it was too delicate, too fragile, to expose it yet to syllable and syntax and time. I smiled. I shrugged. I kept my mouth shut.

They would call it the McKnight Era, when war became police action and identity a media pose, and I saw it born on the television set we bought a few weeks after I moved to Rhode Island. I got hooked by the cathode-ray tube and its Lone Rangers and Cisco Kids, its Cavalcades of Sports and Meet the Presses, its Arthur Godfreys and Ellery Queens. In September, a month after our Nantucket interlude, CBS's *Evening News* covered a speech McKnight made in Kentucky announcing that he had in his hand a list of a hundred card-carrying Communists now employed by the federal government, some highly placed in the U.S. State Department. You could not capture in words what the series of electronically transmitted dots captured of McKnight, and I wondered if maybe Freeman was right and McKnight did own a kind of greatness, wicked as it was.

After the *Evening News*, during the Friday night fights that followed, I found myself whistling along with the Gillette jingle and worrying about how rotten our social and political culture had grown. But what thinking man, drink in hand, had not been troubled by that during his life? Only now I felt estranged from even this dirty world. When you are estranged, you exist right now, for this day alone or for that. Any future, much less a secure one, seems hardly possible. I don't know, maybe the price of the future was corruption, the purchase of life by the selling of soul, and mine went cheap, with a shabby little blackmail that let me function a little longer in a society I'd come to despise.

Over a martini or two, I tried out a wry grin on my grim view, absently watching two pugilists fight it out on screen for my enjoyment. My old Commie pals would accuse me of going existential, but goddamn it, you can only wait so long for the revolution without degenerating into some kind of bankrupt millenarianism. No, I was no longer in tune with my life—I was déclassé, solitary, too much a man of my times to stay in the working class I had once hoped to join. Sitting there in the flickering light of the television, I could even imagine myself in an actual revolution, not on the barricades, but in a fancy apartment in some skyscraper in some big city east of the Mississippi, drink in hand, looking wistfully down onto the streets at the explosions, the gunfire, the tear gas, and I would smile and root for the proletariat, salute them with my half-empty cocktail glass, and watch them. Amused. Interested. But not part of the action.

ACKNOWLEDGEMENTS

Portions of this work have appeared in different form in *Massachusetts Review*, *New England Review*, and *Fifth Wednesday*.

CPSIA information can be obtained
at www.ICGtesting.com
Printed in the USA
FSHW011505121020
74673FS